SAVAGE SURRENDER

As Lettice began to scream, he clasped his hand over her mouth and pressed her back against the wall. Her frantic eyes stared at him over the brown hand that gagged her. His dark, handsome face smiled grimly down at her, his lips parting in his curling beard to show teeth as sharp and white as a stoat's.

Then, suddenly, the gloom was filled with the harsh sound of his breathing. Her body was being crushed by his weight and she was flooded with weakness . . . surrendering, yielding—and grateful. She moaned, hearing herself distantly, and then hearing his voice close, bringing tears of fear and trust to her eyes. Gratitude rushed through her that the wolf who had torn her was to protect her; she had surrendered so much that she must belong to him, or die.

THE
DISTANT
WOOD

Cynthia Harrod-Eagles

A DELL BOOK

Published by
Dell Publishing Co., Inc.
1 Dag Hammarskjold Plaza
New York, New York 10017

This work was first published in Great Britain
by Futura Publications Ltd.
as DYNASTY III: THE PRINCELING.

Dell ® TM 681510, Dell Publishing Co., Inc.

ISBN: 0-440-11703-8

Printed in the United States of America

First U.S.A. printing—October 1982

Bibliography

So much has been written about the political and national side of Elizabethan history that it seems pointless to attempt to single out any historian's works. I would like, however, to mention one or two books I have found helpful on specific aspects and on social history.

Brown, Ivor   *Shakespeare in His Time*
Dodd, A. H.   *Life in Elizabethan England*
Frere, W. H.   *History of the English Church in the Reign of Elizabeth*
Froude, J. A.   *English Seamen in the Sixteenth Century*
Hadfield, A. M.   *Time to Finish the Game*
Purvis, J. S.   *Tudor Parish Documents of the Diocese of York*
Reid, R. R.   *The King's Council in the North*
Rowse, A. L.   *The England of Elizabeth*
Tawney, R. H.   *The Agrarian Problem in the Sixteenth Century*
Trevelyan, G. M.   *English Social History*
Winchester, Barbra   *Tudor Family Portrait*

ORIGINAL SOURCES
William Camden   *Annals of Queen Elizabeth*
William Camden   *Brittania*

Hakluyt   *Principal Navigations*
William Harrison   *Elizabethan England*
The Diary of Lady Margaret Hoby
John Leland   *Itineraries*
The Sydney Papers
Thomas Tusser   *Five Hundred Points of Good Husbandry*

*With thanks to C, T and G,
the real Southbank Trinity—
Et in Arcadia Ego, lads.*

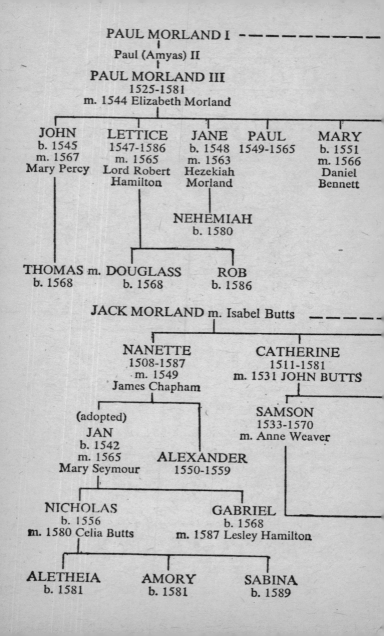

PAUL MORLAND I — — — —

Paul (Amyas) II

PAUL MORLAND III
1525-1581
m. 1544 Elizabeth Morland

JOHN
b. 1545
m. 1567
Mary Percy

LETTICE
1547-1586
m. 1565
Lord Robert
Hamilton

JANE
b. 1548
m. 1563
Hezekiah
Morland

PAUL
1549-1565

MARY
b. 1551
m. 1566
Daniel
Bennett

NEHEMIAH
b. 1580

THOMAS m. DOUGLASS
b. 1568   b. 1568

ROB
b. 1586

JACK MORLAND m. Isabel Butts — — —

NANETTE
1508-1587
m. 1549
James Chapham

CATHERINE
1511-1581
m. 1531 JOHN BUTTS

(adopted)
JAN
b. 1542
m. 1565
Mary Seymour

ALEXANDER
1550-1559

SAMSON
1533-1570
m. Anne Weaver

NICHOLAS
b. 1556
m. 1580 Celia Butts

GABRIEL
b. 1568
m. 1587 Lesley Hamilton

ALETHEIA
b. 1581

AMORY
b. 1581

SABINA
b. 1589

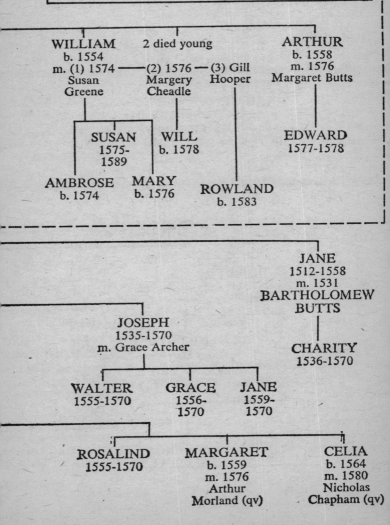

THE MORLAND FAMILY

WILLIAM
b. 1554
m. (1) 1574 —— (2) 1576 — (3) Gill
Susan   Margery   Hooper
Greene   Cheadle

2 died young

ARTHUR
b. 1558
m. 1576
Margaret Butts

SUSAN
1575-
1589

WILL
b. 1578

EDWARD
1577-1578

AMBROSE
b. 1574

MARY
b. 1576

ROWLAND
b. 1583

JANE
1512-1558
m. 1531
BARTHOLOMEW
BUTTS

JOSEPH
1535-1570
m. Grace Archer

CHARITY
1536-1570

WALTER
1555-1570

GRACE
1556-
1570

JANE
1559-
1570

ROSALIND
1555-1570

MARGARET
b. 1559
m. 1576
Arthur
Morland (qv)

CELIA
b. 1564
m. 1580
Nicholas
Chapham (qv)

THE HOUSE OF TUDOR

ARTHUR
Prince of Wales
m. Infanta Catharine
of Aragon

MARGARET
m. 1)
James IV
of Scotland

m. 2) Earl of
Angus

- - - **JAMES V**
of Scotland

**MARGARET
DOUGLAS**
Countess of
Lennox

(illegitimate)
EARL OF MORAY

MARY
Queen of
Scots
m. 1) Francis
K. of France

CHARLES
E. of Lennox

m.2) **HENRY STUART**
Lord Darnley

m.3) James
Hepburn
Lord Bothwell

**ARABELLA
STUART**

JAMES VI
(James I of England)

HENRY VII m. ELIZABETH OF YORK

HENRY VIII
m. 1) Catharine
   of Aragon

   m. 2) Anne Boleyn
      Marquess of
      Pembroke

      m. 3) Jane
         Seymour

         m. 4) Anna of
            Cleves

         m. 5) Catherine
            Howard

         m. 6) Katherine Parr
            Lady Neville

MARY I
m. Philip
   of Spain

EDWARD VI

ELIZABETH I

MARY
m. 1) Louis XII
   of France

   m. 2) Charles
      Brandon
      D. of Suffolk

FRANCES
m. Henry Grey
   Marquess of
   Dorset

JANE I
m. Guildford
   Dudley

BOOK ONE

THE
WOLF

Men must endure
Their going hence, even as their coming hither:
Ripeness is all.

King Lear, Act V Scene 2

CHAPTER ONE

The solar at Watermill House was warm and steamy and fragrant with rosemary and chamomile from the bathwater in the tub in front of the fire. James Chapham was finding it too warm, particularly around the neck where the starched and ruffled collar of his shirt prickled his skin, and he squinted down the smooth, stuffed black silk expanse of his doublet and sighed noisily.

"Not so tight, Matthew," he said. "I shall lose all feeling in my legs."

The servant, Matthew, who was kneeling before him tying the garters that held his nether-stocks and canions together, looked up imperturbably.

"You want them tight, Master, for to get them smooth. It won't show off your fine calves, else."

There was a crow of laughter from the smaller of the two beds in the room, on which James's sixteen-year-old son Jan was sitting, tying his own garters.

"A touch, a touch!" Jan cried. "He has you there, Father, pricked in your vanity."

James rotated the upper part of his body carefully so that he could look at the boy. It was not possible simply to turn his head—the high, upstanding Spanish collar kept his neck rigidly in one position.

"It was no touch," he said, trying to look stern. "I am the least vain of men, child; you should know that."

"Yes, Papa. Of course, Papa. I tremble before your wrath," Jan said, springing off the bed and dropping on one knee in mock humility. "May I crave your indulgence to ask a question?"

"What is it?" James said, managing to retain the frown. It was difficult, though, in the face of this lovely laughing boy. Jan, with his mop of black curls, his shining dark blue eyes, and his fine-cut, impish face, drew love as surely as the moon drew the tides.

"If you have no vanity, Father, why did you buy a new suit of clothes for this occasion, when you had a new suit at midsummer, not three months ago?"

James sighed again and turned the other way, toward the great bed, beside which his wife stood patiently while her maid Audrey slowly and painstakingly tied the points of her sleeves.

'My dear," he said, "are you going to allow me to be baited so in my own house?"

Nanette looked across at him and laughed.

"No, of course not. For shame, Jan! Your father vain, indeed! You know he hates to wear new clothes; and he only shaved off his beard out of compliment to the Queen."

Matthew grinned all the more and murmured, "It's no use, Master, you'll get no help there."

James looked frustrated. "Now, Nan, you know I shaved it off because—"

"Because it was gray and you did not like to appear a graybeard," Nanette finished for him inexorably. James began to smile sheepishly, and Nanette came across to him, half-sleeved as she was, and cupped his smooth jaw in her hand. "You are a handsome man, dear heart," she said, looking with her blue eyes and mischievous smile so much like Jan that it was hard to believe she was not his mother, "so why should you mind who knows it? Being clean-shaven suits you. And this Spanish black suits you. I'm afraid I am like to fall in love with you again."

Their eyes exchanged the private messages of accustomed lovers. "If this doublet and collar weren't so stiff," he said, "I'd kiss you, Mistress Morland."

"What, in front of the servants?" Nanette pretended to be shocked and backed off, returning to Audrey's ministrations.

"And in front of the children?" Jan added, looking across at Mary Seymour, Nanette's young protegée, who was sitting as patient as a rock on the clothes chest in the corner, waiting to have her hair dressed. Mary was ten, a fair, pretty child, with quiet, dainty ways, and Jan always felt protective toward her.

"Quite right, we forget ourselves," James said. Matthew had finished with the garters and was approaching with the short cloak; and James said to him, "Be sure you hang that so that the lining shows at the fold—"

"And be sure, Matthew," Jan interrupted sternly, "that it hangs at exactly the angle of a line drawn from the center of the earth to the rising sun at the autumn equinox. The master will have it so."

Everyone, even little Mary, laughed, and James growled, "Another word, and I shall refuse to come to the dedication ceremony at all!"

"There, Jan, see what you have done with your teasing," Nanette said. "But I still have an arrow in my quiver—if the master refuses to come to the dedication of the new chapel at Morland Place, I shall refuse to come to the dedication of his new school at Akcomb. That will do, Audrey. You had better see to Mistress Mary's hair now—time is growing short. And Matthew,

when you have hung the master's cloak, send for someone to take the bath away and see that the horses are
ready. And find out what's become of Master Simon
and the child."

"Yes, Madam," Matthew said, and departed at once
on his errands. James made no protest at her ordering
of the man, for Matthew was really her servant,
brought with her when they had married, along with
Audrey and four lower servants. Besides, the atmosphere at Watermill House was informal. They did not
live here in a grand way, for it was so small. There was
the great hall in the center, where most of the life of
the house went on; at the warmer, southern end there was
the winter parlor on the ground floor, which James also
used as his audience chamber and steward's room, and
above it on the upper floor the solar with the two beds,
the larger one in which James and Nanette slept, and
the smaller in which Jan and Matthew slept. At the
other end of the hall were the buttery and pantry and
over them the small bedchamber in which Mary slept
with Audrey in one bed, and in the other Nanette's
chaplain, Simon LeBel, with his young charge Alexander.

And that was all, apart from the kitchen, which was
beyond the buttery and pantry in a separate building.
The rest of the servants slept in the Hall, in the old
manner; but despite the lack of grandeur and comfort,
the atmosphere was always very cheerful at Watermill
House. James had a large house in the city, on the Lendal, but they were not often there. Nanette disliked living in York, feeling that it was unhealthy, and she had
some evidence for her fears in the successive plagues of
illness that had struck their Lendal neighbors, her cousins the Buttses.

Nanette's mother had been Belle Butts before she
married and had been born and brought up in the great
Butts house, which occupied a fine site at the end of the

Lendal, its many outbuildings running down to the River Ouse just below the Lendal Bridge. Belle's brother John was the master of the Butts family, and his two sons had married Nanette's younger sisters, Catherine and Jane. Jane's husband Bartholomew and their three daughters had all been struck down by one of these plagues eight years ago, and the youngest daughter, Charity, had survived. Jane had said afterward that it was a pity Charity had not died, too, for the illness had bent and warped her body as if it were soft clay and had left her permanently crippled; and now Jane, too, was dead, killed by the pox only that summer. No, York was not a healthy city; it was beautiful but noisome and stalked by plague and pest.

Here at Watermill House the air was clean, blown in off the moors, smelling of bracken and heather; implicit in it was the sound of curlews crying, the shadow of a hawk's wings crossing the sun, the cold mossy taste of water, cupped in the palms, from a tiny brook that ran between gleaming black lips of peat. The past came to Nanette through the medium of that breath of air; it was all of life to her, the life of the north, of the bleak open places where the sky was huge and the earth reared up to meet it, life that beat with the pulse of the earth itself. Life was the breathtakingly savage fang of winter, when death came in like a dog to lie up against you in the night, and each new day was another won from its jaws; and spring, wet and green and so budding and thrusting with life it was almost painful, like the pain of blood returning to a deadened limb; and the sweet, long, wheaten days of summer, drunk and drowsy, mad as skylarks, when you felt that you would live forever, emperor of the world; and the haunting days of autumn, smelling of wood smoke and bright with the gleam of fruit like jewels, hidden treasure discovered by the turning back of a leaf.

Through those seasons her own life came back to Nanette, brought to her mind as the changing year came to her senses through the scents of the air. From her own springtime came the faces of the bright young people with whom she had shared her giddy youth—the Boleyns, Hal Norys, little Frank Weston and the rest— faces bright and untarnished, blown in from the place where it was spring for them still, from the place where they had ceased to grow old. Her brief summer had brought her love and marriage and, indirectly, a child—Jan, who was her son and no son, who was in some sense the child she and her husband Paul had been given no chance to have.

And now she was in her own autumn, a sweet, gentle season rich with the fruits of years, and wisdom, and love sown long ago and brought to the harvest. Her second husband, beloved James, and their life together here at Watermill House with Jan and their loyal, affectionate servants would have been harvest enough, she felt, for all her gratitude; but a little breeze had turned the leaves, and there was the bright gleam of the unexpected hidden fruit, their jewel, their God-given Alexander.

Nanette had been past forty when she had married James; James was thirteen years older and had been married three times before and three times left a childless widower; and in marrying Nanette he laid down his last expectation of leaving behind him a child of his loins. But six months after their marriage, Nanette had conceived, and in March of 1550, at the age of forty-two, she had borne her first and last child, her son, whom they had named Alexander because it had seemed the only name large enough for such a large miracle. The labor had been hard and exhausting for Nanette—it was then that she had gone gray—but had it cost her her life she would have felt all was paid for by the holiness of the joy she saw in James's face when he first held in his arms the son he had not thought to have.

Now, eight years later, that joy was no less holy. Nanette looked at James's face when the door opened to readmit Matthew, accompanied by Alexander and followed by Simon, who was his tutor; James struggled, not very effectively, to appear stern, for Alexander's lower lip was guilty.

"What was it this time?" he demanded of Matthew.

"It seems we were chasing a cockerel through a muddy part of the yard and soiled our shoes," Matthew said imperturbably.

James examined the trace of moisture on the child's cheek. "Have we seen the error of our ways?" he inquired.

"We have, sir, and been beaten."

"Then there's no more to be said," James replied and held out his arms, and Alexander ran to him and was hugged.

"I wasn't chasing him, Father, I was playing with him," Alexander said, tilting his face upward. "And I forgot about the mud until it was too late, but Master Simon says he wasn't beating me for getting muddy but for going outside when I was told to wait in the hall."

"That's right, my child. Obedience is one of the first things a Christian must learn," James said gently. He was glad that he had passed over to Master Simon both the right and the duty of chastisement, for he doubted if he could ever have brought himself to beat this child, even to save his soul. Alexander's eyes were a brilliant golden-hazel, set on the slant like a fawn's, and luminous with the remains of his recent tears.

"I didn't really disobey," Alexander said judiciously. "I forgot. If I had remembered, I would have obeyed."

James met Nanette's eyes across Alexander's fair head, and she smiled at his dilemma.

"A reason is no excuse, my darling," she said. "The Evil One lays traps for each of us where we are weakest, and your weakness is that you remember what is pleasant to you and forget what is unpleasant." Alexander looked up at her and nodded. He was alwayss more formal with his mother than with his father, for she was sterner than he was and talked about duty and virtue and such other cold words. His eyes now strayed back to his father, and Nanette looked at James, too, and said to him, "It is a good thing for the child that he has Master Simon and me to offset your influence."

"You are right, Mother," Jan added quickly. "Father never beat me once in all my life, and look what has become of me."

Nanette laughed. "God has blessed me in my old age with not one son or two, but three. And a beloved daughter," she added, gathering Mary into the group with a glance. "And now we must go or we shall certainly be late."

"But Mother," Alexander said as they went down the stairs, "you're my mother more than Jan's, aren't you?"

Nanette had always been worried that Jan might be jealous of Alexander, and she looked quickly at her tall, dark boy while she tried to think of an answer. Jan intercepted the look and answered her thought for her.

"Don't worry," he said, "I don't feel that I lack for anything. After all, I've had three mothers—the one who bore me, the one who suckled me and the one who chose me. And do I need to tell you which one I love the best?"

The chapel at Morland Place had been destroyed in 1541, and there had been times when it had seemed that it would never be rebuilt. During the successive protectorates of Edward, the boy-king's reign, the country had been forced further and further down the road toward Protestantism, and Paul Morland, third of that name and master of Morland Place, had not dared to rebuild. Then King Edward had died of the wasting sickness, contracted during his summer progress, and Queen Mary had come to the throne, turned the country about and rejoined the Church of Rome.

But though the religious climate was then right for rebuilding the chapel, the financial and commercial chaos that prevailed had made it hard for Paul to find the money. In the end he had sold some property in the city—the large house on Coney Street and another on Petergate—and later the small outlying estate at Bishopthorpe, and in the end he had still had to receive donations from John Butts and from James Chapham to finish the work.

But now it was done, and the bishop had come to consecrate it and the family and the tenants had gathered to give thanks for the completion of work done for the glory of God. The chapel was beautiful, with its fan-vaulted ceiling, its elaborate column bosses painted blue and gold, its exquisitely carved screen and its richly colored stained glass windows. The ancient wooden statue of the Holy Virgin had been repainted, with plenty of gold leaf; before it had stood on a plinth against the foremost pillar, but now it was housed in a separate Lady-chapel to one side of the main chapel. In the Lady-chapel, too, was the marble memorial Paul had had made to the common ancestors of himself and his wife Elizabeth, to replace the one that was destroyed with the old chapel. It showed Robert Morland and Eleanor Courtney lying, richly robed, full-length upon an elaborately decorated plinth, their feet resting on a wool sack to show the source of the family fortune. Around the frieze of the plinth ran the words: "The brave heart and the pure spirit faithful unto death. In God is death at end."

As well as great pride, Paul felt great relief, for it
was the culmination of a seventeen-year-old vow, which
he had made when the deaths of his father and elder
brothers had placed him unexpectedly at the head of
the family. After the consecration and the mass came
the feasting in the great hall, and sitting at the high table with his family around him and his tenants and
neighbors before him, Paul Morland felt completely
happy for the first time in those seventeen years.

"Well, Paul," James Chapham said when the first
course had been served, "you look like a contented
man."

"As he should be," added Nanette, who was seated
between them. "It's a beautiful chapel. More beautiful
even than the old one."

"It isn't quite finished," Paul admitted. "The screen
has still two panels uncarved, and the corbels along the
north side of the aisle want their decorations, but otherwise—"

Jan leaned forward from the other side of his father
and said with a serious face, "My advice to you, sir, is
to finish it as soon as possible, before we are all asked to
stand upon our heads again."

Paul raised his eyebrows in surprise, and James
smiled with a rather grim humor. "You must pardon
the boy, Paul. He refers to the bad reports we have had
of the Queen's health. It is thought she may be near
death, and if she dies—"

"We shall have the Princess Elizabeth for Queen,"
Paul finished for him. "I have thought about it, I assure
you."

"But why should you be afraid?" Nanette broke in.
"The Princess Elizabeth is no Papist, certainly, but she
is as true a Catholic as her father was. I know her—"

"You *knew* her," Paul corrected. "Pardon me, Aunt
Nan, but you do not know what she may be now, and

the Protestants certainly claim her for their figure-head."

James said quietly, "It's my belief that she may well wish to steer a middle course as her father did; but her father was a man, and a powerful monarch, and he found it hard enough. What chance will a mere, weak woman have?"

Paul's cousin Hezekiah, head of that branch of the family known as the Bible Morlands, joined in. "Besides," he said, "she will have to marry a Protestant prince, for no Catholic prince will have her, and then we shall have war with Spain and France both."

"Perhaps she may not marry a foreign prince," Nanette suggested.

Hezekiah shook his great leonine head. "If she marries a courtier, we shall have civil war, and that will be worse. No, no, it's a bad business altogether."

Suddenly into Nanette's head came the remembered voice of her father, dead these forty years: "There will be no more Queens of England. It won't do, Nanette. Depend upon it, a girl can't take the throne." She remembered the occasion as vividly as if it were yesterday, remembered her father's arm around her and the lovely, comforting smell of him close to her as he explained to Nanette-the-child why King Henry the Eighth needed a son and could not make do with his baby daughter Mary. And behind that contention lay all the sadness of King Henry's life and all the tragedy that touched his wives and all the confusion that gripped his people. That baby daughter was now forty-two and dying, a barren Queen; when she was dead her sister Elizabeth would be made Queen after her, because the only other possible contenders were female, too, the female heirs of the King's sisters.

"There is talk," James was saying now, "that King Philip has already spoken of marrying her when Queen Mary dies, in order to retain control of the country."

"Elizabeth would not marry him," Nanette said abruptly. "The people would not like it—they made that plain when Queen Mary married him and brought the Spanish yoke down on their necks—and Elizabeth would never do what the people did not like. Even when she was a girl, she always had an instinct for what the people wanted."

She had spoken more forcefully than she had intended, and everyone was silenced. James touched her hand warningly and changed the subject.

"The next dedication we shall have will be my school. I hope I can rely on your presence at that ceremony, Paul?"

"Of course," Paul said. "When is it to be?"

"In October, on St. Edward's day. We shall call it St. Edward's School."

"Not Chapham's School?" Paul said with a smile. "I would have thought you would want to be commemorated by it."

"The good work it does will be reward enough for me," James said. He had been increasingly occupied with works of charity over the last few years. "There will be twelve places for the children of the poor, perhaps more later, if I can interest other men of standing in the idea. Alexander goes there from the day of opening, of course, and I hope you will support me and send your children to be educated by my schoolmaster. Come, what say you to sending your younger children along?"

Paul smiled indulgently. "I don't know, James. We Morlands have always been educated at home—"

"Promise me Young Paul, at least, and Mary," James pressed him. "Come, now, Paul, you can't refuse me that, not when I have given you so much help with the chapel. And then we must think about opening a hospital—something must be done about the beggars and vagabonds, particularly the women with young

children. I cannot bear to see them lying out in all
weather along the sides of the roads—"

"One thing at a time, James," Paul cried in defense.
"I will give you Young Paul for your school, but for the
rest you will have to wait. The chapel has cost far more
than I ever expected, and a hospital would need
money—money I haven't got at the moment."

James nodded. "Very well, I'll wait. I shan't forget,
though."

The Queen died in November.

"She believed almost to the end," Nanette said, "that
the growth in her womb that was killing her was a
child."

Elizabeth looked up from her sewing with a frown of
pity. Nanette, attended by Mary and Audrey, had
called on her at Morland Place, for she had recently
been delivered of another son, a small fair child whom
they had named Arthur, who was lying on a cushion at
her feet while she worked. Elizabeth was still drawn
and pale from the birth, and the Spanish black, which
all ladies of fashion wore, made her look paler still.

"Poor lady," she said, and glanced down at her newest child. "It is hard enough to bear a child, but it must
be harder still to want one."

Nanette nodded. "I can't help remembering her when
she was young, before she was disinherited. She was
such a pretty young woman, and fond of dancing and
singing. King Henry had her in to dance before all the
foreign ambassadors. He adored her, although she was
not a boy."

Nanette's sister Catherine, who had ridden in from
the Butts house on the Lendal to pay her first-day visit,
said sternly, "When I think of the late Queen I think of
the screams of those poor Christian souls she had
burned to death, and I thank God she has been taken
to her judgment."

"She did it to save their souls, Catherine, not to please herself."

"To please her husband—" Catherine began, but Elizabeth interrupted more gently.

"Aunt Nan, you don't really believe it is right to burn people to death, do you? You don't really think it does save their souls?"

"I don't know," Nanette said. "The Queen believed it, with all her heart.'

"If it is true, then you must want to have *me* burned to death," Elizabeth said very quietly. Her eyes met Nanette's.

"And me," Catherine added. The Butts family had always been more reformist by nature than the Morlands, and Catherine had followed her husband a good way along the path to Protestantism, further than Nanette liked to think of.

"And," Mary Seymour added shrewdly for such a young woman, "what of your dear Master Cranmer?"

Nanette's eyes filled with tears. The death of her former confessor, gentle Tom Cranmer, had been a blow to her and had seemed so unnecessary, almost ironic, seeing that he had survived the reigns of King Henry and King Edward and most of Queen Mary's and would have received great honor had he lived on under Elizabeth.

"Poor Tom," she said. "Of course I would not wish to see you burned. I think we should leave such things alone and let God judge for Himself. I do not believe He would wish us to torture and torment one another, for whatever reason. We are not clever enough to peer into men's souls and read what is written there."

"Queen Mary thought she could," Catherine said, "and no doubt now the new Queen Elizabeth will think it her duty. Well, we shall be safe enough—but what about you, Nan? What will happen to you when she discovers you are a secret Papist?"

Nanette stared at her sister in surprise, for there was a strain of viciousness in her voice that shocked and dismayed her. Nanette knew that the Butts house was a meeting place for some of the more extreme Protestants in York, but she had not suspected that the taint had so far discolored her sister's thinking.

Before she was able to think of an answer, Elizabeth spoke again. "Aunt Nan will be safe—the Princess would never harm her. Would she, Aunt? You were her mother's friend, and you knew her when she was a child."

Nanette exchanged a swift glance with her maid, as each remembered the years when Nanette had been companion to the Princess's stepmother, Queen Katherine Parr, in whose household the Princess had lived; and the stormy ending to that relationship.

She said calmly, "The Princess will remember, I am sure. She never had an ungrateful heart. Elizabeth, your wool is knotted, child. If you pull at it like that it will never come undone. Here, let me—"

Elizabeth yielded up her work willingly, and Nanette smiled at her. "You were never happy with your needle, were you? Shall you read to us instead, and Audrey can finish off this piece. There is not much to do."

"I am tired," Elizabeth said. "It seems so hard to be a woman. I have been married fourteen years, and in that time I have had ten pregnancies. I love my children, but it does seem that things are arranged unfairly. Men have all the pleasure and women have all the pain."

Catherine looked shocked. "You should be grateful that your children survive," she said sternly. "All of mine died but two. Thank God for your blessings instead of scolding Him for what you please to think of as your pains."

Nanette tried to deflect Catherine's attention. "I have always said it is unhealthy, living in the city, and is it not proof of it, that so many of Elizabeth's bairns survive compared with yours?"

"Aye, I know about this fancy of yours, sister," Catherine said, smiling suddenly, "and why you live like a yeoman's wife at Watermill instead of in proper style on the Lendal. I wonder you ever let Alexander so far from home as Akcomb, and to mix with city children, too. Aren't you afraid he will catch some pest?"

Nanette shrugged, that strange, foreign gesture she had caught in her youth from Anne Boleyn and never lost, and said, "He is a strong, healthy boy. And what God wills for him will come. For myself, I care only that he learns enough to be a useful man, but poor Simon is afraid all his work on the boy will be lost. He questions Alexander like an inquisitor every night when the boy comes home from school and relieves his frustration as a tutor by teaching Mary Greek and astronomy."

Mary smiled, and Elizabeth laughed and said, "Do you remember, Aunt Nan, how Master Philippe grumbled when he was ordered to teach me Greek and Latin as well as the boys?"

"And you learned Greek and Latin much more readily than sewing, as I remember," Nanette said. "There, I have your knot free. Shall you take your work back, or shall I give it to Audrey?"

"No, I'll do it," Elizabeth said with a sigh. "My father always wished I had been born a boy, because I was his firstborn, and I have always concurred with his wishes."

Nanette looked at her sympathetically and thought how many of the misfortunes of womanhood had befallen Elizabeth in her time. She had been sent from home when she was very young to a strange place to be betrothed to Nanette's nephew, Robert, a young man she had never seen before. Robert had been killed before they were wed, leaving Elizabeth a helpless dependent.

Elizabeth had been foully raped during an attack on Morland Place and left pregnant, and Nanette herself had removed the child at its birth so that Elizabeth should never see it or know what became of it. Though afterward she had married Robert's younger brother Paul and become mistress of Morland Place after all, yet continual pregnancy was no easy lot, even though all but three of her children had so far survived.

All this, Nanette thought, when Elizabeth had always loved riding and hunting and hawking, the free life of men. But even as she looked at Elizabeth, there was a sound of horses and men's voices in the courtyard, and Nanette saw Elizabeth's face light up. There were compensations to being a woman, and one of these had just ridden into the yard.

"It is John!" Elizabeth exclaimed and got up and went to the window. She looked down, and her face colored as she waved to the person below, smiling with a tenderness that would not have looked strange on the face of a lover. She turned to Nanette and said, "Jan is with him. They must have met up on the way back. They are coming up."

"Good," Nanette said. "Then Jan can take us home, and we need not disturb your servants."

There were running footsteps on the spiral stair, and then the door was opened and Elizabeth's firstborn son came in, laughing, followed by Jan.

"Look, Mother, look what I have for you!" John said, cradling something with difficulty in the bosom of his jerkin, something that wriggled and made strange mewling noises. Jan stood, hands on hips, watching him with a grin of amusement.

"Have a care, I warn you! It will nip off all your fingers. I told him to leave well alone, but he would not heed me, he would bring it home."

"What is it, Jan?" Nanette asked, reaching out a hand to him. He came to her and took her hand and

knelt to kiss her, and then, with a casual hand on her
shoulder, he watched, laughing silently as young John
took his wriggling jerkin to his mother.

Jan was tall, but young John, at thirteen, was already
taller than he, promising to be a giant of man like his
great-grandsire, Nanette's first husband Paul. He was
strong, too, and broad, and yet he had more gentleness
than a woman and had a great tenderness toward small
creatures and anything hurt or injured. His tow-color
forelock fell across his eyes as with a serious frown he
knelt beside his mother, on the other side from his baby
brother, and unwrapped his gift.

"What is it?" Nanette asked again.

Jan pressed her shoulder and said, "A fox kitten.
Take care, Cousin Elizabeth, their bites have a nasty
way of turning bad."

Elizabeth glanced up at Jan and then away again,
blushing a little. She never quite knew how to take his
words, for he had a disconcerting smile, and he always
made her feel strangely uneasy. There was something a
little mysterious about him; no one knew where he
came from or who his parents were, except, presumably, Nanette and James, and they would never reveal it
to anyone. He was never anything other than respectful
and friendly to her, and yet Elizabeth could never relax
when he was near. But she heeded his warning and
drew her hands well back as her son drew out the little
auburn-coated, mewling beast and held it in his firm,
big hands, holding it toward her so that she could see it.
It made no attempt to bite John, though it bared its
tiny needle teeth at the world at large and made absurdly small noises of ferocity. Her heart went out to
it—so helpless and yet so brave.

"Where did you get it, John? Oh, be careful, don't let
it bite you."

"He won't bite me, Mother," John said with careless
confidence, holding it against his chest and giving it his

little finger to suck. "He's hungry and afraid, that's all. Can I ask for some milk for him? Can I keep him?"

"But what of his mother? Where did you find him?"

"His mother's dead, and all his litter," John said, and there was a brief flicker of anger in his face.

Jan took up the story. "The dam was caught in a trap and had starved to death," he said. "She seemed to have been suckling her kittens to the end, and presumably this one was the strongest of them and so survived the longest. I would have put it out of the way for him, but he would bring it home."

"Jan's dogs found him," John said, caressing the small creature lovingly, "and I expect they would have killed him, but he snarled at them and kept them all at bay."

Jan laughed delightedly. "You should have seen it, Mother," he said to Nanette. "My biggest, fiercest hounds, backing off before that tiniest scrap of a thing! John would keep it, though I told him you can never tame foxes. They always run off in the end."

"But may I try, Mother? Please?"

Elizabeth, who loved John more than all her other sons put together, reached out to stroke his forelock out of his eyes and straighten his velvet cap. "You may try, but you must see that it doesn't bite anyone or make a mess."

"How went your hunting, Jan?" Nanette asked. He had been out hunting with his foster brothers, the sons of the woman who had brought him up until he was eight and Nanette and James had adopted him. Jan smiled at her and cocked his head toward John.

"We shall have fresh meat tonight, Mother, but I would not like to tell you about it while John is listening. He has been haranguing me all the way here about the wickedness of killing wild animals and birds. If I had met him before the kill instead of after, we would be supping on cold beans again tonight."

"But Jan—" John began to protest, and then saw he was being teased. The strange gentleness in John that made him unwilling to kill any creature, however dumb and low, responded to the more normal gentleness in Jan. The two were friends, and John looked up to Jan more than to anyone else except his own father.

"You had better take that nurseling of yours to the kitchen before it dies of hunger," Jan said kindly. The fox kitten had fallen asleep clinging to John's jerkin as if to its mother's flank, and it neither woke nor snarled when John stroked its head with one finger. "And Mother, I will escort you home, if you wish it, but we must go now or there will not be time to dress the kill before supper. Will you go? Mary? Cousin Elizabeth, will you forgive me for taking them away? But I'm sure you need rest on your first day up."

It was kindly said, so why did Elizabeth feel embarrassed at his oblique reference to her recent delivery? She remembered her manners and said the right things, but she was glad when he was gone, even though it meant taking Nanette with him.

CHAPTER TWO

Though there was no certainty to the claim of Princess Elizabeth to be the next occupant of the throne of England, she was accepted without opposition, and the few murmurs of the most obdurate of the Papists were drowned by the hearty acclaim of the people who, when she rode into London for the first time as Queen, cried out "Remember King Harry!" at the sight of her.

The date for the coronation was set, after consultation with astrologers, for Sunday, January the fifteenth, and Nanette and James attended it. The Queen did not forget her old friends. She asked Nanette to come to Court and serve her, and though Nanette begged to be excused, the Queen showed her continuing favor by making James the Warden of Rufford Forest and granting him part of the revenues.

They arrived back at Watermill House at dinnertime on the day after Candlemas, and as they rode into the courtyard, Nanette knew at once that something was wrong. She felt it in the air, in the quality of silence that hung over the house. She looked at James for comfort, but his expression was puzzled, too, and Matthew swung down from his horse and yelled for the servants. Belatedly one of the women, Agnes, appeared, wiping her hands on her apron. She dropped a curtsy and looked up at them with frightened eyes.

"What is it?" Nanette asked. "What's happened? Where is everyone?"

"Oh, Madam, thank God you've come. Oh, sir—"

"Where's Jan?" Nanette asked, flinging herself from her horse and almost falling as she landed awkwardly. Matthew steadied her and took the bridle.

"Oh, Madam, it's the young master—" Agnes began, and at her own words she started to cry. Nanette went white.

"Jan?" she said. James had dismounted, too, and at a glance from him, Matthew moved an unobtrusive step closer to his mistress. Agnes said through her tears, "No, Madam. Master Jan has gone into the city to fetch a doctor. It's Alexander—oh, Madam, the poor young man—Father Simon's with him—no one knew about it—it was an accident, you see—"

"Where is he?" Nanette interrupted the flow, and then picking up her skirts, she ran past the weeping servant and into the house with James at her shoulder, and Mary and Audrey followed, leaving the men with the horses. They crossed the silent Hall, where the fire was low and needed tending, ducked under the lintel of the staircase door and climbed the short flight to the bed-chamber. Within it was very hot, and there was a smell of sickness. Simon LeBel was sitting on a stool by the side of one of the beds, and he looked around as they came in and said in a low voice, quick with relief, "Thank God you are come. I thought I heard voices."

Nanette rushed past him and bent over the bed. Alexander's face was flushed and his eyes were tight shut, and he stirred and muttered with fever. Nanette pushed the sweat-darkened hair of his brow and felt his skin scalding hot. At her touch, his eyes opened a slit and then closed again fretfully as if the light hurt him. Her eyes met James's anxiously.

"What happened?" she asked. Simon leaned forward and carefully pulled back the bedcovers. Beneath his bed gown, Alexander's leg was lightly bandaged.

"He fell from his pony," Simon said as he drew off the bandages. "He was riding down the steep scarp of Popple Height, for a wager with one of the other boys from the school, as it seems. The pony lurched and fell, and as far as I can gather, the pony fell on top of him and scraped him along the ground."

The last of the bandages came away, and Nanette caught her breath. The whole knee was black with bruises, and where the skin had been ripped away the flesh shone glutinously, but that was not the worst. From the knee downward the leg was swollen clear to the ankle, and red and hot to the touch, and the edges of the ragged wound were yellow with pus. The boy groaned deliriously as Nanette laid a flinching hand on the grotesque, swollen limb, and as she bent forward the stink of putrefaction came to her nostrils.

"When did this happen?" she asked in a whisper, unable to command her voice.

"Five days ago," Simon said. "The boy didn't say anything to me. One of the servants bandaged it and, I suppose, did it badly. It wasn't until yesterday when he couldn't mount his pony that I discovered he was hurt. And this morning he grew feverish. Jan has gone into the city to fetch a doctor. He should be back any moment."

As Nanette straightened up, a blind, fumbling hand reached for hers and gripped it so tightly that it hurt her. James's mouth looked strangely twisted, his face gray and old, and in the sudden rush of pity her own anguish was for a moment forgotten. The wait seemed interminable, and yet it could not have been more than

a quarter of an hour later that there were footsteps on
the stair and Jan came in followed by Dr. Cranthorn, a
large, burly man in his thirties who looked more like a
wrestler than a physician. He was the assistant to Dr.
Wykeham, the physician that Nanette usually called in.
She looked sharply at Jan.

"Why did you not bring Dr. Wykeham?" she asked.
Jan looked weary and suddenly grown up with the unexpected and undesired responsibility that had descended on him in his parents' absence. He made no
comment on their return home. He shook his head at
Nanette's question, as if he were shaking off a rebuke.

"Pardon me, Madam," Cranthorn answered for him,
"but from the nature of the case as the young man de-
scribed it, it seemed better that I should come. I have
more experienece than Master Wykeham in some
fields. And now, if you please—" He pushed his way
gently but firmly past them to the bedside and bent
over the boy. Nanette watched him, dazed with her
emotions, and James's hand tightened harder on hers at
the doctor's sharp intake of breath. The big, blunt
hands moved lightly over the injured limb, and then the
powerful young man straightened and turned to the
parents with a stern, almost accusing look.

"This is very bad," he said. "The wound is mortifying. The leg must come off."

"No!" Nanette cried aloud, pressing her fingers to
her mouth.

Cranthorn's face did not change. "Yes," he said.
"The wound is mortifying, I tell you. Look where the
infection is creeping upward—here, and here." He
pointed to the streak of redness running up the inside of
the boy's thigh.

"Please—" Nanette whimpered.

James said in a voice she would not have recognized
as his, "If you cut off his leg—he will die."

The doctor looked at James just slightly more compassionately. "There is a good chance he will live, if we have caught it in time. Almost half the patients live in cases of amputation. If we do nothing, he will certainly die. Come, let us waste no more time. Madam, will you retire? I will need someone to help me, and plenty of rags. This room must be cleared."

He made a shooing motion with his hands and then turned back to strip the clothes off the bed. Nanette stared for a moment longer and then took command of herself. She looked around at the faces of the onlookers and came to a decision.

"I will help you, Doctor. Simon, will you stay? Jan, James, go. Mary, Audrey, go and fetch rags. There is clean linen in the chest in the solar—tear that up. Be as quick as you can. Get anyone to help you."

The doctor had turned back from the bed and was staring at her.

"Madam," he said, "I cannot permit you—this is no place for a woman. One of your footmen can assist me."

Nanette rounded on him fiercely. "I am his mother—who has better right? I will stay; I and the priest. Now tell me what you need."

Cranthorn studied her a moment longer and then accepted the situation with a shake of the head.

"A trestle, to lay on the bed," he said. "I need a flat surface on which to operate."

Nanette sent for one of the hall trestles, and the footmen brought it, their eyes round with sympathetic horror, and Nanette and Simon lifted the child between them while the men laid the board down on the bed. Then Nanette drove them from the room, and the doctor said, "One of you hold the leg up like this, to drain it of blood, while I set out my tools."

The child cried out as she laid her hand on the black-

ened, swollen flesh, but he did not open his eyes, and
she prayed that he was too delirious to know what was
happening. The stink of pus made her eyes water, and
the thing that she held seemed strangely impersonal, as
if it belonged neither to the boy nor to any human creature. Beside her, Simon stood, his eyes fixed like her,
his lips moving in prayer. She said to him, "James
would have been no use. Besides, I wanted to spare
him—he loves the boy so much."

A woman is close to her confessor, in some ways
closer than to her man. Simon nodded in assent. He did
not point out that she too loved the boy. He understood: a woman's love is different from a man's.

The doctor came back and took the limb from Nanette.

"Speed is of the essence now," he said as he tied the
tourniquet. He looked at Nanette with a curious cock of
the head, a speculative look. "Will you faint, or
scream? Say now if this is too much for you."

Nanette shook her head. "I will not hinder you," she
said.

"Then do you hold the boy, both of you. Keep him
as still as you can."

And then he set to work. His knives were sharp and
gleaming and sliced through the blackened flesh as easily as through the skin of an orange. At the first touch
of the blade, the child screamed, a high, thin, unearthly
shriek, as remote and irrelevant as the leg had seemed,
but as the doctor peeled back the flaps of skin as if from
a monstrous red and bleeding fruit, the screaming grew
deeper and closer. Nanette's mouth filled again and
again with the hot saliva of nausea, and she swallowed
and choked, trying to fix her mind on prayer. Her
hands were trembling now and her legs began to shake,
and she dragged her eyes from the doctor's work.

The boy stopped screaming and began to groan and
babble. She looked down at him, and at the same mo-

ment he came fully to consciousness. His eyes stared into hers in frantic supplication, his body writhed under her hands and his mouth opened, shapeless with agony and fear.

"Mother—please—not my leg—"

Tears scalded Nanette's cheeks. There was a new sound, a revolting rasp and and squeak as the metal teeth of the bone saw bit, and the child shrieked again and struggled for an instant with almost lunatic strength. Simon's prayer became audible, and out of the corner of her eye Nanette saw his hands trembling, too, before the child lapsed into unconsciousness.

It was all over. As the doctor had said, speed was of the essence, and she saw now the value of his youthful and burly strength. The matter had taken minutes only, but those minutes had seemed a lifetime long. Now he was tidying up the stump and binding it. Alexander was unconscious, his face so white it looked almost green, his skin dull and translucent like that of a corpse, and Nanette and Simon were mopping up the blood and mess with the rags, keeping their eyes firmly turned away from the rag-shrouded object on the floor. The smell in the hot room was indescribable, and now that it was all over, Nanette could at last run through to the garderobe with an apologetic glance at Simon and vomit up everything in her stomach.

She remained in there for some minutes, resting her hot forehead on the cooler wall, and when she came out again the scene was calmer, less lunatic and hellish, and the doctor was standing by the bed, his square hand over the child's heart, counting.

"Will—he be all right?" she managed to ask.

The doctor looked up at her. "If the wound does not mortify again. His heartbeat is steadying. You had better send servants to clear away these rags. They must be burned at once—do not allow them to linger unburned,

for they are covered with infection—and you had better
rest. I will sit with the child for a while."

Nanette shook her head. "I will"—she stared down
at herself in distaste—"change my clothes, and then I
will come back."

Audrey was waiting for her in the solar and helped
her without a word to change into a clean gown. Nanette looked briefly into the polished silver mirror that
Audrey held up for her and saw a face that did not look
like hers, a white, drawn face with glaring eyes, and she
tried consciously to moderate her expression before
going down to the winter parlor, where the rest of the
family were waiting. James looked up as she came in,
and Jan came to her and took her hand.

"He sleeps," she managed to say. "If the wound does
not mortify, he will be well."

James stood up and held his arms out to her, and
regardless of the presence of the servants she went to
him and let herself be folded into his embrace. She discovered that she was still trembling, and for a moment
she allowed herself to lean against him and draw
strength from him, until she realized that he was weeping, and she knew that it was she who must give comfort to him.

The next day brought a great many inquiries after
"the young master" from tenants and neighbors, many
of them—often the poorest—bringing small gifts, all of
them promising to offer up their prayers for Alexander's recovery. Some Nanette received and some James,
and to all the same news was given, that he was sleeping quietly.

"God bless him," said one cottager woman, her eyes
brimming, "he was such a pretty young gentleman, and
always had such pretty ways. He always used to bid me
God's day as he passed my patch."

Nanette was surprised to find how many people had

the same words to tell. Had it been Jan, with his outgoing manner, she would not have been surprised, but Alexander had always seemed so quiet that she would not have expected him to make so many friends among the poor people.

As the day wore on and the news spread, visitors came from further afield, and noon brought representatives of the family. From the city came Nanette's sister Catherine, accompanied by poor crippled Charity, their sister Jane's only surviving child. Both traveled in a litter, and Catherine complained bitterly about it.

"Bumped almost to death I was, and I would not have come at all, sore troubled as I am with the dropsy, but when I heard the news, sister, I could not stay away. I felt it was my duty to come and comfort you, and Charity would come, too, though I wondered if the sight of her might not upset you—"

"Charity is always welcome here," Nanette said firmly, giving the girl a look of sympathy, for Catherine never noticed whose feelings she bruised with her loud and tactless comments. Charity was twenty-two now, but so thin and undersized that she might have passed for no more than fourteen, and she was so pale from continual confinement to the house that she looked more sickly than she was. Nanette was suddenly aware that she had not done strictly right by her dead sister's child in leaving her so completely in Catherine's charge and at Catherine's mercy. "In fact," she went on, "I could wish that she was here more often." As soon as there was a breathing space, Nanette decided, she would ask to have Charity to stay here for a long visit—perhaps even permanently.

Catherine continued to talk, settling herself on the only chair in the Hall and looking about her for a footstool. "Well, for all that, she would come, and I thought since both my sons are down at the wharf and both my daughters are too great with child to travel, it would

have to be me, sick as I am. I see no signs of dinner,
sister. Have you finished already? But no matter, any
little thing will do for me—a couple of small fowl or
rabbits, and perhaps a bite of mutton, and any little
kickshaws you have ready—you must not go to any
trouble. Now if only I had a footstool to lift this leg off
the ground—is that you, Mary Seymour, skulking
there? Come forward, girl, and find me a stool. You
must learn to be helpful to your elders, child—don't
you trouble, Nan, the girl can fetch a stool for me. You
have enough to occupy you, with your only son lying at
death's door."

Nanette opened her mouth to reply and then shut it
again, knowing the futility of selecting any one comment from the many that needed refuting. A little later a
more welcome visitor came in the shape of Hezekiah,
who rode over from Shawes with the pick of his store
apples, which he had thought might tempt an invalid's
appetite, and he took over from Nanette, with his gen-
ius for seeing where he could be of most use, the task of
entertaining Catherine.

Then came the visitors from Morland Place—the
two eldest children, John and Lettice, in the charge of
their governor, the Morland Place chaplain Philippe
Fenelon. Elizabeth and Paul were still in London, and
the younger children were in the care of the governess,
Mrs. Stokes. Lettice, a vividly pretty girl of almost
twelve, had come out of a desire to be anywhere but
home, and Nanette quickly sent her off with Mary to
make sure the latter got a few moments of relaxation,
for she was overconscientious and had not left Nanette's side. John, however, was genuinely concerned
over his cousin's plight and had brought his young fox,
Toddy, on a leash and begged to be allowed to take him
up to show Alexander.

"It would cheer him up, I'm sure, Aunt Nan. Please
may I go up? I'll be very quiet, I promise."

"I'll see if he's awake," Nanette said doubtfully. She did not think the child would be strong enough to be visited, even if he was conscious. But when she went up to the bedchamber, where James had been keeping vigil, she found that Alexander was awake, lying back on his pillows so weakly that he appeared to have been flattened against them by some enormous weight. James was holding his hand and telling him a story but broke off when Nanette appeared.

'How do you feel now, my hinny?" Nanette asked.

Alexander smiled feebly. "All right," he said. "Just tired, Mother. And my leg hurts."

"Your cousin John has come over from Morland Place," she said. "Would you like to see him? He has brought Toddy to show you."

A glimmer of enthusiasm greeted the words. "Yes, please," Alexander said.

James raised an eyebrow at her and withdrew with her to the door. "Is it wise?" he asked in an undertone.

Nanette shrugged. "I don't see that it can do him any harm. It might entertain him for a moment. You can send John away when you think he has had enough. He's a very good, sensible boy."

"Alexander doesn't know—about the leg," James said even more quietly. Nanette's eyes opened wider. "He doesn't remember—and he can still feel it. The doctor said that he might."

"Oh God—"

"Hush! Don't cry; he is watching."

"Oh, James—"

"Hush, my darling, I know. Send up the boy—but warn him first not to speak of it. It is better for the moment for Alexander not to know."

John remained above for a quarter of an hour, and when he came down again he was subdued. He avoided Nanette's eye and pretended to find something amiss with Toddy's collar that occupied his attention for some time. When he straightened up again, he had regained control, though his cheeks were wet.

"It seems so unfair," he said to Nanette. "Why did God punish him like that? What did he do?"

"I don't know, John," Nanette said. "We mustn't question the ways of the Lord. Things often seem unfair, but it is His way, and we can only trust Him."

"But—it seems so—*wrong*." Toddy thrust his sharp muzzle up between the boy's knees, sensing his distress, and John stroked his ears absently, his eyes on Nanette's face with a puzzled frown. Suddenly she felt her own control slipping. She reached behind her for the wall and gripped tightly at the edge of a timber.

"I know," she said. "I know. I don't understand it either. Oh God—"

John's expression sharpened into anxiety, and he stared at her for one second more before turning and running, dragging Toddy with him. "I'll fetch Jan" he cried over his shoulder. Nanette held onto the wall and waited while her world disintegrated around her.

The following morning the infection had reappeared, and the wound began to stink again. Dr. Cranthorn took Nanette and James and Jan aside and regarded them with pity.

"There is nothing I can do," he said. "It is sometimes thus. I am very sorry."

Nanette frowned. "What do you mean? You must do something—you cut away the infection before—"

"You must do something or he will die," James said hoarsely.

Cranthorn shook his head. "I am sorry. There is nothing that anyone can do. The infection has too strong a hold, and it is creeping upward toward his heart."

As the words sank in, Nanette became aware of Jan standing close behind her. His hand was at her waist, lightly resting but ready to be strong. She met the doctor's eye.

"How long?"

"It will not be long, I think," he said gently. "He is very weak. Tonight or tomorrow."

"What will happen?"

"He will grow more feverish, then he will lapse into a coma, and then the end will come." He made a small gesture with his hand as if he would touch one or both of them, and then drew it back and folded it with the other over his gold-headed cane. "I think that he will not know much about it. He is not in much pain."

It was meant to comfort, Nanette knew, but she could not speak past the agony in her own throat.

Jan spoke for her. "Is there anything to be done to ease him?"

"No, except to keep him happy. As I said, he is not in much pain, and if he is not told, he will know no fear."

Nanette's head went up. "But he must be told—he must prepare himself. The last rites must be performed."

"It serves no purpose but to distress," the doctor said. Nanette crossed herself at the blasphemy, and seeing it, the doctor turned away. "I can only advise you. You must decide for yourself what to do."

"We will," Nanette said angrily, and then, aware that he had done his best for the child, "Thank you, Master Cranthorn. We would be alone now."

The doctor bowed and left them, and Nanette turned to look wearily at James, feeling suddenly all the weight of her years. After each crashing wave, the ship righted itself, but it became harder and harder, and one day she would not recover but founder under the burden of troubles placed upon her.

"Simon will not frighten him," she said at last. When there was something to be done, somehow one did it.

James was staring at her as if he did not see her.
"He's only eight years old," he said at last. "How can it
be right? How, Nan? He has done nothing to deserve it.
He has hardly had a life." His voice broke harshly as he
cried out, "He is everything to me!"

He put his hands over his face, and a tearing sob was
wrenched from him. Jan reached forward, his fingers
plucking at James's sleeve.

"You have me, Father," he said, but James pulled
himself free roughly and stumbled from the room. Her
throat hurt too much with unshed tears to speak, but
she held out her hand, palm up, and after a long moment Jan came back and placed his own over it, and
together they went back to the bedchamber.

Alexander grew more feverish as the day wore on,
and by the evening he was delirious. He babbled about
school and his friends and his pony and his hawk, and
Nanette and Jan soothed him between them, for James
had shut himself away in his chamber below, alone with
his grief. Simon administered the last rites at midnight,
but it was doubtful whether the child knew what was
happening to him, and so in the end both sides of the
argument were appeased. Shortly afterward he lapsed
into unconsciousness, both hands clutching his mother's, and at the darkest hour before dawn on that bitter
February morning he died.

CHAPTER THREE

One hot summer day in 1560 Elizabeth Morland rode over to Watermill House, accompanied by her son John. Since the Watermill estate abutted upon the Morland, it was possible to do the journey without ever leaving Morland land, and so Elizabeth didn't take a servant with her, which would have annoyed Paul had he known. But Paul was out on the hills that day, supervising the painting of the ewes' backs with a salve made by boiling broom flowers in a mixture of urine and brine, and as Elizabeth said sternly to her favorite child, "What your father knows not will not grieve him."

"Yes, Mother," John said dutifully, and then added, "but you must not think of riding home alone. If I am not there to bring you, you must ask Aunt Nan for a servant."

"Yes, John," she said demurely, and they both laughed.

Matthew received them at Watermill—he was to that small house steward, chamberlain, butler, bailey and, nowadays, almost master as well—and directed them to the small walled garden on the south side of the house, where he said they would find the mistress.

"And the master?" Elizabeth asked hesitantly.

Matthew shook his head just perceptibly and then said in a neutral tone, "The master is in his study and gave orders not to be disturbed. Will I have someone take you to the garden, Madam?"

"No need, Matthew. Don't let me keep you from your duties."

It was a peaceful scene in the little garden. The heat was trapped there, reflected off the soft, flaky red brick of the walls, and the air was drowsy with the sound of bees, attracted by marigolds and lavender that had been planted there to fetch them; for fruit will not be borne without the bee, and the garden was given over to fruit. All around the walls were espaliered apricot, peach and fig trees, and in the center were squared beds of strawberries, currants and sweet little muskmelons.

As they entered they were greeted by one short sharp bark from Zack, Nanette's greyhound, who rushed up to them and whirled his tail almost in a circle as he bowed ecstatically and then thrust his muzzle up into John's brown hand. Nanette, at the far side of the garden, turned to see who it was and then came across with a smile of welcome. At home she had taken to wearing very simple clothes, the straight gown of the countrywoman with the barely stiffened busk and comfortable small collar, her hair contained in a neat cap of starched white linen, and Elizabeth reflected that they seemed to make her look younger. From a distance, with her small-boned, slender body, she could have been taken for a young woman.

With her, carrying the long gardening basket, was Mary Seymour, who was just approaching her twelfth birthday and was already quite a little woman. She was small and plump and pretty, with a fair complexion and curling golden hair, and the wide straw hat she was wearing to protect her delicate skin did not cast a deep enough shade over her face to hide her blush as she saw John beside his mother. Elizabeth noted it and smiled inwardly. Ran the stream that way? Well, for the present John would not notice her unless she dropped down and ran on four legs, but sometime in the future, if Paul had not grander plans, Elizabeth would have no objection to a match between them.

"My dear Elizabeth," Nanette was saying as she came across the garden to kiss them both, "how good it is to see you. Look, here, the first little fruit from the apricot. Taste it—it's small, but so sweet."

"Small indeed," Elizabeth laughed. "How can you tell it's an apricot and not a bean, Aunt Nan?"

Nanette tried to look offended. "Just taste it— Morland Place apricots never tasted so sweet, did they? God's day, John. Mary, where are you? Come and say hello at least."

Mary nodded shyly but could not be induced to speak, and John gave her a cousinly salute but was certainly more interested in Zack's caresses.

"How cool and easy you look, Aunt Nan. It must be pleasant to be able to dress like that. I am in fear of my life because I rode over with no servant."

"And what occasioned such haste?" Nanette asked, turning and walking with Elizabeth toward one of the stone benches. They sat down, and Nanette gazed up at the blue sky fringed with the branches of the apple trees in the orchard beyond the wall. Already they were heavy with the little green-gold pearmains.

"John is restless because Toddy hasn't come back yet," Elizabeth said. "I told him he should not look for him to come until the snow—perhaps not even then."

"But Mother, he always came back before," John said passionately. 'When he ran away last summer, he was back by now. And then in spring he was gone only a month—"

"But John, you can never tame a fox, you know that. Why else do we say wild as foxes? Toddy has gone back to his own kind," Elizabeth said gently. "Why do you not ask your father for a dog-pup instead?"

Nanette looked from one to the other sympathetically. "So you came here to divert him?" she said, smiling. "Or was it that you hoped we might have news of Toddy?"

Elizabeth said, "I thought perhaps he could go out with Jan, riding or swimming, something to take his mind off Toddy."

"I think Jan is going fishing with the Smith boys," Nanette said. "Mary, dear, run in and see if Jan has gone yet and ask him to come here."

"Yes, Madam."

"Oh, and you could take in the strawberries as you go. Matthew will give them to the cook."

"Yes, Madam." Mary ran off. Nanette often used her for messages, for she was quick and clever, more reliable than a servant.

John wandered away to the other side of the garden and Zack followed him, and Elizabeth asked Nanette in a low voice, "Matthew said James is still in his study. How is he, Nan?"

Nanette shook her head. "Not well, I think. He eats very little, and he is grown very thin, but worst of all is the silence. He rarely speaks, never laughs or sings as he used to. He does not work, shut up there alone all day. I have looked in sometimes, quietly so he did not see me. He just sits there, staring at nothing."

"Is he grieving still?" Elizabeth asked carefully. It was a year and a half since Alexander's death, but she knew that the wound was not healed entirely.

"For the boy? I don't know. I thought so, and yet there is something else there, too. I think he has turned his mind more and more to other questions. It makes life difficult at times."

"Religion?"

"Yes. He has forbidden any of us to attend the Mass. Not the servants, not Jan, not me—not any of us."

"Because of the fine?" Elizabeth asked in surprise. There was a statutory fine of a hundred marks for attending a Catholic Mass, but it was very rarely enforced, especially here in the north. There was also a fine of twelve pence for not attending church on Sunday and on the major feasts, and this was generally collected. Since it was such a small sum, those Catholic families who did not want to attend the official church paid an annual or quarterly sum to their local justice and continued with their lives in the old way. But in fact the Queen and Archbishop Parker between them had combined enough of the elements of both sides into the official service for all but the most rabid Pope-Catholics to be able to attend without offense, and non-attendance was more frequently a result of laziness than of a tender conscience.

"No, not because of the fine. It is hard to discover what is in his mind, for he says so very little, but I have the feeling he is beginning to think that the Protestants are right after all. He makes us all attend the church, he says, out of loyalty to the Queen, and yet he does not take his duties as Warden seriously in any other way. Sometimes I think—" Nanette stopped.

Elizabeth prompted her gently. "Think what, coz?"

"Sometimes I wonder whether his grief over Alexander may have turned his mind."

There was nothing it would have been proper for Elizabeth to say at that point, so she said instead, "So do you not take the Mass anymore?"

Nanette permitted herself a brief smile, though there was not much humor in it. "I was born and brought up a Catholic," she said, "though I have been no Papist for most of my life. King Henry's religion is good enough for me, as I believe it is good enough for the Queen. You know that Matthew Parker writes to me from time to time? He tells me that the Queen resists strongly any attempt to strip the church of its regalia, and the Queen's own altar has a crucifix and candles and flowers just as Queen Mary's had."

She had lost herself, and laughed properly now. "I have forgot what you asked me," she said.

"About the Mass," Elizabeth prompted.

"Ah, yes. Well, my dear, I have a chaplain, my sweet Simon, and what else should a chaplain do? I think James would like to be rid of him, but he is my servant and not James's, and our marriage settlement gave me control over my own servants, so there is nothing he can do about it. Now, hush, John is coming back." She raised her voice. "What did you find to interest you so long there, chuck?"

"A spider, Aunt Nan, with such colors on his back— like a pigeon's neck," John said. A large fat bee landed on the sleeve of John's doublet, and he looked down at it and smiled. "Look at this fellow; his legs are heavy with pollen. He looks like an ass with panniers. Come now, small brother," he said, holding out a finger, and the bee, as if it understood, climbed onto it and sat astride it while John lifted his hand to his face to look more closely. "You should go home—enough is enough for one journey," he said and held his hand up over his head, and the bee took off and flew straight as an arrow over the orchard wall.

Nanette and Elizabeth exchanged a glance.

"They never sting him," Elizabeth said. "He gets the honey out of the hives for me at home, and he goes with no nets or smoke or anything, and yet they never sting him."

"But why should they?" John asked. "They know I won't hurt them."

Just then the garden gate opened again, and Jan came through with Mary behind him.

"Ah, Bear-cub, see who has come to visit," Nanette said, standing up to receive her tall son's embrace. "Elizabeth wondered whether you would take John out with you."

"You were only just in time," Jan said, smiling at Nanette. He did not look at Elizabeth, for he knew that for some reason she did not like him, and it was not his way to antagonize people. "Rob and Jackie have come, and we were on the point of setting out when little Mary found us. If she had not such light, flying feet, she would have missed us." He gave an affectionate look at Mary, who blushed and looked at the ground. "John may come with us and welcome, but I think he will not like it. We are going rabbiting at Harewood Whin."

"Harewood Whin?" John said excitedly. "But that is where we first found Toddy, don't you remember?"

"Is it indeed?" Jan said, opening his eyes wide in amazement. "I had forgotten. Well, then, perhaps while we catch rabbits, you can look for Toddy. But don't be putting your hand into any holes without looking first unless you want to leave your fingers behind."

John bid a joyful good-bye to his mother and Nanette and, quite forgetting Mary, started for the door.

Nanette called Jan back softly. "Where *were* you going, Bear-cub?" she asked.

He grinned at her. "Akcomb Moor, but what matters it? A rabbit is a rabbit, wherever it burrows."

"Bless you, my darling," Nanette said, laughing. "Good hunting, Bear-cub. Don't bring back a hare by mistake."

"As if I would. I'm Morland enough to know better than that," he said, and in a moment he was gone, swinging with his lithe, light step out of the garden and leaving a quietness behind.

In the quietness Elizabeth's thoughts turned to something that the sight of John and Jan together often provoked in her mind. John was not her firstborn child; she had had another before him, a child which, had it lived, would have been about Jan's age. The child had been taken from her at birth and she had never known even whether it was a girl or a boy. Nanette had taken it away, and Nanette was the only person who knew what had become of it. It was for that reason that for many years Elizabeth had been uneasy in Nanette's company. Well, age and better sense and a large healthy family had done away with that unease, and yet she still wondered from time to time, and the peaceful atmosphere in the garden prompted her suddenly to ask the forbidden question.

"Nanette," she said abruptly, "what happened to my baby?"

Nanette, who had been fondling Zack's ears and smiling to herself about Jan, stiffened, but she said in a neutral voice without looking up, "What good can it do you to know that?"

"I don't know," Elizabeth said. "Yet man is born asking questions."

"Some questions may be better not answered. What could you do if I told you what happened to him?"

"Him? So it was a boy-child?" Elizabeth seized on this eagerly.

Nanette sighed and straightened up. "I should have thought you would have forgotten it all by now. You never asked before."

"I have forgotten much," Elizabeth admitted. She frowned, a little puzzled. "There are great gaps in my memory, as if pieces are missing out of my mind. I've tried to remember, but there are places where there is nothing. Perhaps that is best. And yet I do wonder from time to time what happened to the bairn. He would have been about Jan's age. It was that that set me thinking. I was wondering if he would have been a hero to John, the way Jan is."

"Elizabeth—" Nanette began, but Elizabeth leaned forward and took her hand and squeezed it hard.

"Please, Nanette—tell me."

Nanette looked steadily into the younger woman's eyes. "He died," she said. "Of the pox, many years ago."

"When?" Elizabeth asked. Her eyes werre challenging. She did not believe it—she was looking for the signs of untruth in Nanette's face.

"When he was a year and a little more. He is dead, Elizabeth."

For a long moment their eyes locked, Elizabeth's defiant, Nanette's quite and steady, and then with a little broken sigh Elizabeth dropped her gaze. Her shoulders slumped a little, and she stared at her hands in her lap.

"Oh," she said in a small voice. "I never thought of that. I always supposed—but of course he was as like to die as to live."

"And do you feel better for knowing?" Nanette asked sternly.

Elizabeth looked up with a half-smile, recalling for a moment the wild, undisciplined girl she had once been, a tangle-haired girl who had dared a beating to run off with the shepherd boy and play all day in the soft Dorset hills of her home.

"Yes," she said defiantly. "I do."

"Well," said Nanette. "Shall we help Mary with the figs? I get stiff if I sit too long on a stone bench." And as they walked she made a mental note to confess the lie to Father Simon that evening. A lie is a sin; but as you get older you come to see that there is often no choice but between one sin and another, and all you can do is to choose the lesser.

* * *

The boys came back at dinnertime, and it seemed their expedition had been a success, for Jan had eight fat buck rabbits in his bag, and though John had not found Toddy, he had spent some pleasant hours trying to get close to a pair of hares that lived in the whin. He told Elizabeth all about this while Nanette went out to have a word with the Smith boys, who were waiting at the door. They took one of the rabbits, and Nanette gave them also a castoff dress of Mary's to take home to their mother.

"She can make it over for your sister Betty," Nanette said, "It is not much worn, and there's a deal of embroidery in it. Or if it won't fit Betty, she can keep it by for Sal in a few years' time."

"Thank you, Mistress," the elder boy, Rob, said. "Mother will be right grateful for it, I know."

"You may tell her I shall be over to visit her soon. How is your father's foot?"

"It's almost better, Mistress, thank you. Mother tried the poultice like you said, and that fettled it right off, though he weren't happy to think of puttin' blue mold on it, but Mother said 'at it were no different from him puttin' spiderweb and stuff on the horses' legs when they cut theirselves, and that proved a canny cure. So he held his tongue and now he's hoppin' like a martlet."

"I'm very glad. Off with you now, then, and God go with you."

"And with you, Mistress."

The boys set off for home, and Nanette and Jan turned to go in.

"They are good lads," Nanette said.

Jan nodded. "And Mary and Dick are good folk. And discreet. Every time I go there I ask Mary questions, and she never tells me anything. They are the only ones, apart from you, aren't they, Mother, who know who I am?"

Nanette sighed inwardly and sang a line of an old song: "Little chickens, little chickens, coming home to roost." Aloud she said, "Why, Janny, all the world knows who you are. You are Jan Chapham, Master Chapham's eldest son."

"Mother, you know what I mean," Jan said, for once not smiling with her, refusing to be diverted.

Nanette put a hand up and cupped his smooth cheek—like his father, he went clean-shaven. "Don't ask me, Bear-cub. I told you before not to ask me."

"You said you might tell me one day."

"Maybe one day. Maybe never. You are my son, my only son now, so be content in that."

"I'm sorry, Mother," he said, stooping to kiss her brow. "I forgot for a moment. It was thoughtless of me. Come, shall we go in? Do you know what I thought I might do with the skins of those bucks? I thought I might make Mary a pair of fur gloves. Do you think she would like that?"

James did not appear at dinnertime, and Matthew, who went into the winter parlor to speak to him, came out with the message that he would not eat anything and that they were to dine in the Hall and not trouble him. Jan sat in the master's seat and did his best to cover the awkwardness. John and Mary were deep in conversation together—at least, John was talking and Mary listening as he told her about the hares.

Elizabeth said quietly to Nanette, "I wonder sometimes if it is quite natural for John to be the way he is. This business about not killing animals—it is passing strange in a boy of his age, do you not think so? And look at the way he can pick up bees without being stung. And Toddy—no one can tame a fox, but look how devoted Toddy was to him."

"I think John is a fine lad," Nanette said comfortingly. "I do not think you need to worry. There seems to be a strain of gentleness like that in the Morland

family, and it comes out from time to time. Hezekiah
has a little of it—"

"Yes, that's true," Elizabeth said. "He was always
very tender with my babies when they were newborn—
and he still dotes on my Jane, who's such a little, quiet
thing. But he will hunt and hawk with the best of them.
Who is going to fill my winter pots if John will not kill
a deer or a dove?"

"There are menfolk enough between us to hunt for
all," Nanette said. "Besides, won't John be going away
soon? I should have thought Paul would want him to
have his time at Court before he gets much older."

"He has spoken of it," Elizabeth said, "but time goes
past and he does nothing about it. I think perhaps he is
unsure of how much influence he still has. I am happy
that he does nothing, though—I do not want John to go
to Court,"

"Why not?" Nanette said. "It would be the best opportunity for him."

"I think perhaps she is afraid that the Queen's eye
will light on him," Jan said, "and that he will not come
back again. It is well known that she likes good-looking
young men around her. That is why Mother has never
taken me to Court, Cousin."

"The Queen is well satisfied with her horse master,"
Elizabeth said.

Nanette shook her head sadly. "Robert Dudley," she
mused. "Tainted by treason in every generation, the
Dudleys' and yet the Queen has this one by her and
defers to him in everything."

"She will marry him in the end," Elizabeth said.
"She waits only for his wife to die."

"She will not, then," Nanette said indignantly. "Elizabeth Tudor would not stoop to marry a commoner,
and particularly not one from an attainted family. She
is too proud."

"Aye, Mother, I know how you defend her like a lioness, and yet you know how this Dudley put about that his wife was dying of a tumor, and it was proved to be a lie."

"Yes, a lie so that when he had her murdered, no one would suspect," Elizabeth said.

Nanette cast a glance warningly toward the children. "Enough of such talk," she said sharply but quietly. "Whatever Dudley does or says, the Queen had nothing to do with it, you may believe me. She may be fond of him and like to have him by her, but to suggest that she would help him murder his wife so that she could marry him—! I won't have such talk in my house, and so enough of it. Remember you are speaking of the daughter of King Henry."

"Aye, and the daughter of your friend Queen Anne," Jan added. "Did you really hold the Queen in your arms when she was born, Mother?"

Nanette smiled unwillingly. "I did, Bear-cub, as I have told you a hundred times at least; if you wish to divert me, you must be more subtle. However, I consent this time to be diverted. Mary, did you hear what Jan proposed—to make you a pair of gloves from the rabbit skins? How shall you like that?"

After dinner Mary played for them on the virginals and they sang part-songs, and while they were thus pleasantly occupied, James finally emerged from the winter parlor and stood at the door, looking at them like a man woken from a long sleep and not quite sure where he is. Elizabeth, who had not seen him for some time, was shocked at how ill he looked. He was as thin as a wraith and far more stooped than she remembered; his hair was quite white, and his face had an unhealthy, greenish pallor, and though it was quite cool inside the house, his skin was shiny with sweat.

"God be with you, Cousin James," Elizabeth said,

rising and curtsying, as did the others. "I hope I see you well?"

James looked at her as if he did not recognize her and then with an effort said, "I am cold. I came to see if you had a fire."

"In August?" Nanette said before she could stop herself, and then, seeing how unwell he looked, she hurried toward him. "Husband, how is it with you? Are you feverish?" She reached out a hand to touch him, and he flinched away, glaring at her.

"I am well enough. Stand back from me. Jan, fetch me a cloak—any cloak will do. I will walk in the garden a little."

The little group waited in silence while Jan ran for a cloak and draped it over his father's shoulders.

"Let me come with you, Father," he said quietly. "I will walk with you—the walled garden is pleasant and warm at this time of day."

James looked for a moment as if he would refuse, and then he sighed, an infinitely weary sigh.

"Well, if you will. But be silent. I do not wish to talk."

As soon as they had left the hall, Elizabeth turned to Nanette, her eyes wide.

"Nanette—I did not know—!"

Nanette shook her head quickly and said, "Shall we go on with our song? Mary, play again from the beginning."

A little while later Jan came back alone. His face was white, and he looked distressed, and without waiting for permission he came to Nanette and dropped onto one knee in front of her and put his head against her shoulder.

"What is it, cubling? What has happened?"

"Oh, Mother, I think he is going mad," Jan cried, his voice muffled by Nanette's arms. "He walked in silence for a while, and then he began to mutter. I asked his pardon, thinking he was speaking to me, but he said nothing that made sense to me, only muttered like a man in a fever. Then he cried out something about Alexander and clenched his fists in the air as if in anger. I said something, I don't know what, to quiet him, and he turned on me. He called me Devil-spawn and cursed me that I had lived and Alexander died. And then he said—"

"What?" Nanette asked, her face drawn with anxiety.

Jan lifted his head and looked into her face. "It made no sense. He said that you were never his, and that I made it sure; and then he said, 'I have married three times and have no son. A Morland will inherit my patrimony.'"

There was a long silence. Nanette tried to speak and failed.

"Mother, what does he mean?" Jan asked at last.

She pulled him gently toward her and laid her cheek against his, rocking him gently. She moistened her lips with her tongue and said with difficulty, "I don't know, hinny. It must be his grief speaking. He would not wish us hurt, cub, you know that."

Jan held her tightly for a moment, and then she released herself gently.

"I had better go to him," she said.

As she reached the door of the walled garden she heard him coughing, a harsh, wrenching sound, followed, as she flung open the door, by a choking silence. He was a few yards from her, his back to her, his head bent, his hands up to his face. As the door opened, he turned abruptly. She saw his tawny eyes bright with—fear, was it?—and below them a mask of blood, brilliantly red, shocking against the whiteness of his cheeks. His hands were red, too, and the gravel of the path, and the orange marigolds that edged the path were streaked with red.

"Oh sweet Jesu—" Nanette whispered.

James stared at her, his red hands suspended halfway from his face guiltily, like a child caught stealing eggs.

"Nan—go away—" he cried harshly. The sound of his voice unfroze Nanette's limbs. She ran to him, pulling up her apron as she ran to thrust the end of it into his hands, and while he wiped his hands, she fumbled with the strings behind and pulled it off and reached up to wipe his face; but her hands were trembling too badly, and he took it from her and turned away with a curious shyness to clean himself up.

"I did not want you to know," he said, still with his back to her. "Not this way—"

He turned back. Where he had missed streaks of blood, they were already darkening to rust against his colorless skin. There was one bright spot of color on each cheekbone, and sweat beaded his upper lip.

"You had no right!" she cried, her voice high with anger. "How long have you known?"

"Since April. Cranthorn—"

"Cranthorn!"

"I swore him to silence."

"You had no right. Oh James, James—"

He held out his arms, and for the first time in months they embraced, though he turned his face carefully away from her, and after a moment he pushed her gently away.

"Nan, my heart, you know that it is contagious. You must keep away from me. I have tried to keep myself apart. God knows, it was hard to do. You understand—"

"I understand only that I love you, and I want to be with you," she said. Her voice was ugly, and she put her hands to her mouth as if she could reshape the sound. They stared at each other, very still. An afternoon breeze stirred in the apple trees and fluttered the sash of the bloodstained apron that hung from James's hands. "How long?" Nanette said.

"Perhaps—three months, more or less."

"Oh God—"

"Nan, don't cry, I can't hold on if you cry. Listen to me—I love you. I want you to know that, whatever happens. But I must keep apart from you, and the boy, from now on. I will have a bed made up for me in the winter parlor, and no one must come in there."

"No!"

"I have rewritten my will. Watermill goes to you for your lifetime; then everything is Jan's. I had left all the city property to Alexander—"

"No!"

"Nan, *please*—"

"I can't let you go!" Tears came at last, scalding her cheeks, breaking her control. She was too old to cry easily or gracefully; it was harsh and ugly. Then, because perhaps it did not matter very much anymore, he let drop the thing he held and sat down on the bench and drew her onto his lap. He put his arms around her, and she hid her face in his shoulder and he held her until the tears stopped. She had always been small and light; she was like a child still to hold. He closed his eyes and rocked her.

Afterward they were quiet for a long time, so quiet that a blackbird flew down onto the wall just in front of them, flipped his tail and set his head back to sing, a fountain of silver notes in the warm golden air. A leaf yielded to the tug of the breeze and planed down to the path; its edges were curled and yellow-brown. It was August, but there was the first smell of autumn in the air. Autumn is for endings, he thought. He felt the small, light-boned thing in his arms and remembered his first sight of her, a lifetime ago when she was seventeen, with skin like a rain-washed pearl and hair as black as night hanging loose to her waist from under a maiden's cap. He thought he had got over the pain, but

it rose in him as freshly as his memory, and he closed
his eyes against it and held her tighter. The blackbird
flew off, and there was silence but for the leaves rattling along the path.

Nanette stirred. "We must go in. You will catch
cold," she said. He did not point out that it hardly mattered now. She stood up and held out her hand to him,
and when he hesitated, she said, "Come, take it. I have
nothing worse to fear."

He stood up and took her hand. It felt so cool against
his burning skin.

"Nan," he said, "when—the end comes—" It was
hard to hurt her, but he must. "I'll have none but
Thomas Markham." Thomas Markham was a Protestant minister. Nanette let go of his hand. "Promise me,"
he said. Her mouth turned down with pain, but she
nodded. "Say it," he insisted. Her blue eyes lifted to his,
and his undoing was in them.

"I promise," she said. He was breaking apart, but
there was no longer any reason to hold on. Now it was
he who held out his hand. How could it be suddenly so
dark? Where was the sun?

"Take me in, Nan. Oh my hinny bird, take me in."

It was an autumn of indescribable beauty, warm lan-
guorous days of liquid gold, long luminous twilights,
vivid fiery mornings edged with brilliant frosts that sugared the fallen leaves and made them crackle underfoot. The smell of fruit was in the air, and the wood-
smoke smell of autumn, and the days were filled from
dawn to dusk with bird song. The trees changed their
coats, and winter was coming on in scarlet battalions,
the crimson of the creeper, the jewel brightness of the
swags of rowanberries, the deeper blood red of the holly's fruit; but the summer warmth held on, pushing
back the limit of the year as if it might hold back time

itself and make last forever this twilight of piercing sweetness.

Then November came, and on St. Erkonwald's Day the dawn broke gray and bitter, flushed along the horizon with winter's pink. Along the roof tree sparrows bunched, fluffing out their feathers against the cold, and the great willow tree trailed its bare fingers along the surface of the pond as the last yellow leaf fell to the black water. Inside Watermill House the fires were built up and the air was sweet with apple smoke, and the smell was proof that summer was over at last. Matthew went into the winter parlor just before dinnertime to make up the fire and found his master lying in his bed, looking out of the window.

He chattered lightly as he made up the fire, turning the half-consumed logs so that the flames sprang up, golden and blue, and the sparks spat and cracked up the chimney.

"Going to be a very cold winter, Master, by the look of it. There's a lot of berries on the holly, and that's always a sign of a hard winter. And there was a flight of geese over this morning, flying very high—did you see them? Too high to shoot at. Always a sign, when the geese are that high. Oh, and one of the men was over from Morland Place a bit since with a mutton, and he told as how the young master's fox had come back; turned up this morning, did Toddy, bold as brass, and trotted straight up to the kitchen door."

Matthew swept the last of the ashes in under the dogs and stood up.

"I'll be bringing your dinner to you in a while," he said, turning toward the bed. "Are you warm enough, Master? Shall I bring another rug?"

But his master did not answer, only continued to stare out with unseeing eyes at the bare tree and the winter sky.

CHAPTER FOUR

On St. George's Day 1562 the family all came together at Morland Place to celebrate. Mass was said in the chapel very early for the household and those of the tenants—a large number of them, in fact—who cared enough for the Old Faith to attend; but since it was not only a Saint's Day but a Sunday it would have been unwise for the Morlands to draw attention to themselves by not attending church. Paul and John, therefore, rode into York with a handful of servants and attended the early service at the church of the Holy Trinity within the gates.

The church had been the Priory church, and since the dissolution it had fallen into disrepair. Ten years back a violent storm had brought the campanile tower crashing down through the roof to ruin the chancel, and for some time the church had stood open to the elements until the parishioners had collected enough money together to roof over the nave for use as the parish church. There was barely a shadow left of Holy Trinity's former glory; but the Morlands had always attended it, and many of them had been married and buried there before the chapel had been built at Morland Place, and so it was still the church where they chose to make their official attendances.

When Paul and John returned from York, the celebrations began. Paul still insisted on the traditional archery practice on a Sunday for all his family and household, and so the big straw targets were set up in the Long Walk across the moat, but since it was a feast day, it was made into a competition, free to all to enter, and fine prizes were put up—a black piglet, a pipe of good wine and a copper cooking pot were the best. All the Morland children were expected by Paul to be able to pull a bow and to attain a performance consonant with their age. Elizabeth had not been taught archery in her childhood at Hare Warren, and though she had taken it up since her marriage to please Paul, she was not accomplished in the art and took no more than a nominal part in the proceedings. She preferred to sit on one of the benches and watch, enjoying the pride and security the weekly display of her family gave her.

There was Paul, her husband: a small man with the very upright carriage common to small men. His uprightness was emphasized nowadays by the stiff Spanish ruff he wore, which permitted no bending of the neck, and the bombasted doublet, which severely limited bending at the waist. He was very conscious of his image and dressed always in the latest fashion, and insisted that Elizabeth did, too. He had the Morland coloring— dark hair and beard and light skin—and wore much black, relieved by sapphire blue.

Elizabeth had been sent north as a very young girl to marry Paul's brother and had ended up marrying Paul. It made little difference to her—a woman must marry where she was sent, the match was good and matters had turned out well enough for her. Paul was a kindly man, though strict, formal, perhaps a little ponderous;

gaiety and laughter sprang up more readily when he was
away from home, as he frequently was; but he was
never cruel or unjust, and he was liberal with his gifts to
her. She had thought once, at the very beginning of
their marriage, that she might love him, and perhaps if
they had been simple folk, a yeoman and his wife, she
would have. But the master and mistress of Morland
Place were king and queen of their small country, and
dignity and formality came first.

That the marriage had been successful, however, was
patently obvious—ten children, of whom seven were
surviving. Elizabeth surveyed them as she sat in the
fragile April sunshine that day and thought what a fine
brood they were, all healthy and handsome, all but two
with the family coloring—dark hair and blue eyes. Arthur, at four the youngest and her special pet, had a
reddish tinge to his darkness, and his eyes were the
violet-blue of the auburn-haired. He still had his baby
chubbiness, but conscious of his newly donned manly
clothes, he was doing his best to pull the bow of eight-
year-old William.

William was the odd one out in looks, with hair so
fair it was almost white; it glittered like silver in the
sun. Mrs. Stokes, the governess, called him the angel-
child, not only for his great beauty but for his sweet
temper, biddable nature and pure treble voice that
would bring tears to the eyes even of a hardened sinner.
With great patience now he was supervising Arthur's
baby endeavors with a bow that was too big for him,
and when, looking up, he caught his mother's glance
upon him, he smiled radiantly. He loved everyone and
everything quite effortlessly, and he seemed to have a
natural talent for doing and saying the right thing.

Mary came next in age, being eleven, and she was
practicing side by side with her sister Jane, who was
fourteen. In looks they might have been twins, both

dark haired and blue eyed, and while Mary was tall for
her age, Jane was very slight, so they were much of a
size; but their natures were very different. Mary was
like her mother, bold tempered and fearless, often led
into error by high spirits, hasty and careless. Since she
had been attending St. Edward's School she had been
improved by the stricter discipline, but she still loved
best to run wild with the village boys who shared lessons with her, and Mrs. Stokes shook her head over her
and wondered if Mary would ever learn to be a lady.
"Give her another year," Elizabeth would say. "When
she is twelve she will be a woman—that's time enough
for her to be a lady."

Jane was a puzzle to her mother but a source of
pride to her governess, for she was quiet and obedient
and as ladylike as could be wished. Father Fenelon
called her a scholar, and Paul called her Nonnette;
Elizabeth laughed at them both, but there was about
Jane a great fund of thoughtfulness and serenity that
seemed almost unnatural to Elizabeth. Jane rarely
laughed, but she was not sullen-tempered; she seemed
to contemplate the world from within a stronghold of
calm and assurance, drawing on some secret source of
spiritual refreshment. Elizabeth felt that she might have
benefited from attending school, but she had always
been taught at home.

Young Paul was the other Morland who had been
sent to St. Edward's School. Coming between the girls
in age, at thirteen he was the plainest of the children in
looks and the most turbulent in nature. He grasped at
life with the clumsy energy of a child grasping a broad-
sword, and more often than not he grasped the wrong
end and cut his fingers. He was always in trouble, always to blame, always misunderstood, and his errors
did not seem to stem, like Mary's, from high spirits but
from a kind of clumsiness or ill luck. He had no friends,

was always involved in fights with the other boys at
school, quarreled violently with Mary and Lettice and
was, paradoxically, Paul's favorite child. Elizabeth could
not care for him—she had a natural affinity for what
was happy and lucky and beautiful—but Paul lavished
on him a tenderness he showed to no one else.

Young Paul, smoldering along on his own wild track,
stumbling over obstacles he never managed to see in
time, had no time for his father's tenderness. He wanted
to be admired and respected, and he resented his father
for seeming to love him *in spite* of what he was and not
because of what he was. Young Paul loved only Jane
and his hawk. His hawk he handled with great skill, and
the vicarious slaughter of small birds eased some of the
frustration he felt in coping with a life that seemed to
fit him so badly; and to his gentle sister he turned for
peace and soothing.

At the target nearest to where Elizabeth sat were her
two eldest children. Lettice was now fifteen and in the
first flush of what promised to be an almost extrava-
gant beauty. Her skin was white as milk, with the delicate bloom of wild rose petals; her eyes the pale, swooning blue of forget-me-nots; her long curling hair soft as
silk and dark and shining as polished jet. She was smiling to herself as she drew back her arm to take aim at
the target. She was good with the bow, just as she was
an excellent horsewoman, a superlative dancer, and
played elegantly though in a limited way upon the virginals. Whatever suited her image of herself, whatever
added to her appearance of being elegant and accomplished, Lettice applied herself to, and because she was
by no means stupid, she excelled at it. But she had no
real learning, was lazy, ignorant and incorrigibly vain.

Well, what mattered it? Elizabeth asked herself. All
Lettice dreamed about was marrying well—better than
her mother for preference—and tomorrow she was to
go to Court to further that career. Elizabeth had no

doubt that some foolish young man would fall in love with her, and if Lettice had enough wit to hold him off and he had enough control of his fortune, she would be married within the year. Elizabeth would be glad to see her gone: she both disliked and envied Lettice, and her presence galled her. Elizabeth turned her attention to her firstborn, who was talking to Lettice and shooting with her; John was going to Court, too, to seek a place, and was not happy to be going. Contemplating him, her heart turned over in her with love and wonder.

How could she, she wondered for the thousandth time, have produced out of her own body this glorious, godlike creature, this golden giant? She was no more than a woman's height, and Paul was small and slight for a man, and yet John Morland at seventeen stood six feet and a handspan tall and was broad and strong in proportion.

His sheer physical size was awe inspiring, but along with it he had great beauty. His fine features were cast in a mold of lovely benignity in which there was no trace of weakness; his soft, straight hair was barley fair with a glint of gold that matched the golden fairness of his skin; his eyes—lucky eyes, the people called them, for one was hazel gold and the other hazel green—held an expression of tenderness and wisdom that made him seem more than his age. The golden giant was a gentle giant, too.

The people recognized in him what animals had always known about him. The child whom bees did not sting or fox kittens bite, who could handle any horse or hound, had become the man to whom poor folk for miles around brought their ills and troubles. It made Elizabeth feel strange to see a woman of the village put her sick baby into John's big, gentle hands and look up at him with an expression of absolute trust. The smaller and weaker a creature, the more tenderly he would handle it, and there was healing in his touch. He could

stroke away a headache for Elizabeth and cure young
Paul's choking fits.

As he had grown, Elizabeth's love for him had
changed. She loved him now with a wonder and trembling, a passion that no other man had ever called forth
from her; he was more than a son to her, and like him,
she did not want him to go to Court. She contemplated
life here without him and saw it blank. He glanced at
her now and, with his usual quick sympathy, came
across to hunker down before her.

"Is something wrong, Mother?" he asked. "You had
such a strange expression just then."

"I was thinking of tomorrow," she said. "Half of me
hopes that you do not get a place."

John's odd eyes searched her face. "All of me wishes
it," he admitted. "I have been talking to my sister—"

"Rather, she has been talking to you," Elizabeth
said, managing a smile.

"She is so much looking forward to it. I admire her
vitality and her courage so much."

Elizabeth tried not to look surprised. "Vitality and
courage, you call it?"

John leaped straight into the center of her thoughts.
"You are wrong about Lettice," he said. "She has many
qualities that are not immediately apparent. But look,
father comes."

He stood up quickly as Paul approached. The movement looked almost guilty, and Elizabeth was forced to
restrain a smile as father and son confronted each
other, Paul standing up so straight and John trying to
slump down and not to show it, for to tower over his
father or to appear to notice that he did were equally
offensive.

"Come, are you ready?" Paul said. "We must start
the competition. John, I think it right for you to help
me to judge but not to take part—you have an unfair
advantage over the others of your age."

"Yes, Father," John said meekly. He was very good at target practice, though he never applied the skill, for he would not kill any creature.

"We will not wait for the Buttses to arrive," Paul said. "Ah, I see Hezekiah there, and Jan, just come. Well, let us begin or we shall not finish before dinner."

Paul dashed away, and John was about to follow when Hezekiah saw him and Elizabeth and bellowed a greeting, so he waited. Hezekiah was just back from one of his sea voyages, as his brown skin and rolling gait betrayed, and it always took him awhile to moderate his voice to landsman's pitch.

"What ho, coz," he cried. "God's day to you, little Elizabeth. And John—why, God's me, you have grown again! I thought I was to be the giant of the family, but all my growing has slipped sideways these last years, while yours goes on upward like a sapling. God bless you—both. How do you do?"

Elizabeth greeted him affectionately. She was fond of the big bluff sailor and envied him his footloose life. Hezekiah was the great-grandson of the notorious Richard Morland, who was reputed to have walked three times around the whole of England barefoot and to have wedded a wild woman from the dark wastes of Scotland who spoke no word of any tongue intelligible to man and bore her children upon the open heath like a wolf. Whether these stories were true or not, Hezekiah had the urge to wander right enough and had spent most of his adult life at sea, returning between voyages to Shawes, the estate he had inherited from his father, which he farmed vigorously and ingeniously until the sea called him again. At twenty-nine he was a big, broad man with a huge smile and a vast, spreading beard from which sun and sea winds had bleached the color.

"Now I have a chest of presents at home for you and all your pretty bairns, and if you will have me to stay awhile, I will come tomorrow and bring it," he was saying now. "I hear tell your man is to London tomorrow, and if I can supply his place and get me some female company into the bargain, I shall be content."

"Of course you can come, and welcome," Elizabeth said, "presents or no presents, but you must not break my maids' hearts while you stay—I know what you sailors are."

Hezekiah spread his hands innocently. "As if I would—"

"My maid is quite mad for you, Hezekiah, ever since you brought her a shell comb from the Indies, so be careful what you say."

"I will, I will. God's beard, is that my little cousin Jane over there? Elizabeth, will you excuse me? I have such a pretty thing for her—but bless me, it is at home still with the rest. Yet I'll tell her about it—"

Elizabeth and John smiled at each other as he hurried off. He had always had a soft spot for the quiet one of the family. John was again about to follow his father when Jan, who had held back while Hezekiah was talking, came across the grass, waving to attract his attention.

Jan gave a respectful bow to Elizabeth and then held out to John a bundle of cloth. "I'm glad I caught you, John. I wanted to show you something."

"What is it, Jan? I cannot stop long—my father is calling me."

"Cannot you guess?" Jan asked, grinning. "Did I not promise you, weeks since?"

John's face lit up, and he held out his hands. "The pup?" he said, unfolding the cloth. A fat gray-brown whelp stirred and sneezed and wriggled toward John's fingers and, finding one, took it in his mouth and sucked on it. John held the little thing, enchanted. Jan watched with satisfied amusement. The friendship between the two, unlike though they were, had never fal-

tered, even though Jan was now master of his estate
and therefore had less time to himself to seek out John.

"What is this?" Elizabeth asked, and her voice was
sharper than she had meant, for though she had never
liked Jan, she always tried to conceal it, for John's
sake. "Haven't you dogs enough, John?"

"Why, no, Mother," John said, looking a little surprised. "They are my father's dogs—I haven't one of
my own. Jan promised me one of this litter because it
would be very special. Don't you remember me telling
you? He tethered out his hound bitch when the wolves
came down, and the whelps will be half hound and half
wolf."

"The best of both strains, cousin," Jan said politely
to Elizabeth. "The courage and faithfulness of the hound
and the strength and cunning of the wolf. And this is the
pick of the litter. It seemed to me a good progression,
from a fox kitten to a wolf cub. No doubt he'll be
taming a wildcat next."

"Thanks, Bear-cub," John said, and though his
words were few, his eyes conveyed his gratitude to his
friend. "But I must go—my father is beckoning. Will
you take the pup again?"

"One thing more—I will keep him until he's ready to
leave his dam and then bring him to you again—but
will you do something for me?" He put his hand into
his breast and brought out a letter. "Will you see that
this gets to my mother when you reach London?"

"Of course," John said, and exchanged the pup for
the letter before running off to obey his father's increasingly irritated summons.

The competition got under way at last and proved
very enjoyable. Jan Morland, who was one of the best
marksmen in the country, provided some amusement by
pretending to shoot very badly and with one of his shots
very skillfully sent an arrow through Hezekiah's bonnet,

which its owner was waving in the air to encourage
him. The black piglet was won by Lettice, which
pleased Paul very much and did not please Lettice at
all, until Paul promised to exchange it for a bracelet or
some other such toy. Jane Morland also won a prize,
one of the lesser ones, and that too caused some amusement, though a different sort, for Hezekiah stood behind her at each shot, bent her bow for her, took aim
for her and did all but make the shot himself; and had
it not been that she feared to hurt her cousin's feelings,
the "Little Nun" would have refused the prize as being
undeserved.

Then the Butts family arrived, and it was time for
dinner. Catherine, fatter than ever and wearing widow's
weeds, for her husband, old John, had died the year
before, came in a litter attended by Charity, and with
her came her sons Samson and Joseph and their wives
Anne and Grace, and a governess and a very elegant
number of nursery maids attending the children. The
Butts family, as Catherine put it, had been struck by a
plague of girls: Samson had two, eight-year-old Rosalind and two-year-old Margaret, his four sons having all
died in infancy; and Joseph had two, Grace and Jane,
aged five and three, and one surviving son, Walter, who
had struggled through to his eighth year without ever
having looked as though he would survive to adulthood.

Nanette, of course, attributed the death of the
Buttses' sons to the unhealthiness of York, and she and
Catherine argued on that subject whenever they met.
Now as she was led into the hall to take her seat at the
high table for dinner, Catherine felt the lack of someone
to argue with and filled the gap by complaining about
Nanette herself.

"That sister of mine, running off in that fashion to
Court—unseemly, I call it, with her poor husband not
cold in his grave, and at her age, riding about the coun-
tryside on horseback, leaving her estates to that boy of

hers to handle—and the good Lord only knows where *he* came from—what's that?" as Hezekiah murmured something urgently to her, "Yes, yes, I know he's here. Short of sight I may be but not yet blind, though I'm fifty-one come Michaelmas and a martyr to my legs. Yes, I'll have some of that brawn, and a cut off the mutton—plenty of fat—and some of the little fowls. Just three or four—too many bones in 'em for me. I prefer in nice fat partridge, but you can't tell Elizabeth— she will have these dainty meats. Nan's another of 'em, and not a pick of flesh on her for it, as you know. Well, she'll have fine fare enough at Court, though for all the dainties in the world I could not sit at the table with the Queen. King Harry's daughter she may be, though there's plenty will tell you there's doubt about *that* enough to hang a man, but when a woman in her position makes her horsekeeper her lover and bids him murder his wife so she can marry him—is that sauce sharp, hey? Put it here beside me then, where I can reach—though I doubt that it'll be sharp enough for me. I may be an old woman, but I have a refined palate all the same. It comes of being a lady, and if I were Elizabeth I'd not send that girl of mine to Court, even to get her a husband, for who knows but she might lose more than she gains—"

In desperation Hezekiah began to talk very loudly to Jane, and in response to a little prompting he began on a series of stories about his sea voyages to exotic places, adding such color as he went along as seemed most appropriate and urged on to flights of invention by Jane's gravely attentive face. Gradually he gathered up the rest of the table for his audience, and at the end of a particularly exciting story about a battle with a sea monster, Elizabeth broke into ironic applause and cried, "Well done, coz, indeed, but you had better be more sparing with your effects, or what will you do for adventure next year and the year after?"

"How can he know, Mother, until it happens to him?" John asked.

Elizabeth laughed up at her son. "Why, you don't believe all those stories about far-off places, do you? He makes them up for our better amusement while he sails peacefully to and fro between Rye and Calais, doing scrimshaw work and watching for dolphins."

"Why, I hadn't thought of that," John said, while Hezekiah roared with laughter at Elizabeth's idea of shipboard life.

"I believe them," Jane said stoutly, feeling he needed defending. "Cousin Hezekiah would never tell a lie."

Hezekiah looked at her oddly. "Do you then, Puss?" he said gently. "Well, I can't pretend that I've never slipped a little off true before now, but I'll say this—I'll never lie to you, Mistress Jane Morland, as long as I live."

"A toast," Jan called out, laughing. "To the reclaiming of a sailor's soul!"

Amid the laughter and the drinking of the toast, John and Elizabeth exchanged a glance that said all manner if inexpressible things, and then Paul spoke to the company in general: "We shall have a musical evening with so much talent here today. Hezekiah shall sing us some of his shanties, and Jane and Lettice shall play to us, and William shall sing, and Jan shall give us one of his own songs for a treat. But now let us be quiet and seemly while we have a reading from a book of devotions. Clement," to the steward, "fetch the book. Father Fenelon, will you read to us?"

When the family retired for the night, Elizabeth went up first while Paul had private words with John and with Lettice in the steward's room. Elizabeth undressed quickly and got into bed, pulling the curtains around for privacy, since others would have to pass through the chamber to reach the other bedrooms. The bed she

slept in was the great Butts bed, which had been made
for Paul's grandparents on their wedding. All Elizabeth's children had been born in it. It was a splendid
affair of cedarwood, every inch elaborately and delicately carved. The tops of the four pillars were cornu-
copias whose spilled fruit and flowers made the upper
frieze, which carried the tester and curtains. The pillars
were wound about with fruiting vines and wine butts
hidden amongst the leaves, canting reference to the
original bride's name.

The head and base panels showed fauns, satyrs and
maenads disporting themselves—fairly modestly, all
things considered—in a luxuriant garden. The hangings
were of crimson velvet in winter and red-and-gold
striped sarcenet in summer, and when the household
moved to Twelvetrees for the annual sweetening, the
Butts bed was dismantled and carried over to the other
house on oxcarts, for Paul would not be parted from it.
To him it was the essence of the headship of the family,
and having been brought up as a younger son, he was
that much more careful of his dignity.

Elizabeth settled down on her side and pulled the
covers up, hoping to be able to feign sleep well enough
when he came to bed for him not to want to wake her.
His demands on her body were not excessive, and he
was always careful and courteous as a lover, but Elizabeth dreaded the occasions when he did not immediately settle to sleep. Her youngest son was four, she reasoned, and she could not hope to be lucky forever. She
felt a little guilty about terming it "luck," but though
she was proud of her children she would be glad not to
have any more. She was thirty-six and had had ten
pregnancies, and she had a number of potentially fertile
years ahead of her. She did not want to be worn out
with pregnancy; most of all, she did not want to die in
childbirth.

As for the consideration that sexual intercourse

might ever be anything other than a duty for the purpose of procreation, it did not occur to her. He was not the man who could have roused her to bliss, and it was beyond her sympathy with him to suppose it was anything other than a duty to him, either.

Her luck was out that evening. Though she closed her eyes and breathed deeply and evenly when Paul came through the curtains and closed them after him, she knew at once by the sound of his breathing and his touch on her body that tonight was to be one of the nights.

"I shall be going away tomorrow, and I shall be gone perhaps for a month," he said, putting a hand lightly on her shoulder. He trembled as in his mind's eye he saw himself unlacing her bed gown and touching her bare, smooth flesh. He waited, hoping that she might say she would miss him, that she might fling herself against him, strain him to her, speaking words of love, whispering sweet, lascivious things in his ear as she took what he offered her. It was, as always, a forlorn hope. Elizabeth only lay passive, waiting for him to act, and the pang of disappointment and pain was followed quickly by disapprobation from the strict moralist in the other half of his brain, who told him that the marriage act was for the creation of children and not for pleasure.

Chronically ambivalent, he took her, trembling, waiting all through the brief conflict for some response from her; longing for her to love him while he condemned himself for loving her. For he did love her, as he had from the beginning, hopelessly, utterly and from a great distance, humble suitor at the feet of the embodiment of all female virtue. When it was done, cold reaction set in and he rolled away from her, bleak and lonely, and they settled to sleep with as much of the bed between them as they both could manage.

"You need not rise to see me off tomorrow," Paul said. "We shall be leaving very early."

Elizabeth murmured something in consent. It did not occur to her to wonder if he wanted her to argue with him over the matter: she accepted his edict, which was comfortable to her, and they both went unsatisfied to sleep. Her dreams were uneasy. She searched all night long for something she had missed, while not knowing what it was, and a sense of sadness pervaded her that made her weep in her dream, she knew not why. She did not dream of a perfect lover. She had known no other lover but Paul; she had no way of knowing what love might be like.

It all happened very quickly. They were in the crowded corridor outside the audience chamber, waiting for the Queen to arrive, Paul and his patron, the young Duke of Norfolk; John; and Lettice dressed from head to toe in her very best and looking as nervous as she was beautiful. Around them were other people of varying degrees waiting their chance to beg a boon of the Queen or merely to get themselves seen, but Norfolk was the Queen's kinsman, and the Morlands had a place at the front of the crowd.

There was a bustle and excitement, running before its cause like heath fire running before a stiff breeze, and suddenly they were bowing and curtsying and the Queen was there, was passing, paused, and stopped before them. A clear, cold voice said with surprised emphasis, "God's death, who is *this*, Cousin Norfolk?"

The white-faced, copper-haired young woman, magnificent in crimson and gold and pearls, who was their Queen, extended a finger toward the Morland party.

"The name is Morland, Your Majesty—you may remember Master Morland here was seeking to recommend to Your Majesty's service—"

"Ah, yes, Morland. They must be kinsfolk of yours,

Nan," the Queen interrupted, turning her head to where Nanette stood a little behind her among her ladies-in-waiting. The Queen swept a brief and uninterested glance over Lettice, who, still down in her curtsy, dared to lift her eyes at that moment. "Hm. A pretty face enough. We have too many pretty maids at Court. But who is this extraordinary young man?"

John looked up, his face burning. The imperious, beautiful face was opposite his own even though he was bent double in a bow; the remote, dark eyes looked into his with a strange curiosity. In response to some message in them, he straightened up to his full height, and as he passed it the white face tilted upward with him, the eyes never leaving his own.

"That is John Morland, Your Majesty," Nanette offered, "the eldest son and heir to the Morland estate."

The little smile that was playing on the Queen's lips was flirtatious, but there was nothing of that in the eyes that sought and questioned something in the depth of John's. What did she want from him? He was only afraid that it was something it would tear him bloodily to give her. Abruptly, almost in a movement of anger, she extended a long white hand to him. His gaze unwavering, John took it and kissed it in a manner that held nothing of submission.

"Let him come to Court," the Queen said. "I shall do what I may for him."

A little murmur of surprise and interest fluttered upward like disturbed pigeons from the spectators of this strange scene, and the Queen passed on into the audience chamber, leaving behind an astonished Paul, a bemused Duke and a tearful Lettice.

"She barely looked at me!" she wailed when the Queen had gone. "It's not *fair*. John didn't even want to come to Court, and it's him that she has noticed."

* * *

John arrived home at Morland Place late one night on a foundered horse, having ridden as though the hounds of hell were after him. The outer gates were locked, and the steward had to be roused to authorize their opening to let him in.

"Where is my mother?" John asked as a groom took his lathered horse from him.

"The mistress has retired," Clement said, "but I believe there is still a light in her chamber."

"Thank you." He started to move and then checked himself, remembering. "Look well to my horse. See he does not get a chill." Then he was gone, and Clement stared after him, perturbed. It had to be something serious for the young master to leave his horse to someone else's care.

John ran up the stairs and flung himself into the bedchamber, pushing the door closed behind him and leaning against it as if to shut out some pursuer. His mother was seated before her mirror of polished silver, while her maid brushed out her long silken hair that reached almost to the ground. She turned as he came in, half rising from her seat in anxiety, and her lips made his name though she made no sound. John shook his head and then drew breath to say, "No, all is well. I've come home. You almost lost me Mother, but now—all is well."

Elizabeth dismissed her maid, and when they were alone, she held out her hand for him to come to her to be comforted. He crossed the room in a quick stride and knelt and held her hand to his cheek for a moment; she felt him trembling and smelled the dust and sweat, the man-smell of him, so potent in the closed and candle-shadowed room. Then he took the brush from her hand and, standing up, began to brush the silken tresses. Elizabeth watched his face in the mirror and waited.

"Lettice has her place," he said at last.

"I'm glad," she said. Then, "But what of you?"

"I had a place. The Queen wanted me to stay, and it was a great honor—everyone said how great an honor it was to be noticed. But I felt like an animal in a trap. Of course I must accept, my father said—but I knew I must, though I despaired. Then—"

"Tell me," Elizabeth prompted him gently. He told her.

"The second audience—it was very hot that day, stifling hot, and the press of bodies—we must stand, of course, for the Queen never sits. She strolled here and there, or stood on the dais under the canopy of state, and always at her shoulder that proud-looking, richly dressed man. Sometimes she rested against his shoulder like a lover, and when he spoke in an undertone, she laughed as if his words amused her uniquely."

"Master Dudley?" Elizabeth hazarded. John's face solidified out of the flowing candle shadows as he bent forward toward the mirror.

"Aye, Master Robert Dudley. There was such a closeness between them—almost more than lovers. Twin brothers, perhaps. Then toward the end of the audience she sent for me, and when I came to her, she waved off everyone, even Master Robert, who moved away with very ill grace. I had to stand close to her— there was so little room. I was so close to her I could smell her scent, and looking down into her face, I could see the little fine creases of her skin under the face paint, the soft wrinkling of her eyelids and the fine golden down on her cheek."

He met Elizabeth's eyes in the glass, and his hand slowed in its brushing.

"Her eyes are dark, like deep water, and the thoughts move remotely in them, like carp swimming far down. She looked at me awhile and then said, 'You are proud, Master Morland.' "

"I said, 'A man would be proud to be chosen to serve Your Majesty.' "

" 'Aye,' she said, 'a man would; but not you. Why? No, don't answer,' she went on quickly before I could speak. 'You are not a courtier, and the truth might hurt.' "

"Hurt her, or hurt you?" Elizabeth asked.

John shook his head, swallowing before he could go on. His throat was dry with dust and talking.

"I don't know. She didn't say. She looked at me for a long time, and then she smiled suddenly. She said, 'My good friend, Master Dudley, does not wish you to come to Court. You may guess why.'

"I said, 'I am flattered, Your Majesty.'

" 'And so you might be,' she said. 'Sometimes I oppose Master Robert for his own good, but just now I have a wish to please him—and in doing so, to please you. And so, if you wish it, you may go home, without fear of my displeasure.'

"I did not know what to say, and there seemed some shadow of sadness on her. She said, 'I set you free, you see, though I could have kept you, like a bird in a cage given me for a present. Enjoy the freedom I give you. God bless you, John Morland,' she said. 'Don't forget me.' "

Tears rushed to his eyes, and his face worked as he tried to hold them back. Elizabeth kept very still.

"That was when you almost lost me," he said at last, his breath dragging against the tightness of his throat. "Not before she set me free, but afterward. I saw then such a need in her—such loneliness—" He could not find the words. "Then I wanted to stay. That was the ensnarement. If I had stayed of my own will, I could never have left her."

He brushed and brushed, taking care even in his passion not to hurt her. His hands on her head were so strong and so tender that Elizabeth trembled.

After a long while he said, "My father said she was like her father." A pause. "When he said it, it was in disappointment."

He spoke no more, and the silence settled around them like birds that had been disturbed coming to roost again. Elizabeth leaned back until her weight found the hard warmth of his body, and she rested against him and slowly closed her eyes. Gradually the rhythm of his moving hand slowed and then stopped, and at last he put down the brush with a delicate click, and his arms came around her from behind, and his head came down to rest on her shoulder.

CHAPTER FIVE

John, on his way to the stable yard, met Jane coming from it, carrying a covered basket and looking upset. Her expression was usually one of perfect tranquillity, and John asked in surprise and concern, "Why, Jane, what is the matter?"

"It is nothing," she said, looking down. "I should not be so vexed when I cannot have my own way—and yet—" She sighed.

"What is it you want, little sister? I'm sure it is not something entirely selfish. What is in the basket? Did you want something taken somewhere?"

"There is no one to ride with me," Jane said unwillingly, "and that is all my trouble."

"Where did you want to go?"

"To Shawes. A servant came this morning to say my cousin Hezekiah has an ague. I wanted to take these things to him." She lifted a corner of the cover to show him what was in the basket, and he counted them over with amusement.

"Some neat's-foot jelly—rosemary jelly—some honey. What's this? Quince jam? And some patties, of your own making, I expect. Well, child, cannot a servant take them for you later?"

"Oh yes, of course. That is why I said I should not wish to have all my own way." Jane tried to look cheerful.

John stooped and kissed her cheek. "You are a good little girl, my Jane, and put us all to shame. I understand you—you wanted to go yourself. Well, run and put on your cloak, sweeting—I am going over to Watermill House, and I can take you by Shawes as I go. You will not mind waiting there until I can collect you again, will you? Jan has a colt he is breaking, and he wants me to help him, so I do not know how long I will be gone."

Jane's face lit up. "Oh, thank you. How good you are! And it doesn't matter a bit about being late. I can stay at Shawes until you are ready to come for me."

"Run along, then. I like to see that smile on your face. I will go and see to the horses. Who will go with you—Zillah? Call her, then, but be quick."

"Oh, she is all ready. I will meet you in the stable yard," Jane said, running off lightly to call her maid and fetch her cloak.

Hezekiah's ague was not feverish, and he came out to meet them himself.

"God bless you," he cried, slapping John heartily on the back. "How good of you to come and see me." Jane he greeted more quietly, lifting her from her pony and setting her down as if she were made of Venice glass and might shatter if handled too roughly. "How now, Puss? Hast 'a come all this way to see thy worthless old cousin?"

"God's day, Cousin," Jane said, looking a little ruffled. "You are not old or worthless, and I wish you would not say so. It grieves me."

"Well, I shall not then, for I would not grieve you for all the world. What, John, are you going already?"

"Aye, I came only to bring your physician. I am going to Watermill. Will you keep her until I come again this afternoon?"

"Of course—I would show her my herb garden, which I have put in better order since she lectured me so thoroughly last time." He smiled down at Jane, who blushed and lowered her gaze. "But you need not trouble to call back for her—I will ride home with her myself. My ague is not severe, and it is time I called on your mother."

"I smoke your purpose," John smiled. "You want to sup at someone else's table. Well, I shall see you at home, then. Jane, I leave you in good hands."

"I know," Jane said, making it literal by placing one of her hands in Hezekiah's in a gesture of simple trust.

When John reached Watermill House he found Jan out in the orchard, helping Mary Seymour pick apples. It was not strictly necessary, for Agnes was holding the basket and the footman, Digby, was up the tree, and all that Mary had to do was take the apples from Digby's hands and place them in the basket; but as John came through the gate with the young half-wolf pup at his heels, he thought Mary looked so pretty in her wide-brimmed straw bonnet trimmed with long blue ribbons that it was no surprise that Jan felt he should be there. The sunlight filtering through the leaves of the apple trees dappled Mary's face and almost concealed the fine blush that colored her cheeks as she turned and saw John. Kithra, the hound pup, raced ahead, his tail swinging madly, and thrust his muzzle up at Mary, then ran to Jan and barked happily.

"Down, Kithra! Come here!" John commanded sharply. Kithra ran back to him and then made tight circles between his master and Mary, lashing his tail and licking his lips in delight, his big pointed ears pressed flat ingratiatingly.

Jan laughed at the sight. "There's nothing of the wolf in that one!" he called, coming across to meet John. "He's as soft as a mouse's belly. What, sirrah, thy father would be ashamed of thee!"

"But his mother would be proud," John said, catching Kithra's collar and pulling him to heel. "God's day, Mistress Mary. You are back, then?"

Jan answered for her. "Aye, my mother is come home. We shall go and see her later, but first we must get on and see to this colt. I fear I must leave you, Mary. I hope you can manage without me?"

But Mary, taking her eyes from John's face for a moment, said, "Agnes and Digby can see to the apples. I will come and watch, if you do not mind it?"

"By no means. I would be honored," Jan said, surprised and pleased. He led the way to the home paddock and took great pains to seat Mary comfortably on a fallen log where she could see but be out of harm's way, and then he and John fetched the colt. It was a big, leggy, shaggy creature, full of fire but intelligent, the hardest sort to break.

"I don't want to break his spirit," Jan explained to John, "and that is why I wanted your help. You are so good with animals—they trust you."

"I will do my best," John said. He took hold of the head collar and soothed the nervous, excitable beast while Jan fetched the saddle. Then he sent Kithra to lie down with Mary, and they began.

It was a long, hard struggle, heartbreaking in its way, for all that was wanted was some way of explaining to the colt that no harm would come to him, but that was impossible. John, combining his huge strength with his strange sympathy for all dumb creatures, held the colt's head and tried to still him while Jan first saddled and then mounted; the colt screamed, kicked and reared, its nostrils wide and eyes rolling in fear and anger. The two men grew weary, sweaty and dusty, and lather broke out on the colt's shaggy neck, while Mary sat holding Kithra's leash and clenching her fists in anxiety until the fingernails dug into her palms. Then finally the colt reared up and struck out, throwing Jan off backwards and hitting John on the shoulder, spinning him around and felling him.

Mary jumped up with a cry, and as the colt trotted off to the far corner of the paddock, she struggled with the gate and ran across to where the two men lay supine in the dust. As Jan sat up, groggily shaking his head, he saw Mary kneeling with fine disregard for her skirts and trying to help John sit up.

"Are you all right?" he called, getting slowly to his feet. John sat up and held his right shoulder, wincing with pain, while Mary, her eyes huge, pressed her fingers to her mouth.

"Yes, I'm all right. He caught my shoulder a blow— thank heaven he was not shod. It's just bruised, I think. Get down, Kithra, stop washing my face. Thank'ee, Mary, I'm quite all right. Jan, we must catch the colt before he treads on the reins."

Between them they cornered the colt, and then Jan said firmly, "That's enough for the day. I will put this little youth away. You go in and get my mother to look at your arm. Mary, will you go with him?" He said this rather wistfully, for Mary had not taken her eyes off John for a moment, not even to inquire whether Jan was hurt from his fall. "Take Kithra—I'm sure he is pulling John's arm painfully."

Jan watched the three of them crossing the paddock and disappearing around the side of the house. The colt was quiet now, exhausted with his rage and struggle, and as Jan stared thoughtfully after John and Mary, the colt pushed at his shoulder with his soft muzzle and blew in his ear and then tried a tentative mouthful of his hair, which effectively woke Jan from his reveries.

"All right, young one, we'll go and find you some hay." He stooped and picked up his velvet cap, and then on an impulse put his arms around the colt's neck and rubbed his ears. The colt, after an initial start away from him, relaxed and blew again, this time affectionately. "Aye, you love me really, don't you?" Jan said. "But it can be hard when love struggles against something else—in your case, self-will, and in mine—" He paused. "Well, we shall get over it, I dare say. Come then, little one, we'll go home." And he led the colt slowly toward the stables.

When he reached the solar, Jan found John sitting on the floor at Nanette's feet, having his shoulder bound with cold cloths while Mary brushed the dirt off his jacket for him. They were talking about Elizabeth— Nanette had evidently just asked how she was.

"Well enough," John said, "though she finds pregnancy tiresome, I know. She doesn't complain aloud, but her temper grows short, and sometimes I can see she has been crying."

His concern was in his voice, and Nanette, tightening the cloths so that he winced a little, said, "Don't worry, John, she will be happy again once the baby is born. I remember how when I was young I always wondered how women could ever bear to be pregnant. It seemed such a disagreeable process." Her voice was calm and cheerful, and Jan, looking at her across the room, wondered how she could be so strong. No one would guess that she had lost her husband and her only born son. She looked up and caught his gaze and smiled, making her face seem young again.

"There, that will do—put your clothes back on," she said to John, and then, "What about you, Bear-cub? Where were you hurt? Have you anything that needs bandaging?"

"Nothing but some hurt pride, Mother, that needs

your kiss to soothe it." He crossed the room and stooped to kiss her smooth, unlined forehead and be kissed in return. He straightened up and looked at her with satisfaction. "It is good to have you home. The house misses its womenfolk—" He cast a shy glance across at Mary, who did not look his way. "You should come home more often."

Nanette smiled, reaching out to brush some dried mud from Jan's sleeve. "Home," she said musingly. "It seems I have had little practice in my life in thinking of any place as home. When I was younger than you, Mary, I was sent away to Kentdale to live, and then when I came back I was sent off to Court. Morland Place was my home for a little while, and then I went back to Court, and then I came here, to Watermill." She paused as Audrey came to take away the bowl of water and the spare cloths soaking in it; the air was sweet with the scent of the lady's-mantle she had put in the water to ease John's shoulder. Nanette remained thoughtful for a while and then continued, "My life seems to have been built around other people, always; and now it is built around the Lady Anne's daughter. And you, of course, Bear-cub: I hope you know it is not because of any failing in my love that I share my life between you instead of devoting it all to you?"

Jan met her eyes. "I can hardly begrudge you to the Queen, can I, Mother? After all, you knew her before you knew me; and perhaps she needs you more."

John, standing by the window slowly working his way down the buttons of his doublet, looked thoughtfully at Jan, remembering the dark, lonely eyes that had called to him. It was said she had her mother's eyes: no wonder then that Aunt Nan had devoted her life first to the mother and then to the daughter.

"I love you, Janny. You are my only son," Nanette said. "But she *does* need me. It is hard to be Queen, and lonely. She has good, loyal counselors and faithful servants, but sometimes she needs a friend as well. So you forgive me?"

"Of course I do, Mother, so that you come home whenever you can. It is not in that way you are cruel to me."

"In what way am I cruel, chuck?" Nanette asked, keeping a solemn face.

"Why, in keeping Mistress Mary from me, of course," Jan said. He did not look at Mary, but from the corner of his eye he saw her blush painfully: she had very fair skin, and her golden hair had a reddish tint to it, which meant she blushed easily. He was sorry to pain her, so he quickly went on, "And in keeping from me the thing I have always wanted to know."

Nanette grew serious. She said, "Bear-cub, you know I have always said that I would tell you if I could—"

The answer was no better. Jan despaired of it. "I know, Mother. Look, the sun has come out again. Shall we go into the garden and see if there are any more of those late strawberries? Then John could take them home to Cousin Elizabeth. I know women crave these things at such times."

He offered his arm to Nanette, and she rose and took it, and they went out, followed by Nanette's greyhound Zack and Jan's hound bitch Fand, who was Kithra's mother and who had been majestically ignoring the pup's attempts to chew off one of her ears. Behind them John offered his arm to Mary, and they followed, with Kithra bouncing irrepressibly between them. Jan, turning at the door, was just in time to catch Mary's smile as she looked up into tall John's face, and as they walked down the stairs he called to the lagging dogs with unnecessary sharpness.

When John arrived home for supper, he was aware at once, from the air of suppressed excitement among the servants, that something had happened. His mother met him as he went in and led him into the winter parlor, looking distracted.

"What is it, Mother? What has happened?" he asked. She turned to him, still graceful in a loose gown despite the growing bulk of the child.

"Thank heaven you are here, John. It's Jane—"

John's heart turned over. "Merciful God, she's not harmed?"

"No, no, she is well enough. Hezekiah brought her back an hour since. He—Hezekiah—it seems—"

She hesitated, staring at her tall son with a troubled air. John, remembering how he had left them, began to have some inkling of what she wanted to tell him.

"Is he still here?" he asked.

"He is with your father in the steward's room. They are talking."

"And Jane?"

"With her sister in the solar. John—"

"I think I know, Mother. Hezekiah has asked for my sister's hand."

"You knew? It was not well done of you, my dear, to keep it from me. But what do you think of it?"

"Has she said what she thinks? Will she have him?"

Elizabeth spread her hands impatiently. "It seems they settled it all between them in the herb garden at Shawes."

John could imagine the scene. If there was any place on earth that suited his idea of his little sister, it was an herb garden. "I didn't know of it, Mother; only now you tell me it seems surprising we did not guess before. You know he has always adored her, and she has admired him since he first picked her up from her cradle. He could not have a better wife, and she will be happy where she chooses, for she has the judgment of a woman twice her age. But what will my father say?"

"I think he will consent, with Lettice at Court. He will think it a good thing to tie Shawes more tightly to us. They are talking, I believe, of settlements."

John cocked his head at her and came across to touch her shoulder and lay his fingers against the base of her neck where the pulse beat. "What is it, Mother? Shan't you like it?"

"She is so young. And he is so little at home," she said, and then burst out, "I hate to think of her wed so young and pregnant!"

John looked at her with consternation and then guided her to a bench and made her sit. The pulse in her neck was throbbing.

"You are in pain," he said. "What is it—a headache?" She nodded, closing her eyes. The tears seeped out from under the lids. John laid his hands on her brow and began to stroke the pain away, outward toward the temples, and he felt her relax under his touch.

After a while she opened her eyes again and smiled a little tremulously. "It is better now," she said. "The pain is eased. John, will it be all right?"

He looked down, trying to understand her trouble, longing to ease it. "I think so," he said, in answer to whatever question she was asking.

Just then Paul came in briskly, moving too quickly as always to notice the atmosphere in the room. "Ah, John, there you are. Your mother has told you, I suppose, of Hezekiah's visit? Well, I have told him that I will consent to the match, if she really wishes it. She trusts you, John. Will you go to her now and ask her what she feels? She is too young to be wed to him against her will, and she might perhaps tell me what I wish to hear instead of what her heart says."

"Of course, sir," John said, and went willingly on his errand. Jane was sitting in the solar with Mary and Zillah, sewing and waiting for the summons, her inward agitation showing only by the unusual size and clumsiness of her stitches.

John beckoned her away from the curious stares of her sister and her maid and took her to the window. "Well, Jane?" he asked gently.

She looked up at him with a face so radiant that he did not need to ask anything more.

"We were walking in the garden," she said. "He took my hand as we stopped by the lavender and asked me if I could learn to love him, in a few years when I was older. As soon as he let me, I told him that I loved him dearly and would be his wife as soon as he wished it."

"Don't you think, dearest, that it might be wise to wait a little—a year, perhaps—to see if your feelings alter?"

"Oh, no," she said with such quiet assurance that he was satisfied. "I shall not change. I love him and I know that he loves me. When I said I would marry him, there were tears in his eyes. I think," she added inconsequentially, with a curious little smile, "that I shall always love the smell of lavender."

John smiled, too, and rested his hand on her shoulder. "I will speak to Father for you, then. I only want you to be happy, and I'm sure you will be. He will have a wife to beat all. Go down to the winter parlor, *ma nonnette*, and I will go and fetch your lover."

Mary, straining her ears, heard that word, spoken as John and Jane turned toward the door, but Jane ran past her in a flurry of skirts, her face hidden, and before Mary could ask him, John had gone, too, darkening the door as he stooped under it; so Mary was left to her own speculations, aided by the smile of quiet knowingness on Zillah's moonlike face, until they were called to supper, when the sight of Hezekiah and Jane sitting together with smiles of identical satisfaction would have told all but the stone blind what had been going on.

* * *

In October the Queen fell gravely ill with smallpox, and it was thought that she would die. Some of the younger maids were sent home, partly to avoid infection and partly to have them out of the way should the expected upheaval come: for the Queen was unmarried and childless and had not named her successor. The struggle for the vacated crown between the several possible rivals would be bloody and bitter.

Lettice came home with her serving woman, Kat, and told what little she knew to the assembled family.

"The Queen's condition is very grave," she said. "She is not expected to live. It's said that the Queen was told she was dying but still would not name her successor. So we were sent home."

"And my mother?" Jan asked in anguish. "And Mary Seymour?"

"Your mother will not leave the Queen," Lettice said indifferently, "and Mary will not leave your mother. Aunt Nan and Kat Ashley nurse the Queen—she'll have no one else."

There was silence while everyone considered the plight the country was in. At last Paul said, "There can be no doubt that the Queen of Scotland *should* take the throne—"

"King Henry and King Edward both named the Grey girls as heirs in their wills," Hezekiah pointed out.

"But the throne is not the King's to will. It must fall by right of succession," Paul objected.

"Aye, but who can determine that right?" Hezekiah said.

"The Queen of Scotland is descended from the elder sister of King Henry, and the Grey girls from the younger sister," Paul offered.

Elizabeth broke in, "What matters that? She is Pope-Catholic and kin to the French."

"The choice of Protestant heirs is too wide," Jan said. "It would cause faction."

"Lady Catherine Grey is the obvious choice—" John began, but Paul snorted in disgust.

"That tainted family! Besides, the girl is a mere cypher—whoever had custody of her body would manipulate her."

"A male heir is what is needed," Hezekiah said. "Margaret Douglas has two sons, and she is descended from King Henry's elder sister, too. Her older son—what's his name? Darnley—did you see anything of him at Court, Lettice?"

"Oh yes, he was there," Lettice said. "A very pretty young man. The Queen had him almost as a prisoner."

"Would to God the Queen had married," Paul said bitterly. "If she had a child—even a girl child—it would at least be the undoubted heir."

"There would always be some to doubt, if it were a girl," Hezekiah said, "And some to reach out for power, if it were still an infant. No, the only thing that would save us would be for the Queen to stay alive. If she dies, we shall have civil war again."

The news that came next from Nanette was glorious news for them all: the Queen had not died. Her amazing vitality had brought her back from the brink of the grave, and the fear of war retreated a few steps. But in January when Parliament resumed, the fear was still close enough for the Speaker to be prompted by all the members to exhort the Queen to take a husband as soon as possible. Look what had almost happened, he pointed out. She must get an heir, lest her people be left without a shepherd. The Queen listened patiently and then answered in the way she was already becoming known for—an answer that was no answer, which told nothing and promised nothing.

Lettice wrote home to her mother that it was said that the Queen had told Master Cecil that she liked the virgin state so well that she intended to live and die in it; but, Lettice said, her own opinion was that the Queen intended to marry her master of horse, Robert Dudley, as soon as the scandal over his wife's mysterious death had been forgotten.

Lettice's letter arrived shortly after her mother had given birth to her eleventh child, a son, who was christened Henry. By the end of January the babe was dead, and by the middle of February Elizabeth was pregnant again.

In April the weather was still cold, but the sun was shining from a frosty blue sky for Jane's wedding day. She was delighted to learn that she must marry Hezekiah twice: once in a public ceremony in the church, and a second time privately by the old Mass in the chapel at Morland Place. Hezekiah himself seemed too dazed almost to know what was going on. His big form was dressed to great advantage in white velvet with gold trimming and scarlet ribbons cross-gartering his knees. Jane, in his opinion, looked like an angel in a dress of white sewn with yellow daisies and green leaves, the big stuffed sleeves stiff with gold lace. Elizabeth privately disagreed, for she did not think white suited Jane, making her look too pale. Jane had just passed her fifteenth birthday but looked much younger. Her black, curling hair hung loose for the last time from under a little heart-shaped coif of black velvet trimmed with gold lace. It signified her virginity; after that day she would be a child no longer.

Elizabeth hated to think of that aspect of it. Her own sister Jane, who had married the Londoner Joseph Cooper, had died in January in childbirth; Elizabeth's twin, Ruth, had died in childbirth fifteen years ago; and though Nanette was of the opinion that these deaths

could often be avoided and were caused by clumsy mid-
wives and the unhealthiness of towns, few agreed with
her. It was just a hazard of being a woman. Elizabeth
was uncomfortable in her present pregnancy, suffering
greatly from indigestion and heartburn, which was not
helped on the wedding day by the tightness of her bombasted stomacher. Her dress was of the still-fashionable
black silk, with a high Medici collar, designed princi-
pally to show off the Morland family heirloom, the
priceless black pearls, which glowed with a weird and
sullen beauty against her creamy throat.

The feast was lavish, with various entertainments,
tumblers and jugglers, a small orchestra, singers, an al-
legorical mime and then dancing. Hezekiah danced a
galliard with his diminutive wife, who afterward, as if to
emphasize her small size, danced with big John, and
then with Jan, who, though he could not match his
cousin's stature, was still taller than average. John
danced with Mary Seymour, whose porcelain complexion took on a delicate rose flush; Hezakiah danced with
Nanette; and Jan came and led out Elizabeth. John's
intimacy with Jan had forced her to overcome her dislike of him, and she had to admit that there was nothing on which she could fix her dislike, for he was perfectly courteous to her, and his merry high-spiritedness
seemed perfectly innocent. Yet with his black curly
hair, black curly beard as tight as a ram's fleece, his
dancing, dark-blue eyes and his little white teeth so often flashing in a smile, he was altogether too impish for
her to feel at ease with him. He was also in black: black
velvet slashed with watchet-blue silk, a black velvet hat
whose band glittered with tiny sapphires and a very
large lace ruff that tilted his face upward so that he had
to look down at Elizabeth through his long dark
lashes—a very provocative pose. Elizabeth was glad
when her set was over and she could plead her belly
and go and sit down with her sister to talk.

Elizabeth's last surviving sister, Jane's twin, Mary, had come to the wedding with her husband Tom Bennett, and their only child, Daniel, who was sixteen and would inherit Hare Warren when Elizabeth and Mary's father, Luke Morland, died. That day could not be far off, for Luke was sixty-five, and though the Morlands were a long-lived family, he had been suffering more and more from coughing and difficulty with breathing. Elizabeth was older than Mary, but Luke had passed over her for Mary's sake, feeling Elizabeth's children were well enough provided for. Besides, Daniel had been brought up at Hare Warren, and his father, Tom Bennett, had worked Hare Warren ever since his marriage to Mary.

While sitting talking to Mary, Elizabeth, glancing around, saw Paul, deep in grave conversation, ushering Tom Bennett toward the steward's room. He wanted to converse in private, obviously, and Elizabeth's lively mind sprang ahead over the possibilities. A marriage? Paul, she knew, was eager to preserve contact with anything that might one day be Morland land, and she knew also that he had been angry that Luke was leaving Hare Warren to Mary's child and not to Elizabeth.

Daniel Bennett was eminently marriageable. Who then? Not Lettice—Paul was intending a very grand marriage for Lettice, which was why she had been sent to Court. Hare Warren and the Bennett boy would not be good enough for Lettice. Mary, then. Elizabeth smiled at her deduction. Paul would bring her the news like a gift, hoping to surprise and please her, but he never could surprise her. Pleased, though, she would be. It was time Mary was married—she was too forward and bold to be kept in the schoolroom—and Elizabeth would be glad for one of her children—and the child most like her—to go back to her own country.

* * *

A month after Jane's wedding the weather turned fine and warm. The house seemed very quiet with the loss of all its daughters—Jane gone to her new household, Lettice gone back to Court and Mary gone to Hare Warren with her aunt and uncle and her prospective husband to learn the ways of the house. The fine warm weather brought on the spring flowers at last, and the first day of sunshine found Elizabeth sitting out of doors in the sunniest part of the herb garden, tatting in the company of one of her maids. She had just sent the girl into the house to fetch some lemonade when John came out to her, having just returned from his morning's hunting.

"Was it good hunting?" she asked him, pushing Kithra's inquisitive muzzle away from her work.

"Aye, if you can call hunting good. Jan got the stag he was after, and now he's in a ferment of worry because Fand has a tiny scratch on her flank where it caught her with an antler tip."

"Well, my dear," Elizabeth said reasonably, "the deer do bark the fruit trees, you know, and kill them."

John smiled. "You sound like Aunt Nan. But they have a right to live, too. Mary was saying—"

"Mary Seymour was out with you?"

"Mary and Aunt Nan both. I can understand why Aunt Nan comes—she is a savage kind of lady—but Mary seems as unhappy as me about killing deer. I have to do my duty by the house and provide fresh meat—but I don't know why Mary comes with us if it upsets her."

Elizabeth looked at him sharply. No, he really didn't know, she thought. While she was wondering what to say, he flung himself down onto the grass at her feet and smiled up at her, squinting a little in the sunlight.

"What is it you are making? I never see your fingers still—they are always flying nimbly about some work or other."

"Only some lace," she said. "To trim the baby's shirt." She sighed unconsciously with the words, and John leaned his face against her knee for a moment in silent sympathy. "I wish the next months were over, so that I could ride out with you again. You don't know how lucky you are, John, to be a man and be free."

He looked up at her then, and she saw she had distressed him. "My father," he began and, wisely, stopped. "I do know," he said instead. "Every time I ride out I know I am blessed, and I thank God and Our Blessed Lady. I hate to think of you imprisoned—*thus*—" He could not go on. Elizabeth knew what he would not say: imprisoned by my father's lust. He hated his father for doing such a thing to his mother when there was no need. He could have been satisfied with the children he had and left her alone—his face darkened when he thought of it.

Elizabeth watched him wonderingly. He resented her loss of freedom on her behalf. It was impious, strange, wrong that he should resent Paul's lawful sway over her body—impious, but oddly satisfying to her. He was so beautiful, she thought as she looked down into his face, tanned a sweet honey color by his exposure to the weather. She loved the way the tender fans of his eyelashes brushed his cheek as he lowered his eyes in thought, and the way his silky-firm lips lay in a long crescent, lightly together and almost smiling. She loved the way the sunlight picked out the gold in his barley-fair hair, an odd strand of it slipping down over his smooth brow. She could not feel that she was his mother, that she could have had anything to do with creating this supreme wonder. She wanted his love as badly, and was as uncertain of it, as if he were a strange man she had just met and fallen in love with. No wonder Mary Seymour—

He looked up suddenly, and she felt herself blushing absurdly. On the tail of her last thought she said, "Has it occurred to you that now that the girls are all settled, your father will be looking for a wife for you?"

He raised an eyebrow. "You can't spare me," he said. "Who will run the estate if I am off courting girls?"

"Have you anyone in mind?" Elizabeth asked lightly. If he cared for Mary Seymour, she must try to persuade Paul for her, though it would be difficult. The girl had no family and no money, unless Nanette and Jan gave her a dowry from the Chapham estate.

But John rolled over onto his elbows and roughed Kithra's head relaxedly. "Oh no," he said, and she knew it was true. "I love all girls the same—little soft things, like baby birds, to hold in your palm. But there's only one girl in my heart, and that's the one closest to me now." He leaned against her knees, rubbing his face against the velvet of her skirt like a cat. She leaned forward to stroke his hair and was arrested by a burning like the beginnings of indigestion. "No," he went on, "I don't want to be married. I am happy as I am."

"Still, you must marry sooner or later," Elizabeth said. "The only reason you have been spared so far is that your father has not found a good enough match for you. If you do not marry and have a son, who will carry on at Morland Place after your father?"

"Any of my brothers," John said, getting to his feet. He leaned over to kiss her, and as he kissed her he placed a hand over her belly. "Mayhap even this one," he whispered in her ear. Elizabeth laughed in delighted shock, and he straightened up and said, "And now I must go and tell Clement about the venison and see the bailiff and the factor and all the others who clamor for my attention. God bless you, Mother. Come, Kithra, heel."

"God go with you, John," Elizabeth said absently. Her feeling of sickness was growing, like nausea, and she sat still and concentrated on fighting down the desire to vomit. Then, with devastating swiftness, pain streaked through her, making her gasp and clutch at her chest. Not childbirth pains, was her thought, before thought dissolved. It was as if a spear had been hurled into her chest, a point of steely fire that was followed by a dull, grinding agony as the shaft was forced inch by inch into her heart. She could not draw her breath; she tried to rise and fell to her knees and then onto her side on the grass.

Everything was sinking away from her, and though she tried to call "John!" she could make no sound. Even so he must have heard something. He had been at the door to the garden and came racing back, pushing Kithra away, rolling her onto her back with his great strong hands, propping her against his knees while he yelled for the servants.

"Fetch help. Call my father, and Master Philippe. Quickly!" she heard him saying to some servant who had appeared. Then his voice close to her ear, though far away, strangely distant, "Mother what is it? Can you speak? Is it the babe? Mother!"

She opened her eyes; their eyes met; she strained to communicate with him, urgently, for the iron bar seemed to be swelling inside her, forcing out her breath, forcing out her life in a vast, breaking agony. His hands were on her face, pushing off her headdress, pushing her hair back. She loved the touch of him, but even that was fading before the pain that was everything, that was all there was for now and forever. She tried to speak. *He knows,* she thought. *I'm dying.*

"Mother!" John cried frantically. Her lips were blue. They moved, saying something—what? He held her tighter as if he could keep her back by the force of his love. They were coming now, running from the house with cries of alarm like disturbed birds, but the staring eyes were empty, they were too late, the blue eyes reflected only the sky, and she was gone forever.

CHAPTER SIX

Death was a part of life, close to everyone, touching the edges of daily experience as night touches the edge of day. The Morlands grieved, and grief like a kindly, wholesome rain washed away pain so that they could go on again, living and growing as the green things of earth grow over a fire scar, softening and eventually covering it. But for John the good, cleanly grief was held back from him by shock and guilt and horror. Useless for the old women of the house to tell him that it was sometimes thus with women who were with child: the suddenness of Elizabeth's death seemed to him a judgment. He sat day after day unweeping in the herb garden where she had last been, staring at nothing, shut away in the black pit that was his heart, falling endlessly. It was not the absence of God that prevented him from praying, that appalled him: God was there in all His awfulness.

John had loved his mother, but he was aware, as he had gradually become aware over the years, that the love they shared was not normal love between parent and child. He had loved her in a more than filial way, and he saw now that he had been guilty of impiety; at the very moment of her death he had committed an impious act, and he could not free himself from the dread that it was this impiety that had occasioned her death. God had struck her down; she had died unshriven with all her sins upon her; she had died because he loved her too much, because he had resented his father's possession of her. Useless for Philippe Fenelon to urge him to prayer, to offer him the comfort of faith. John was cut off from both by his guilt, as he was cut off from the grief that could have healed him. Hour after hour he sat alone, his great frame rigid, struggling in silence for understanding, and the family and the servants watched helplessly from a distance, unable to comfort the young master.

Full summer came, bright and rich, but John's eyes were dulled to it. Jan, visiting one day and seeing John sitting alone and brooding, with Kithra dejectedly watching his face, decided that the time had come to act, and the next day he brought Jane to Morland Place. He knew John perhaps better than anyone else, knew his nature, and hoped that a gentler influence might reach further than the stern voices of logic and reason.

Jane found John sitting in the herb garden mending a piece of harness, with Kithra at his feet, nose on paws and tail tucked out of the way. The dog jumped up as she came out from the house and greeted her with ears out sideways and tail swinging, but there was a cautiousness about the greeting that showed his overtures had not recently always been accepted gladly. John welcomed her without reserve, but Jane could see there was a dullness in him where once his joy in life had shone out.

"I'll swear you have grown two inches at least since you were married," John said, stooping to kiss her. "Come sit here in the sunshine with me. Married life seems to agree with you—you are looking happy."

Jane sat beside him and settled her skirts with her usual calm carefulness. She wore a very simple gown of russet wool with long, close sleeves over a high-necked kirtle, and there was hardly any stiffening in the stomacher. Her hair was knotted up behind, and she wore her usual stiff linen cap, its heart-shape curves framing her face. There was no richness or show in her attire: only the beauty and purity of her face made her look like a queen. She looked at John carefully, as yet concealing her anxiety.

"I am very happy," she said. "My only fear is that I shall have my temper spoiled by too much petting. Hezekiah is so kind to me and the servants so respectful that I have nothing to vex me at all."

"So it should be, little one," John said. "You are the one person who could not be spoiled by attention."

"But you, Brother, how goes it with you? I am sorry to see you looking so—" She paused, not knowing quite how to put it. "You look uncomfortable," she concluded at last.

John looked down at the ground. "You cannot be surprised," he said. "I cannot forget her."

"None of us will ever forget her," Jane said, "but you must not begrudge her to God. He had His reason for taking her."

"I know why she died," John began, and Jane saw the bitterness in him.

"You may think you know," she said firmly, "but you do not. It would be a poor thing if men were as wise as God."

"But to die thus, with all her sins upon her, and—"

"And?"

"And mine," John said, very low.

Jane looked stern. "Dear Brother, think what you are saying! Is God less just than we are? All that is good in us is only the shadow of His goodness. He knows all her virtues and all her faults to the last minim, as you cannot. You must trust Him and let your faith comfort you."

"If only I could understand—" John muttered, but she could see she had reached him. She touched his hand lightly.

"If we understood everything, where would be the need for faith?" she said. "It is not for us to know or understand more than a little. We are given life to serve and praise Him, until it pleases Him to call us home again. Everything that lives must die, and God knows the time for each of us."

John shook his head. "I would I had your acceptance," he said. He glanced up at the calm beauty of Jane's face as she looked up at the sky; the reflection of the sky deepened the blue of her eyes, just as it had always done with his mother's eyes; and in that moment he saw that Elizabeth was not lost, that she was here and all around him still, real but invisible. The revelation lasted only a moment, but even when it was gone, it comforted him. Jane turned her head and smiled at him, and as he smiled back, she saw that some of the brightness had returned; the healing had begun.

"Acceptance will come in time," she said. "Prayer will help, as will sunshine and bird song and the sweet air. Take one step at a time, John."

He nodded and lifted her hand to his mouth to kiss it, and then held it in his lap. After a while he sighed, and some of the aching tenseness went out of his body, and when he spoke again it was in a voice so much lighter and more like his own that Kithra lifted his head and beat his tail softly at the sound of it.

"It is a lovely day," he said. "When you go home, I think perhaps I shall ride with you. I have not ridden Jupiter for days—he will be forgetting all I have taught him. Perhaps I may take him around by Watermill and show Jan how he is coming on."

* * *

In the autumn there was much coming and going at Morland Place by messengers so richly clad that they might not have been taken for servants at all had it not been for the Percy badge on their sleeves—a lion and a crescent and the motto *Esperaunce*. Clement, the steward, made much display of the Morland hare-and-heather badge on his own sleeve and gave orders to the other servants in a terse bark unlike his normal voice to let them know that they must not let him or the master down in front of the strangers. He was proud of his position in the family and proud of the family itself, and he wished it to be known that his household was run with as much efficiency as even that of the Earl of Northumberland could show.

Clement knew, of course, the reason for the comings and goings: the master was looking for patronage and particularly for a match for the young master. The Morland family had been for a long time under the patronage of the Duke of Norfolk, but the religious schism was changing that. The Pope had recently ruled that it was a mortal sin to attend a Protestant service; new legislation had been passed by Parliament more rigorously to exclude the religiously unorthodox from public office. The Justice of the Peace, whose duty it was to enforce orthodoxy, had been deprived of his office and replaced by a less lenient man, and now there would be more fines, more old ways suppressed—no candles on Candlemas, no palms on Palm Sunday, no ashes on Ash Wednesday, no creeping to the cross on Good Friday, no lighting of the Paschal Candle on Easter Eve.

And those who, like the Morlands, tried to hold to the old ways would be more closely watched, perhaps punished. The Old Catholics and the Protestants were being forced further apart—and the young Duke of

Norfolk was a Protestant. It was not surprising, therefore, that Paul Morland was seeking a new patron or
that he should look in the direction of the Catholic
Percy family. North of the Roman Wall the Queen's
writ did not run, and there was an old saying about
those wild lands on the border of Scotland—North of
the Wall, no King but Percy. There had been attempts
to bring the north under the same rule as the south but
they had failed. Clement knew his master's plans and
approved. The heart is nearer than the foot, ran Clement's thoughts. Up here in Yorkshire, a Percy's favor
might prove more useful than the Queen's.

There came the day when the master and the young
master went to attend upon the Earl of Northumberland himself in his town house in York. Percy's Inn, as
it was known, was a large and handsome house on
Walmgate in the marshy northern part of the city,
where many small streams drained into the Fosse to fill
the city's conduits and fish ponds. Within, the house
was sparsely furnished, and though it was grand, it had
the unaccommodating air of a house that was rarely inhabited.

Lord Percy received the Morlands in his presence
chamber, which was furnished in the old style with a
single chair for the lord, a table covered with a Turkey
carpet and a huge, tapestry-draped bed. Northumberland was three years younger than Paul but looked
older; a gaunt, weatherbeaten man with a grim and
lined face and the cold eye of an autocrat. He had lived
hard and fought hard in those bitter lands on the edge
of the wilderness. The Prince of the North was richly
dressed, and around his neck he wore a chain studded
with a fortune's worth of jewels, but his life was harsh
and loveless, and he regarded John's great height and
gentle expression with the cold curiosity of an eagle sur-
veying some potential prey. Paul he glanced over with
no interest at all.

He began abruptly. "I have a cousin—a distant cousin, but blood kin for all that—who holds land on the border. Will Percy is his name—they call him Black Will, though whether for his countenance or his heart I do not know—and his wealth is cattle. He commands three hundred men." In the Borderlands a man's standing was told by the size of his private army, an old-fashioned reckoning that had died out elsewhere in the country. Northumberland went on. "Black Will has no son born in wedlock, so all will pass to his daughter. She must have a husband, and the husband will rule her lands in fact as she rules them in name."

Percy's jeweled fingers began to drum upon the lion's-head arm of the chair.

"I am minded that Mary Percy should wed John Morland. How say you to that?"

John was troubled and showed it, but he had more wit than to speak. Paul Morland smiled with diplomacy.

"I say that my lord is generous with his patronage, but he will surely want something in return for his influence."

Percy smiled, a smile devoid of humor. "You are right, of course. But for the moment let us say that all I require from you is your—loyalty. You are Catholics anl hold the Mass in your private chapel in defiance of the law—oh yes, I have my sources of information. You need not deny it. You supported the late Queen against the Protestant usurper. I should be glad to have the son of a good Catholic family controlling the lands Black Will leaves his daughter, and I should be glad for the Morland men to be Percy's men. For the time being, that is all."

"But when the time comes?" Paul suggested carefully.

Percy's cold eye fixed him like a spear. "The Morland motto, I believe, is *Fidelitas*?"

John shot his father one agonized glance. His mind was full of a memory of dark eyes, dark eyes that demanded his love and loyalty; but his father was smiling and nodding, understanding as well as John did the implication of those last words.

"You are right, my lord. The Morlands are faithful to those to whom they owe gratitude. When the time comes, we will be ready."

"Then it is settled," Percy said. "I will send you word when and where you will meet Black Will, and I will send men to go with you to him."

"That will not be necessary, my lord," Paul began, but Percy laughed harshly.

"You underestimate the lands to which you travel," he said. "If I sent no men with you, you would not reach him alive. Think on that, Master Morland, if ever you are tempted to go back on your word."

John and his father rode back through the crowded, noisy city in silence, each wrapped in his own thoughts, until they reached the bridge at King's Staith. Here they were held up behind the usual press of packhorses and wagons waiting to file across the narrow bridge between the overhanging houses and shops. There was always a crowd here, and passage was made more difficult by the crowds thronging to buy fish at the stalls set up all across the bridge. The noise and the stink were almost overwhelming, and the surface of the road was slippery with innards and blood as the fish were gutted on the spot for the customers.

Protected a little by the din, John at last spoke out to his father, spilling the doubts and anxieties in his mind. Paul listened to him grimly.

"You heard what my lord said," he interrupted John at last. "He could have you killed as easily as you or I swat a fly. And if that does not trouble you, think of the danger you could put upon the rest of the family."

"But Father—our motto—*Fidelitas*—we owe allegiance—obedience—"

"Aye, but to what? To whom?" Paul said fiercely.

"To the Queen," John said helplessly.

"And if she marries a Protestant, and destroys our faith, and outlaws us? What then? Do we not owe loyalty first to the Church? Do you, my son, not owe loyalty first to your father?"

"How can I choose between loyalties?" John asked. "To keep one faith and break another? The Queen has spared us—Aunt Nan says she is a Catholic like us and will hold back the Puritans and save our church—"

Paul shook his head. "She stands on middle ground and must slip one way or the other. Without the Catholic succession, we drift further and further into heresy. You see how she has drifted already. You see how my lord of Norfolk has drifted. The Queen will follow her husband, and she cannot marry a Catholic, so what choice is there? No, John, we must stand by what we know; besides, this is a good match for you. The girl will bring us land and power."

"But Father—" John said again.

Paul fixed him sternly. "The choice is not yours, John. Your first obedience is to me, your father. Beyond that, let me decide. I will hear no more of this."

He kicked his horse on, and John followed, his worry unabated.

The emptiness of the northern lands was awesome. Though the moorlands of Yorkshire were wild and solitary enough, here the distances seemed darker, the hills more desolate, having nothing to do with mankind: here the patient stag bred for the wolf, the rabbit for the crow and mountain fox, the hare for the raven and eagle. Once there had been forest here as far as the eye could see, but now the hills were bare except for

bracken and heather, and the woods were confined to
the lower places; oak and birch woods dark with undergrowth, where lived wild boar, and wild cat, and danger.

The Morland party kept to the higher ground, riding
close together, accompanied by the armed men sporting
the Percy badge which was their safe passage. Their
horses' hooves made no sound on the rough turf and
the silence of the high hills was all around them, a silence made up of many small sounds—the murmur of
bees among the heather bells; the cold small chatter of
water over stones, near but out of sight; the singing of
the upland wind against the ear; the swish of Kithra and
the other hounds brushing through the burnished
bracken.

They saw no other men or sign of human habitation
save once, in the distance, a thread of blue hearth
smoke, until the hot, still gray day when they came over
the breast of a hill to a glen through which a thread of
white water purled down over broad gray stones, making still pools here and there that reflected the flaming
swatches of rowanberries in the trees that flanked them.
Their leader halted them, and at once a cloud of flies
descended on them from nowhere, and the horses fretted their tails and stamped irritably.

"We are close now," the man said. He spoke southern English perfectly but with a care that suggested it
was not his native tongue. The glen was bound on the
east side by a great, round-topped, gray-green hill.
"Ravens' Knowe," he told them it was called. "And on
that side, Tod's Knowe—" a smaller hill, rough and pit-
ted and sloping backward more shallowly until it
merged with the uplands. Ahead the glen ran on into
the darker, purplish heights and the Scottish border.
"Around the flank of Tod's Knowe is Black Will's
steading. Someone will meet us soon."

He rode on, and they followed, John leading the

packhorse onto which was loaded the bride gifts they were bringing as a sign of good faith. There was no one but themselves to be seen, but as they slithered down into the closed stillness of the glen, John had the sensation of being watched, and even Kithra ceased his ranging abroad and ran close to Jupiter's heels, his tail down and his ears pricked warily. Their guide was leading them to a place where the river ran over foaming shallows, where they could cross it on a natural stone causeway. On the further side a steep bank of raw red earth showed where there had been a natural fall not long ago. On the near side the ground was soft and boggy, its bright greenness betraying it, and they had to ride single file along a thin strip of firmer ground.

With terrifying suddenness a pack of great, heavy-necked dogs burst over the red bank and sprang at them, snarling and baying. The horses reared and screamed in fright. Kithra and the other dogs sprang forward snarling to defend them, and the Morland party struggled to control their mounts and reach for their swords. Then, just as abruptly, a figure on horseback appeared at the top of the bank, and a cold, imperious voice called the dogs off. For a moment confusion reigned, and then everything quietened, the two dog packs drew apart and their noise sank to warning growls, and the figure on the skyline was joined by other, rough-looking men armed with spears, riding on small hairy ponies.

But John's eyes, like those of everyone else in the party, were fixed on the firstcomer. It was a boy, a boy young enough to be beardless; he was dressed in a thick quilted doublet of midnight blue with a jeweled belt into which was stuffed a long, gold-hilted dagger, and thigh-high riding boots of soft leather; he rode upon a superb gray stallion caparisoned in crimson anl gold, a horse fit for a king, which arched its great crest and flexed its bit, shifting its forefeet restlessly and lashing

its banner of a tail against the flies. The boy checked
the horse's movement minutely with one strong, narrow
brown hand. The other rested on the hilt of his dagger,
and he frowned down at the Morland party with the
authoritative calm of a princeling.

"Who are you? What do you want here?" he demanded. His voice was light but carrying, a voice used
to command and to being obeyed. His face, tanned a
pale gold by the weather, was beautiful with a strange,
wild beauty that John could hardly comprehend. The
cold purity of the profile, the large eyes, gray as clear
water, set at a slant above high cheekbones, the slight
frown between fine, fair brows were in some odd way
foreign; his hair was covered by a cap of crimson
leather with long side flaps, but the few hairs that escaped it were silvery and as fine as a child's. He was as
different from the dark, rough men behind him as his
white horse was from their coarse native ponies. John
stared, entranced and bewildered.

"We come to seek Black Will Percy," the guide was
answering for them. "We are to meet him, by the will of
Lord Percy, Earl of Northumberland."

"And what business have you with my father?" the
princeling demanded. Paul and John exchanged a
glance. So that accounted for the boy's assumption of
authority—some bastard son of Black Will's, the more
careful of his pride because he was not lawfully got.
Paul checked their guide with a small movement of his
hand, and the princeling's eye came around to him.

"Our business is with Will Percy alone and not to be
told to anyone else. By what right do you demand to
know his business?"

The white horse, carved out against the gray sky,
fretted again, and the boy checked him; his curved wrist
and pliant back and strong thighs made a living spring
against which the great power of the stallion was delicately buoyed as lightly as silk and as strongly as iron.

The gray eyes moved now to John's face, and they widened slightly as if with recognition. For a moment they seemed to look through him and into the secret places of his heart, and he felt weak and confused; and then the eyes went back to the guide, and he spoke again, abruptly.

"I will take you to my father's place. Follow behind, and be careful what you do. My men are armed. And if I find you have no lawful business here——" He did not finish the sentence but parted his lips in what was not quite a smile. His teeth were sharp and white. Then he whirled his horse about and rode up and over the bank, and the dogs leaped after him, leaving the dark, scowling men to surround and escort the Morland party.

It was not far——over the bank and around the flank of the hill, and there in a sheltered niche in the hillside, guarded by the river and a birch wood and a great wooden stockade, was the steading of Black Will Percy, a cluster of roofs from which smoke rose, an orderly confusion of men and women and children, dogs and swine and fowls, horses and cattle: the stronghold of a border cattle lord. As soon as they entered the stockade they were surrounded, hands were on their horses' bridles and they were obliged to dismount. Kithra stood pressed against John's legs, growling, but no hurt was offered them, though the people seemed strange and dark and unfriendly, the place rough and comfortless. They were led right away to the largest of the buildings; as they ducked inside they found themselves in the great hall. It was dark and smoke filled, for the fire was on a raised hearth in the center, and the smoke drifted up to the smoke holes in the roof. The rushes on the floor were noisome with human and animal filth, and there was no furniture but the trestles stacked against the walls and the long benches on which various people were sitting, mending harness or carving wood or waiting for their lord's attention.

At the far end was a raised dais, and as they were ushered toward it they saw that their host was waiting there for them, his hands on his hips, watching them warily. He was a small man in height but made up for it in breadth, a tough, stocky, barrel-shape man with a huge chest and shoulders like an ox. His hair and beard were jet black and as coarse and full of life as a pony's mane; his face was as dark as fumed oak, his eyes dark and gleaming with life. He balanced his weight lightly on the balls of his feet, and as they approached, he bared his brown-stained teeth in a ferocious grin.

"Come forward, then, strangers!" he roared. "Show me your credentials—and if they are not good, we'll feed you to the ravens!"

The papers were produced, and Black Will glanced only at the seal before handing them to the boy, who stood behind his shoulder. The boy glanced them over quickly—Paul guessed that Black Will could not read—and handed them back, speaking a few words in a voice too low to be heard. At once Will stepped down from the dais and came toward them, spreading his hands.

"All is in order—you are well come to my house." He clapped his hands to a servant and barked out an order. "They will bring the welcome cup—you must forgive our rough ways here, but a stranger too often brings death to be allowed past without great care. God's greeting to you."

He shook hands with them both, and a servant brought a large bowl full of wine from which they all drank, pledging friendship. A warmth and vitality emanated from Black Will that both Morlands found irresistible, and though he was so small in height he seemed to fill the hall, making John feel small by comparison. From the friendly greetings and the pledging the princeling held back, and John found his eyes drawn again and again to him, wondering at him, pitying his lonely pride. It must be hard to be a bastard son and see everything that might be yours passing to a female heir.

Black Will himself conducted the Morlands to their quarters, giving orders for the fetching of their bundles and the housing of their horses and their servants. He was cheerful and friendly, admiring their mounts, questioning John eagerly about the breeding of Kithra, promising them some hunting the next day.

"We have hunting here such as you southerners will not imagine," he said. Paul held his tongue, though it was strange to be called a southerner when all his life he had himself despised the soft life of the south. "I should have known you, even without your papers," he went on, "for I was told that the Morland heir was as tall as a young tree. If that do not melt my daughter's heart, nothing will. She is everything to me," he said, suddenly serious. "Her mother was as beautiful as a star and died when Mary was not two years old. I never married again, though I could have had my pick from both sides of the border. But there was none like my Mary—except her daughter. Nothing but the best is good enough for her," he said, eyeing John up and down. "At least I can offer her the tallest man I ever came across." He laughed suddenly and clapped Paul on the back with a hand that felt like an iron hammer.

"Come," he said, "let us go in to the hall. Dinner will be ready, and you must be hungry."

The Morlands followed him back through the warren of passages and rooms that John despaired of ever understanding and into the hall, where the servants were dragging the tables and benches into position. The high table was already set up on the dais, though bare of the plates and salts and breads and other accouterments of civilized eating that the Morlands were used to. Black Will sat himself down on the bench in the center and

motioned the Morlands to sit one on either side of him,
and servants came to put down wooden plates and pewter mugs before them. There was a smell of meat in the
air, and the hall was thronged with people and dogs, all
adding their own smells, and there was so much smoke
from the big fire that it was hard to see right to the end
of the hall. Black Will drew out his dagger from his belt
and set it on the table before him. This was evidently
his only eating tool. John felt foolish using his own
elaborate set of knives, which were neatly contained in
a leather case embossed with gold, so he drew his own
dagger likewise and laid it on the table.

"When shall we have the honor of meeting your
daughter?" John asked Will, straining to be heard
above the noise without shouting.

Black Will grinned with a grin slightly less villainous
than usual. "You have met her already, though you
have not been introduced. Mary, come here, my hinny,
and bid our guests welcome," he called, leaning back
from the table. John turned his head to look in the
same direction and saw the tall young boy standing a
little way off, watching with that same cool, imperious
stare and the same little frown between his brows.
John's heart leaped with sudden, giddy knowledge even
before the princeling stepped forward at Black Will's
command and with a smile more savage than humorous
tugged off the crimson leather cap. The soft hair, pale
and bright as moonlight, tumbled down and, shaken
out, reached to the jeweled belt.

"My daughter, and heiress, Mary Percy," Black Will
said. "I believe her first act upon meeting you was to
set her dogs on you?" And he burst out into roaring
laughter, while Mary Percy, her slender hands on her
hips, continued to stare at the strangers with wide, rain-
gray eyes that seemed to turn John's bowels to water
with love and pity and longing.

* * *

They stayed a week, hunting, hawking and looking over the estates and trying to get used to the strange, rough people and the crude way of life. Asking for hot water to wash in was the first mistake the Morlands made, and there were others of a similar kind that made it clear that Northumberland men and Yorkshire men were very different. As to the reason for their visit, it was never mentioned; the gifts were examined, praised and accepted, but that was all, until the supper feast on Hallowmas Eve, when they had been there a week.

For that feast Mary Percy had, how unwillingly they did not know, put on woman's dress. The gown was of rich material, damson-blue velvet, and the underkirtle was of gold-brocaded silk, but though it had been carefully looked after, it was obviously not new, for the style of it was thirty years out of date: square-necked, loose-sleeved and bell-skirted. Her fabulous pale hair hung like a skein of silk to her waist, and on her head she wore a halo-shape French coif as far out of date as the gown. John thought he had never seen anything so lovely as her in all his life, and his face showed it as clearly as if he had spoken his thoughts aloud; but Mary Percy, as unbendingly proud as ever, would not look at him or smile at him, seeming to need even more aloofness to protect her outside the safety of her boy's garb.

When the first courses were on the table, Black Will said to Paul, "Well, my friend, you will have to be going south soon if you are not to be staying here for the winter. Once the weather closes in, there'll be no moving until the spring thaws. I suppose we had better get down to business."

Though the gifts had been accepted, Black Will seemed reluctant even now to discuss the proposed marriage, and Paul wondered whether it was bargaining

tactics, a feigned reluctance designed to put up the
price.

"As you please," he said casually, spearing another
joint of grouse from the serving dish with the point of
his knife and dipping it in the sauce. "Perhaps after
supper we can retire to some private place and discuss
the terms."

Black Will shot him a curious look and then said,
"Oh, it is not a matter of terms. My daughter, you see,
is a pearl beyond price. She has been son and daughter
to me. Before she could walk she rode in front of my
saddle, and when she was but four years old she had a
pony of her own and rode by my side wherever I went.
What price can any man offer for such a jewel?"

Paul frowned and looked toward John for inspiration. John, leaning forward to look at her where she sat
at the other end of the table, said softly, "There is no
price a man can offer but the love of his whole heart,
and his service, all his days." The quiet words carried,
and Mary Percy looked up suddenly, surprised, and her
wide gray eyes met his for a moment, questioning and
perplexed, before she looked away again.

Black Will observed everything without appearing to
and went on casually, "Aye, that seems as good a price
as may be had. What says my dove to that?"

Mary straightened a fraction more and looked away
down the hall as if she disdained to meet any man's eye.
The little frown was back between her brows, and she
said only, "No."

Paul looked at Black Will, who seemed amused by
his daughter's defiance. "Not marry this tall young man
who loves you? Come, Mary, my hinny, where shall
you find a better man?" His words sounded ironical to
Paul, but he could not be sure enough to take excep-
tion.

"I will not marry a southerner," Mary said fiercely,
and she addressed herself to her meat again.

"And is that your last word, my bird?" Black Will asked wheedlingly. For the least part of an instant, her eyes flicked back to meet John's gaze, and then she said, "Yes." But was there a slight hesitation?

Black Will turned to Paul. "You see, she will not have him. And before you speak, let me tell you I would not force her to it."

Paul was at a loss. "Then what's to be done? Lord Percy said—"

"Aye, true, and we must not offend Lord Percy, the Prince of the North. So what's to be done?" He looked from one to the other, enjoying the situation and the helplessness of his guests. Then he thumped his fist down on the table, making the wine jump the rim of his tankard. "I tell thee what, Master Morland! How shall it be if thy son bides here with us and woos my daughter? If he has charms enough he may win her heart. And if he wins her heart, he may have her."

Paul opened his mouth to give a furious refusal, but John cried out first.

"Oh, yes, Father, let me stay!" He lowered his voice. "I shall have no peace or joy anywhere but here. Let me stay and win her, if I can."

Black Will's laughter drowned out anything Paul might have said, and between the girl's cold fury, John's passion and Black Will's amusement, he saw himself being outmaneuvered. How far had it been planned? he wondered. For in this way John remained behind as a hostage, Paul's promise of support to Lord Percy could not be called back, and yet there was no marriage, no surety, no dowry, not now and possibly not ever. John could be kept there dangling on a thread of hope for years. He could forbid John to remain, but even as he looked at his son he saw it was no use. John would be stubborn, would refuse to leave, would set Paul's authority at naught. The only thing to do was to give in gracefully and hope that John could win the girl and wed her and bring the dowry and the lands into the family. Paul glared from one face to another, but there was nothing he could salvage but his pride, so he forced a smile to his lips and lifted his cup.

"Very well," he said. "Then let us drink to success and the future joining of our two families."

Black Will lifted his cup and drank noisily, and on either side of the fathers, the children sat in silence, Mary Percy looking at the ground and John looking, longingly, at Mary Percy.

CHAPTER SEVEN

The ceremony that surrounded the Queen was elaborate, dazzling and very wearying; but Queen Elizabeth knew, as her father had known, that it was necessary for a prince to appear a prince, so everything in her Court was done with the greatest attention to etiquette and the correct procedures of ceremonial. It extended right up to the door of her bedchamber, and stopped there: within, the Queen could become, briefly and for refreshment, Elizabeth Tudor, and no one was allowed beyond that door except her two closest ladies, Kat and Nan, and the servants who made her bed and emptied her slops. The two ladies had their own functions within the chamber—Kat's was to chatter and gossip to amuse her lady, and pet her and fuss over her and flatter her like a nurse. Nanette's was to soothe her and calm her and listen to her and advise her. Both, of course, had also to love her, but that was less a duty than a pleasure.

It was a heavy day in August, hot and damp, with a gray sky but no rain, the worst kind of day to endure. Ceremonial clothes were heavy, and the Queen's were the heaviest of all, sewn as they were with pearls and

embroidered with bullion thread, and when Kat and
Nan lifted the dress off, the Queen's slender body
seemed to straighten up like a blade of grass that had
been pressed down. In her white linen chemise she sat
down before her mirror, rested her elbows on the little
table that held her brushes and pots and sighed.

Kat glanced across at her. "Never mind, my precious
lady, Kat will come and bathe your face in a moment.
But you must not lean upon your elbows, my darling.
I've told you a hundred times. You will mark them and
make them ugly."

"Don't fuss, Kat," the Queen said, continuing to
lean. "Nan, come and brush my hair for me. No one
has a touch like yours with hair, and it will soothe my
head."

Nan left the dress to Kat and crossed the room to
obey, while Kat said anxiously, "Have you a headache,
my lady? I had better get you some rosemary water to
breathe."

Elizabeth opened her mouth to say no and then
changed her mind. "Yes, do that, will you, Kat? And
bring me some lemonade, too."

There was silence in the chamber when Kat had
gone, and without speaking Nanette took the pins out
and let the red-gold hair tumble free and then began
gently and carefully to brush it out, watching as bit by
bit the Queen relaxed. After a while she opened her
eyes again and said, "Nan?"

"Yes, Your Grace?" It came more easily to her than
"Your Majesty."

"What am I going to do about her?"

Nanette was too quick to think she meant Kat.
"Whom, Your Grace?"

"The Scottish queen," Elizabeth said and grimaced.
"My cousin, Mary Stuart, Queen of France and Scotland, as she styles herself. And Queen of England she
would like to style herself."

"She cannot be that," Nanette said calmly. "As long as you are here and—"

"And what?"

"You know, Your Grace. As long as you remain unmarried."

Elizabeth nodded. "Yes, as long as I remain unmarried, each man will decide for himself that I will marry eventually the person he favors. But what of her, Nan? Unmarried she is trouble enough to me. Married, she would be far worse."

Nanette saw which way her mind was working. In these conversations they had, Nanette had always to keep ahead and suggest the thought that was already in the Queen's mind. It reassured her in some way that she needed, and though Nanette did not understand it, she recognized it and played the game.

"Unless she married the right person."

"But who would be the right person, Nan?"

This was harder. "Someone loyal to Your Grace?" she hazarded. Yes, that was the right answer, but Nanette could not guess which way this subtle mind tended. Who was loyal to the Queen? Nanette's mind ludicrously offered her the name of Elizabeth's staid, elderly statesman William Cecil, and she almost laughed. "I do not know, Your Grace," she said at last, brushing out a long strand and keeping her eyes on it so that she did not have to meet the dark eyes in the mirror. "It would be a great honor."

"And a great risk." Elizabeth waited, but Nanette offered her nothing more. "I was thinking, Nan—Mary is said to be very passionate. It would have to be someone with whom she would fall in love, someone who would make for her a demanding lover."

"You want to keep her occupied," Nanette smiled. "But he would need to be a Protestant, too, or he would only fire her Romanism."

"True. And then, think of it—their child might be heir to my throne—a half English heir at least. One might stipulate that he was to be brought up in the church of England if he was to be heir. And then, if the man in question was loyal enough to me—"

"He would make an excellent spy within the Scottish Court for Your Grace." Nanette's mind was working again now.

Elizabeth picked up one of the silver-backed brushes and toyed with it with her long white fingers—so like her mother's, was Nanette's involuntary thought.

"But who could this man be, Nan? Who is loyal to me, not a Catholic and handsome enough to make Mary fall in love with him?'

Nanette still could not imagine whom the Queen meant. She shook her head, and the Queen straightened up suddenly and rapped Nan's hand painfully with the back of the brush.

"Stupid Nan! Why, there is only one man that fits the description, don't you see? My dear Robin. He shall be the one."

Nanette's wits were agile enough for her not to gape at the idea, but it seemed to her as ludicrous a one as she had ever heard. My lord Robert Dudley, to wed the Queen of Scotland? Elizabeth's passion for her Master of Horse was known throughout Christendom, but it was not likely anyone else of her rank would share it. Carefully Nanette brought out the only inoffensive objection she could think of.

"But Your Grace, his rank is not high enough. It would be—forgive me—an insult to the Queen of Scotland to offer her a commoner to wed."

It was dangerous ground. Elizabeth frowned. "An insult—Robin?"

"Gracious Majesty, *you* would not, could not marry a commoner. How then could your royal cousin?"

Better. Elizabeth liked it to be thought that she did

not marry Robert Dudley because he was a commoner; better that than because he had murdered his wife. The frown passed like clouds clearing the sun, and Elizabeth's dark eyes met Nanette's merrily. "Well then, we shall have to do something about his rank. We'll make him an Earl. Earl of Leicester I think would sound well. And then we shall send him to woo proud Mary."

"He will not like it," Nanette said.

"He will do as he is told," Elizabeth said. "We shall send a great train of courtiers with him, the rich and the beautiful. Nan, that niece of yours—what is her name?—Lettice? She shall go. She is very beautiful—and she may make a good match there. Some of those Scottish lords, though they are rough, are very rich. How will that please you, Nan? I know it will please your proud nephew, Master Paul Morland of Morland Place."

Nanette smiled at the Queen's humor and allowed the subject to be changed. Could she really be contemplating sending Dudley to the Queen of Scots? Nanette could not imagine it, but so much of this subtle young woman's thinking was beyond her that all she could do was wait and see.

In October Lord Dudley was made Earl of Leicester and was told the plan. He accepted the Earldom but was furious at the idea of being offered by his Queen to the Queen of Scots, and for a time there was a falling out between Robert and Elizabeth that both seemed in some strange way to enjoy. Kat said privately to Nanette that one of the reasons they needed each other was that no one else could quarrel with either of them quite violently enough. It was rather like a quarterly purge they took for their health's sake.

Nanette, however, was not in a position to enjoy the quarrel, for shortly afterward she became ill. At first it seemed like nothing but an ague, but then it turned fe-

verish, and Nanette took to her bed and grew steadily
weaker. Audrey and Mary Seymour nursed her, Zack
lay across the foot of the bed and never took his eyes
from her, Simon leBel came in three times a day to
pray with her and Kat came once a day from the Queen
to inquire. At first Nanette smiled and apologized
hoarsely for being so much trouble; but then she lapsed
into silence broken only by incoherent mutterings as the
fever mounted.

One evening Mary was sitting beside her holding her
hand when Nanette abruptly opened her eyes and said,
quite clearly, "Paul, what will become of us all? What?"
Then her eyes closed again and she moved restlessly on
her pillow.

Mary looked at Audrey anxiously. "He was Madam's first husband. Long ago—I was just a girl," Audrey said.

They looked at each other for a moment, and then
Mary said, "You had better call the doctor. And send
word to the Queen. And"—she swallowed—"you had
better call Master Simon in."

Audrey stared a moment longer and then ran.

Late that night, when her business was finished, the
Queen herself came to Nanette's chamber, despite the
doctor's warnings that the fever might be catching. She
strode to the bed and took Nanette's hand and pressed
it, and Nanette opened her eyes, and after a moment
she smiled.

"She knows you," Mary whispered. "She is rational."

"Nan, dearest Nan, what ails thee?" the Queen said
gently. "They tell me you are sick unto death, but that
cannot be. I need you—you and Kat look after me."

"Kat—and me," Nanette said, her voice gone to
nothing but a hoarse whisper, and when she spoke there
were long gaps between the words in which her breath
whistled in and out like a laboring ox. "When your fa-

ther died," she said, "I remember—I thought it was so sad that there should be no one left but Will Somers and Tom Cranmer. It is sad to have outlived all your friends."

She stopped speaking, but her thoughts traveled back through the years and she saw how her life had been lived, always for someone else, never for herself—years of service and living vicariously, through Anne Boleyn, through Katherine Latimer, through Elizabeth Tudor. As if her own life was suspended somewhere just out of reach, to be taken down and lived only once, those few brief months with Paul, whom she had loved, whom she loved still. Paul, taller than a tree, strong and dark as a great oak; she saw again how his height darkened the doorway when he came in; she felt in her memory his strong arms holding her, his lips kissing her; remembered the smell of him, sweet and manly, leather and clean linen, man-sweat and horse-sweat when he came in from hunting, chamomile and lemon balm when he was dressed for feasting.

He was so real to her, though she had outlived him—outlived them all, husbands and children, Kings and Queens, friends and relatives. Like old King Harry, she was alone in her generation, a last survivor, and it was lonely. The Queen held her hand, demanding her service, calling her back; but close beside her, in the darkness behind the eyes, Paul was waiting for her, smiling, arms open for her. She saw his great dark shining eyes, and they grew larger and larger until they were dark pools into which she could slip down and drown without struggle.

The Queen released the hand and looked around the room. "She must not die," she said. "Is there no one who could make her want to live? Was there not a son?"

Audrey clasped her hands in sudden hope. "Yes!

Master Jan!" Then her face fell. "But he is in Yorkshire. It is a hundred and fifty miles away." The Court was at Hertford for the hunting.

Elizabeth straightened, and her face was determined. "Riding post, I can have a messenger there in less than two days. With my warrant, he can be back with your Master Jan in four. I shall go and see to it at once. And you"—her eye gathered everyone in the chamber, the women, the doctor and the priest—"You will keep her alive until then."

They would not let her dream—they called to her, dragging her up from those quiet depths of dark water where she could float weightlessly—tormenting her with remedies, bleeding her, blistering her feet with hot irons to draw out the evil humors, clapping on steaming plasters, forcing noxious potions down her throat at all hours. The fever did not abate, but the pain kept her from drifting. They talked to her, but she understood little of it.

Then came the night when a new presence came into the room, a smell she remembered of damp air, refreshing in the stuffy room, the smell of moors and open air and damp leaves. A hand gripped hers, hard, a lean strong hand with calloused palms, not a woman's or a priest's hand. She opened her eyes, and her heart panicked in her, for Paul, her husband Paul, was kneeling there gazing at her, but Paul was dead, long dead. He was crying, tears were running down his cheeks from his eyes—his blue eyes? No, Paul's eyes had been dark as night. Dark blue eyes—her mind cleared, and she smiled.

"Jan—Janny—"

"Mother. Oh, thank God! I have ridden like the hounds of hell, and I was so afraid—but you will get well now that I am here. You will start to get better."

She loved the feeling of his hand around hers, the

strength and life of it. She loved his bright, beautiful face; his hair curling so vigorously; his strong dark beard; his virile, muscular body.

"Bear-cub, I cannot. I am too old and too tired. But I am glad to have seen you again. I should not have liked—to die—without—"

She was too tired even to speak. Her eyes began to drift closed. Jan gripped her hand harder. Mary and Audrey and Simon stood near, watching, willing him to succeed.

Jan racked his brains for some way to reach her. Desperately he said, "Mother, all my life I've wondered—tell me now—you must tell me now—" he dropped his voice to a whisper and leaned closer. "You are my real mother, aren't you?"

Nanette opened her eyes again. His loved face was close to hers, and she read in it not what his words had said but other things. She smiled faintly, weakly, and Jan's smile echoed hers, but more strongly, his strong white teeth shining in his dark beard.

"Mother, you cannot die without telling me who my mother was."

"Then," she said slowly, "I will not die."

Love claimed her; the same love that called her from the grave drew her toward life. James had once said that love is not a closed circle; the dark eyes were near, and she was very, very tired; but she could not yet lay down the burden of her life. Jan was Paul, as James had been Paul and Alexander James, as Elizabeth was Anne Boleyn; love was a duty, love was her life, and she was born to serve her love until it set her free to lay down the burden.

"Stay near me, Bear-cub," she said. "I will sleep awhile."

By morning the fever was abated, and she began to mend.

* * *

While Nanette was recovering, Jan spent a lot of time with Mary Seymour, and though it may have seemed accidental to her that whenever she sat down somewhere with a book or a piece of work, he appeared, she was the only one who did not know what was going on. Since coming to Court she had grown up a great deal. She had begun to use henna on her hair, so that the red-brown of it had deepened to the color of a chestnut. She plucked her eyebrows and used a whitening powder on her face and touched her lips with rouge and, at sixteen, was a perfect lady. To Jan she was beautiful—her little snub-nose, pout-mouth face and golden-brown eyes were his dream, a complete contrast to the cool elegant beauty of his mother, and the more lovable for that. He sought her out one day where she was sitting in a window seat with a piece of embroidery and, aware that his time here was limited, he said, "I have not seen very much of you since Mother came back to Court. Watermill House seems empty without you."

"It is kind of you to say so," Mary said, "but we are home quite often, are we not?"

"Not often enough for me," Jan said.

Mary smiled down at her work. "Yes, you must miss your mother," she said.

Jan tried again. "Do you think of it as home, Mary?"

"Of course. I have lived there since I was four years old. I remember no other."

"Would you like it to remain your home, all your life?" he asked.

Mary still did not look at him. "It would be pleasant," she said. "But I suppose one day I must marry. And if I did not—"

"There is no need for marriage to take you away from home, Mary," Jan said. He put one foot up on the seat beside her and leaned on his knee, and now her attention to her work was deliberate, and her white skin took on a rosy glow.

"How could that be?" she asked carefully.

"I think you know very well. Mary, look at me."

"I cannot," she said, so low that he hardly heard her, and then after a moment she did glance up briefly, embarrassed.

"My mother knows I am speaking to you now, and she approves—in fact, it has always been her wish. There is no one else whose permission is needed, so— Mary, will you be my wife? I will take care of you, and honor you, and love you all the days of my life. I have loved you for a very long time now—I am sure you must know that. And now that—"

Now she did look up and met his eyes earnestly. He carried on with difficulty.

"Now that John has gone away to be married, there is nothing to stop you from considering me."

"You know about John? You know how I felt about John?"

"Of course," he said, and smiled. "Why else do you think I invited him so often to the house, when I could more easily have gone to him?"

Mary stared in astonishment. "You say you loved me—yet you would have helped me to win John?"

"If I could. Because I love you, Mary. I wanted above all for you to be happy. Now that there is no hope of your marrying him, I dare not trust your happiness to anyone else. Dearest, loveliest Mary, let me offer you a home, and my heart, and my service always. I swear no other man could ever love you more."

Her golden-brown eyes were very bright as she looked up at him in wonder and perplexity, and he dared to take her hand and, caressing it, said very gently, "Dear Mary, how clearly your thoughts show in your eyes! I would fain keep your admiration, but hon-

esty compels me to tell you that I am not in the least
noble and self-sacrificing, just very much in love.
Come, you know you like me, and we have such fun
together. Who has taken care of you, and mended your
toys, and wiped away your tears all through your childhood? Say you'll have me."

Her soft red lips curled into a smile, and she said,
"Jan, I must have time to think." But her white hand
rested in his as trustingly as it had all through her childhood, and her eyes looked confidingly up into his face,
and he knew what her answer would be.

Young Paul rode his pony through the Micklelith
Bar, waving casually to the sergeant on guard, pleased
that he was beginning to be known. He dropped a groat
into the bowl of the nearest beggar, too, happy to be
able to bestow charity as his father did, and trotted up
the road. On his right was the high wall of what had
once been the priory gardens, all now privately owned.
He passed the partly ruined church of the Holy Trinity,
with its stocks—empty now—in the graveyard, then the
twin churches of St. Martin on the right and St. Greg-
ory on the left, and then the road narrowed between
two rows of houses and the King's Staith bridge was
ahead.

It was hard to tell when you actually passed onto the
bridge, for there were houses and shops all across it,
their upper stories overhanging the causeway, and what
little space remained was crowded with open stalls—
this was one of the city's fish markets—and jostling
people. The weather had been bad recently, snow and
frost week after week, but now the air was mild, a thaw
had come, and underfoot was slush and mud to add to
the normal refuse; once or twice his pony skidded a little, its iron shoes ringing on the stones as it scrambled
for footing. The river was very high, the thaw having

swollen it, and the smell of it was strong—many people had built their privies to empty into it, and with its gradual silting up, the refuse did not pass downstream as quickly as it should.

Once across the bridge the streets narrowed even more ahead, and the smell became strong enough to make the eyes water, but Young Paul turned his mount to the left past St. Michael's into the wider Spurriergate. As he did, a noise like the screaming of a thousand martyrs erupted from the yards between St. Michael's and the river, and out under his pony's hooves galloped six young black pigs, with two grubby children in hot pursuit. Young Paul's pony reared and snorted wildly— most horses hate pigs—and Young Paul had a to-do to calm him, and by the time he had his mount under control again, the pigs and the children had disappeared up an alley toward Peter Lane. He cursed a little and rode on. Pigs were the bane of the city, adding greatly to the smell and filth and always escaping. No one had ever yet devised a way to keep a family of pigs in, and many of the poorer people deliberately let their pigs out to forage on the rubbish in the streets in order to save the cost and trouble of feeding them.

Spurriergate broadened into Coney Street, where once the Morlands had owned a large house, and again into the Lendal. This was the quieter, wealthier end of the town, and here again the street was bordered with the high walls of the gardens that surrounded the richer houses. Then he reached the end of the Lendal and his destination, the Butts house. Had there not been houses built right across the bridge, he could have seen the Butts house from there, for it ran down to the river with its gardens and outhouses, next to the elegant Guildhall, and he would have seen the private barge tied up at the waterfront. What he did notice as he rode into the yard was the smell of the river, and the servant who met him

told him that the river was so high it had lapped over
into the lower part of the gardens and flooded a couple
of the outhouses.

"And we can see the cracks in the bridge from here,
Young Master. Frost and thaw and frost and thaw and
there's cracks a man could put his fist into."

"Lendal Bridge, you mean?"

"No, Young Master, I mean t'other bridge. River's
so high the big boats can't get under the arches anymore. Master's had to go down to the warehouses a-
horseback today, and that didn't please him."

"I imagine not," Young Paul said.

"Will I rub him down, Young Master?" the man
said, taking the horse's head.

"No, just hold him for me, will you. I shall be back
soon."

"Oh aye—taking Miss Charity out for a ride again?"
the man said approvingly. Paul said nothing but strode
off into the house.

The friendship between him and Charity had grown
since last Christmas and puzzled everyone, though it
pleased everyone, too. Young Paul found Charity's admiration refreshing, while her advice was very sound,
and she was always willing to listen to him and help
him with his problems. For her any attention was balm
to her spirit. Young Paul, discovering that she could
rarely go out, and then never except in a litter, had begun that summer to take her out on horseback. She
could not ride alone, her legs not being able to grip, but
she could ride pillion behind him and hold on around
his waist, and in that way he had taken her to places
she had not seen in almost twenty years. This was the
first time in weeks that the weather had been good
enough for an outing, and Young Paul found her waiting for him as eagerly as any prisoner waiting for release.

He stayed to take a cup of mulled ale with Charity and Anne Weaver, and to admire Anne's new baby, another girl, whom they had christened Celia, and then Charity was wrapped warmly in her thickest cloak and hobbled out into the yard to be hoisted by a couple of servants into the pillion seat behind Young Paul.

"Where shall we go?" he asked as he rode his pony up to the street.

"Can we go out toward Micklelith Stray?" Charity asked. "If you don't mind."

"I don't mind where we go," Young Paul said, turning the horse back the way he had come.

"You cannot imagine how good it feels to be out of doors again," Charity said. "Or, if you can imagine that, you surely cannot imagine the sense of freedom it gives me to move at such a speed. I feel almost as if this horse's legs are my own."

"That gives me an idea," Young Paul said. "Have you ever tried swimming?"

Charity laughed. "Not since I was a child," she said. "I'm afraid it is too late now. It would not be seemly."

"I wonder," Young Paul said. "If a secluded pool could be found, and serving women set all around to guard against intrusion—"

'Please, Cousin, you are embarrassing me. Please do not speak of it," Charity said.

"Very well," Paul said, but privately he determined to find some way around the problem. He was sure it would be delightful for his cousin to swim and feel the freedom of the water, even though grown women never swam. The streets seemed more crowded than ever on the return journey, and when they reached the bridge they were held up for some time. People and children and dogs and pigs and geese and cats surged around them. Oxcarts, loaded asses and saddle horses shuffled forward very slowly. That was when Young Paul no-

ticed the rats—huge, slime-gray giants as big as rabbits—slipping across the road like shadows under the
very feet of the horses. There were always a lot of cats
on the bridge because of the fish offal, but—

"Look, do you see?" Charity said. "Rats! Where are
they coming from?"

"From the cellars of the bridge houses, it seems. But
how strange. They don't normally come out in daylight."

They were halfway across when the strange noise began—a terrible grinding roar, building up rapidly to a
crescendo. Simultaneously the ground beneath them
seemed to move, as if they were upon the back of some
monstrous creature that was waking up and writhing to
shake them off, and as the amazed silence of the crowd
broke up into shrieking, the houses on either side slid
apart, and the bridge sagged downward in the center. It
was terrifying, a nightmare in which inanimate things
came to life. The air was filled with the screaming of
people, the lowing of beasts, the shrieking of horses and
the muttering rumble growing to a deafening crash.
Young Paul kicked his pony on frantically, and it
scrabbled desperately up the sloping roadway toward
safety. Slates and stones and pantiles crashed down
from the collapsing houses, smashing in the road and
spraying them with splinters of stone, and the pony's
hooves slipped and skidded on cabbage leaves and fish
heads.

Then, almost it seemed in slow motion, the center of
the bridge crumpled, and the great stones of the arches
and the houses above fell into the river, sending a huge
wave of greasy brown-gray water flying over the ruin
like a horse leaping a hurdle. The thunder of the col-
lapse drowned out every other noise, even the panic-
stricken screams of those still on the bridge struggling
for the safety of the banks. Hands reached out, grab-

bing, tugging, and astonishingly, they were safe, they had gained firm ground, and Young Paul could slip from the saddle and lean trembling against the sweating, terrified horse to regain his composure while he looked back at the still-falling masonry and the churning, debris-scattered water.

The two middle arches had gone, and about a dozen houses had completely disappeared into the river, while those houses on either side of the breach were severely damaged, leaning at crazy, drunken angles, poking split beams and torn frames at the sky. The crowd was quiet, awed by the size of the catastrophe, except for those who were weeping for missing friends or relatives. How many people had fallen in could not be guessed, but it was sure that anyone who had fallen into the water would be dead by now, drowned or crushed or both. At either end of the bridge the survivors packed the entrances, staring silently at each other across the gap. Only the ubiquitous pigs kept on squealing.

Young Paul looked up at Charity, where she sat white and trembling, holding onto the saddle, and he reached up and took her hand and pressed it comfortingly.

"It's all right now. It's all over. We're safe."

She shook her head at him, unable to speak, but thinking of the poor wretches who had been killed and their grieving families left behind.

Young Paul tried to think of something to say to comfort her. "What a pity the Lendal Bridge didn't fall, too—then you'd have to come and stay with me at Morland Place," he said, hoping to make her laugh. But she looked horrified at the jest and began to cry.

"Take me home," she gasped. "I want to go home. Take me home."

"All right, I will. Please stop crying, Charity. It's all right; we'll go back now. Don't cry anymore."

She shook her head, and, her voice choked with tears, she said, "I don't want to come out with you again. Not ever again."

He looked up at her and then closed his mouth and began to lead the pony through the crowds. He could ride along the southern riverbank, cross by the Lendal Bridge and have her home in a quarter of an hour. It was only that she was upset by the accident, he reasoned. She could not mean it. She would be all right when she had rested. What interested him more than her state of mind was his own—that he should care so very much at the idea that she might really not want to see him again.

CHAPTER EIGHT

Lettice had sometimes boasted at Court of her superior ability, as a northerner, to tolerate the cold; now that sin of pride was being punished, for in February 1565 she was included in the large train that accompanied Henry Stuart, Lord Darnley, on a visit to the Court of Mary, Queen of Scotland. Darnley, in common with most people in the realm, believed that he had thought of the idea and had persuaded Queen Elizabeth to allow it, but Nanette, looking on, saw the culmination of a devious plot on Elizabeth's part. So Darnley was to be the loyal, Protestant husband who kept Mary of Scotland occupied? Nanette saw, too, that it was fitting for him to provide the half-English heir to both thrones, for he was the grandson of King Henry's sister Margaret, and he and his brother were the only surviving males of Tudor blood.

But the Queen would never have admitted any of this, and Nanette must of course watch in silence and keep her understanding to herself. So Lettice went north knowing only that she was honored in being cho-

sen and that she must keep her wits about her and perhaps secure a rich Scottish husband. Attended by her
woman, Kat, and herself attending upon and in the
charge of the elderly Lady Soames, Lettice rode north
in a dream of the impact her beauty and sophistication
would make on the Court of Scotland, and of the handsome Earl who would fall madly in love with her and
make her a Countess.

The Scottish Court was assembled at Wemyss Castle,
a bleak gray edifice on top of a cliff overlooking the
Firth of Forth. A wind like a whetted knife blew in off
the North Sea and passed unimpeded through the un-
glazed windows to howl down the bare passages and
mock the trivial heat of sulky braziers. On a bitter cold
seventeenth of February, Darnley's party was received
in the great hall by the Queen of Scotland, and when
Lettice's turn came to kneel and put her stiff, blue fingers to the white hand of the Queen, she realized that
she did not yet know all there was to be known about
the cold.

She backed away to take her place again near Lady
Soames, trying to push her fingers surreptitiously into
her sleeves, and, miserably conscious of her red nose
and blotched face, tried not to sniff. There was much to
observe to keep her mind off her chilblains: the clothes
all seemed strange to her, for the Scottish Court dressed
in the French fashion; the people seemed strange, too,
speaking French but with outlandish accents and in
voices as harsh and uncultivated as if they had been
peasants and not the high nobility of the land. There
was Lord Moray, the Queen's bastard brother, a little,
terrifying man like a gargoyle carved roughly out of a
piece of stone. He, it was said, was the real power in
the land and thought he ought to reign in Mary's stead.
Wemyss Castle was his own, and it was filled, to Lettice's horror, with the beautiful relics and treasures of
the Catholic Church which he had stolen.

Then there was the Queen herself—a giantess, she seemed to Lettice, for she was six feet tall, and big-boned, too. But she was very graceful and beautiful, with her long, mobile face, large violet eyes always ready to brim over into tears, charming smile and sweet laugh; and her dainty, well-bred ways were thrown into relief by the general uncouthness of those surrounding her. Lettice thought it must be lovely for her to be receiving Lord Darnley, for he was as tall as she, which must in itself be a rare experience. Lettice wondered what she would have made of big John; the Queen seemed very struck with Lord Darnley, however, and it was not to be wondered at. Darnley, at nineteen only a year older than Lettice, was as handsome as a god, went clean-shaven to show off his looks and perfect skin and moved as elegantly and gracefully as a dancer. He stood at the Queen's right hand and they chattered and laughed together in rapid French in well-modulated, musical voices. It struck Lettice suddenly that, except for the difference in their clothes, they could have been twins.

A feast followed, and Lettice had a good seat for observing, in the center of one of the long tables. Her eyes were often on the Queen and Lord Darnley, but when they wandered they were drawn to a stocky, bull-shouldered man who was in conversation with Lord Moray.

Lady Soames had been several times to the Scottish Court, knew everyone and loved to gossip, and she was very satisfactory to ask questions of. "Ah yes," she said in answer to Lettice's inquiry, "that's Lord Bothwell—a very disreputable man. He is only here by virtue of being a friend of Moray's. A fine soldier, but wicked and uncouth. He's been in prison more times than I can remember."

Lettice's attention had passed on to a man at the cor-

ner of the table opposite who had already looked more
than once in her direction, and she inquired casually
about him.

"Lord Hamilton," Lady Soames said. "Rob Hamilton, one of Moray's friends and very rich. He's been
married twice and widowed twice, and there's talk that
his second wife's death was not entirely natural." Lettice felt a thrill of excitement. Rob Hamilton was big,
heavy-built and darkly handsome, with a fierce, fine
face like something beautiful but untamed. He caught
her eyes on him and suddenly flashed a smile at her, his
teeth showing whitely in his dark beard, and Lettice
dropped her eyes to her plate, feeling her face burn and
her heart pound uncomfortably under her tight busk.

"Now, there, look," Lady Soames was saying, "just
come in—see how Moray hates it? That's David Rizzio,
the Queen's secretary. He came over from Italy in 'sixty-
one with the ambassador of the Duke of Savoy. He is
a musician, and he stayed on to make up the Queen's
quartet—he has a fine bass voice, though you wouldn't
think it from his build—but he soon became her confi-
dential clerk. Now she has made him her secretary, and
he is never out of her presence for more than an hour.
He even goes into her bedchamber, and she takes his
advice in everything. Moray loathes him. I think for
two pins he would have him poisoned."

Such shocking talk was new to Lettice, but she soon
found that it was the norm in the Court of Scotland.
The Court stayed at Wemyss until the end of the
month, and between her woman Kat and her protec-
tress Lady Soames, Lettice was soon apprised of all the
gossip. Lady Soames told her that the Queen was fascinated by Henry Darnley, but that Moray had called
him "that beardless boy", while pirate Bothwell had
said Darnley was more of a woman to men than a man
to women. Kat told Lettice that Lord Hamilton had in-

quired about her, wanting to know who was the beautiful girl with the swooning eyes.

The Court was a strange, rough place. Manners were crude, the men unruly, loud-voiced, often drunk and always foul-mouthed; the gossip was salacious and the behavior unlicensed. Lettice was used to the well-regulated, morally strict atmosphere of Queen Elizabeth's Court, and she was shocked, but stimulated and fascinated. It gave her, at least, something to keep her mind off the aching cold.

At the end of February the Court moved back to Edinburgh, that fairy-tale city built all of honey-color stone and crowned by its stronghold upon a black rock like a stranded whale. Edinburgh was not as cold, but it was damper, and that made the cold harder to bear. However, Holyrood Palace was much more comfortable than Wemyss, with smaller rooms and more adequate heating and, by comparison, considerable luxury. Lettice learned there what she had begun to suspect at Wemyss, that there were two Courts: the mannerly French Court of the Queen and the Protestant, tough, harsh Scottish Court of Lord Moray. Within the French Court they lived quite comfortably, with fine food and elegant French furnishings, but the brushes with the other court were frequent and chilled like a touch of frost. And between the two only Darnley passed easily, every man's woman and every woman's man, agile as a spider, charming as a songbird, elusively desirable as a marsh light.

Jan and Mary Seymour married in April, in the chapel at Morland Place, amid much celebration. It was a match to make everyone happy and to offend and deprive none; Nanette was especially delighted, first that her beloved son had won the woman he loved, and second that her protegée was settled so well and so comfortably for life. Already the change was apparent in Mary: she held her head a little higher, looked the world in the face with a bolder stare and smiled more often, secure in the knowledge of Jan's love and her future prosperity.

"One wedding brings on another, so they say," Jane said to Nanette afterward at the feast. "Whom do you think it will be? I suppose we must look to see Young Paul settled soon—he is sixteen now, and if John does not come back—"

"Your father will bear that in mind," Nanette said. "He will be looking high."

"Not too high, I hope," Jane said dryly, "having made one mistake—or at least, I should not say mistake but one miscalculation." They both looked across at Young Paul, who was standing by the door with William talking to the troupe of actors who had been hired for the occasion to make entertainment. Young Paul was fascinated by the actors, but it seemed that some of the actors were fascinated by William's angelic beauty and were making more of a fuss of him than was strictly good for him.

As they watched they saw Young Paul turn his head, looking around for someone, and as he found the eye he sought he smiled and his face lit with a rare beauty. Nanette followed the direction of his eyes and said thoughtfully, "A strange friendship that, between Young Paul and Charity."

"It has changed him," Jane said. "My cousin has gentled him, I think. He thinks far more now of others and less of himself. He had much to do to win her confidence again after the accident on the bridge, but he persevered. He does a great many good works to try to win her approval."

"Like his activities at Paul's hospital," Nanette said,

and then looked curiously at Jane. "What is it between them, Jane? You were always his confidante."

"I don't know," Jane said. "He loves her, and we must suppose that love comes from God, for it is not base. It has made him a better man."

Nanette wondered whether she knew more and would not tell or simply did not know. "And what does Charity feel about it?" she asked. "It must be strange for her after so long to have such a very persevering champion."

Jane looked at Nanette swiftly and uncomfortably and seemed to hesitate over whether to speak. "Aunt Nan," she began, and then, "do not speak of it, but it is my belief that Charity will be glad when Paul is married. I think she would wish to be left alone, but she will not turn him away, now she sees it does him good. But Aunt Catherine——" She hesitated again.

"Aye, I know. Catherine has a way of making everyone uncomfortable. I always meant to have Charity to live with me, but now that I am at Court so much— perhaps I should have a word with Jan and Mary. They could have her to live at Watermill."

"Not yet," Jane said. "It would place her nearer Morland Place and Young Paul."

Nanette raised an eyebrow. "Is it that serious?"

"Only look at her," Jane said.

Nanette did look then, and again and again through the day. Young Paul was almost always at her side, talking earnestly to her. She smiled and conversed, but there was an uneasiness about her. At one point Nanette saw her half rise from her chair, making some vehement protest at something Paul had said, but he took her hand and continued to argue the point, and after a while she was silent, only a little whiter than before. Shortly afterward when Nanette looked again, Charity was alone, and Young Paul nowhere to be seen.

* * *

Paul stared at his second son in amazement, not sure
if he had heard aright. Young Paul stood just inside the
door of the winter parlor, where he had followed his
father, asking for an audience, standing very upright
and defiant but poised as if ready to run.

"Are you mad, boy?" Paul said at last. "You cannot
have thought what you are saying."

"I have, sir, truly I have. I do not know why you
should be so surprised. I have made no secret of my
affection."

"Affection! Aye, a cousinly affection, and a Christian charity that everyone has approved in you," Paul
said. "But—"

"Sir, I beg of you to consider. I must marry soon,
that is plain."

"You must," Paul said grimly. "And I shall not
waste your marriage, you may be sure."

"But sir, my love and my honor both are pledged.
There is none but my cousin that I could ever wed
now."

Paul's face suffused with anger. "None that you
could wed!" he bellowed. "You forget yourself! It is
not for you to choose. You will wed whomsoever I
choose for you—"

"Father, things have changed since your day—"

"Things have changed indeed when a boy can tell his
father what he will do or not do, when a young man
can wish to marry a barren old woman. Where is your
sense of duty? Would you betray your family and your
heritage?"

Young Paul's eyes filled with desperate tears. "Father, please, don't say such things! I love Charity, and
she is the only wife I want—"

"She is past thirty, and a cripple!" Paul shouted.
"You will marry a young woman—a rich young
woman—who will give you sons. It is your duty!"

In the brief silence that followed they stared at each

other. Young Paul was weeping, and as Paul's anger cooled he felt a stirring of pity toward his son. He knew what it was like to love, and he knew how lucky he was that love and duty had coincided. "Come, child, control yourself. You know what you ask is impossible. What does the lady herself think of it? I warrant she did not agree with you."

Young Paul looked uncomfortable. "She—"

"She has too much sense to accept your proposals."

"I am pledged to her!" Young Paul cried.

"No, you are not, then. If she does not accept the promise, it is no promise." He reached out and put a hand on his son's shoulder, and Young Paul flinched under the touch. "Forget this foolishness, my son. Go back to the feast and forget it."

"How can I? How can I ever meet her eyes again?"

"Don't look at her. She will know without any words from you."

Young Paul stared a moment longer, and then with a choking cry he broke away, wrestled briefly with the door and was gone, running out into the yard and toward the stables. Paul contemplated for a moment sending after him and then decided to leave him alone. Let the boy ride out his passion on the moors and return more submissive. And when he returned, Charity should be gone. He could at least see to that. He went back into the hall, and the first eyes he met were those of the crippled woman, trapped in her chair on the dais. She looked questioningly into Paul's eyes, and he gave an infinitesimal shake of his head. Charity's shoulders moved in a sigh, and her sad gaze moved away to fix on the players. She was twenty-nine, and it was the only offer of marriage she had ever had.

For John that first winter was like a dream, with a dream's mixture of unreality and desire. There was a bleak, wild beauty about Northumberland that sus-

tained him through the hardship of cold and hunger
and discomfort, so that looking back, he remembered
not the dark and noisome buildings, the reek of smoke
hanging like a dark flag under the low roofs, the blaz-
ing fires that burned the front of you while the back
froze from the clammy cold, the tough and inadequate
food: what he remembered was the sound of the wind
rioting over the bare brown back of Ravens' Knowe;
the smell of the black crumbling earth under the wet,
dead bracken; the breathtaking dagger of frost silvering
the world so that each blade of grass became an indi-
vidual work of jeweled perfection and the woods in the
valley were like a silversmith's masterpiece.

He spent more of that first winter out of doors than
ever before in his life, riding guard on the herds, fighting off attacks from the border raiders and ever and
ever hunting for food, Kithra at his heels, his pony, Jupiter, beneath him and his throwing spear light in his
hand like an extension of himself. By the end of the
winter he could bring down a bird in flight with a single
throw. He had always had a good eye, and now necessity had removed his scruples over killing animals. He
took pride in killing swiftly and mercifully, but he knew
his place in the world was that of a predator.

And always, running through his memories of the
time, running through the experience of every day like
a thread of gold running through a tapestry, was Mary
Percy, her presence or absence alike, the fact of her
alone enough to weave his life into a pattern. After that
first time he never again saw her dressed in a woman's
clothes, and he soon forgot it. She was the Princeling to
him, slender and proud, fiercely possessive of herself
and her honor. In the house he saw little of her, but she
was as much outdoors as he, riding always at the head
of the group as a king rides at the head of his army.
Her white stallion, Houlet (the local word for an owl),

bore her with a matching pride, his bridle always decorated with swags and tassels and little chiming discs, and she always had about her some flash of color, like her scarlet cap, so that she should be seen more easily, for that was her pride, to lead her people and take the first blow.

John was amazed that her father let her go into so much danger, but gradually he learned that Mary was Black Will's son to him, and he rejoiced that she was everything that he would have wanted in a son. Besides, he would deny her nothing. She ruled him with the clear, steady gaze of her rain-gray eyes. John was utterly under her spell, and when she was not near him, he was haunted by her, his mind filled with images of her, her proud, sculpted face, the parting of her lips as she drank the wind upon some hilltop, the quiet strength of her slim hand on Houlet's reins, the hard spring of her sapling body controlling the weight and power of her mount. At night he dreamed of her, and awake there seemed little difference, for he was drowning painlessly, as in clear crystal water, in the fact of her, so that it scarcely seemed like love, though he did not know what else to call it.

As for her, she treated him as she had from the first with cool indifference, although as time went on he wondered sometimes if he did not perceive occasionally a flash of gold from within the crystal. All the other women in the steading looked on him with admiration, for he was the handsomest and by far the tallest man there, the best rider, the deadliest with spear or longbow, the softest-spoken; and Mary Percy was, in spite of everything, a woman. Riding, hunting, fighting, in the great hall singing and playing the little Northumberland harp, dancing, storytelling—whatever he did to charm her, she held him off, her eyes as inhospitable as the gray northern skies; yet there was a watchfulness about her, as if she kept guard not only on him but on herself. If she did not feel her fate in him, as he did in her, what need had she of such careful custody?

He did not expect an answer, but an answer came one April day when the snow was still on the ground and John and Mary and a handful of men were out beyond Tod's Knowe on Girdie Fell hunting for deer. Mary was leading the way as usual, with John riding a pace or two behind and to the side where he could look at her face, glowing with cold from within the hood of her gray wolf-fur mantle. She checked, and then, bidding them remain where they were, she rode Houlet on up a steep, crumbling scarpside to a vantage point twenty feet above them and for a long time remained there, looking down into the deep ravine of the Kielder Burn. The ponies shifted from foot to foot, restless in the cold; Kithra lay down in the shelter of a patch of untrampled bracken, brittle as potsherds, and looked up reproachfully at his master; the men talked quietly among themselves in their own language, incomprehensible as bird song; and John thrust his aching-cold fingers into the rough of Jupiter's mane to warm them and looked up at Mary.

Even from this distance he could see there was a strangeness about her: her face was etched against the heavy sky with a doomed clarity, and she looked so sad that it made his chest ache with the longing to ease her. Then suddenly everything changed: she became alert, stared away at something out of their sight and then, whirling Houlet on the spot, she came back down the scarp at such a speed that they would surely have fallen had Houlet's small hooves not been as sure as a mountain sheep's.

"Raiders," she said abruptly as she reached them. "Coming from Wauchope direction. I suppose they

thought to creep up behind us and come down by Cat-
cleugh. We will surprise them—come."

There were ten or twelve of the raiders to eight of
them, but they had surprise on their side, and position,
coming down on them off the fell side as they picked
their way along a shallow ravine. The Tod's Knowe
men raised a yell, the dogs sprang out from ten feet up
and landed on them like four-legged hawks, and then
they were doing battle. The raiders—little, tough men
like tree roots, inconspicuous in their earth-color
plaids—were fierce fighters, hard and quick and able to
take wounds unflinchingly, but ambushed, they knew
themselves beaten, and after a short hard battle they
turned in flight.

Last to run was their leader, a man with a mass of
hair and beard as tawny as a fox's pelt, whose cloak
was held at the shoulder by a massive brooch of silver
set with huge amethysts. He held back until his men
were away and then drove his little hairy pony straight
for the ravine side. Something in that struck a chord
with Mary, and she cried out, "That one is mine! Wait
here!" and spurred Houlet after him. The white stallion
went up the steep slope like a cat jumping a wall and in
a few paces had caught up with the raider, and he
turned and swung with his sword. Mary was coming at
him from below, and his speed in turning his pony and
striking took her unaware. John knew she was struck by
the movement of her body, and his heart cried out in
him; his spear was in his hand, and even as Mary
ducked away to make room for her own sword-blow, it
was singing through the air and took the raider square
in the chest, so that he toppled from his mount without
a sound. The cry came from Mary, a high shriek of
anger and pain, and as the raider's pony scrambled
panicking away up the ravine side, she turned Houlet
and spurred him down toward them.

Her wolf fur was sliced through at the shoulder and bloody, and the tip of the sword must have caught her cheek in its descent, for one side of her face was a mask of rowan-bright blood. But worse was the fury of her expression. She did not look at any of the other men—she knew that it was John. Her gray eyes flashed like an angry cat's, so that he shrank back for a moment in reaction.

"He was mine! He was mine, and you killed him!" she cried. "You dared to interfere—aye, and that is how it would be! That is how you would keep my honor bright, if I were foolish enough to marry you!"

John knew that he must not apologize, even if he could.

"It was swifter than the thought," he said. "It is not easy to do nothing."

"You would not have done it to my father!"

"Perhaps I would, or perhaps I would not," John said, trying to keep his voice steady. "But at all events, your father would not have minded."

Her mouth curled bitterly. "My father would not have needed to," she said, but it was an acknowledgment that they were both right and both wrong. She stared at John for a long moment, and he felt that for the first time she was looking at him and seeing him. Then she gave a shuddering sigh and put her hand up to her face to explore her wound with her fingertips.

"Are you much hurt?" John dared to ask.

"A flesh wound only." She wriggled her shoulder to test it. "It is nothing. We'll ride on. And in future"— her eyes were distant again, and she spoke from behind her customary mask—"obey orders."

John smiled and shook his head. "I cannot promise not to try to save the life of a comrade, be it man or woman, but in all other things I will obey you."

*   *   *

Lettice was growing up rapidly, forced out of her shuttered ignorance of everything but herself by the pressure of life, as a chick is forced out of its shell. She ceased to be able to restrict her quick mind, though she would have liked not to notice the things she noticed. She was living in a world within a world, and she wished she did not have to see how thin the barrier was between her world and the menace outside.

There was the Queen—immensely tall, with endless hands and feet, long white face, rich and somber clothes—laughing and chattering and dancing, playing with her little dogs, *tête*-à-tête with little dark Davy, who clung to her skirts like a pet monkey, devout at her prayers, flirting with Henry Darnley; but Lettice could not prevent herself from seeing the fear behind the charming mask, from reading the apprehension, almost terror, in the Queen's eyes whenever the door opened or a distant sound impinged upon them.

Then there was Lord Darnley—slender, girl-faced, as sweetly pretty as a rose, graceful as a roe deer, dancing, smiling, attending on the Queen with a display of lovely and proud deference, like a god stooping to a mortal. Yet Lettice looked at his soft curling lips and saw brutality; smelled under his perfume a rankness that made her mouth run water. If he came close to her, her skin crawled and the hair stood up on the nape of her neck with a horrified disgust that she could not explain and could barely mask.

But at least here, in the court-within-a-court, there was a kind of safety of familiarity. Mass was said three times a day as it was at home in Morland Place, and kneeling, telling her beads, murmuring the litany, hearing the familiar, exotic Latin rolling over her like a warm wave, she felt a temporary haven. Servants moved about in an orderly fashion, people spoke in quiet, cultured voices, and there were no abrupt move-

ments or harsh sounds. The day's activities were familiar from the English Court, the rising, praying, eating,
working and playing falling into place like the seasons.
Outside, like something dimly perceived in the dark
corner of a large room, just beyond the circle of candlelight, the other world went on its inexplicable way, a
world of men, of dark, hard, dour men dressed in
strange, drab plaids and outlandish spiky jewels; men as
arrogantly, brutally sexy as dunghill dogs, men with
cock's feathers in their caps and daggers in their belts
and dirks in their stockings; men with lowering faces,
untrimmed beards, harsh mocking voices, who scorned
silks and perfumes, who laughed at women with a brutal laughter devoid of humor.

Within Queen Mary's fragile, hollow world, brightly
colored and frangible as a blown robin's egg, the
women clustered together like harbored deer, wrinkling
their soft noses and glancing sidelong in fear and fascination at the circling wolves. For Lettice, one wolf
passed close by more often than the others, and her
eyes followed him, unwillingly, whenever he was in
sight. For his part Rob Hamilton looked with dark,
powerful amusement on the prettiest of the maids-of-
honor, and a certain curve to his lips suggested that he
was wondering how long the honor would keep the
maid a maid.

Kat, Lettice's woman, more frightened than her mistress, had woven herself a powerful fantasy under
which, like a blanket, she could hide her head when the
shadows in the corners jumped for no discernible reason, and the dark, fascinating Hamilton was part of it.
Whenever they were alone together, Kat poured ideas
into Lettice's head, as all through Lettice's growing
years she had poured vanity and ignorance. Rob Hamilton was bewitched by her; Rob Hamilton was ready to
be her slave; Rob Hamilton could not take his eyes off
her whenever they were in the same room together, so

much so that the Queen had looked at him in anger and
spoken sharply to him at dinner; Rob Hamilton was so
much in love that the slightest encouragement from
Lettice would bring forth an honorable offer of marriage and a generous settlement, for he was certainly
rich.

Lettice listened, but for once she sorted and dis-
carded. He was interested in her, certainly; and though
the feeling he aroused in her was mainly fear, yet there
was a fascination about the sheer black power of him.
Besides, her native cunning and common sense suggested that in a world of menace, in a world dominated
by brigands who obeyed no rule but their own will, the
best course of action for a potential victim was to secure the protection of one of the strongest of the brigands.

So matters stood in May when the court went to Stirling Castle on the moors for the early hunting. It was
Hamilton's own country, and against the background of
the gray moors he seemed to stand out more clearly, as
if he were etched against the horizon. He behaved here
more politely than the rest, was less often drunk, spoke
in a softer voice and with the seeming of mannerliness.
Kat saw in it the salutary effect of Lettice's beauty, but
to Lettice it was the smile of the wolf. But other things
were changing; storms were coming closer, and she
must start looking for shelter. At Stirling Lord Darnley
caught the pox and was dangerously ill for some time,
and when he recovered it was clear that the Queen was
so far gone in love that she meant to marry the girl-
faced youth, against all reason. Lord Moray quarreled
violently with her, and when she refused his demand to
legitimize him in the event of her marrying, he left the
court in anger, threatening to bring force of arms
against her. On Darnley's advice, the Queen sent for
Bothwell, who was in France, to take command of her
defense, and Lettice saw that the Queen had herself de-

cided to seek the protection of a brigand against the brigands.

July came, a hot and damp and sulky month. At the end of the month the Queen was to marry Darnley, who already displayed the insolence of a king and was now drunk every night instead of every other night. Bothwell was traveling back and would arrive in a few weeks, and Moray was at Wemyss gathering an army: Lettice saw the fragile world beginning to crack against the pressures outside. The dark eyes of Hamilton watched her; there was something frighteningly attractive about the restraint he had imposed on himself, like a raging torrent held up by a dam that must at last break. One day as she passed through the hall on an errand for Lady Soames she saw Hamilton just leaving, alone, by another door, and on a mad impulse she followed him.

Stirling Castle was a maze, a rabbit warren of passages, which he knew and she did not. She was soon beyond her very limited knowledge, and pattering breathlessly behind him, she hurried to keep up, not to lose him, for to be alone and lost seemed at the moment worse than to be with him and lost. She saw him turn a corner ahead of her, and as she hurried around it in his wake, she was seized and dragged through a door: he had waited for her.

They were in a storeroom, lit only dimly by the sullen light that came in through an arrow slit. Hamilton shoved the heavy door closed, and as Lettice opened her mouth to shriek, he slammed his hand across her mouth and pressed her back against the wall.

"Oh no you don't," he said. "No shrieking, my lass. It will do you no good anyway." Her frantic eyes stared at him over the brown hand that gagged her. His dark, handsome face smiled grimly down at her, his lips parting in his curling dark beard to show teeth as sharp and white as a stoat's. Lettice's nostrils were wide, dragging

for breath, and she could smell him all around her, a
powerful odor of man and sweat and leather and sex,
and it terrified her so that she felt her legs buckling, her
insides turning to water. His hand smelled of meat, and
its skin felt lightly greasy against her face and made her
want to vomit. He pushed his legs against her, holding
her to the wall easily with the hand over her face and
the bulging muscles of his thighs, and with the other
hand he began to pull up the heavy skirts of her gown.

Realization came to her that he really meant to do it,
and a squeak, like the sound a mouse makes when the
owl strikes, worked its way past her gag. He smiled a
little more, and his tongue licked his lips. His tongue
looked very pointed and muscular, somehow terrifying
and obscene. As if he knew what she had not said, he
answered her.

"It's what you wanted lassie—I know that. I've seen
the way you looked at me. Why else did you follow me
now? I can't, you say?" He made a mockery of listening
to her, as someone might listen attentively to the mur-
murings of a sick person in a fever. "Oh but I can, and
I will. And if you think you can complain afterward,
you might remember that your own behavior wants
some explaining—wandering around here without a
chaperon—shameless girl!"

His hand was working its way down her body while
his hard, inexplicably bulging lower body nudged her to
the rough stone wall. He went on talking while she grew
dizzier with fear and nausea.

"Oh lassie, I'll wager you have a lovely body, dainty
wee breasts like a little deer, but with this busk and all
this stiffening, I'll have to wait and see, won't I? But
here now, here's something to feel. Oh, lassie, that's
soft. Soft and warm as a woman should be. Hush now,
don't struggle or I'll have to hurt you, and there are
better ways to hurt you than that. Bide still now and

you'll find you like it. There—" as she wriggled in demented anguish against the slippery touch of his big dark hand, "that's where it is, the quick of you, the tenderest thing in all God's universe. Still now, lassie, that's for me. You're ready for it, too, like a wee cat— bide still now.'

One hand still holding up her skirts, he took his other hand from her mouth, but before she could draw breath to scream, he clamped his own face down over hers, and the pungent, intrusive taste of his tongue filled her mouth so that she almost choked, and with one movement, as easily as if she were as small as a child, he folded her off her feet and lay her down on the storeroom floor and went down with her. His powerful legs forced her knees apart, and he lowered himself onto her, his free hand jerking at the laces of his codpiece.

Suddenly her face was free of him, he was holding her down with both hands and she could have yelled now, called for help, for what good it would have done her; but the gloom was filled with the harsh sound of his breathing, her body was being crushed by his weight and a savage pain was tearing her apart. She could not cry out, could not make any sound at all; worse than the pain was the great brutal maleness of him, the sense of being invaded, taken over, blotted out by his person; no more herself, only a broken-backed mouse hanging from the claws of an owl. Her body was filled with him so that all she was was battered out of her, and there was no sense except that hot, swollen point of pain.

And then, quite suddenly, it was over, the crisis, the struggle, and she was flooded with weakness, surrendering, yielding, feebly grateful that the pain was gone, wanting only to do his will, to be no more herself and suffering, but his and safe. She moaned, hearing herself distantly, and then his voice, close, bringing tears to her eyes, tears of surrender and fear and trust.

"Aye, lassie, aye, lassie," he crooned. "That's it now."

She began to sob, and he moved again, settling himself and waking the pain to raw burning again. "Please—" she said, but she didn't know any longer what to ask for. She opened her eyes and saw his wolf's smile hanging above her.

"And if you have a boy," he said, "we'll call him after your father. That should make him give you a good big dowry."

For a moment she did not understand, and then weak gratitude flooded through her again that the wolf who had torn her was to protect her; she had surrendered so much that she must belong to him or die from the shame of the surrender; and she shut her mind to everything and called it love. I love you, she said in her mind, though not aloud. The only sound she made aloud was a wail of pain and loss a moment later when he drew out of her.

BOOK TWO

THE
UNICORN

The Gods are just, and of our pleasant vices
Make instruments to plague us.

King Lear, Act V Scene 3

CHAPTER NINE

When Elizabeth had died, much of Paul's life died with her, and now it seemed as if his whole world was falling apart. He looked back on the time when she had been alive and his family was around him, healthy and happy, as Adam must have looked back on the Eden from which he was forever excluded. One by one his children were deserting him: Jane, of course, had given no cause for complaint; she had married well and visited Morland Place several times a week. And Mary was in Dorset still and was to be wed to Daniel Bennett next year. But what of the others?

First John, his pride, had gone against his wishes, abandoned his inheritance to live in Northumberland in the hope of marrying Mary Percy, faint hope though it seemed; then Young Paul, his joy, had asked to marry his cousin Charity, and since Paul had refused, had become wild and sullen, staying away from home for days at a time and getting drunk in city taverns night after night. And now Lettice, pretty, silly Lettice, who had been doing so well at Court that she had been chosen to go to Scotland, had been fornicating with a Scottish baron, so that Paul had to agree to a marriage between them.

Not that, in some ways, it was a bad match—Hamilton was wealthy, of good rank and standing in his own country—but when all was said, he was a foreigner and a Protestant, and above all, Paul did not like to find his hand forced.

"I had plans for her," he told Nanette on one of her visits from Court, "and they did not include leaving her to rot in a barbarian castle. What influence can she bring from there? She will have to leave the Queen's service—and that's another thing: it was not pleasant having to ask permission of the Queen for what was known to be a *fait accompli*. If it had not been for your intervention—"

Nanette spread her hands. "I did nothing; the Queen was not averse. Once Lord Darnley had married, it did not much signify what happened to the maids."

"That is almost worse," Paul said, determinedly gloomy. "That the Queen should be indifferent—"

"Well, do not think too badly of the girl," Nanette said. "I wonder if it was all her fault. I heard from Lady Soames that Hamilton had made inquiries about Lettice and about her family some time before it happened. It seems as though he must have set his mind on the match and then done what he could to bring it about. It may be that Lettice had no choice in the matter."

"No choice—" Paul looked shocked, and then his griefs came to him anew. "Oh, Aunt Nan, she is lost to us now. Married to a Protestant! She is lost to us and to herself forever."

"Who knows," Nanette said comfortingly. "We must pray for her, pray that God will give her strength to keep faith. Hamilton may let her follow her religion, so that she does it secretly."

"But their children—"

"We must wait and see. It is not beyond possibility that she might influence their minds sufficiently."

But Paul continued to mourn her as lost, though he made a show of accepting the match and made the settlement on her that was required. Then, at Christmas of that year, 1565, the worst blow of all fell. Young Paul, riding back drunk from the city, fell from his horse and lay all night in the snow before he was found. He took the lung fever and, his health impaired by drinking, he had no strength to fight it off. In two days the best loved of Paul's children was dead.

Paul fought hard to shake off the crippling blow, for though joy was gone from his life, he was still master of Morland Place and had its fortunes to guard. In the house still were the youngest two boys—William, just twelve, and Arthur, who was eight—and though it made the place seem even emptier, Paul determined to seek a place at Court for William, for it was necessary to regain the Queen's favor, and William, the angel-child, was the best suited to do it.

So in February 1566 William went to Court, where Nanette promised to keep a distant eye on him. Then Paul persuaded Joseph Butts to send his only son, Walter, who was ten, to be educated at Morland Place with young Arthur, and to fill the nurseries he also persuaded Samson Butts to send his two youngest daughters, Margaret, age six, and Celia, age two, promising his help in settling them when the time came for them to marry.

In January 1566 Jan and Mary's son was born and was christened Nicholas, and as soon as mother and son were fit to travel the first place they visited was Morland Place. After the first visit they were there often, and Jan spoke casually about the possibility of sending his son and heir to Morland Place when he was out of petticoats. Neither he nor Mary gave any hint that Nanette had written to them on the subject. She also wrote to Jane and Hezekiah, and when the good weather came they, too, were at Morland Place more often than at home. Paul's spirits revived. With people coming and going and children and babies in the house, Morland Place seemed to be coming alive again. Then came the news that Lettice was pregnant.

Though life was not easy or entirely pleasant, Lettice continued to feel that what had happened to her was for the best. She was Lady Hamilton, mistress of Birnie Castle in Stirlingshire and Hamilton House at Aberlady, a few miles from Edinburgh, between which two places she divided her time, following her husband as he moved from one to the other. Best of all, she was out of the service of the Queen and for the most part away from Court, attending only when Hamilton required her presence at a feast or ball. The terror that had stalked her in Holyrood and Stirling Castle had withdrawn to the other side of a closed door, which Hamilton guarded. She had nothing to be afraid of but him, the wolf she had shut herself in with.

The nature of the wolf, however, was puzzling, and the longer she lived with him the less she felt she understood him. Why had he wanted her? For her beauty? For her dowry? Neither seemed entirely adequate as a reason. He made her give up her religion, which was a distress to her, but she dared not defy him, only continuing to say her rosary when he was absent from the house, and even then only when she was alone and in the dark, for she dared not trust any of the servants except Kat.

She discovered, too, that she was stepmother to two small daughters, Jean and Lesley, the children of Hamilton's former two wives. No one would tell her what had happened to the girls' mothers, but she remembered Lady Soames saying that it was thought Hamilton had done away with Lettice's predecessor. There were traces of the two women in both houses—a work frame here, an inscribed book there—but no one ever spoke of them, and she dared not ask. She had little to do with her stepdaughters. They were brought up in a separate establishment within the house, and Lettice came into contact with them only formally, when they were brought to her by their governesses. She tried to be friendly with them, but they watched her with sullen, frightened eyes and addressed her as Madam. That was when Rob was away. When he was in the house they seemed to become numb with terror.

Lettice found his presence a heady mixture of fear and desire. He treated her, in public, with overt respect, which seemed to conceal a dark and malicious humor. Everything he said could be interpreted in two ways, and the more alert Lettice seemed to this ambivalence, the more it seemed to amuse Hamilton to torment her with it. In the privacy of their houses he ignored her most of the time, leaving her to her own devices and to, she was sure, the supervision of his servants, whom she believed to be spying on her. Only in the bedchamber did he pay heed to her, and his behavior there was as puzzling as elsewhere. Sometimes he would talk to her, telling her news of the Court, discussing politics and business with her as if she were a man and a friend. At other times he would mock her, insult her, call her an ignorant Papist whore; but whatever his mood, it ended always in bed.

Lettice was sure, in her inmost heart, that what they did together was a sin, and she was sure that Hamilton did those things to her partly to shock her. What shocked her more than his nature was her own, that she should, despite herself, enjoy it; and Rob seemed to delight in breaking down the barriers of her pride and her upbringing and bringing her to a state of frenzied abandon. He introduced her to grosser and grosser pleasures, leading her with a grimly mocking smile over

the terrain of sensuality he had explored in his own
youth, and with each new excess Lettice's love for and
hatred of him increased, hardening an inner core of
resistance to him even while externally she surrendered
more and more completely.

Outside her house, troubles increased, and she
looked on with detached pity as the Scottish Queen discovered the true nature of the weak and evil creature
she had married and made King. Her own wolf, Bothwell, was proving an effective guard against the rest of
the pack, and in August of '65 he beat off Moray's first
armed attack and drove him over the border to New-
castle. The Queen returned to Edinburgh, leaving her
wolf patroling the border, and in December it was announced that she was pregnant. The child she bore
would in all probability be heir to the throne of both
England and Scotland: but she had by this time become
incapable of disguising her disgust and distaste for her
husband, and her preference for Davy Rizzio's company led the drunken King to accuse him of being the
child's real father.

Bothwell defended her verbally as he had physically;
but in February he married Bonnie Jean Gordon, and
while he was away celebrating his nuptials, the King
took his drunken revenge. He broke into the Queen's
apartments where she was closeted with Davy and held
her arms behind her back while his friend Ruthven
hacked the little singer to pieces before her eyes. She
was six months pregnant.

Hamilton kept the news from Lettice at first, because
she, too, was pregnant, having conceived in January,
and was unwell, suffering from nausea and headaches,
and by the time she was well enough to be told, much
had happened. The Queen had been imprisoned by
Morton and Douglas until Moray arrived with an army,
and Hamilton told Lettice that the whole business had
been engineered by Moray. He could not keep the wolf

from slipping away, however, and Bothwell got to Dunbar, gathered help and contrived to get the Queen and Darnley out. A week later Bothwell marched on Edinburgh and drove the rebels to flight. The Queen disgraced Darnley and hanged the ringleaders, but she pardoned her brother, feeling unequal to spilling sibling blood.

All this Hamilton told her, and Lettice listened carefully, unable to determine where her husband stood in all this. He had fought on neither side, yet she had always known he was friendly with Moray. She looked at him curiously, and he saw her look and flashed his white and wicked smile at her.

"Wonder away, my lass, so that you bear me a son. Aye, and the Queen, too—what will she have? She must be a tough one not to have miscarried. There's something forbidding about a woman as hard as that. But if she has a boy, he will be King, and she'll be of no account."

"Then you—" Lettice began, and bit off her words quickly.

"Bothwell's a pirate," Hamilton said, "and a bonny fighter, but he and the Queen and that stinking boy of hers can't make up one statesman between them. So we'll bide our time, lassie, me for a king I can serve and you for childbirth."

It was the closest she had ever come to understanding him, and more than ever she knew she had been right in her choice of wolf. She never ceased to fear him, and she knew that her very life hung by the thread of his favor: but he was a canny predator, and if she continued to please him she would be with him when he came out on top. Whichever side won, that would be the side Rob Hamilton was on.

In September Lettice gave birth to her first child, a son, born after great travail but greeted with great joy. He was a tiny, wrinkled baby with a yellow skin, so that he looked like a store apple except for the thatch of black hair. Lettice was shocked to discover that Rob expected her to breast-feed him herself, but it was found she had no milk, and so after three days a wet nurse was found and the potential crisis was averted. Rob was delighted with his son and paid more honor to Lettice than ever before or after. The child was christened Hamil.

The Queen of Scots had also borne a son, named James after her father. He was born in June, and almost immediately after his birth it was rumored everywhere that the Queen and her border wolf were lovers. The King was still in disgrace and completely estranged from the Queen, spending his time in drunken debauchery in what amounted to imprisonment in Stirling Castle. He was suffering from syphilis, and a certain amount of tacit encouragement seemed to be given to his excesses. Hamilton thought that the Queen and Bothwell hoped his style of life would carry him off so that they could marry. Lettice, basking in the light of a new security and an unexpected gentleness in her husband's treatment of her, heard him distantly, like hill thunder.

In December Prince James was christened at Stirling Castle in a very elaborate ceremony at which a great many foreign ambassadors, including some from England, were present. Lettice and Rob were there, and Lettice saw for the first time what had become of Darnley, the pretty, beardless boy. He looked twice his true age, raddled and sick and almost out of his wits with drink and syphilis. Shocked, Lettice concluded that he would not live long. On their return home from Stirling to Aberlady, however, all other considerations were driven out of her mind by the news that her son was sick. Rob and Lettice sat up together with the baby for two days, but in vain. A week before Christmas he died in his father's arms.

* * *

The two horses, one white, one bay, picked their way up to the highest outcrop of Oh Me Edge and stopped, and their riders gazed out northward over the wild lands. It was a fine May day, the sky high and blue and filled with running wind, and in every sheltered pocket on the hillside the small brave flowers of the upland were growing—fragile rockroses and harebells, two-colored toadflax, rose heather and wild thyme and purple-blooming sage—where the bees browsed while the sweet damp wind stroked their thick-pelted backs. Lower down gorse and broom burned like pale golden fire, and lower still the hanging woods of the Kielder's ravine were blurred with the tender green of young foliage.

Kithra, five years old now, heavy-necked and proud in the fullness of growth, stood on the very edge of the scarp and looked out over the view, too, his huge ears pricked alertly, and Mary Percy's little brown mongrel bitch, Mowdie, who had adopted her at the steading, nosed around in the short, tough grass for insects. For a long time the two riders were silent. Then Houlet shifted his feet restlessly and made a downward snatch to graze, and the jingling of his bridle decorations broke the silence.

"We'll let them graze for a while," Mary Percy said, swinging lightly to the ground. John followed suit, and they sat on a warm rock and let the horses graze to the length of their reins.

"Scotland," John said after a while. "Who knows where it begins or where England ends? Somewhere out there"—he nodded at the bare uplands—"we decide almost at random that one country ends and another begins. A line drawn between two blades of grass with the same root, and suddenly it is a foreign land and the people enemies."

Mary stirred and glanced at him. "It sounds foolish and simple. But they are different They are enemies. The same grass feeds their flocks, the same sun warms them, but their hearts are closed to the Faith and to all human decency."

John smiled at her. "Even those of the Faith can behave badly. What of Queen Mary?"

It roused the Princeling instantly to anger, anger like the flash of gold of a coin falling through sunlight. "It was nothing to do with her. I cannot believe she had anything to do with it. It was Bothwell's doing."

"Protestant Bothwell," John smiled, having achieved his object. "You are so beautiful when you are angry."

A different kind of anger now. She turned her face away. "You are not to speak to me so."

"You are my captain, I your faithful lieutenant," John agreed. "But you cannot do without me now, and it would be seemly of you to admit it." But he saw he had distressed her, so he changed the subject quickly. "Strange, is it not, the similarity between the cases of Queen Mary and Queen Elizabeth. With Queen Elizabeth, there was the mystery over Amy Dudley, and it was supposed that she contrived at her lover's wife's death so that she could marry him. And now with Queen Mary, her husband is mysteriously murdered, she is abducted by her lover, and they marry."

"By the Protestant rite—it is no marriage."

"The difference is that Queen Elizabeth did not marry her horse master, and Queen Mary—"

"That proves nothing," Mary said hotly. "No one doubts that it was Bothwell who blew up the King's house, but to say that she knew anything about it—"

"I do," John said.

"You do what?"

"I have doubts. I don't think it was Bothwell. The King, you remember, was strangled, not killed by the explosion. A foolish way to go about things—and Bothwell is no fool by all accounts. No, I think it was Moray who arranged it all to bring the Queen into disrepute. Blowing up the King's house made sure that everyone knew about it, drew attention to it so that it could not be kept secret. If Bothwell had killed the King, he would have made a better job of it. Besides, it was foolish—he would soon have died anyway."

Mary absorbed all this and then said, "But why, then, do you think the Queen guilty?"

"Not of the murder, but her abduction by Bothwell was clumsy and cowardly. If she wanted to marry him badly enough to do it, she should have done it openly. The pretense at coercion only makes her look a fool and a poltroon. But then she is only a woman. I have been spoiled for other women by too good an example of female courage and honor."

"Don't, please don't," Mary said quickly. John smiled inwardly. Once she would have said it scornfully, sharply, as though reprimanding a servant. Now she said it softly, breathlessly, like one who saying no would fain say yes. He reached out his hand, and she flinched from him.

"Mary, how much longer?" he said abruptly. "How many years must I serve for you? You know now that you could not do without me. Your people look to me as their King as they look to you as Queen—"

An unfortunate choice of words, it seemed. The softness left her face and she stood up, her eyes taking color from the sky. "There was another Queen Mary who was foolish enough to name her husband King," she said. "Come, let us ride on. We have a way to go yet."

So we do, John thought, and in silence he pulled up Jupiter's head and mounted and rode behind Mary down the scarp side toward the burn and the woods. In a little while she regained her temper and said pleasantly, as if to make amends, "You heard from your sister recently, I believe?" John nodded. "Did she say anything of interest?"

"She writes very circumspectly, as you can imagine. She is in fear of her husband and does not know on which side he stands, though he is often seen talking to Morton, who is one of Moray's men. If she said too much, or the wrong thing, she might be in danger of her life. So much I understand from her cautious hints."

"Her husband, you think, would kill her?" Mary said, surprised. In her life she had ruled men and had never been afraid of any of them.

"Not at the moment—she is pregnant again. But his previous two wives died, and he is a violent man."

Mary threw him a look that said as clearly as words, you see what happens to women foolish enough to marry, and John gave a rueful smile and, taking the reins in one hand, held out the other to her, palm up, for inspection. "What could that hand harm?" he said.

Mary felt a smile tugging her lips, and rather than allow it to be seen she spurred Houlet on suddenly to a trot and drew ahead of him. The way was steep and rough, and soon their descent became a breakneck race, the exhilaration of danger going to their heads. The dogs barked in excitement and raced each other, too, picking their own steeper way toward the fierce little burn in its precipitous valley. Houlet was the better horse and Mary the better rider, and there was never any doubt that she would win the race. At the bottom of the scarp they pulled up, panting, flushed and laughing, and then rode on in companionable silence.

They crossed the burn at a place where a steep gray cliff came right down to the burn side and a rock fall had made a natural dam across the top of which they could cross, the horses stepping carefully on the mossy flat stones, snorting at the swirling, bubble-streaked wa-

ter. Here rowan trees grew close on either side, making
an arch of branches over the water; below the dam the
water foamed white into a small, deep pool which reflected the sky and the woods above, and there was a
small mossy lawn between the pool and the thick, choking trees and undergrowth that spilled down the ravine
side beyond. It was a still and silent place, despite the
mocking chatter of the water. There should have been
insects dancing in the air over the water, flies settling
and taking off from the warm moss lawn, lizards and
snakes basking on the flat gray rocks, butterflies and
birds decorating the air with their graceful galliards:
but there was nothing, only the shadow of the cliff, the
silent woods, the still pool and the white teeth of the
water.

Looking up, John saw, a long way above, the outcrop on which Mary had paused on the day they had
surprised the raiders. He glanced at her now as she
waited for him to cross the burn. Down her left cheek
ran a thin red line, the scar of that day, fading a little
now; but what other scar was there that he did not
know about? She was looking at him, but she was not
seeing him: there was an expression on her face of distant apprehension, as if she were seeing an approaching
shadow of fear or grief. Reaching her, he checked her
as she was about to turn and ride on.

"What is it, Mary?" he asked. "You look so—
afraid."

She raised her eyes to his and seemed about to deny
him, and then changed her mind. She glanced around
out of the corners of her eyes like a wary deer.

"It is this place," she said. "It is nothing, but—"

"Once before I saw you look at it with that expression. You were up there—on that gray rock. Do you
remember?" She looked up at the outcrop far above.

"It is called the Old Man, that rock. And here, this

place, is called the Standing Pool. My people say that it is a magic place, that the pool is a window through which you could see the future. It is nonsense, of course—but it is too quiet here." She looked at him, her gray eyes wide with fright, making her look very young. No air stirred the soft down of silver hair on her brow, the fronds that had escaped her cap. She might have been a boy of fourteen. The strength of her was subdued, and she was as vulnerable as a fawn cornered by mastiffs.

"I dream of it at night," she said suddenly, as though the words had been pulled out of her.

"What do you dream?" he asked gently.

"I don't know. In the morning, when I wake, I have forgotten everything, except that it is this place, and that I feel—oh, such sadness, as if it is the end of everything, and—"

She would say no more. John longed to put his arms around her, to tell her that now and forever he would hold her, keep away dark and danger and evil, throw the mantle of his love around her so that the shadows beyond the candlelight could not touch her. But it was not time yet; he felt her moods and desires with his mind as he felt the air on his skin. In a moment, without speaking again, she turned away and led the way up the other side of the ravine.

At the top they turned parallel with the burn and rode along the rough path between the trees, the dogs coursing excitedly from side to side, following game smells, noses down. Mary's spirits lightened, and soon her head was up again and she turned to him with her customary imperious look and said, "Well, and how much further is it to this place where you said you saw the wildcat's lair? I have known these woods all my life, and I never saw it."

"We will be there soon," John said, smiling inwardly

with relief. "Now you have brought us this far, perhaps I had better lead the way?"

Even to his own eyes, he had changed in the years he had spent here, and the difference was brought home to him just then, as if he were seeing himself from outside with a stranger's eyes, between the tall gentle boy he had been at home, dressed in the commoner's simple gown of rough wool, performing the innocent business of the farmer and landlord; and the lean, hard man he was now, still gentle within but with an air of authority and alertness, king of his people in all but name. The Tod's Knowe folk had accepted him, though Mary had not. It was to him as much as to Black Will that they brought their problems, their quarrels and especially their sicknesses. His ability to heal and soothe had not deserted him, and perhaps more than anything it was this that had reconciled the hard Northumberland men to a southern lord.

And here he was, riding along a track that was hardly a track at all, knowing his way by minute signs—an oddly shaped branch, a patch of lichen on a stone, a particular grouping of trees; mind, eyes and ears alert to the sounds of the wild, sorting them effortlessly into those that meant normality and those that meant danger. They were coming near the place now, and he signaled Mary to stop and called the dogs close.

"We had better go on foot now," he said quietly. They hitched the horses to a dead tree and leashed the dogs. Mary stepped close to him but a little behind, accepting his leadership with the quiet discipline of a fighting man, and his heart lurched anew with the recognition of her differentness: whether she eventually accepted him or not, he knew that he could never now love any other woman, for no other woman was like her. Stepping as quietly as stalking cats, they moved off the path and through the undergrowth, the dogs pad-

ding softly at heel, both used to the routine of hunting.
They went slowly, taking care with each footfall to snap
no twig and rustle no dead bracken, and soon they were
at the edge of the clearing, and they sank down on
their haunches to look.

It was a small clearing, and on the other side was an
outcrop of rock, jutting up like a gray stone beehive.
Grass and small bushes grew from the base and hollows
of it, but before it was a bare patch where the vegeta-
tion had been worn away by something jumping down
from the small dark opening higher up. There was a
strange smell in the air; Kithra salivated and whined
very softly, and John checked him and looked at Mary.
She was crouching on her heels, so still in her brown
jerkin, boots and leather cap that she became almost
invisible in the muted light against the undergrowth.
Her eyes were wide and clear; her fine brows, pale as
her hair, drawn slightly together in concentration; her
nostrils fluttering, searching the air for danger; her lips
lightly closed. Desire thudded suddenly in his belly, and
he pushed the thought away.

They watched for a while until they saw a squirrel
run lightly down from a tree and pause at its foot for a
moment before flirting its tail with a ripple like shaken
foil and running around the bole. Everything was still
and calm.

"Come," Mary said. "There is nothing here. Let's go
and look closer."

Carefully they worked their way across the clearing,
pausing every few steps to look and listen, but there
was nothing. The dogs were quiet, though wary. They
reached the rock, and before John could prevent her,
Mary had sprung lightly up the rock to look in at the
opening. It was barely a cave, more like a wide fissure.
She stared in and then turned her face, enchanted, toward John.

"Come down," he whispered urgently. "Don't be foolish."

"You were right," she said, ignoring his words. "There is a lair, and two kittens." She turned to look again and then frowned. "I think one is dead, John. One moves and looks at me, but the other—oh, it is growling! Such tiny teeth, like the finest embroidery needles. I think—"

But suddenly the dogs were bristling, and Kithra began to growl.

"Mary, come down, quickly!" John cried. She turned, recognizing the urgency and authority of his voice, but even as she reached downward with one hand and foot, from behind John like tawny lightning came the cat, crossing the clearing with unbelievable speed and springing through the air to land on Mary's back.

It was her cap that saved her. The wildcat's hind claws scrabbled for hold on her leather jerkin, but its foreclaws and teeth fastened on her cap, which came off, throwing the cat off balance. They both fell, the cat turning in mid-air in the way of its kind, so that as Mary hit the ground shoulder and thigh and rolled over, it was on her back again instantly. Both dogs leaped forward at once, snarling and barking wildly, so that the cat paused. John had brought Mary here only to observe; he had never intended killing the cat; but now there seemed no choice. As the cat struck out at the dogs and Mary struggled to get her hand to her dagger, John sprang forward with his own knife and drove for the creature's heart.

Icy cold followed by burning was the pain, and he glanced down in surprise to see his forearm laid open and bleeding, the cloth of his sleeve lacerated. Mowdie shrieked, too, and limped aside, tail between her legs, but the cat was backing off before Kithra, while Mary,

having the sense to keep her back, the less vulnerable
part of her, to the cat, had drawn her legs under her
and was crawling away. Kithra, all the ferocity of his
wolf ancestors aroused by the smell of the old enemy,
was a bristling and horrible sight. He was bigger and
heavier than the cat by far, but the cat was quicker.
Even as Mary gained her feet and turned, crouching,
Kithra sprang. There was a whirlwind of snarling, snapping, slashing fur and teeth and claws, and then the cat
sprang up to its rock and stood defiantly, teeth bared,
yowling hatred, while Kithra fell back, still snarling, the
side of his head laid open and his shoulders torn and
bleeding.

This was the chance, and John seized it. "Run," he
said to Mary. "Quickly."

She obeyed him, snatching up the limping Mowdie
and running for the trees. John called Kithra, and when
he backed a pace from the rock, John grabbed his collar and tugged, and the two of them turned tail and ran.
The cat, as he had guessed, stayed put now she had
gained her lair, but her howling followed them, defiant
and furious, raising the hair on their necks.

The horses were restless, jerking their heads and rolling their eyes, but they had not broken away yet, thank
God, and without need of words John and Mary tugged
the reins free, vaulted up and rode at a gallop along the
track, Mary still clutching Mowdie in her arm and
Kithra running behind. When the cat's howling had
faded in the distance, they pulled up the sweating
horses and slid to the ground to inspect their wounds.

Kithra was the worst hurt, but he would not let even
John touch his wounds, and after trying for a while
John let him be.

"He will probably heal the better for being left
alone," he said, and Kithra, when he saw he was not to
be molested, flopped down at a distance and tried to
reach his wounded shoulders with his tongue, but in

vain. In a moment Mowdie limped across to him and lay down beside him, and after a moment of warning growling at each other they began companionably to lick each other's wounds.

The humans did much the same. Mary was barely scratched, her leather doublet having taken most of the rending, though her neck and shoulders were sore. John's arm was bleeding freely from four bloody runnels, and the muscle was exposed in one place. Without a word Mary took off her doublet, dragged up her shirt, tore a strip off it and proceeded to bind John's forearm tightly.

"There," she said at last. "That's the best I can do for now. We must get home, and then I can bind it properly. But that should stop the bleeding a little." She looked up at him with an oddly furtive expression. "John," she said hesitantly, "I'm sorry. It was my fault, what happened. I should have let you tell me. I was wrong."

She met his eyes frankly and candidly, and he saw how much it had taken for her to apologize. With her cap gone, her moon-color hair had fallen loose down her back, fine and soft as a child's. Under her torn shirt, barely concealed by her chemise, her tender young breasts moved softly with her breathing, and at the hollow of her throat was a warm, white place, untouched by the sun, where the blood beat softly. She was very close to him, one hand still on his bandaged arm, and as he looked down into her face and saw the slightly questioning look she gave him, he felt the quality of her resistance alter, as hand-to-hand wrestlers will.

All her life she had commanded men and feared none. Now she feared him, because he had made her want to surrender, and if she surrendered, it would break her pride and her heart. She could not live without the sense of her honor her strange upbringing had given her. He remembered, suddenly, the colt that he and Jan had tried to break in, and the tragedy of its inability to understand what was wanted. Words, he thought, we have words. There must be a way to make it known.

"Mary," he said. Her nostrils were fluttering with the same wariness he had seen before, but in her gray eyes was a gold light of pure desire. "Mary, I would take nothing from you. I would not fetter you like a kestrel. I would give to you, serve you, honor you. If it was by your own will it would not be a defeat."

Had she understood? Her face was very close, her lips parted, dragging in the breath shudderingly as if she were wounded and near death. His own control snapped. He folded her into his arms and pressed his face against her hair, her cheek, her neck. She was rigid in his arms, brittle, and he could feel her shuddering. Then her arms came around him, awkwardly, like someone unused to the gesture, and her small breasts were against him, their hard nipples pressing into him through his shirt. Love and desire flamed together like two bushes set alight, indivisible now.

He pulled his head back to kiss her and stopped at the sight of the struggle still going on in her face. "What is it?" he whispered. "Say it. Mary, Mary. Say it."

Her lips moved soundlessly, rehearsing it once or twice, and then in a falling cadence she said, "I love you."

He gathered her into his arms, and she was as soft and unresisting as a child. She clung to him weakly, and he lay her down on a smooth patch of turf at the foot of a tree and stooped over her, and in the last moment before their lips met he paused again and said, "It changes nothing, Mary. You are king and queen." Yielding and suffering were in her face, and desire, too, but not yet the joy of yielding.

"It doesn't matter," she said. "I love you." Then he kissed her, and their two bodies turned to flame, creatures of fire, joyful as salamanders springing to the consummation of death at whose heart is the seed of life; the death of two and the birth of one.

Afterward they were still for a long time, consumed with the silence of nature of which they had become a part. There was no room in either of them for any thought or sensation, so at one were they with the pulse of the earth. But there is no gain without loss, and no happiness without a shadow of sadness, and they did not speak for fear of knowing it. They lay still, wrapped in each other's arms, and at a little distance Kithra and Mowdie went on quietly licking and licking at each other's wounds under the dappled shadows.

CHAPTER TEN

For a time, after the baby died, Lettice had begun to think she might grow closer to her husband. He was more distressed by Hamil's death than, in her limited experience of people, she had expected a man to be. He sat silently brooding for hours at a time, while Lettice, too afraid to speak, sat by silently working. Kat, in their few private moments together, told her it was a wonderful sign that he wanted her to be there at all, that he did not shut himself away from her company.

"He takes comfort in you, my precious, you see that," Kat said as she brushed Lettice's hair or laced her busk. "He begins to realize your worth. It may be that the bairn's dying like that was the best thing that could happen."

Emboldened by Kat's words, Lettice went so far as to seek her husband out, though still she had not the courage to speak unless he spoke first to her. But she would walk with him in the long gallery or sit near him sewing, and sometimes she would look up from her work to find his eyes fixed on her in a way that made her blush to her collarbones. Yet though he slept with her every night, he did nothing more than caress her

before falling asleep, always with one hand touching
her, resting on her throat or shoulder, as if he wanted to
make sure she did not escape in the night. Once, when
he was stroking her face and breast, she thought to encourage him to begin another baby, but he pulled back
from her abruptly, almost roughly, and for a moment
she thought he was afraid. She dismissed the thought—
Rob Hamilton afraid?

Then one morning she woke and found him gone
from the bed, and later that day one of his servants
came to tell her that he had gone away.

"Gone away where?" Lettice asked sharply.

The servant's face was impassive. "I dinna ken, mistress. The master didna see fit to tell me."

No one would tell her any more than that, and she
began to be worried. Her worry increased when orders
came from Rob for her to be removed to Birnie Castle,
and when she learned that the rest of the household,
including her step daughters, was staying put at Aberlady, her fears began.

She came to look back on those long months at
Birnie as the worst in her life. Alone but for Kat in that
bleak place, with no word of her lord or of her family,
she would have been lonely if it had not been that her
fear drove everything else out of her head. She tried at
first out of pride to hide her fear, but one wild, windy
evening when Kat was brushing out her hair she broke
down at last and began to cry.

"Why, my precious lady, what is it? What's the matter? Tell Kat."

"Oh, Kat, I'm so afraid!"

"Why, what of?" Lettice made an incoherent answer.
"It's only the wind, my lady. Just like the sweet wind at
home at Morland Place, blowing in off the moors."

But at the mention of Morland Place Lettice sobbed
more loudly, and at last Kat made out the words, "I
shall never see Morland Place again." Lettice lifted a

tear-stained face to her servant. "Oh, Kat, I'm so sorry to have brought you to this. It is not deserved."

"But to what, my precious? What is it? All this storm of grief?"

"Oh, Kat, I'm afraid he means to kill me."

"Your husband?" Kat whispered, her hand going to her throat as the possibility came home to her. Lettice nodded, staring up earnestly, her eyes enormous in her pale face.

"That's why he has sent me here, and alone. Have you not seen how the servants watch me." She shuddered. "I hate them! They are like those horrible faces carved on the buttress ends in the church at home, that stare down at you out of the shadows like devils. What happened to his other two wives? Why will no one speak of them? Haven't you ever wondered, Kat?"

"Why yes—but my lady—"

"They did not give him a son, so he poisoned them. Yes—don't deny it! I know it's true. And he has sent me here, shut me up here alone with his loyal henchmen, and he will have me poisioned by and by, because I gave him a son that died."

Kat could not reason her out of her fear, and true enough, Kat believed it herself. There was no way of escaping, either, even had they the courage to contemplate it, two women alone as they were. The doors to the castle were kept locked and barred always in that wild country, and it was necessary to get the steward to unlock if one wanted to go out. In any case the two women were never allowed out alone.

No word came to them of Rob, but gossip filtered upward from the servants, tales of the grim and terrible happenings in Edinburgh, the murder of the mad, sick King, the "abduction" of the Queen and her marriage to Bothwell and the announcing of her pregnancy. All the inhabitants of Birnie Castle, in common with most of the populace of Scotland, believed that the Queen and her border wolf had contrived the murder between them so that they could marry. They were all Protestants, and there was no love for or sympathy with the Catholic Queen: only Lettice, trapped in her own fear and remembering the Queen's fragile, threatened happiness, wondered how far Mary of Scotland had had any choice, once she had called the wolf in over her threshold.

Weeks passed, and the blow did not fall, though Lettice's fear grew more rather than less with each day that passed leaving her still alive. She grew thinner, fearing to eat anything that she did not take for herself from the common dish, and wilder, often not bothering to dress or do her hair. She cried a great deal, and prayed a great deal, and sang to keep her courage up, and Kat could do little but follow in her lady's tracks, talking to her and hoping she would not lose her reason, for, white-faced, wild-haired and huge-eyed as she was, Lettice looked fit for Bedlam. Kat even wondered if this, after all, was Hamilton's plan.

In June more news came, that Morton had rebelled again, had captured the Queen and imprisoned her at Lochleven, a castle built on an island in the middle of a lake, from which escape would surely be impossible, and had called Moray home from France. And in July, by what means of force it was not known, there at Lochleven Moray persuaded the Queen to abdicate in favor of her infant son under the regency of Moray. She had miscarried of the child she was bearing, and Bothwell was far away, having fled the country when she was captured. Once again Lettice wondered what choice she had had. Now, Lettice supposed, the Queen, in similiar plight to Lettice herself, would be poisoned, too.

And then, in July, Rob came home. Lettice was in her room one morning, still in her bed gown, her tan-

gled hair down her back, sitting at the window and staring southward, toward the homeland that she knew she
would not see again. She was singing idly under her
breath, a little, repetitive song that her governess had
taught her when she was a child, and her thoughts were
so far away that she did not hear the commotion of ar-
rival downstairs. She heard nothing, in fact, until Kat's
voice was raised in excitement of some kind in the
outer room, the door burst open and Rob was there,
filling the doorway, big and black and solid and real,
smelling of the sweet damp wind, of earth, of sweat and
horses.

Lettice jumped up in terror, her eyes stretching wide,
and she opened her mouth to scream. Rob was across
the room in one astonishingly swift movement and had
seized her by the throat, clapping a hand over her
mouth in time to stop the sound. He was grinning a
white and savage grin that, despite her fear, woke longing in Lettice; and between fear and desire she did not
notice the faint trace of wistfulness in that dark, sardonic face.

"What now, my lady; what do I find? I go away and
leave you shut up safely here where no harm can come
to you, and you break your willful heart, like a tethered
unicorn. Hush now, hush, don't struggle. Be still and
I'll let you go, but I cannot have you screaming. I was
drinking until late last night, and my head is tender this
morning. Will you be still?"

Lettice nodded, nothing of her face showing above
Rob's huge hand but her wide violet eyes. Carefully
Rob lowered her to her feet and removed his hands,
and she stood, hunching her shoulders like a frightened
bird, shivering, but never taking her gaze from his face.

"Now then, what was all this for?" he asked. His
voice was rough and mocking, but the sense of the
question was kind. Lettice's lips moved a few times before she framed the right question.

"Why did you go away?"

"I had business to attend to. I came to a decision and acted on it."

"Decision—about the Queen and—and Lord Moray?"

Rob smiled, a gesture a little less hard than his grin. "Even frightened out of your wits you have much sense, lady. Aye, and that's one of the things I like about you. About the Queen, and Moray, aye. Well, it's done now, and we have a governor for the country that can govern, and will, that has both the power and the right."

"And you—"

"I helped."

"But what will happen to the poor Queen?" Lettice said abruptly. Her mind was working quickly. How could they leave the Queen alive, to be the figurehead of rebels? "They will have her killed."

"I do not know," Rob said seriously. "It is not my problem."

"She's shut away, and none will know when she dies," Lettice said. "They'll lock her up and poison her, just as—"

She stopped abruptly, clapping her hand to her mouth in a disarmingly childish gesture. She must not let him know what she feared. Rob stared at her, his mind working just as quickly.

"So that's what you feared, was it, my wee unicorn? That I had tethered you here to saw off your horn and poison you with it?" There was pity in his face for just a moment before he hid it with his usual sardonic grin. "I shut you up here alone to protect you, you damned wee fool, while I was on dangerous business. You were too vulnerable at Aberlady. It is impossible to guard that house as this place can be guarded. They told me when I arrived that you had determined to break your heart and die, and that nothing they could do would stop you."

Her eyes were fixed on his face, and all her thoughts were in it so transparently that he laughed aloud.

"Aye, well, and now I'm here, I'll teach you to despoil my property like that. You are my wife, and my property, and I'll thank you to take better care of what is mine."

"Rob, I—you—"

"You and I, that's right, my hinny. And now you have work to do."

"Work?"

"You've a son to bear me. And I've a son to get. So let's be about it."

She did not speak, but her face told him of her consent, and more than consent, and with a jubliant laugh he put his arms around her and swung her up easily and carried her to the bed. She was light and fragile and white, but her eyes burned like blue torches, and when he flung her down on the bed and began to unbuckle his sword, she laughed, too, with gladness and relief that the long night was over.

Paul had grown so used to the situation that he scarcely cared when the news arrived that John had finally married Mary Percy. To him John seemed as irrevocably lost as Lettice and Paul, for whether he married her or not, it was sure that he would remain in the border country. Paul had disinherited him, and the whole estate would pass to William, and there was an end. Yet he had been proud of his son, and he could not but be excited at the prospect of seeing him again, and he consented very willingly when John wrote to ask if he might visit, with his wife, in the autumn of 1568. Their first child was expected in July and they thought to visit in October when Mary would have recovered, but as it turned out, the birth was hard and Mary was so ill after it that the visit had to be postponed to the following spring.

That October in York was not without its excitement. Queen Mary of Scotland, having made a spectular escape from her island prison at Lochleven, had arrived in England with nothing but the clothes on her back and a handful of faithful servants in May of that year, demanding sanctuary of her cousin Queen Elizabeth and help in redressing her wrongs.

"That puts the fox in the henhouse!" Nanette had exclaimed when she heard the news. If Queen Mary was unwanted in Scotland, how much more unwanted was she in England, where Queen Elizabeth was still trying to reconcile her Catholic subjects to her non-Catholic rule. The best and simplest thing would have been to have her put to death, but Elizabeth would never spill the blood of an anointed Queen, even if she had not also been a relative, so the best she could do was to imprison her cousin with as much comfort and honor as possible. A trial was arranged for Queen Mary to answer for the various crimes laid against her, and this took place in October 1568 in York. All of York was agog to see this astonishingly tall and beautiful woman, to hear the details of her notorious wickedness and to discover what in the end was to be done to her, or with her. The trial was not completed. Elizabeth had ordered it at York to keep it as much as possible out of the way of her subjects' curiosity, but when Maitland suggested that the best thing to do with Queen Mary was to marry her to the Duke of Norfolk, whose blood, many thought, was more royal than that of either of the Queens, and send her with an English army to recapture Scotland, naming her children by Norfolk heirs to the English throne, then Elizabeth decided it was time to remove the hearing to Westminister where she could have more control over what was said and not said.

*   *   *

On a sweet May day in 1569 John and Jan were riding side by side from Morland Place down toward the great south road. It was all open champaign through which they rode—the only enclosed fields were on the higher ground, where the sheep grazed now with their new lambs—and away on every side stretched the broad strips, curving with the folds of the land, of green rye, of barley and of fallow. They rode along the banks of the Holgate Beck, where there were hay meadows and where children tended geese and goats on the common grazing. All along the flanks of the Hob Moor was a sea of pink-flowering sainfoin, some set aside with hurdles for haying, some being grazed by the milch cows.

"Your father has grown very interested in improving his farming," Jan said. "I think he reads Tusser more often than the Bible, and he's full of ideas about how to keep stock through the winter."

"Is that the reason for all this sainfoin?" John asked, waving a hand toward it.

"Yes—I grew a great deal last year on my little pocket handkerchief of land over at Watermill, and your father was green with envy when he saw how fat my kine were in February." Jan shot a look at his tall companion and said, "I think he misses you, John. I am but a poor substitute."

John shook his head. "I was never his favorite. But in any case, I cannot come back, if that's what you ask. The raids were very bad through the winter, and it's only now for a short while that I dare come away. Once the calves have been dropped, we will be riding around the herds day after day."

Jan shook his head. "What a strange life it must be. I try to imagine it, but my imagination fails. Do you really ride into battle for your own herds? And with Mary beside you?"

"She's a bonny fighter," John said proudly. "She's saved my life more than once. You see this scar?" He lifted the hair from his forehead to show a white seam and a dent. "That's where I was hit with the blunt end of a battle-ax. I fell from my horse and would surely have been killed. But Mary jumped down and stood over me, fighting off everyone who came at her, until I recovered my senses. Her arm was laid open from shoulder to elbow doing it."

Jan shuddered. "Dear God alive! Imagine me riding out with my Mary beside me——"

"It is different——" John began.

Jan smiled. "Oh, save your tremendous frowns, coz. I know it is different. It was no discourtesy to your wife I meant. Oh, John, it is so good to see you again! You have changed a great deal, you know." To Jan's fond eyes, John had grown from a slender gentle-eyed boy into a heavy-shouldered man with a firm-mouthed, authoritative air; very much a general and leader of his people. "You have grown up."

"I would I could say the same of you," John said with a smile. He looked around him. "This is such a fat land. Though it is my home, it seems strange to me now—the quietness, the gentleness, the luxury—above all, the luxury! Chimneys, and furniture, and dainty food, and baths! It is like another world in the Borderlands."

Jan looked at John and saw the shadows in his eyes where he was seeing not the sunlit meadows around him but the place where his heart now was, and try as he might, Jan could not visualize it. John knew, too, that he could never convey to this dainty and bejeweled man the brooding silence of those great naked hills, the low, soft skies, the smell of the upland, the mysterious trilling of the curlew and the kee-wick of the hunting kestrel; and the shape and texture of his life there, the darkness and sudden light, the smell of smoke within doors, the violent excitement of the turnout in the middle of the night, to ride with a soft thunder of hooves over the black turf where a fired thatch made a great yellow-red blossom in the night, the sound and smell of frightened cattle with the firelight glowing in their eyes, the sound and smell of the raiders, little fierce men with long knives like bee stings but much, much more deadly.

At the ford Jan drew rein and John followed suit, and they sat looking down the slight slope toward the road.

"Well, there it is—my father's monument, and now yours," Jan said. St. Edward's School was a small, neat, red-brick building with tall chimneys, and beside it now, sharing one boundary wall, was the hospital Paul Morland had taken the major part in founding and building. The hospital was built around a central court-yard, with its bridewell for unwed women and their infants on the further side nearest the school and its bedlam for the insane on the further side, where the high wall shut out the view of Hob Moor.

"The choice of name occupied much thought for many weeks," Jan said, "but in the end they settled for St. Edward's Hospital, so they might have saved their trouble. It has forty beds—everyone is immensely proud of it."

"Where did the money come from?" John asked.

"Oh, it is properly endowed, never fear. Your father gave property, and so did many other notable families of the town—the Buttses, and the Archers, and the Weavers, and the Conyngsbys."

"And you?"

"No, I had very little to do with it. The school is my interest. I gave the house my father left me, on the Lendal, and he, of course, endowed it with considerable

property, so that we can afford good wages for the
schoolmaster and usher. There seemed to me no point
in having a school unless we have a good schoolmaster.
In deference to my father's idiosyncrasies, there is only
a modicum of beating, so it needs a good man to control the children, especially those of the Bridewell
women."

"But is it all worthwhile, you think?"

"See for yourself—the vagabonds and beggars are
gone from the roads. The sick are tended, the vicious
are reformed, the idle are given work and the children
are taught to read and write and then sent to an apprenticeship in the town. Come, since we have ridden so far,
let us pay a visit to the school."

John was the amused but admiring onlooker as Jan
was greeted with great exuberance by the children of
the school. He appeared to know most of them by name
and was obviously a popular hero with them. He spoke
aside to the schoolmaster and usher, tested one or two
of the girls and boys on their progress and then addressed the school at large on the subjects of endeavor
and obedience.

When they left, John said, concealing a smile, "You
seemed to be well known to them."

"Oh, I am there quite a lot, one way and another,"
Jan said, trying to look casual. Then he grinned. "In
fact, I am there several times a week, and sometimes I
take small groups of them for special lessons. And of
course I organize the Founder's Day celebrations, so
they remember me for that."

"My friend Jan Chapham, the great benefactor,"
John said and smiled.

Jan led the way back across the ford. "Why, I have
to have something to set in the scales against my great
wickedness. Come, let's gallop. I long to be home to see
your wonderful Mary again."

Though the Morlands had expected Mary Percy, it could hardly be said that they were prepared for her, and when she rode in at John's side, mounted on Houlet and dressed in britches and long boots and a man's stuffed doublet, most of them failed at first to recognize her. Before they had come down, she and John had discussed the matter of clothes, and John had tentatively suggested that she might put on a dress while she was at Morland Place, only to withdraw the suggestion at the first flash of her quick anger.

"You are right, of course," he said pacifically. "It would be a sham, a lie. You are what you are, and I love you as you are. I will support you."

She needed his support, for it was a shocking thing to the inmates of Morland Place to see a woman, a married woman who had borne a child at that, dressed as a man. After the shock had worn off, reactions varied. The older people, Paul and the grown-up Buttses and Hezekiah, thought it bad and wrong; Jan thought it grotesque; Mary Seymour thought it silly and wondered how a woman as beautiful as Mary Percy could bear not to wear pretty clothes and jewels, could bear to wear her moon-pale hair in one thick braid behind instead of curled and frizzled, could bear to risk her looks in battle with men and naked blades. What Jane thought, no one knew. She kept her counsel as always and behaved toward Mary Percy with the same unvarying courtesy and kindness she showed everybody. The children—Jan and Mary's Nicholas, the Butts children and Arthur—thought it impossibly romantic as well as wicked, and ten-year-old Margaret Butts became Mary Percy's shadow and longed so for a scar on her own cheek that she tried to produce one with the end of a slate pencil but had to give it up when she discovered it hurt.

The only person who seemed really to understand

was Nanette. At sixty-one she was still active and energetic, loved to ride and hunt and still, after the fashion
of her own youth, rode cross-saddle, which Mary Percy
found a comfort. Nanette had been her father's eldest
child and therefore in many ways had been his son; she
understood the longing for freedom that afflicted
women from time to time: she remembered Elizabeth's
unhappiness at having to exchange riding and romping
for quiet modesty and stillness. Moreover, Nanette had
lived with kings and queens and understood better than
the rest of the family could the duty that was laid upon
the soul of one who was leader to the people. She understood that Mary Percy was her people's Prince, and
Mary, responding to that felt sympathy, was easier in
Nanette's company than in anyone else's.

On the morning that Jan and John rode down to the
hospital, Mary Percy stayed behind, sitting in the herb
garden with Nanette and Mary Seymour and Jane, sewing. At least the other three sewed while Mary Percy,
a little self-consciously, mended a bridle strap that had
worn on the journey. She would much sooner have
ridden with John, but she understood that he could not
have the easy conversation with his childhood companion that he wanted if she was there, and so she
had stayed behind. Kithra stayed with her, for he had
developed a sore pad on the long ride from Redesdale
and needed rest. He lay at her feet with Mowdie, growling horribly at Nanette's little greyhound Zack whenever the poor beast moved a muscle.

They talked, at first, of babies. Mary Seymour's firstborn, Nicholas, was now three and was doing lessons in
the Morland Place schoolroom, and her second son,
Gabriel, was almost eighteen months old and promising
to be a very forward child. Nanette was very proud of
and delighted with her grandchildren and was happy to
talk about them at any time.

"Jan is already teaching Gabriel to ride," Nanette said. "He would have done the same with Nicholas if Mary had let him. The earlier they learn the better for them. I keep telling you that, Mary, but you will not understand it. Don't you want your sons to be good horsemen?"

"I don't want them tumbling off and killing themselves. I had sooner have a live son, even if he is not the world's greatest master of horse," Mary Seymour said crossly, her eyes on her work. Jane glanced quickly, anxiously at Nanette, remembering how Alexander had come upon his death, but Nanette's face was serene. Age had been kind to her, and though the flesh had fallen away a little, showing up the sharp bones of her face, she was very little lined, and her eyes were as blue and bright as ever. She concealed her hair entirely, now that it was white, with a pretty little whelk-shell cap, and with her high collar hiding her throat, there was nothing visible but her smooth, sharp-boned face, so that she had an alabaster beauty that was very enduring.

"What does Mary think about it?" Jane asked, turning to the visitor in politeness.

Mary Percy looked up and encountered the kindness of Jane's regard.

"My own Thomas I had up on the saddle before me as soon as he could support his head," she admitted. "He never had the least fear of horses."

"But weren't you afraid he would fall and be killed? And then—all that labor for nothing," Mary Seymour said. "I believe you had a hard time of it, did you not?"

Mary Percy nodded, not wishing to speak of it. The labor had been so long and hard that it had seemed several times that she would die. The child was big, and her muscles strong with riding. The combination, so the midwife said, was a bad one. At any rate, it seemed unlikely that she would ever have another, which made

Thomas the more deeply loved by both her and John. "It never crossed my mind that he might be hurt," she said. "Besides, God has his own plans for him. If he is meant to die young, there is nothing we can do about it."

Mary and Jane exchanged a glance at this, and Nanette said, "I wish I could ever have accepted matters as easily as that. But tell me, have you heard recently from Lettice? I believe she writes to John sometimes?"

"Not recently. The last time she wrote was in the autumn, to tell us of her delivery. She had a daughter, born almost on the same day as Thomas. They have called her Douglass. She never tells us much—I think she is unsure always what it is safe to say."

"But her husband is something powerful in the regent's council, is he not?"

Mary frowned. "He was, I know; and from hints that Lettice gave in her letters, I think that Lord Hamilton helped Lord Moray to power. But—" She stopped abruptly and said no more. Nanette did not press for it. John would tell Jan, she knew, and she would hear from Jan later what the new development was.

"I think," she said, to cover Mary Percy's silence, "that we shall have trouble now the Queen of Scotland is here. What a foolish, wicked woman she is! The pity of it is, my lady is too tender-hearted to have her put to death, so she will live on to make misery for us all."

"Aunt Nan," Jane said, gently reproving, "you should not wish for vengeance on the poor lady."

"Poor lady!" Nanette said. "A murdress and an adultress."

"It is not proved," Jane said.

Mary Seymour threw Jane a malicious look. "And besides, she is a Catholic, is she not, cousin Jane?"

"So are we all, Mary," Jane said quietly. "It is only a matter of degree."

"I wish to God that is all it was," Nanette sighed.

"Why cannot everyone accept the religion we were given, that the lord King labored so long and lovingly over? Why must everyone argue and contend and try to destroy each other?"

"Man was born asking questions," Mary Seymour said. "All everyone wants is the truth." She and Jan were far nearer to the Protestant religion than the rest of the family.

Mary Percy leaned forward to stroke Kithra's rough head. "That is what everyone wants," she agreed. "But how will any of us recognize it?"

At that interesting moment they were interrupted by the children, released from their lessons for dinner, which was imminent. William was still at Court, so eleven-year-old Arthur was the young master at Morland Place, but he was a quiet, phlegmatic boy without the spirit or ambition to challenge Walter Butts for supremacy. Walter was fourteen, and Nanette felt it was high time he was sent away, for he was bumptious, sly and bullying and took shameful advantage of Arthur's docility. Margaret Butts, now ten, followed close after the boys, imitating what she fondly imagined was a boy's walk, her eyes going to Mary Percy to see if she approved. Mrs. Stokes came after, leading Celia Butts, a very pretty child, by the hand, and with Nicholas, a year younger, beside her, and last came a nursery maid carrying Gabriel, a very bonny, lusty baby.

"May I hold him?" Mary Percy asked Mary Seymour when the latter had inspected her offspring. "I miss my own Thomas so much."

Mary Seymour passed him over with a raised eyebrow which, to Nanette, implied quite clearly that she was glad to see Johns' wife had some normal instincts. Jane's face was impassive as she talked to Nicholas and Celia, not looking at the baby at all. She and Hezekiah had been married for almost six years with never a sign of a pregnancy.

John and Jan arrived back then, and soon everyone went in to dinner. It was an elaborate meal of three courses and many dishes, for Paul still took pride in keeping a good table, and whatever the reversals of fortune he would never forget that he was master of Morland Place. There was a shoulder of veal, a leg of mutton stuffed with garlic, a capon boiled with leeks, venison pastries with sugared mustard, stewed pike with Dutch sauce, spiced stuffed cabbage, roast blackbirds and pigeons, a very delicate salted beef, roast pears, syllabub, roast apples stuffed with curd cheese, orange and lemon pudding with bitter sauce and three different color jellies. The children dined separately in the winter parlor, but Walter was brought in to the hall during the first course to read aloud to them from a book of devotions—Paul was too old-fashioned to have the scriptures read, as was customary in the Butts house—and during the second course Nicholas Chapham and Celia Butts came in to sing a part-song which they managed very creditably, in spite of some initial nervousness.

After dinner Nanette challenged Jan to a game of chess, and when they had secured a quiet corner of the chimney place for themselves, she was able to have the private conversation with him that she had anticipated.

"Come now, tell me all," she said. "I know John will have confided in you."

"Mother, how can you suppose that I would break a confidence?" Jan teased.

Nanette reached across the board and rapped the back of his hand. "You know very well what I mean. I want all the news. Come now, tell!"

"Very well—where shall I start? You know all about the baby by now, I am sure."

"Not all. That they adore him, yes, but I could have guessed that for myself."

"John, I believe, suffered even more than Mary with

the birth. It seems that her life was despaired of. He and Mary are closer than twin brothers, and he could not contemplate life without her. What a strange marriage theirs must be!" he added in parenthesis.

Nanette looked at him shrewdly. "Do I hear envy in your voice, child?"

"By Our Lady, no!" Jan shuddered. "I should not like to bed with a scar-faced boy who might knife me as soon as speak to me if I did the wrong thing. He did not precisely say so, but I gathered that she is as thorny as a quickset hedge, and he has much ado to please her. And yet—there is something strangely appealing about the love that abides between two soldiers, fighting side by side. When that is combined with the love of man for woman—" He sighed. "I am well contented, Mother, with my own bonny Mary and my sons. She is the flower of womanhood—and I have you to thank for that. You brought her up to be perfect."

"I could not do less for the daughter of an old friend, could I?" Nanette said, glancing across to where Mary Seymour sat talking to Jane. "I often felt that she was my own daughter. I could not love her more if she were."

"A daughter who is no daughter and a son who is no son," Jan said, smiling sympathetically. "You have had to do with substitutes all your life, have you not, Madonna?"

Nanette looked at him sharply. "I know what your next question is to be and I will not answer it, so you may as well save your efforts for the game."

Jan shook his head sadly. "You are a hard-hearted tyrant, Mother. When will you tell me what I want to know?"

"It can do you no good to know."

"But man was born asking questions."

"Now I know where Mary gets that expression. She said it today."

"She is a dutiful wife and even copies my language."

"And while we speak of dutiful wives, tell me about Lettice and Lord Hamilton. Mary Percy almost let fall a hint of some trouble between Lord Hamilton and his masters."

Jan gave a circumspect glance at the company and then said in a lower voice, "It seems from the hints Lettice let fall in her letter that Rob Hamilton had something to do with the escape of the Queen of Scotland."

"But I thought he was one of Moray's men?"

"So he was, and helped Moray to power. But John thinks Hamilton was afraid that Moray would have the Queen put out of the way and would not give his consent to that, even tacitly. So he helped her escape. Some suspicion has fallen on him, and while he is not exactly in danger, he is out of favor and no longer in the inner circle of power. John also thinks that he was very disappointed that Lettice's baby was a girl, and Lettice is worried about that, too."

Jan paused a moment and then went on, his face very grave. "Mother, you must be aware that there is trouble brewing. You come from Court—you must have heard rumors there."

Nanette nodded. "Because of the Queen of Scots coming here? Yes, there have been rumors. Rumors of a marriage between her and my lord of Norfolk. Even— rumors of rebellion. We do not disregard them, though I wonder how serious the threat is. Can anyone seriously think a rebellion in favor of those two would succeed?"

"The threat is not from them, though they will be the excuse. Mother, don't you understand that whatever happens to the country—and I believe your mistress is strong enough to survive anything—our family is ready to split open like a fissured rock? You are an old Catholic, though not a Pope-Catholic, but you are outside the conflict, protected as you are at Court. But there's Paul, old Catholic, too, and stubborn in it, though loyal to the Queen; the Buttses, growing more Protestant year by year; Jane and Hezekiah much like Paul; Mary and I somewhere between the two; and then there's Lettice, married to a Protestant, and John and Mary Percy, both fanatical Pope-Catholics and ready to fight for it."

"But Jan—"

"It's true! You must not shut your eyes to it."

"But John is loyal to the Queen as well."

"He was. Now he is Mary Percy's other half and serf to my lord of Northumberland. When the men of the north march against the Queen, to put Catholic Mary on the throne, they will march, too. And then what will Paul do?"

"I don't understand."

Jan's face was frighteningly grim. "Paul has you at Court, and young William at Court, and he holds the old Mass here, so he is in a delicate position. But he also made a bargain with my lord of Northumberland to aid him if John married Mary Percy. I think Paul has forgotten that over the years, but Lord Percy will not forget. He will call for that aid, for the terms of the bond, and if Paul refuses, he will destroy him."

"Jesu save us," Nanette breathed.

"Aye, you see it now," Jan said. "Treason to the Queen, or treason to Percy? Either way could be death. I would not have Paul's choice to make for all the gold of the Indies."

CHAPTER ELEVEN

Through the summer tension increased. Nanette was back at Court and, with faithful Kat Ashley, was staying close by Elizabeth's side as rumors flew about the corridors like disturbed bats, for she needed to have about her those she could trust absolutely. One such was Henry Carey, now Lord Hunsdon, who was the son of Anne Boleyn's sister Mary and therefore the Queen's cousin. Nanette liked him immediately, finding him a gentle, unpretentious man who, despite his higher rank, treated Nanette with great respect because of her many family connections with the Boleyns.

By the time the Court went on progress at the end of July to avoid the unpleasantness of London in the heat and to hunt through the grease season, when the deer are fat, the rumors had merged into one: that the plot was that same idea suggested the year before at the trial of Queen Mary. She and Norfolk were to marry, and with a show of arms they were to persuade or force Elizabeth to acknowledge their children as heirs to the throne. It was an open secret that both Mary and Norfolk had consented to thus much of the plot.

"But of course it would be impossible for it to end there," Elizabeth said to Nanette in the privacy of her chamber on the evening the progress reached Guildford. She had dismissed the maids, and they were alone. The Queen sighed heavily and leaned her elbows on the dressing table, staring at her reflection in the looking glass that always traveled with her on progress. Nanette, knowing how tired and worried the Queen was, came forward quietly to remove the Queen's wig and unpin her hair and brush it out, which she knew always soothed her.

The Queen was approaching her thirty-sixth birthday, and her red-gold hair, like her sister's before her, was fading to sandy; Nanette noticed, with a pang of pity, that there were one or two silver threads on the crown now. She lifted and brushed the mass of hair tenderly, looking in the mirror, too. Anne Boleyn's daughter was a grown woman now, and the bony, uncompromising face in repose was thinner and older, less like her mother's, more like her father's; but then Elizabeth's eyes met Nanette's in the glass, and she smiled, the magical dark eyes transforming the pale tired face. "Nan, dear Nan, what's to do?"

"My lord of Norfolk must be stopped, of course. Perhaps Your Majesty should arrest him."

Elizabeth frowned. "No, I am loath to do that. He means no harm to me, I am sure. In his person he is loyal to me—and besides, much of the same blood flows in our veins. I do not want him harmed. If only he could be persuaded to come to me—if I were to hear it from him first, we could say that he always intended to ask permission, and then it would be no treason." She met Nanette's eyes again. "There are many who would like him dead. I do not wish to give them the opportunity."

"You do not think, then, that he is party to the rest of the plot?"

"Ah, no, not Norfolk. He is vain and silly, but not vicious. Perhaps I have been too distant with him. Perhaps I should have taken more pains to befriend him; then this would not have happened."

Nanette arranged the long hair over the Queen's shoulders. "It is impossible to know what would have happened, Your Grace. And Mary of Scotland? How far do you think she is implicated?"

"I would believe anything of that woman," Elizabeth said sharply. "Would she had stayed put in Scotland! Nanette, is it true that your niece's husband had something to do with her escape from Lochleven?"

The question, abruptly put, startled Nanette. "Your Grace—I do not know—it has been suggested, but I do not know if there be any truth in it. But how—?"

"How did I know? It is my business to know everything, my Nan." The large, dark eyes caught up Nanette's regard in the looking glass. Their expression was serious. "You have relations also in other parts of the country. It would be very difficult for a person whose loyalties were pulled two ways, between duty and family." Nanette did not know what to say. She was surprised the Queen knew so much and did not know what she was implying by these words.

"Your Grace, if I hear anything, any rumors—" she began.

Elizabeth smiled, though a little grimly. "You need not say anything. What I mean is, dear Nan, that I hear everything from another quarter, and you need not therefore betray either loyalty. I would not wish to lay that burden on you."

Profoundly grateful, Nanette knelt and kissed the Queen's hand. When she had resumed her self-appointed task of brushing Elizabeth's hair, the latter said, "But to the point. What is to be done about my lord of Norfolk?"

Nanette frowned in thought. "Perhaps, your Grace, if

you were to hint to him that you know everything already, it might frighten him enough either to admit his plan or to withdraw from the plot."

"Hm. I shall think about it. I cannot, just at present, think of any other way to proceed."

The Queen's hints, however broad, produced no reply from Norfolk, though he looked nervous and depressed whenever he was seen in public, and in the Queen's presence he seemed to find his ruffs rather too tight for his neck. The progress continued, and the hunting was good, but when the Court reached Titchfield a new development came to light. The indefatigable Cecil had a private audience with the Queen, and immediately afterward she sent for Robert Dudley, Earl of Leicester, her lifelong favorite. The messenger returned to say that my lord of Leicester was so ill that he had taken to his bed and was, to his great regret, unable to rise from it to obey the summons.

The Queen's face became grimmer than ever, and she sent again, requiring Leicester's presence at a private audience at once. This time the summons was obeyed. Nanette heard about it afterward when, alone with her and Kat, Elizabeth paced about her chamber in a fury.

"He was in on the plot from the beginning, the ungrateful traitor!" she cried. "So this is how he repays all my love, all the honors I have heaped upon him. It was he that persuaded Norfolk to it in the first place, else the fool would never have thought of it." She bit her lips with rage, clenching and unclenching her hands as if she longed to have them around Leicester's elegant neck.

Kat threw an alarmed glance at Nanette and then said, "But sure, my little lady, he did not do it to harm you? What reason did he give?"

"He has his excuses ready, you may be sure!" Elizabeth said with a snort. "He must have been thinking them out while he lay on his sickbed, too ill to rise! He *said* he did it only to release me to marry him. His part in the plot was only to tell me the proposition, but that he had been having doubts about the propriety of it all and therefore hesitated. What he means, of course, is that he was too afraid to tell me—and rightly so. God's death, these Dudleys! Generation after generation, they are not to be trusted. Cecil was right."

"But my lady," Kat wheedled, "you know that he loves you to distraction. It was as he said, he was driven to it by his dear love for you, love that made him foolish. He knows how you love him and would marry him if only—"

"Oh Kat!" Elizabeth cried in affectionate exasperation. "No more of that. You have been pouring that sweet poison into my ears too long now."

"But you do love him, my dear lady," Kat said anxiously.

Nanette said quietly, "You have known for long, Your Grace, how far you can trust my lord of Leicester. I cannot believe this comes as a surprise to you."

Elizabeth paused in her pacing and looked at Nanette. Then she relaxed and smiled.

"You are right. I know what he is—none better! And I love him as he is, for all his faults. Well, Norfolk must be persuaded one way or another to withdraw himself from this tangle. And if he will not be persuaded—"

She left the rest unsaid.

At the beginning of September the Court was back at Windsor for the deer hunting, and the Queen sent for Norfolk, realizing that there was little time left to call off the planned uprising. Rebellions always took place in the autumn after the harvesting was finished, so from October onward one might expect trouble. Norfolk announced his guilt on receiving the summons by fleeing home to Kenninghall and there feigning illness, just as Dudley had done. It served him no better than his mentor. The Queen sent again and told him that he could either come to her at Windsor or go straight to the Tower, as he pleased. He came to her, and after a long and emotional interview, he wrote a letter to Neville and Percy, the Earls of Westmorland and Northumberland, calling off the rebellion and repudiating his part in the plot. He swore to the Queen that he had never intended treason, wanting only that his heirs should be acknowledged after the Queen's death. Elizabeth punished him no further, allowing it to appear that she believed him.

"Truly," she said to Nanette, "I don't think he knows himself how much he intended. He is such a mixture of vanity and fright and ambition and vacillation that he is able to convince himself of one thing at one moment and another thing the next."

Nanette wrote in haste to Paul to tell him that the plot was ended, phrasing the letter so that it appeared merely as good news she was relating, for she did not know how far Paul was involved, if at all. She laid out a considerable sum of money to send the message posthaste, which should be warning enough if warning were needed, and after that, like everyone else, she could only await events.

The rebellion should have ended with Norfolk's defection, but his sister was married to Lord Neville and was ashamed of her brother's weakness and hesitation, and she persuaded her husband that the plan should go on, with or without the Duke. The purpose of the rising, she said, was to restore the Old Faith, and they did not depend on Norfolk for that. And so, on the thirtieth of September, the muster took place as originally planned.

*　*　*

A hundred and fifty men rode out from Tod's Knowe, mounted on their surefooted shaggy ponies, bred at home and raised from birth by their riders so that they could almost read their minds. The men were dressed in leather jerkins and steel helmets and armed with lances and light bows, and they rode behind the Percy standard. At their head rode Black Will and behind him came John Morland, wearing a surcoat over his breastplate on which were displayed the Morland arms, with his cadency mark, the label of the eldest son. Beside him rode Mary Percy, carrying their son Thomas in a sling in the crook of her shoulder, under her cloak. Her face was set with fury, for they were riding first to Alnwick to meet up with the rest of the Percy contingent, and there she and the boy were to be left in the safety of Alnwick Castle. Her husband and father had both agreed that she must not be risked in battle, and all she had to salve her pride were her father's words: "We must not all be killed, hinny. There must be one of us to rule, till the boy is grown."

At Alnwick a brief and embarrassing exchange took place between John and Lord Percy. The latter's eyes were attracted to John by the distinctive black-and-white Morland arms, and he beckoned John over and looked him up and down with a freezing stare.

"Your father," he said harshly, "has not sent word of his support. Does he mean to help us or no?"

"I do not know, my lord," John said steadily, forcing himself not to stoop, for he towered over the Earl. "I do not hear from my father."

"Yet you wear the Morland arms."

"These are my arms, my lord, and my pride is in them. I am not in my father's counsel. I can only answer for myself."

Percy stared a moment longer. "A good answer," he said abruptly. "Perhaps your father has been deceived by Norfolk's letter." And he strode away, leaving John to wonder whether the last remark had been in jest.

On the tenth of November the joint armies of Percy and Neville rode into Durham, where they were greeted warmly, and there the Earls celebrated a full Roman Catholic Mass in the cathedral. Then they rode on to Ripon, celebrated the Mass again and sent out a call to all Catholics to join them in restoring the True Faith. But already at Ripon they were too far south. The men of Yorkshire had grown too comfortable and domesticated for rebellion and had been their own masters too long to yield readily to the demands of a feudal overlord. Men did not flock to the standards; the army marched on to Tadcaster, but it numbered only six thousand.

At Tadcaster the news came that the Queen's army was not far away to the south, under the command of Lord Hunsdon, an able soldier. Reinforcements had been expected to arrive at Hartlepool from the Duke of Alva and the plan had been to march on London and celebrate the Roman Mass in St. Paul's Cathedral by Candlemass. But the reinforcements did not arrive from abroad, and there was not so much as even a message of support from the Catholic countries of Europe, so at the end of November the Earls decided to withdraw northward so as to make their stand on more familiar ground.

The weather, which had been cold and bright, turned foul, and the army marched back the way it had come through torrential, freezing rain, laboring day after day through greasy mud sometimes stirrup-deep. In the murky half light of the wet days under leaden skies, the Yorkshiremen who had joined them slipped away again like shadows to go home to comfort and sanity. By mid-December the Earls had reached Durham, and they were back where they had started, reduced to the numbers of their own personal supporters, and with Huns-

don and the army recruited from the men of the Mid-
lands coming on relentlessly. The rebellion was over,
and the Earls announced to the bedraggled captains
that they were to disperse.

Black Will brought the news to John where he waited
with the Tod's Knowe men. They were bivouacked outside the town in the open fields, and the men had hud-
dled on the lee side of the ponies for shelter. John was
even wetter than the rest, for he had slung his cloak
over Jupiter's back, fearing for his weary horse's health.
When Black Will told him the news, he looked up from
the contemplation of his mud-splashed boots with a
dawning of hope.

"Then we can go home?" he said.

Black Will scowled. "No, by Our Lady. We march
on."

"March on? But where? How? The Earls—"

"They must save their skins—they'll be across the
border by the week's end," Black Will said, faintly contemptuous. "Their hearts weren't in it from the beginning—it was their womenfolk that set them on. Well,
let them run with their tails between their legs. We'll go
on."

"But where?" John asked again.

"Dacre's men are still coming on, marching up from
the south. We'll go across country and join them. We
cannot go home without drawing our swords."

John stared at him in despair, and the older man
spread his feet and stuck out his rough-bearded chin
like a small round rock determined to weather any
storm.

"But it's hopeless," John said. "To go on is hopeless.
You must see that. Much better that we go home and
make the best of things."

Black Will smiled a grim sort of smile and put out a
hand to pat John's shoulder.

"Why aye, and maybe it is hopeless, but Black Will's

not one to sheathe his sword until the fight's done. Laddie, you go home. Go home to Mary and the boy and take care of them. They'll need you. You'll have men enough left up there to keep Tod's Knowe. But I'm going on. You're young, and change is easy for you. I am an old man, and if the old world is dying, I'd sooner die with it."

"The old world dying?"

"Aye, that's what they've been saying. They say that's why no one joined our standards, because our world is finished and gone—the old ways, the old loyalties, the old honor. We're like ghosts, marching out of the past to fight for a world that's already passed away." His grim old face did not waver, though there was a terrible sadness in it. "Well, lad, I won't be a ghost in my own world. I know only one way, one faith that our forefathers gave us, and I'll die by it as I've lived by it, for I don't know how else to do."

John put his hand over the gnarled hand on his shoulder. "In God's name, I'll go with you," he said. Black Will stared a moment and then laughed, his own old, fierce laugh, booming out with all the force of his barrel chest.

"In God's name, th'art a true son of Black Will's, even if th'art a damned Southerner! No, lad, no, this fight's not for you, though God bless thee for saying it. You must go back and keep the land and protect your son. If trouble comes you can slip across the border until it dies down, but I doubt any will be foolish enough to send after you into Redesdale. Take care of Mary— she's proud and fiery, but she's full of honor. By Our Lady, it was a good day's work she did when she set the dogs on you!"

The next day Black Will marched the Tod's Knowe men away, leaving only ten of the younger men to escort John back north. He gave John a father's blessing before he left, and at the very last he regarded John curiously and said, "You marched with me, though you had no stomach for it, though you thought it foolish, and even wrong; still you kept faith. Maybe the new world won't be so different from the old, if there are men like you in it. Give Mary my love, and the bairn. Tell her I'll be home in the spring."

He turned his pony and trotted out to the head of his band, and John and his followers turned and rode the other way, toward the north.

Lord Leonard Dacre's private army reached Carlisle in January, and there at last battle was joined. The rebels fell upon Hunsdon's army and after ferocious fighting were defeated in what was almost a massacre. One or two of the rebels managed to flee, and some were taken prisoner, no doubt to be hanged later for an example. None of the Tod's Knowe men came back.

The crisis had blown over, and with no immediate harm to Morland Place or its inhabitants, but the whole business had shaken Paul badly, and it was then that he began to be old and to rely more and more, without realizing it, on Jan Chapham. Walter Butts had gone back home to the house on the Lendal to learn the family business from his father Joseph, for he was the only heir and all the business would be his, though all the little Butts girls would be wealthy. This left, besides the girls, only Arthur and Jan's two sons in the nursery, and Arthur was not the child to win a peevish and nervous father's affection. Paul began to pay more attention to Nicholas and Gabriel, particularly to the former, who was a gentle and intelligent boy and, with his blue eyes and black hair, bore a remarkable resemblance to Paul's beloved, much-missed wife Elizabeth.

In March the last was heard of the rebellion, when 750 rebels, almost all Yorkshiremen, were hanged. The roads were lined with gibbets, from which the dead bodies hung to be picked at by crows. For weeks Paul

kept to his bed, not needing to feign sickness, for there
were plenty who must have known that he had been
solicited by Percy for help, and who could tell if his
eventual nonparticipation had been enough to save
him? Sickness also saved him from having to face a decision that was now presented to all Catholics. A Papal
Bull had been issued that excommunicated Queen Elizabeth, proclaimed her a bastard and a heretic and ab-
solved all her subjects from obedience to her. It was a
nonsensical document, for among other things it condemned the Queen for taking the title of Supreme
Head of the Church, a title she had specifically refused;
but still it was a Papal Bull.

It was now a mortal sin to attend any service other
than the Roman Mass; equally, it was by the laws of
England a treasonable offense to attempt to reconcile
anyone to Rome or to be reconciled to Rome oneself.
Catholics must now decide which way to move, and the
comfortable compromises that had been open were now
to be taken away. Paul hid from the decision through
his illness, and while he was confined to his bed, Jan
took command at Morland Place and instructed Father
Philippe not to say the Mass in the chapel until the master was well enough to order it himself. Philippe saw
the sense in this and obeyed, but those old Catholics in
the household and on the estate saw the beginning of
the end in the move.

So the year went on with its timeless routine: in
April the cattle going up to the summer pastures, in May
the early haying and the hedging and ditching, in
June the shearing, washing and winding; the routines of
the days and weeks interspersed with the festival
days—the pageants on St. George's day, maying and
morrising on May Day, the bonfires and feastings on
Midsummer Eve. By May Paul was back on his feet
again, and by June he was as nearly normal as he
would ever be, pottering about the herb garden, poring

over Tusser's *Hundred Points of Good Husbandry* and
contemplating which of his fruit trees to graft, riding
out to the pastures and the mill, consulting with his
steward and bailey and holding his manor court. But
the difference was that he was an old man now, bent-
shouldered, graying, at times fidgety and querulous;
and in the chapel the sanctuary lamp burned steadily,
but there was no Mass said.

Then, in the heat of July, plague broke out in York.
There had been many plagues in the city, some brought
in from outside but often arising in the city itself, for its
water supply was notoriously foul, and though the
Council of the North under Sir Thomas Gargrave had
put aside money to improve it, nothing had yet been
done. For the first week news came out of the city, until
the worsening situation caused the council to station
sergeants on all the gates to prevent ingress or egress so
that the plague should not spread, and the city was cut
off from those outside.

The plague began in the center, in the most crowded
and squalid places, and spread outward to where the
houses stood on extensive grounds behind high walls.
The Butts House on the Lendal was neither one thing
nor the other. It was a very old house, a rabbit warren
of buildings and outhouses jumbled together in the
space between the Lendal and the river. Between the
main building and the landing stage were gardens and
courtyards interspersed with henhouses and pigsties and
store sheds and barns; inside the house were long dark
passages, short flights of stairs, a multitude of different
levels and different ceiling heights, and even in summer
the smell of the river permeated all the rooms. The water was drawn from a well in the main courtyard. At the
best of times the water had a peculiar taste which, in
her perversity, Catherine Butts had often declared was
preferable to the bland, tasteless water at Morland
Place; at the worst of times the sewage from the river

seeped into the well and the water had to be boiled to be drinkable.

The children caught it first. Grace and Jane, who were thirteen and ten, began vomiting as soon as they woke one morning, and it was assumed they had been eating secretly after they had gone to bed the night before. They denied it but were given a purge anyway by their nurse. Within the hour they had a violent flux and a high fever and were still vomiting. Their nurse purged them again. Jane began voiding blood and was dead by suppertime; Grace died during the night. The following morning Charity and the two elder children, Walter and Rosalind, were all feverish, and the family realized the plague had reached them. It was on that day that the city gates were closed, and so no word could be sent to Morland Place where Rosalind's two sisters, Margaret and Celia, were still living.

Matters deteriorated swiftly. The servants were no more immune than the family and succumbed to the fever, flux, vomiting and terrible sores that broke out on the skin. Soon the house was filled with the smell of sickness and smoke and the sounds of the feverish ravings of the stricken. It was like a scene from hell. Catherine, who had always complained of her health, hung on grimly, organizing those servants who were still fit, trying to tend to the needs of the dying and to oversee the laying out of the dead, but it was a hopeless task. Samson and his wife Anne Weaver caught it, leaving no one but Joseph to help her, and Joseph would not leave the bedside of his son, the only Butts heir. When Walter died on the third day, Joseph lost hope. He brought up a half-dozen bottles of wine from the cellar and drank them all, one after the other, through the evening. He fell unconscious in his chair by the unlit fire, and such was the confusion reigning in the house by that time that he was not discovered until two days later, lying dead on the floor.

Those servants who were still healthy began to slip away from the house, hoping to flee the sickness and if possible escape the city. A number of people were escaping down the river at night, while others got away through the marshes in the north of the city by boat. By the time Catherine died at the end of the second week, only a handful of servants were left.

The Court was on its summer progress, and the news reached Nanette at Northampton. She went straight to the Queen and in some distress asked leave to go home immediately.

"The whole family? Oh Nan, I am so very sorry. Of course, you have leave for as long as you need it."

"Thank you, Your Grace. If I ride hard and start at once, I can be there in time for the funeral. I would like to be there—my only sister—"

"Of course. But, Nan, is it wise to try to ride the whole way? Forgive me, but at your age—"

"Your Grace, by God's will one day you will be sixty and more. I wonder what you will say to anyone who dares suggest you are not fit to ride a horse?"

The Queen laughed and patted Nanette's hand. "Who would dare, indeed? Well, go on then. God go with you—and come back as soon as you can. I cannot do well without you."

So Nanette rode, accompanied by Matthew, Audrey, Simon and another servant, and by the time she reached Morland Place she was well aware both of the age of her bones and of the difference between riding in a park, or even riding to the hunt, and slogging along the roads hour after hour for as long as daylight lasted. She did not wish to admit even to herself how exhausted she felt, and it was perhaps as well for her pride that she arrived to walk into the middle of a family quarrel. The adults were gathered in the solar, and as Nanette came in, Jan turned an impassioned face to her and cried, "Mother, thank heaven you are here. Now you will be able to make my cousin see sense!"

Nanette looked at Paul and was shocked at the change in him. She had first known him as a young man, and without realizing it she had always thought of him thus. Now she saw an old man with white hair and a lined, bitter face who turned to her with an expression of helpless rage.

"Paul, what is it?" He only shook his head—it was Jan who answered.

"He wants to have them buried by the Catholic rite!"

"Well, indeed, I should hope so," Nanette said.

Mary Seymour broke in almost before she had finished. "But they were not Catholics! Everyone knows the Buttses were all Protestants—far more reformist even than we are."

"Nevertheless, Paul is right. To save their souls—"

"I am head of the family," Paul said. "The decision is mine."

"Not the head of the Butts family," Mary said. "Margaret is the oldest surviving Butts."

"Margaret is a child and in no position to make any kind of decision."

"If it comes to that," Nanette said firmly, "my mother was a Butts, so I must be the oldest member of the family, and I agree with Paul. Whatever their errors during their lives, we can at least see to it that the proper Mass is said for them and offer prayers for their souls."

"Mother—!" Jan cried in exasperation.

"Do you want them to linger in Purgatory?" Nanette cried angrily.

"There is no Purgatory!" Mary shouted. "It was abolished!"

"How can any law of man abolish Purgatory?" Paul shouted back.

Jan spoke over them, his eyes burning blue at his mother as hers burned at him. "You cannot do it Mother—to go against everything they believed, when they are unable to answer you. You had Alexander given the last rites, against my father's wishes. You gave him a Catholic burial, against his wishes. You must not let Paul do this. Apart from the matter of conscience, don't you see that you are risking imprisonment, even death?"

"It is a matter of conscience," Nanette said firmly and quietly. "When I was a child there was one faith, and we were all held by it. Now there are a hundred false prophets. I hold by what I know, as does Paul, and if to do what is right and good is not enough to keep us alive—well then, by Our Blessed Lady, I do not care to live!"

"But how do you know it is right?" Mary Seymour cried. Nanette was startled by her vehemence, and she looked from Mary to Jan and back again.

"Now I see," she said slowly. "It is not you, Jan, who taught Mary, but she you. Why have you left the faith of your fathers?"

"My father had doubts before he died," Jan said. "He was beginning to see the truth—the new truth. The old ways are dead, Mother—you must see that. There is a whole new world opening up, and we are part of it. We cannot let the past fetter us."

Nanette stared at him, at his vivid, handsome, Morland face, and knew that she had lost him.

"Also," she said slowly, "you are hereditary warden of Rufford Forest, and any taint of recusancy would lose you your position. Yes, I see it now. Well, that must be your decision—just as the matter of the burial is Paul's and mine."

"There will be a proper Catholic burial," Paul said,

and as he spoke his shoulders straightened a little, and the old pride and vigor of the head of the Morland family shone from him for that moment. "And the chapel at Morland Place will continue to celebrate the Mass of King Henry, as it has done all my life. We can only do as we know."

Jan glanced at Mary and then said, "Then I will have to take my sons away. I am sorry, but I cannot have them endangered."

That struck Paul hard, and the light went out again. "Take away Nicholas?" he said.

"Oh, Jan!" Nanette protested, and as she met her son's eyes, she saw they were filled with tears.

"Mother, I never wanted this, but what can I do? Just as you say, we can only do what we know. But I love you still, just as I always have done. It doesn't change anything."

"It changes everything," Nanette said sadly. "You know that. But you are my son, and I will pray for you, and for your sons."

When they had gone, Paul sat down on a stool by the fire and looked up at Nanette like an exhausted, cornered fox.

"The family is being split in half," he said. "He will take away my little boys; and John is gone, and Lettice; and Young Paul is dead. Morland Place will be deserted. Aunt Nan, what will become of us?"

Nanette sat down slowly and stiffly on the opposite stool.

"I don't know," she said wearily.

CHAPTER TWELVE

In January of 1570 Lord Moray had been murdered, and Lennox had taken his place as Regent of Scotland and guardian of the infant King with Morton at his right hand. Lettice heard the news with fear and horror: during her time at Court, the two people she had found the most repulsive of that frightening crew had been Morton and his henchman Ruthven. They had seemed to her not quite like human beings—more like ravening beasts, utterly heartless and ruthless, without fear of pain or pity for suffering.

Rob Hamilton had been widely known as one of Moray's men, and Lettice supposed that the change would be the worse for him. The news reached her late, for she was at that time at Aberlady with the children, and the murder took place at Linlithgow, on the other side of Edinburgh; but still it arrived a little before Rob, who came galloping in from the City just after the gates had been closed for the night. There was much to do to get the gates opened for him, for the servants were naturally nervous, and Lettice herself when she heard the hoofbeats outside thought they probably announced her end. Over the years she had spent in Scotland, she had become accustomed to the idea of death being only a step away: the women and children of these savage foreigners were the natural target for revenge or punishment.

So when she heard the sounds without, she gathered her stepchildren—thirteen-year-old Jean and eight-year-old Lesley—and the baby into the solar, along with Kat and Mackie, the chamberlain, whom she had come to trust. They had their orders and would carry them out on a command from Lettice: death was not so much to be feared, being a thing they must all face sooner or later, but it was well known what the assassins did to young women and girls before they killed them. Kat and Lettice were armed with long knives, Mackie with a short sword. If the intruders were assassins, the three children would be quickly dispatched before they could be taken and made sport of by a gang of hired murderers.

When the door opened to reveal Rob, mud-stained and bedraggled from his hard ride, Lettice dropped her knife and ran to him with a cry of relief. She put her arms out to embrace him, but he caught her and set her aside with hard hands that bruised her upper arms.

"Peace, wife, there's no time for that," he said harshly.

"Oh, I am so glad to see you," Lettice cried, but quickly controlled herself, biting back the stream of relieved babble that sprang to her lips. Her family would hardly have recognized the vain, silly, lazy Lettice they had known in this alert-eyed young woman, so calmly ready to execute her children if it were necessary.

Rob's eye took in those preparations without surprise, and his only comment was, "You have heard the news, then."

"Only an hour since."

"You must prepare to leave. You will be safer in

Stirling. You will ride tonight—there is a moon from midnight, and if we move quickly we may stay a step ahead of danger."

"We are ready," Lettice said calmly. "We need only change our clothes. There is danger then?"

Rob gave a grimace. "When is there not, lass? But there's a circumstance that may tilt the balance our way. The killing was no matter of policy."

"No?" Lettice said in surprise. "But I thought—I assumed—was it not Morton, then?"

"No, though at present everyone thinks so. But in fact it was a murder for private reasons, and the murderer was a cousin of mine, Hamilton of Bothwellhaugh. It seems Moray raided his house at Roslin, turned out his wife and stole the estate, and Hamilton killed him in straight revenge. This I know through some of his servants who fled to me for aid. I sent them over the border and then came here. When it's out that it was Hamilton did it, it may give me a foothold on the new council."

"Lennox is to be Regent?"

"Aye, but he will not last long. Morton will rule him and then kill him. Morton's the one to keep in with. But for now you will all be safer at Birnie."

"And you, my lord?" Lettice asked anxiously. Her heart was beating fast at his sheer presence, for she had not seen him in six weeks, and every absence made him dearer and more exciting to her, especially as every time he went away, she never knew if she would see him again. One day word would come of his death, and then what would she do? Flee, she supposed, like everyone else, over the border. If she could get as far as Redesdale alive, John and Mary would help her.

"I will trust to my right hand to keep me alive," he said, patting his sword hilt. "If it cannot, then I am not fit to live."

"Oh, husband, take care," she breathed. He looked down into her face, meeting her eyes for the first time, and she saw his nostrils flare as his familiar white grin broke through his dark beard. He read her face, as always.

"We have a little time before you must leave—time to eat at least. You will not eat again until you come to Birnie. Mackie, go and prepare food. Madam," to Kat, "take away those children and get them dressed, and then take them to the Hall and feed them. We will join you there. Get you gone, all."

Mackie hurried out, followed by Kat carrying the baby and chivvying the children. When the door had shut behind them, Rob turned to Lettice with that same white, wicked grin that made her skin burn and her throat tighten between desire and fear.

"And now, lest we do not meet again," Rob said, coming toward her, "let us say our farewells as we said our first salutations."

Lettice tilted her head back, her eyes closing, and his mouth came down on hers while his strong fingers pulled at her lacings. When they were both naked, he laid his dark hands on her white body here and there, firmly but with a look of wonder on his face that moved her so that she seemed to turn all to water inside. Rob's breath was whistling harshly through his nose, as if he labored to draw breath.

"By God, lady, but you are white and tender," he whispered. "Lie down and let me look at you."

Obediently she backed to the bed and lay down, and while he looked at her, she looked, too, unable to drag her eyes away from his square, broad, hard body, so dark-skinned, black-haired, so alien to her white curving softness, so pulsing with a fierce and terrible life. She felt the blood pounding all over her body, and half of her wanted to hide her eyes in shame and terror, while the other half bid her again, as always before, to surrender to this overwhelming, crushing, invading power. He read her face and, trembling, he crouched over her, hard as a rock, and yet as much a victim of his passion as she. He could not control his desire for her; he was led on by the agony of wanting of his body, so that as he drove into her he flinched, just as she did, as though those parts of them were unbearably painful.

Thought retreated before the wildness of passion that grew wilder each time, because for each of them it was a yielding of self that was intolerable. Rob held her down by the shoulders, his teeth gritted as though it were a battle he fought, as he thrust into her harder and harder. And, "Give me a son," he cried through it, though he did not know his own words. "Give me a son, lady!" And Lettice, driven before him, flushed out of the coverts where she hid herself, goaded, hunted by their unbearable love, cried out in surrender and hate and defiance, "*You—give me*—a son!"

They reached Birnie in safety and settled down again to the enclosed life of semi-exile. By Easter the situation had resolved itself. Lennox was established, with Morton at his shoulder, and Rob Hamilton was back in favor and in the inner circle. And Lettice was pregnant. With the utmost secrecy she continued when alone to say her rosary and to pray in the old form, calling upon the Blessed Virgin to watch over her pregnancy and give her the son that she and her husband so desired. She prayed, also, that Rob might bring her back to Aberlady where she could be near him, or that he would come to see her, for since that January night he had not come near her, and she saw what would be the pattern of her life: the long, lonely times, month after month after month, waiting for him to come, between the few brief moments when he was there, giving her a reason for her life.

She gave birth in October, in Birnie Castle, to a son, and a messenger was sent with all speed to summon Rob. His delight in the boy was almost painful to Lettice, outweighing her own joy. The baby was christened Robert after his father and grandfather. Matters of state called Rob away almost immediately, and he never saw his son again, for the child's brief candle flickered out barely three weeks later, on Hallowmas Eve; and Lettice did not see Rob again for almost a year. By then Lennox had, as he had predicted, been murdered, Morton was regent, and Rob had changed sides.

It would not be true to say that William had forgotten Morland Place, but his home was so remote to him now that he hardly ever thought of it. He supposed, vaguely, that one day he would have to go back to take over his inheritance, but he preferred not to think about it. He was happy at Court and dreaded having to leave what seemed to him the hub of life for the remote and wild lands of Yorkshire.

He had done well at Court. His fine singing voice had brought him preferment while he was still a child, and he had been often in the Queen's presence. He had been taught to accompany himself on the lute and the cittern, could compose and write lyrics for his own songs and had also learned the trumpet and hautbois, so he was an accomplished musician, which in a musical Court was a clear way to advancement.

In 1571 he was seventeen. He had been lucky in that when his voice broke it hardly changed but remained very light and pure. He could not quite reach the achingly high treble notes that had been his fame as a child, but he had lost scarcely half an octave from the top and was the finest countertenor in Whitehall. His beard also remained very light, so that he needed to shave no more than twice or three times a week. At first he had been distressed by his inability to grow a beard, and the other pages had mocked him, but as he grew older he came to accept what was and to make a virtue of necessity. He shaved and made a fashion of clean-shavenness that was all his own, and he in turn mocked the other young men for spoiling their smooth skin with ugly, coarse hair.

His childhood beauty, which had earned him the name of angel-child, was in no way diminished. He was small in stature and very slender; his skin was very fair, and his cheeks were always delicately flushed; his hair was as smooth and pale and bright as primrose silk and hung down behind in long lovelocks, curling at his brow and over his ears. His eyes were a pale, bright blue, set on the slant, which gave his face a piquant, strange, appealing look, as though he were a faun or some other fairy creature from a mythological garden. The Queen liked to have good-looking men around her, and though her taste had always tended to the big, hearty, outdoors kind of man, yet she appreciated the purity of William's looks, the sweetness of his temper and his great musical skill so she had him a great deal about her.

The women of the Court made a great fuss of William, and adoring him almost became a cult. He would have been horribly spoiled had it not been for his natural modesty and sweet temper, and also the fact that he did not like the ladies. There was something about them that horrified and repulsed him: he hated their stiff, unnatural, heavily decorated clothes; he hated their painted faces that made them all look the same, dead white faces with black-rimmed eyes and red mouths like birds of prey; and when he got close, as he often did, drawn against a woman, unwillingly, by her grasping hands, he would see under the paint the little wrinkles and lines and imperfections, smell under the heavy scent the unwashed, sour smell of their bodies.

From this loathing he excepted two women. One was the Queen: he was afraid of her, as was everyone, but he loved and respected her for her great intelligence, her straightforwardness, her power, her magnetism. She, too, was stuffed and painted and primped and frizzled, but William sensed that with her it was a mask, a disguise, donned for some better purpose than mere vanity, and she looked out from underneath the disguise a clear-cut, admirable person. Also, she was clean. On the few occasions he came close to her, she smelled of nothing under her scent. For the same reasons he also loved his great-aunt Nan, who was the Queen's constant companion and who kept a stern eye on William, advised and instructed and disciplined him. Great-Aunt Nan did not wear paint, and her clothes were simple, scarcely stiffened or stuffed at all. Her hair was concealed under a simple linen cap, and she smelled deliciously of soap and roses. She did not spoil or pet William. She spoke to him straightforwardly, gave him good advice, and when she praised a song of his, he knew that it really was good, for she never flattered.

But best of all he liked the company of the young men of the court. He loved to pull a bow, to play at bowls, to dance the exacting, high-leaping English dances, to play tennis, to hunt and hawk, to box and wrestle. He loved to loll at his ease in a window seat in the long gallery and pick out delicate tunes on his lute while the other young men lounged around him and gossiped. His beauty and his popularity had at first made the other young men suspicious of him, but when they saw that he did not care for the women and was not a rival for their affections they took him to themselves as a slightly eccentric but acceptable companion.

When he was sixteen William was promoted to the post of Gentleman Usher and thereafter had a great deal to do with the Master of Revels, the official at Court whose business it was to arrange all the entertainments. William was an excellent dancer and was given good parts in all the ballets and masques, as well as being called upon to play and sing, and sometimes—a great honor—to compose music especially for an occasion. Best of all, William loved the times when bands of traveling actors were hired to perform plays before the Queen and the Court. While the masklike dissembling of the Court women horrified him, the dissembling of the actors fascinated him. He loved the comradeship between the actors, the esoteric jokes, the private language, the shared memories. He longed to be part of a group, he who seemed to have been designed to fit in with no society. He loved the plays, the songs and the characters, the ranting of the villain, the nobility of the hero, the exquisiteness of the heroine, the wild tragedy, the uproarious comedy, the anarchy of the clown.

In May of 1571 a troupe of actors was hired by the Master of Revels to perform three plays during the Whitsun celebrations. William had not met this particular troupe before. They were called the Southbank Trinity Players. Most troupes bore the name of their patron, always a well-to-do man, who was their guarantee of respectability, and there was a rumor that Parliament was to pass an act banning all groups of actors who did not have such a patron, for they were thought to be rogues and vagabonds. But the troupe that had originally been hired for the occasion had been stricken by an outbreak of smallpox, and the Master of Revels had had to hire another troupe on short notice.

William was deputed by the Master to welcome the players and escort them to their quarters, a task that he was very willing to do. The players seemed disposed to be friendly toward him, and to him they glittered with the glory of their trade, so that their kindness to him seemed like the condescension of gods.

"What's your name, lad?" asked one of them. He was a tall and handsome man with a strangely old-young face, as if he were either very young and had suffered great hardship or old and had led a very easy, untaxing life. William could not decide which. He was, it seemed, the leader of the troupe.

"William Morland, sir," he said. The tall man grinned, showing even, white teeth. He had yellow hair, too, but the yellow was brassy and ended a little before the scalp.

"Don't call me sir," he said, flinging a casual arm around William's shoulders. William glowed. "I'm John Fallow, the great tragedian, and you, my boy, shall call me Jack."

"Thank you, sir," William said, delighted.

Behind him another of the troupe, a squat, middle-aged man with a loose, ugly mouth and a large, open-pored nose that was clogged with old makeup, chanted shrilly, "Tack-about Jack, comes in from the back. Beware of the squall—keep your back to the wall."

"Take no heed," Jack Fallow said, throwing a warning glance behind him. "That is Augustine Hoby, who specializes in old women, minks, priests and soothsayers. He speaks so often in rhyme that he forgets himself sometimes. How old are you, boy?"

"Seventeen, sir," William replied.

Jack Fallow raised an eyebrow. "So much!" His voice, rich and deep, held more modulations than William would have thought possible, and now expressed enormous surprise. He scanned William's face closely, and William, inexplicably, began to blush. Jack removed his arm from his shoulder and asked in a stage whisper, "Tell me, Will, do you shave?" William's blush deepened, and Jack threw a glance of significance to his companions. "I only ask because you have such fine skin. Do not be ashamed."

"Oh, he has some natural modesty, then," said a third actor, a tall, thin young man with a face like a skull and overlarge, popping eyes. He was looking most unpleasantly at William and Jack. "Beware the honest slut and the smiling crocodile, Jack—that's what you have always told me."

"Hold your tongue!" Jack snapped, his face darkening and clearing instantly as he said to William, "That is Richard Johnson, who is apprenticed to us and plays the women's parts, and does one or two other things."

"One or two others things being more important than his women's parts," Hoby broke in with a horrible laugh. "If he had women's parts enough, Dick would take his pricks with more philosophy."

"Peace, babbler," Jack said, but Hoby capered on the spot and chanted again.

"Though Dick was a vessel with a voice so shrill, now Jack makes for harbor with a Will."

They had reached their quarters now, and William slowed to a halt, looking from one to another of these godlike creatures. There was a great deal going on that he did not understand, but apart from Dick Johnson he sensed no ill will from them. In fact, they seemed to be looking at him with interest.

"These are your quarters, gentlemen," he said, throwing open the door.

"And very fine, too," Jack said, walking in and looking around him. "If we do well here, we may find ourselves growing used to luxury of this sort."

William thought he was speaking ironically, for the room was not very grand or comfortable, and he said hesitantly, "We have much ado to house everybody here, sir—"

"Bless you, child," said another man, "we are not complaining." He was older than the rest, with a sensitive face and the voice of a gentleman. His eyes were kind, without hidden messages. "I am Christopher Mulcaster," he introduced himself. "I try to keep my companions in order, but without success."

"Kit is our clown," Jack explained.

"Well, this is better than a flea-ridden pallet in the Seven Stars," Dick Johnson said, flinging himself down, all angles, on one of the beds.

"Don't get too comfortable—you won't be sleeping there," Kit said.

"You won't be sleeping much anywhere," Hoby said, *sotto voce*.

"Enough, Austin. Go away, over there. I want to talk to Will," Jack said, and putting his arm around William's shoulders again, he led him to a corner. "Tell me, what do you do here? What is your position at Court?"

"I am a gentleman usher, but I also assist the Master of Revels and I am a Court musician."

"A musician, eh? And can you dance?"

"Yes, sir, and sing, and play the lute and trumpet and hautbois."

"Can you indeed?" Jack's voice expressed great interest. He seemed impressed. "And what is your family?"

William told him but broke off short when he heard the bell sounding for evening prayers. "I must go, sir. I was supposed to bring you here and go straight back."

"Well, I will not keep you. But we must have many a long conversation while we are here. Shall we have the pleasure of hearing you perform?"

"Oh, yes, sir—Jack—I have my part in the celebrations. I have composed four songs which I am to sing tomorrow before Her Majesty."

"I'll look forward to that. Well, off you go, then. We'll meet at supper, I dare say."

William hurried away, feeling more excited and happy than he ever had before. The actors had been so kind, so friendly, so welcoming. What would he not give to be one of them!

That evening, after supper, the troupe gave their first performance before the Queen, and William saw them in all their glory of costume and paint, rolling speech and large gesture. Afterward a message came inviting William to join them in their rooms, and as soon as he was off duty he hurried along there. He found them lolling about, some already changed and cleaned up, others half clad, talking idly, drinking, joking and laughing, and all the magical atmosphere of their professional identity wafted over William like a heady perfume. When Jack flung his arms out and greeted William like the one person he had been waiting for all day, William's happiness was complete.

He learned a great deal about them that evening. There were six shareholders in the troupe—Jack Fallow, Austin Hoby, Kit Mulcaster, Ben Withers, Will Bennett, and Reynold Simmons—and six hired men. Besides these there were a number of apprentices, like Dick Johnson, who played parts, mended costumes, ran messages, painted canvases and were paid only a very small wage because they were learning the trade from the great actors, the shareholders.

Jack and Austin were very rich, Kit Mulcaster very poor, because he had several rapacious mistresses and expensive tastes. The others seemed neither one thing nor the other, though they all had tales of hair's-breadth escapes from bailiffs, of dodging creditors, of wild flights over rooftops to avoid paying irate landladies. They seemed very well acquainted with the taverns of the town and used a great many words and expressions that William did not understand at all but which added to the charm of his being there, nominally one of them.

Jack was flatteringly interested in everything William could tell him about himself, his home, upbringing, career, talents and desires, and William, flushed with pleasure and more wine than he was accustomed to, talked freely, and later at Jack's request sang them one of his own songs. When he had done there was a silence of genuine respect. Jack and Kit exchanged looks, Austin grinned to himself and took another large gulp from his own private bottle, and Dick scowled and got up so abruptly to turn away to the window that he kicked over a stool. Everyone then praised William's singing, and he took more pleasure in their praise than in anyone else's ever before. In fact, the only discordant note in the whole evening was the inexplicable hostility of Dick Johnson.

On the last night, after the performance William was invited to sup with the actors, and when he reached their quarters Jack Fallow was waiting for him outside the door and asked him to take a walk with him along the gallery.

"I have something very particular I want to say to you, my boy," Jack said. William accepted the invitation with pleasure. They walked along the silent gallery for a while, and then Jack said, "You did excellently well tonight. Your singing voice is very fine, as you must often have been told. But you also play the trumpet like an angel. I swear I saw tears in Her Majesty's eyes."

William looked down in embarrassment.

"Will, tell me, have you ever thought of becoming an actor?"

The question was unexpected, and William looked up, startled; but at once the notion flooded into his mind.

"Oh, yes, Jack, often and often," he said; and he believed it was true as he said it. "But my father would never permit it. I have to go home one day and take over the estate."

"Pah! You would be wasted as a farmer. You have rare talents, my boy, and you should not waste them. You should be on the stage, presenting them to the world, not hiding them under a bushel. Why do you think God gave you such looks, such a voice, prevented your beard or your body from growing? God's death, my child, don't you see you were born to be an actor? You could play all the great heroines of the stage, and then when you have served your apprenticeship, you could become one of the great tragic actors of all time. Better than me!"

"Better than you!" William cried disbelievingly, for to him Jack was already the fountainhead of talent.

"Come with us when we leave tomorrow morning. Come secretly, for they will not permit you if they know about it. I personally shall teach you everything I know about acting—and let me tell you there are few men alive who know as much about the craft as I do. Within the month you shall be playing Queen Berenice in *Herod's Vengeance*, I swear it!"

William's eyes shone like candles. "Oh, sir, oh, Jack, could I really come with you? Oh please, yes, I want to so much."

"You'll leave everything and come away in secret with us tomorrow morning?" Jack said, putting an arm around William's shoulders.

"Oh, yes!" he cried, carried away with enthusiasm.

"Hush, not so loud! Well then, my boy, you are one of us now, a Trinity Player, and my special friend. Come, seal our bargain with a kiss."

Excited as he was, William did not find this a strange suggestion. Jack turned him about to face him, put his two hands on William's shoulders and stooped from his height to kiss him lingeringly on the lips. Close to, Jack smelled clean and deliciously of verbena oil, and his lips were smooth and firm and not unpleasantly moist. When Jack straightened up he remained looking down at William for a long time, and William, as well as the admiration, respect and love he felt for Jack, had the curious feeling that he was on the brink of understanding something that had puzzled him for a long time, though he could not think what it was.

"Well, let us go back and tell the others," Jack said
at last, and they walked back along the gallery, Jack's
arm casually over William's shoulders again. When they
reached the lighted, noisy room where the actors were
gathered, Jack announced the news, and they all
cheered and then gathered around William to pat his
back and welcome him and give him drinks. He stood,
glowing with pleasure, confused, excited and dumb.
Here at last was a place where he could feel he belonged.

CHAPTER THIRTEEN

The disappearance of William was a terrible blow to Paul. It was not known how he had got out of the palace, or why, but once out, many and various were the fates that imagination could supply for him: he might have fallen ill, met with an accident, been kidnapped, been set about and robbed, even been raped and murdered. For months Paul waited in hope of a message reaching him from his son, calling for help or rescue; but when by Christmas 1571 no message came, no word or even hint as to his whereabouts, Paul gave up hope.

He called Arthur to him in the steward's room.

"Your brother has now been missing for more than half a year," Paul said. Arthur nodded and tried to look intelligently interested. He had been called from his lessons with Father Philippe, which that morning were Latin and rhetoric, and to Arthur very boring. He was fourteen, of small stature yet and good-looking enough in his way, with his auburn hair and dark blue eyes, but there was a vapid expression on his face. He was not in fact stupid, merely uninterested in matters of the mind.

He loved stories, adventures, and since reading was hard work, he loved best to slip off and seek out old servant who could tell him of the adventures of their youth He often rode over to Shawes to hear Cousin Hezekiah tell about battles at sea and strange customs in foreign lands, and his mind, more often than not, was on those things when the absent look came across his face.

Now, however, he tried to look alert and aware as his father spoke to him, for the longer he could extend this interview, the less time there would be for Latin and rhetoric before dinner.

"Yes, Father," he said.

"I have not spoken of this before to you, because we have always hoped that word would come from him," Paul went on.

"Yes, Father," said Arther, varying his tone a little.

"But in all this time there has been no word of him, or from him, and if he were alive he would surely have managed to get some message to us. We are not without influence, not without friends."

"No, Father."

"I am forced, therefore, to the conclusion that your brother—" Paul swallowed. "That your brother William is dead."

"Yes, Father," Arthur said, very solemnly.

"This will make a great difference to you, of course. You are now heir to the entire Morland Estate. You will one day be master here, as I am now."

"Yes, Father."

Paul stared at this youngest child of his thoughtfully. He knew little of Arthur, had never cared to know anything. John, because he was his firstborn, he had taken a great interest in; Young Paul he had loved, perhaps not wisely; but Arthur had always been the baby and beyond his reach. He had never made a friend of any of his children: he had been brought up himself in the

ld school, strictly, where it was no part of a father to be a
riend to his children. But the world was changing, and
the young no longer had the unquestioning obedience to
their parents that he and his generation had had, as witness John's undutifulness, and Jan's; and after all, William would not now be lying dead unburied or in some
unmarked grave had he not left the palace without permission, a flagrant flouting of the rules. So perhaps it
might be wise to attempt to make contact with Arthur,
the last Morland, the last hope. Paul cleared his throat
for the unnatural effort.

"My child," he said, "are you happy?"

Arthur's mouth opened and shut again. He did not
understand the question or the reason for asking it. He
searched the words for some hint of the right answer,
and finding none, he looked for the first time at his
father's face. There was some kind of struggle going on
within the old man, and something naked looked out of
his eyes, which embarrassed Arthur deeply. Adults, like
his father and Father Philippe and Great-Aunt Nan, always behaved according to a predetermined pattern.
They said the same things, espoused the same attitudes,
were unmovable monuments of disapproval. That was
their function; Arthur found it disconcerting that his father should suddenly have stepped out of character. He
looked away from the embarrassing face and said sul-
lenly, "Yes, Father."

"Arthur, I have never had much time to speak to you
about yourself. That was perhaps as much my fault as
the result of too many cares, but I hope now that we
can come to know each other better. Now that there are
only the two of us." No response. Arthur stared at the
floor. "There are a great many things I shall need to
tell you, and many things with which I can help you if
you are to take my place in years to come."

Still no response. Arthur began to think with an unexpected longing of Father Philippe and Latin grammar.

"My son, is there anything you wish to ask me?" Paul tried again.

Arthur thought for a moment and then said hopefully, "Father, may I go back to my lessons?" An expression of cunning flickered across his broad face, and he added persuasively, "I had better work very hard at my lessons if I am to be master, had I not, sir?"

Paul stared a moment and then sighed. "Yes, child, go along. We will talk again at some other time."

Arthur left, and Paul turned away to the window and stared out at the snow-covered walks. He was too old a dog to learn new tricks, and between Arthur and him there was too great a gulf. Had it been John, now—but it was folly to think of that, though he could not prevent himself from thinking, hungrily, of John's child. It was hard, surely, to have fathered ten children and to be left alone without grandchildren to fill his nurseries.

In a small cottage on the edge of the village, Mary Smith lay dying. Spring was not far away—it was April 1572, and the snow was thinning on the ground, so that the grass began to show through, and every day was filled with the sound of the new lamb's high-pitched calling and its mother's deep answers—but Mary would not see the spring. The cold had settled on her chest before Christmastide, and she breathed laboriously now; the mere effort of breathing was wearing her out.

Her man, Dick, was dead some years since, and her eldest boy, Robin, a great heavy-shouldered man of thirty-two, was the smith in his place, a good, steady, quiet man, hardworking and kindly. He was married and had three living children of his own. Her second son, John, who was thirty, had set up in another village and was married and had four bairns. Betty, now twenty-seven, had married a carpenter and had three children and another on the way, and Sal, the baby, who would have been twenty-five next month, was dead two years since of the childbed disease. Her widower had married again, needing a mother for the six children she had given him.

The little, smoke-weathered cottage was full of people, more full than it had ever been in Mary's life, as her children and grandchildren gathered for her death. That was as it should be—that was the way to go to Our Blessed Lady's arms, surrounded by your own family, in your own house, whose every inch you knew better than your own face. Mary's eyes were closed, but she could visualize without difficulty the turf oven; the hearthstone fire; the rows of pewter plates and tankards, carefully scoured and polished with bran; the neat little three-legged stool that Bet's husband had made for Dick, on which in later years Mary had sat while she stirred the porridge; the beautiful oak and ivory crucifix that Mistress Nan had given her when—

Mary's eyes flew open. There was one of her children missing. Robin bent over her solicitously.

"What is it, Mam?"

"Where is your other brother?" At least, that's what Mary tried to say, but through her hoarse and labored breathing only one word came out.

"John's here, Mam," Robin said, puzzled, drawing a little back to let John come forward. Mary closed her eyes and clenched her fists in the frustration.

"Jan," she managed at last. "Bring Jan." And then she collapsed, gasping, from the effort.

The three Smith children looked at each other, and at last Robin said slowly, "John, best that you go. Walk on over to Watermill House and ask Master Chapham will he come. Quick as you can."

But John, who had been to school with Jan and was quicker-minded than his brother, had a better idea.

There was a horse in the smithy next door waiting to
be shod by the apprentice, and Watermill was only ten
minutes away on a good horse. Surely this was an emer-
gency, and the owner could not object. John threw a
garbled message at the 'prentice, mounted the horse
bareback and galloped off.

Jan had seen less of his foster family in recent
years—since his marriage, in fact, for Mary did not encourage him to mix with the Smiths—but he came instantly upon the summons, and when he arrived at the
little cottage he went straight to the bed and knelt there
in tears to take up and kiss the hand of the woman who
had suckled him. Feeling the wetness on her skin, Mary
opened her eyes, and a smile transformed her old, lined
face.

"Jan—Janny—"

"I'm here, Mam. I came at once when John told me.
Oh, Mam—"

"My little Janny—my boy," Mary whispered. She
gasped for breath, and Jan's hand tightened on hers in
sympathetic effort. "Not long now. So glad to see you."

"Mam, I didn't know—I'd have come sooner." Mary
shook her head slightly, and then closed her eyes again,
exhausted. Jan watched for a while in silence. Behind
him his foster kin waited, acknowledging his better right
to be beside her, though they were blood kin and he
none. But he was a gentleman and always their mother's favorite. He was Master Chapham of Watermill
House, and whatever he wanted was his to take, even
their mother's last words. Jan stared in anguish at the
woman whose milk had sustained him as an infant, who
for the first eight years of his life had fed and clothed
and washed and comforted him. Her arms had been the
first refuge he had known, her lap the first citadel of
comfort he had conquered; but she was also the last
person, aside from Nanette, who knew the secret of his
birth.

"Mam," he whispered urgently. "Mam." At last she opened her eyes, and they were filled with unrecognizing pain; for her nothing existed now but the effort to breathe. "Mam—you must tell me—about my mother and father. Who was my real mother? Mam, you must know. Tell me. Who was my mother?"

Mary's oxlike eyes stared at him, and he pressed her hand, willing her to understand and to answer. Mary's mind drifted back to that winter of Jan's birth, a time more distant it seemed than the winter of the Nativity. Scenes appeared before her like scenes from the Mystery Plays—the dark night, Nanette in a cloak, the snow, the mewling newborn babe, the tug at her breast, oh so moving, even now in distant memory. And the events that led to Jan's birth, so shocking, so pitiful. Poor lady! And he, poor gentleman—

"He must have wondered," she whispered. He must have wondered, have tried to work it out, have suspected. How could he not suspect?

"Who, Mam? Who must have wondered?" Jan said urgently. Mary looked at him, her eyes clearing a little. Jan, her darling Janny, was married to that hard little baggage who had taken him away from the True Church, through ambition. She was likely to make trouble if she ever found out. Why did you leave the Church, Janny? Her eyes strained to communicate with Jan, and he leaned forward, his mind not in tune with hers.

"Who, Mam? Who was my mother?"

"Jan," Mary whispered, raising herself a little off the bed with the extremity of her effort to speak. "Forget."

"What?" Jan was startled.

"Forget. It—can—do—no—good."

Mary collapsed back onto the bed, her eyes closed again, and Jan could have wept with frustration, for he had been sure she was about to tell him. After a mo-

ment he stood up and met the disapproving gaze of his
foster kin. He bowed his head, ashamed, and stepped
back to yield his place to them.

"I'm sorry," he said inadequately.

"For what, Master?" Robin said stolidly, and his patience rebuked Jan. He remained, but in the background, until Father Philippe arrived from Morland
Place to give the last rites, and soon afterward he ran
outside to where his horse was tethered with patient
Fand watching over it, mounted and galloped home.

He found his Mary in the winter parlor, sewing. She
sat in her usual seat, facing the portrait of herself that
she had done back in '69 in an attempt to imitate the
pictures of Nanette and Old Paul that hung on either
side of the fireplace in the winter parlor at Morland
Place. Jan had spoiled her plan by refusing to sit, but
Mary was very pleased with the likeness of herself. It
showed her wearing her best gown, crimson brocade
with a great deal of stiff gold embroidery, over an under-
gown of white satin embroidered all over with red roses
and green leaves. She wore a high gold-edged ruff, and
her red hair was frizzed and pinned up under a rust-
color velvet bonnet decorated with mother-of-pearl
daisies and a rust and a white feather. She had on all
her best jewelry and was wearing a very smug expression. Altogether a very successful portrait. Now if
she could only persuade Jan to have his likeness done,
wearing his best black velvet and the bonnet with the
sapphire brooch—

"She is dead," Jan announced starkly as he came in.

Mary put down her sewing and folded her hands in
her lap. "Do you know what I was thinking about, husband?" she said. "You'll never guess—it was those
black pearls! It seems such a wicked waste that all the
Morland jewels are never worn since Elizabeth died—
just lying around wherever it is that Paul keeps them.

Especially the black pearls. Why, they are priceless. Suppose they were stolen, or lost? They ought to be worn regularly, you know—"

"Mary," Jan said patiently, "did you hear me?"

"No, my dear—what did you say?"

"My foster mother is dead."

"Oh, my dear, I am sorry," Mary said placidly. "Did she say anything?"

"Say anything?"

"Well, you know—"

"I asked her." Jan frowned, remembering. "I thought she was going to tell me. She said " 'He must have wondered.' "

"Who must have wondered?"

"She would not say. When I asked her, she grew agitated and said I must forget."

Mary's face was thoughtful. "Now, husband, we must use our wits."

"What do you mean?" Jan walked across to the fire and leaned against the chimney, worn out with emotion. Fand padded after him and flopped down, yawned mightily and stretched her belly to the flames.

" '*He must have wondered.*' Well, so should we all have. We have not been using our wits. Have you never noticed how like you are to your mother, to Nanette?"

"But of course," Jan said impatiently. "But she is not my real mother—she has sworn it, and there would be no reason for her not to tell me if that were true."

"Very well. Now, further, have you not noticed how Nicholas has such a look of Jane about him? And do you not remember how like Jane was to her mother? And have you never thought how alike Nanette and Elizabeth were?"

"Mary, what are you talking about?" he asked wearily.

"Why, simply this, my dear—that all those I have named have the Morland looks. It speaks as plain as words that you are a Morland."

Jan turned and stared at her. "What—"

"Husband, you can be a great simpleton at times. Have you never heard tell of the mysterious mishap that befell Elizabeth before her marriage to Paul? Have you not? Then perhaps there was reason to keep it from you. She had a bairn, and the bairn was spirited away as soon as it was born, and no one ever heard of it again."

"Mary—"

"Wait now. Who do you think took the bairn away? None other, my dear husband, than our mother, Nanette."

Jan's face was white and strained. "Elizabeth?"

"Why not? You have, as we have all remarked, a great look of her. Your age is the same."

"But—no, I can't believe it. Elizabeth my mother? And my father?"

"I don't know," Mary said. "I never heard tell that part. It is all a very close secret, and I heard only from servants. But when Mary Smith said 'He must have wondered' did she not mean Paul? Must he not have wondered if you are not really his eldest son? Is that not why he was so fond of my children? Why he was so upset when you took them away from Morland Place? Oh, husband, it all fits."

"No, Mary, wait, you are going too fast." It was too difficult to contemplate. Elizabeth his mother? He remembered how uneasy she had always been in his presence. Paul his father? But—"If Paul was the father of the bairn, why was it taken away? Why did he not simply marry Elizabeth then, instead of later?"

Mary shrugged. "I don't know. Perhaps it was not his—but Elizabeth's all the same."

"That would make—" John his brother, John whom

he had always loved, all through childhood. And the others—Lettice and Jane and all the Morlands, all his kin. He had a great hunger for kin of his own, the foundling's desire for family. He thought greedily of embracing them all, calling them brother and sister, and for a moment a hardness rose up in his heart against Nanette that she had denied him that. Then his mind cleared, and he crossed to where Mary sat and looked down at her and said, "This is all surmise, and wild surmise at that. From now on we must never speak of it. This conversation must be forgotten between us."

Mary stared up at him as though he were mad. "Forgotten? Have you lost your wits, husband? No, you must go to your mother with what you know and make her tell you everything. If she thinks you know all but a few details she will tell you the rest."

"I should never have spoken of it even to you," Jan said. "My foster mother charged me to forget, and so we must."

"Must? Why so? Of course we must not forget."

"Mary," Jan said, shocked, "they were a dying woman's last words. You cannot disregard the wishes of the dying."

"Popish cant!" Mary snapped her fingers. "There is a great deal at stake here. Do you not realize? Do you not want to be rich?"

"I am as rich as I need be. We have Watermill House—"

"No we have not, then. It is your mother's house, and we live here by her favor. Watermill was part of the Morland Estate once—it can be again."

"What are you saying?" Jan stared at her, horrified.

"Paul has no one left but Arthur," Mary said, speaking quickly, "and he cares little for Arthur. Besides, one life is a slender thread, and who knows what may happen to him? But he loves Nicholas and Gabriel, he would

as lief have them as his heirs, and if you *are* Elizabeth's
firstborn—"

"Mary, be silent!"

"Think, Jan, think—to leave all that to Nicholas, all
of Morland Place, the estates, Watermill, the city property—and Jane and Hezekiah have no child yet,
perhaps may never have—Shawes could be his, too!"

"Mary, be silent!" Jan cried. "You cannot have
thought what you are saying. Are you mad?"

Mary sprang to her feet and faced him, her eyes wide
and her face alight with anger and desire. "No, not
mad, but tired, tired and sick of being poor! Oh, it's all
very well for you—you have what you have always had,
but I, Jan, I was a Queen's daughter. I should have
been the richest heiress in the Kingdom, and I was
robbed of everything I ever had. Robbed! I was left so
penniless that I could only be brought up at all by the
charity of your mother, who once lived by the charity
of mine. So now I want back a little of what was mine.
Is that so wrong? I am sick of being poor. I want to
have what should have been mine—the houses, the jewels, the horses. And I want to leave a good fortune to my
children, so that they should never be beggars as I was.
Is *that* so wrong? If you were a loving father to them,
you would want it, too."

She stopped, out of breath, and Jan stared at her in a
mixture of amazement and pity. After a long time he
said slowly, "I never knew—that you felt that way."

"Well, you know it now," she said calmly, sitting
down again and taking up her work. "And the only person now who knows is your mother, and she is old and
will not live many years longer. You *must* ask her, while
there is yet time." She looked up at him shrewdly.
"Have you thought what it would be like to go to your
grave not knowing?"

Jan turned away and walked to the door, and Fand
came alert at once, jumped up and padded over to him.

"Very well, I will ask her. And now I must go and walk a little in the garden. I want to be alone."

"I will send when dinner is ready," Mary said imperturbably, examining her stitches.

Jan looked at her bent, fashionably crimped head for a moment and then said softly and with pity, "I'm sorry, Mary."

She did not look up and he went out, closing the door softly behind him. Only later did she wonder what he was apologizing for.

The inn yard of the Three Feathers in the village of Fulham had been converted for the time being into a playhouse, and the bills that had been posted advertising the very popular play *King Herod's Revenge* had drawn a full house. Fulham was a popular country resort for the London gentry, and with May being so hot, many of them had come away early for the summer, so there was a good gallery audience, as well as the groundlings, who stood in the yard itself for a penny and were the most difficult audience to please.

The bill outside the inn announced that the play would be performed by Lord Hovenden's Players, and mentioned underneath some of the principal attractions of the production. A tall, square-set, middle-aged man with the air and dress of an upper servant spent a great deal of time studying that bill until he was startled by the sound of the trumpet being blown to announce that the play was to begin. He stared toward the source of the sound, though it was hidden within the inn yard, and then hurried forward to pay his penny and take his place.

Later, after the play was finished and the audience had dispersed, the same man went into the taproom of the Three Feathers to buy himself a tankard of ale. The taproom was low ceilinged and ill lit, murky with the smoke from the fire in the grate and from the fatty lamps that hung here and there. It was close, odorous and noisy, and there was loud altercation, boisterous jokes and some surprisingly harmonious singing. The inn maids bustled here and there with trays of tankards which they balanced aloft on one hand, never spilling a drop. They were neatly clad in white aprons and mob-caps, for it was a decent respectable place, and though there was much noise there was little impropriety.

The man sat himself at a wooden table out of the lamplight where he could see and not be seen, and when the maid came, he ordered a pint of ale and a plate of sausages and pease pudding, for it was past suppertime. When the food and drink came he occupied himself with assimilating it and watching a particular group of actors sitting under a lamp opposite him. If there were to be any impropriety, it would come from this group, for the two men—at tall, good-looking man and a short, ugly, lascivious one—were entertaining and being entertained by a very good-looking, golden-haired woman. She was wearing a dress which, though tawdry with long wearing and little washing, had once been of good quality, and she languished and teased and chaffed the two men like a whore, though her features were fine and her voice, particularly her singing voice, was sweet and well modulated.

At length the man's impassive staring attracted the attention of the group, and after some muttering and sniggering the two men propelled the woman toward him with an ungentle shove. She put a hand on her hip and walked over with an exaggerated air of seduction and, leaning forward over the table, said, "You're a stranger here, aren't you? You look lonely—why don't you buy me a drink, and we'll talk together awhile."

Behind her the other two men guffawed. The man looked up at the painted face. Under the crude make up it was a young, sweet face with strangely slanting pale blue eyes and long golden hair falling out of its pins.

Only a person who had seen the play would know it was not a woman at all but a man, the actor billed as Will Shawe, who had played Queen Berenice in *Herod's Revenge* an hour since.

"What shall we talk about?" the man asked, unembarrassed.

"What would you like to talk about?" the golden-haired one said suggestively. One of the men at the other table made an impolite suggestion.

Matthew stood up and looked down sternly at Will Shawe. "Shall we talk about home, Master William? Or what about your poor father's broken heart? For shame, young Master, for shame to give so much grief to so many who love you."

A slender hand flew to a white throat, and the slanting blue eyes stretched wide as Matthew in standing was lit by the lamp above and was recognizable. The two men at the table behind saw that something was amiss and leaped to their feet, knocking over a bench in their haste, and a sudden silence fell over the taproom as all eyes looked around, fearing or hoping for a brawl.

"Why, Matthew," William said, licking his lips nervously, "how you startled me, my dear."

"What, Will, do you know this man?" Jack Fallow growled, coming up beside William with his hand on his sword. "Is he troubling you?" Matthew's stern eye took in Jack and went back to William as if the former were not worth bothering with.

William felt the tension in his companion and put a hand out to touch him lightly, not wishing for violence. "That I do, Jack. He is the manservant of my Great-Aunt Nan, whom I have told you about."

"The one who is friend to the Queen! Aye, you told us. Much good did it do us, though, for all the patronage we have got by it. What does he here?"

"I've been looking for you for almost a year now,

Master William," Matthew said. "My mistress has laid
out money aplenty to find you, for she had an idea
what might·have become of you."

"Does my father—?"

"Your father thinks you are dead and mourns you,"
Matthew said sternly. William closed his eyes for a moment. "He will be so glad when he finds you are not
that he will likely forgive you your faults."

The eyes flew open. "Oh, no, Matthew, you mustn't
tell him. You mustn't tell anyone."

"What, do you not mean to come back? What of
your duty to your father, Master, what of your duty to
your family? You are heir to Morland Place; you cannot mean to let that go?"

Jack Fallow's arm came down across William's
shoulder, and he glanced up, reading the message in the
face of his protector. He slipped a long white arm
around Jack's waist and nestled up to him with a lithe
grace. He half closed his eyes and pouted provocatively,
and Matthew watched impassively.

"Now, Matthew, good man, can you really see me as
master of Morland Place? Look at me." Suddenly all
pretending fell from the boy's face, and he looked out
from under the paint, fragile and alone. "See, Matthew,
I don't belong there. I don't belong anywhere but here.
No, my dear, I won't go back. Surely you must see that
it is impossible?"

"Aye, I see that it is," Matthew said slowly. "But it is
a mortal shame. Yet I suppose some folks are made one
way and some another. What shall I tell my mistress?"

"Tell her—tell her that I send my love and my
thanks. Good Matthew, you and she—" He swallowed,
and his eyes were unnaturally bright. "Tell her I'm
happy, and that she must forget me. I shall never go
back. You see, don't you, that I am happy?"

Matthew looked from William to Jack Fallow, and
then to Austin Hoby, and then to the smoky, dim tav-

ern. He said, "Let me speak with you apart a moment,
Master William. Just a moment."

William glanced up at Jack, whose eyes were fixed
suspiciously on Matthew, and then gently released himself and stepped a pace or two aside.

"What is it, Matthew? You won't change my mind."

"Master, just this—you may think now that all will
be like this forever. But things may change. If you need
help, or money, or a good word spoke for you, or if
you want to come home, don't hesitate. Send word to
me, and I'll send you money or come and fetch you,
whatever you want. Promise me, Master; promise me
you'll send word to me if ever you need help?"

William stared for a moment and then flung his arms
around Matthew in a hard embrace, and suddenly the
tavern seemed far away and home, Morland Place,
childhood, normality seemed very close and very dear.
Matthew returned the embrace with difficulty, feeling
strange because it was a child and a woman and a man
he embraced, all three. "I promise," William said.
"And now you had better go. Thank you, Matthew, for
everything."

"Good-bye then, Master William." Matthew hesitated, wondering what else there was to say, and then
turned to go.

"God bless you, Matthew," William said softly.

"Matthew turned back. "Do you say your prayers,
Master?"

William looked helplessly at him. "Oh, Matthew—"
he said, spreading his hands.

Matthew shook his head sternly. "Never mind. Say
your prayers to Our Blessed Lady and the holy saints
and put your trust in God. He knows more than we
ever can. You say your prayers, Master."

"I will, but go now. Yes, I will, I promise."

Matthew went, and William watched him out of the
door and then turned back to his companions.

Jack fingered his sword hilt uneasily. "I wonder—will he tell your father? Should we perhaps make sure of his silence?"

William looked shocked. "No, by Our Lady," he said. "Matthew will tell no one but Aunt Nan, and she will keep her counsel. I wish there were some way not to hurt them, but—" But no repining. Matthew was gone, and the tavern had become real again. He was Will Shawe, of Lord Hovenden's Men, the greatest player of women's parts in the world, and Jack Fallow's lover. He would be a great actor, as already he was a great singer. He smiled up at Jack, drawing his arm around him. It was the only place now where he belonged. "Come, my dear, let us drink some of that excellent sack, and then I'll sing to you. And I'll not charge you a penny!"

Jack Fallow laughed and scooped Will up like a girl and carried him back to their table and sat down with him on his knee, while Austin morosely called to the nearest inn maid to bring sack and some cold meats. Those who had not love to comfort them must needs turn to food and drink.

"You were right, Madam," Matthew said to Nanette. "He went with the Southbank Trinity Players, and I think—I am sure—it was of his own free will."

"Yes, I guessed it. I should have known when I saw how he hung about their necks when they were here—"

"You could not have known he would do such a thing. Do not reproach yourself, Madam."

"And he will not come back?"

Matthew shook his head.

"Is he prosperous? Is he happy?"

"They call themselves Lord Hovenden's Men now, after the law against vagabonds, and they seem well thought of. He seemed—well fed and well clothed. He said he was happy."

"And he said he would not come back."

Matthew bowed in assent. Nanette sighed.

"I did not think he would, or he would have sent word before this time. But I hoped——" She mused for a moment and then became brisk. "Well, Matthew, no one but you and I must know about this. He is mourned as dead—let him be so from now on. It would be cruelty if Paul were ever to find out."

"My own thoughts exactly, Madam."

"Good, Matthew. You may go now—and thanks."

Matthew left her, and Nanette continued to muse. From old habit she remained standing—those about the Queen had little practice in sitting down—and her carriage was as upright as ever, but every day it was growing a little more of an effort. Life had been full and rich, but it had brought so many disappointments, so much responsibilty. Now there was the added burden of the secret concerning William to weigh her down. She was like a beast of burden onto whom ever one more and one more bundle was tied. Well, there was solace for that—was there not One who said, "Come unto me all ye who are heavy laden"? She moved slowly into her inner chamber, where, by the favor of the Queen, she kept a *prie-dieu,* and there, a little stiffly, she knelt and made the sign of the cross and began to repeat the comfortingly familiar phrases. But only half her mind was on what she was saying. The other half kept wandering over her crowded life and wondering what more would happen to her before God saw fit to call her home to her long rest.

CHAPTER FOURTEEN

In the winter of 1572 Nanette fell ill again, and in February 1573, just after her sixty-fifth birthday, she retired from Court and went home to Watermill for good. It was hard to part from the Queen and all her friends, some of whom she had known all her life, for whatever happened on the surface of Court life, the minor officials in the background went on doing their duty year after year whoever reigned. It was a tearful parting from the Queen. Elizabeth was thirty-nine, and Nanette had known her from the moment of her birth, and now that she was leaving Court it was unlikely that they would ever see each other again. But Nanette looked thin and frail, and Court life was wearing.

"You must take care of yourself," the Queen said. "You are nothing but bones—you must eat plenty now that spring is coming on and fatten yourself up."

"I shall be better at home. I miss the fresh air and the open skies," Nanette said cheerfully, but she felt that she was going home to die. However, though the journey tired her, her own words proved true, and when she arrived at Watermill House with her small household she felt measurably better and was able to eat a substantial part of the meal that Jan and Mary had had prepared for her. She was alert enough also to notice a strange atmosphere between the young people and to wonder whether it had to do with her coming.

After supper the children were brought in to see her. She was delighted with Nicholas, who was just seven and a tall, well grown boy, advanced in his lessons and with the same bold, bright glance that Jan had had as a child. He had a look of Jan about him, though he had inherited Mary's brown eyes. To Nanette the combination was disturbingly reminiscent of Adrian, the bastard son of her first husband Paul. Gabriel, who was four, was still chubby, and with a snub nose and tawny hair promised to take after his mother. While Nanette was playing with him and talking to Nicholas, she noticed out of the corner of her eye a number of significant glances passing to and fro between Jan and Mary, and when the children had been taken away, she determined to know what was happening. She waved the servants off and said, "Now, Jan, let us be frank with each other."

"Are we not always, Mother?"

"No, my Jan, not always," Nanette said sadly. "Since I have arrived I have noticed that there is something troubling you that is not being said."

"I cannot tell you, Mother, not now," Jan said. Mary opened her mouth to speak, but Jan intercepted her look and she closed it again.

Nanette looked from one to the other. "We had better talk about it. It seems that it is serious," she said.

"Not now, Mother. In the morning. You are tired."

"Oh, for heaven's sake, Jan, let it be said and be done with it," Mary said impatiently. "None of us will sleep for thinking."

Jan sighed. "Very well, then."

Nanette took a place on the window seat, the place where Mary usually sat. Opposite her was the fireplace and above it the portrait of Mary, looking pleased with herself. Though Nanette had no idea what was to be said, she knew that it was of Mary's instigation. It astonished her that Jan, who was so strong in other ways, could be so weak where he loved.

Jan sent the servants into the hall, closed the parlor door and, with difficulty, avoiding Nanette's eyes, told what he knew and what Mary thought he knew. Nanette listened quietly, her eyes on Jan's face, except for once when she glanced at Mary, who was sitting on a stool across the room and fidgeting with her neck chains.

"So you see, Mother," Jan finished uneasily, aware that his narrative had not sounded as good when spoken as it had inside his head, "you must tell me now the truth about my birth."

"*Must* I, Jan? With what do you threaten me?"

"Oh, no, Mother——" Jan began, but Mary broke in impetuously. "Is it not better that you should tell than that he should go to Paul with his suspicions?"

There was a silence after her words, and Nanette's eyes were like blue ice as Mary faced her. "Oh, Mary, that was not well done," Nanette said at last. "Did I bring you up no better than that? Did James and Simon and I teach you nothing but to be bold and heartless and greedy?" Mary dropped her eyes at last, her face red, but not from shame. Nanette looked sadly at Jan.

"Well, Jan, I have heard you, and now I am tired and wish to go to bed."

"But——"

"Not now, Janny, I must think. I will tell you my decision in the morning. In the meantime——" she paused and then shrugged. "I will pray for you. And you pray for yourselves."

Through the night in the intervals between sleep——

for now that she was old she slept fitfully; sleep ran as thin as her blood, though when she was young she had devoured sleep in great black drafts—she turned matters over in her mind, seeing that it had gone far enough, that she would have to tell Jan or Mary would force him to go to Paul, and it would be cruelty for Paul to be disturbed after all this time by those sad ghosts. From a lifetime's habit she could not pray lying in bed. Painfully, trying not to disturb Audrey, she climbed from the bed and pulled a wrapper around her, for it was cold outside the curtains, and knelt on the bare boards to pray. She prayed to God, and to the Blessedly Lady, and to St. Anne, her own saint, the mother of the Blessed Lady, and then, finding her requests hard to formulate, she remained kneeling and repeated the Paternoster again and again, falling after the first few words into the Latin of her childhood. At length, numb with cold and stiffness and repetition, she climbed into bed and slept.

The next morning was bright and cold, and after her morning celebration with Simon she called Jan to fetch her cloak and walk with her in the walled garden.

"I want to be alone with you," she said, "and there is more privacy out of doors. No, not you, Mary," she added as Mary went to put on her own cloak. "This concerns Jan alone."

Mary's eyes locked with hers rebelliously, but Nanette was old in authority, and sulkily the young woman sat down again. Warmly wrapped and moving briskly, Nanette found it pleasant in the garden. For a time she walked in silence, enjoying the clean air and the new-washed look of everything under a clear pale sky. It was the same pale bright blue as William's eyes. Nanette wondered if she had done right in concealing his whereabouts from Paul: perhaps he should be forced to come home now that there was only Arthur? A bluetit flew down onto the wall and stared at them, flipping his tail, and Jan's head went up to follow the movement. Nanette glanced at him sideways, loving all over again his firm, bright face, his lips always ready with a smile, the dark blue eyes looking up at the bird with such a light of laughter in them. She wanted him never to be troubled; she wanted to preserve in him the joy of life he had always had from the time she first brought him to Watermill as James's heir. Why did that brightness always have to fade? Ah, no, not always—Jane had it still. Grace was in her, and radiated from her, for she had never left the sunlit garden of faith. Nanette had not, either, but the difference between them was that she knew that it was only a garden, and had seen the darkness and chaos beyond the walls; Jane had never even seen the walls—to her the garden was the whole world.

"Jan," she began at last, "why do you think I have kept the secret all these years?"

"To protect the woman—my mother."

"Yes, to protect her—but to protect you, too. Do you not think that I would have told you if it had not been better that you did not know?"

Jan's eyes met hers. "And yet can it ever be better not to know? The desire for knowledge is in us all."

"Well, it is too late now. I see that I must tell you. But I charge you to keep the secret. Oh—" she added, seeing his expression, "do not worry. I will not make you swear, for I would not have you add to your sins. I trust that you will see it is better for you to be silent. You—or rather Mary—were right. Elizabeth was your mother."

There was a long silence. She saw that though this had been Jan's guess, he had not absorbed it until this moment. It was a shock to him. He was looking back, she could see from his expression, and fitting the new information in with everything he had felt and experienced as a child.

"She has been dead many years now," he said.

"So you see that I felt you needed to be protected."

"Did she know about me?"

"No. She may have guessed, I suppose, but it's my belief she shut her mind to the whole matter. It was past and dead, and the mind can be surprisingly merciful. No one knew whence her babe was taken. No one knew whence you had come. There was no reason for anyone to connect the two. Except—"

"Except what?" Jan asked eagerly. Nanette frowned.

"Except that you look a little like her. Your foster mother may have been right. Paul knew about Elizabeth's babe—perhaps he has wondered sometimes. But I think it has more often been supposed that you were a misadventure of mine that was cunningly concealed during my long absences at Court." She smiled now, and Jan saw the irony of that particular surmise.

"Well, then, Elizabeth—God receive her—was my mother. But who was my father?"

"That was the shame from which I wanted to protect you," Nanette said, and then in a quiet, steady voice she told him the whole story: how Adrian, the illegitimate son of Paul Morland the first, bitter because he could never inherit the Morland estate, led a band of vagabonds in a violent attack on Morland Place, in the course of which he raped Elizabeth, leaving her pregnant.

Jan was silent for a long time while they walked up and down the turf-edged paths in the sun-warmed garden, and then he said at last, "So Mary was right—I am a Morland."

"A Morland, though not in name."

"But Morland blood on both sides, and kin to you."

"Kin to all of us."

Jan screwed up his eyes with the effort to assimilate the complex family connections, and then he smiled at his mother, a memory of his old, wicked smile. "My grandfather was your uncle—I suppose that makes me a sort of cousin of yours?"

Nanette smiled and then grew serious. "So you see, Bear-cub, that you have no claim on Morland Place. I charge you again to keep this to yourself. Do not tell Mary, for it will only make you both unhappy. If she knows that you have Morland blood—"

"More even that Paul himself," Jan said musingly.

Nanette looked at him sharply. "No, Bear-cub. That is not the way to think. You have your father's estates—be content."

"But if all Paul's heirs fail—" Jan said tentatively. "Mother, I don't wish it, but it could be. There is only Arthur left, and then Mary and Daniel Bennett's children. How could it be better for a Bennett child—and a younger son at that, for the eldest will not leave Hare Warren—to take over Morland Place, than for me, who loves it, who was brought up here and who am a Morland in all but name?"

"Oh, Jan, leave speculation; it is profitless. As you say, there is Arthur—and Jane and Hezekiah may have children. And John may be reconciled with his father. Who can tell? I wish you could forget all this."

"I wish I could, too, Mother, but it is too late. Perhaps it was always too late."

Nanette did not answer. It was too close to her thoughts of the night before.

Mary Percy woke, shuddering and crying, tears on her face, and reached for John. He woke instantly and gathered her into his arms, drawing her head onto his shoulder and cradling her, stroking her hair as he had seen her cradle Thomas after a fall.

"Hush, my hinny, my bird, it's all right. I'm here." When she had stopped shuddering, he said gently, "Was it the dream again?"

"Yes," she said, muffled by his body.

"It comes more often now, does it not? But it is only a dream. It's over now."

"I dreamed you were gone—I had lost you—it was so cold, so empty without you—"

"But here I am, you see, my bird. And you are here in my arms, warm and safe," John crooned. He saw that she was not quite awake, still in the tendril grasp of the dream of loss, and that words meant nothing to her, so instead he set her head a little back from him and began to kiss her. She responded at first softly and sleepily, but in a little she caught fire from him; they felt each other's minds, having no need of words. From the first time up in the hills, they had been apart for so few days, so few hours; apart in spirit never, though she was fierce and proud, for when they fought each other it never touched the inner core of themselves, they who had fought side by side like the children of one birth. Only sometimes this sadness would come, and then, as now, she would cling harder than ever, as if she would be more than close, as if she would *be* him.

They made love and then lay soft and relaxed, their damp skin touching along all their length.

"Is is so hard to bear, this dream?" he said after a while. "We have been apart before, though for very few days. But when I marched with Lord Percy and you stayed behind in Alnwick with the boy—"

"It is different," she said. "Then we were still together. And I knew you would come back."

"Did you? What if I had been killed?" She shuddered minutely: he felt it through his body.

"But I knew you would not be. When—I have the dream—it leaves me to feel that I can never be close enough to you, whatever we do or say."

"Do you feel it now?" He felt her frown.

"It goes away—but it comes back again, with the

dream. I wonder sometimes—" she did not finish, bu[t]
he knew what she thought—she wondered if the drean[m]
came from God, a warning that human, mortal love wa[s]
not to be desired too much. "I never loved, befor[e]
you," she said at last. "And when I first saw you, I fel[t]
as though an end had come, as though I must die. [I]
resisted you, though I knew what my fate must be. [I]
had been Mary Percy, and myself, and I was afraid to
let that go. Can you understand it?"

"Yes," he said, though it was with his mind he understood, for he had never felt that sense of the single-
ness of himself. "I loved, before you."

"Your mother," she said. There had been nothing
held back between them in the years they had been together.

"Yes. And she was the forerunner—she prepared me
to love."

"Then, perhaps—"

"What, then?"

"Perhaps all our love, all our human love, is only to
prepare us? Perhaps that is why it is so—" She paused
a long while, looking for the word, and in the end said
inadequately, "So sad."

He did not rebuke her or tease her—not for them the
lovers' delight in misunderstanding and explanation. He
knew what she meant by *sad,* though it was not the
right word. They had great joy in each other, but even
in that joy there was something like sadness, as if they
were straining to reach something through each other
that was forever beyond them, glimpsed as a shadow
always turning the stair a few paces ahead. Even her
beauty, its very purity, had a delicate poignancy about
it as if, like a tethered unicorn, she looked at the golden
chain around her neck and said, surely I was made for
something other than this?

But these were thoughts for the quiet times. When
morning came they rose from the bed together and

heard Mass and broke their fast and the days came crowding in on them, filled with incident, duty, responsibility. They were king and queen of their small country, with all that entailed. Then there was the boy. Thomas was five years old that summer and already grown taller than other boys of his age. He was his mother's son, with her clear, gray eyes and light hair, bleached in the summer to silver white, but he promised his father's height and strength and also some of his father's gentleness and strange affinity with animals. Already at five he could ride any horse and handle any hawk or hound. Mary had given him a horse of his own, half-brother to her own Houlet, and he rode it bareback, often not even bothering with a bridle, for the horse seemed to know his mind without instruction.

He handled spear and bow easily, was quick at his lessons and was accepted as leader of the other children without having to fight for it. John saw in him the qualities that he would need to survive up there in the Borderlands—all but one: he seemed to have inherited his father's lack of ambition. It did not seem to matter to him that he would one day be lord of all he surveyed. He did not talk about it or plan what he would do when it was his. He had no curiosity about his father's lost inheritance. His interest seemed to lay all with riding and hunting and climbing trees and splashing in the burns and watching the wildcat's lair and taming fox kittens. He seemed to have no curiosity about the world of men. John wanted Thomas to be perfect, for Thomas was the culmination of his and Mary's love, the product and outcome of it. He loved Thomas with a painful intensity, never attaining the careless ease with which Mary loved her only son. For John felt more and more strongly as the boy grew that he was what they had been for, he and Mary and all their love. His own life had taken on a pattern, a routine—breeding and selling cattle and horses, hunting for food, fighting off raiders, protecting and ruling his people—that seemed likely to go on unbroken for the rest of his life. But what did life hold for Thomas? Perhaps the child's strange detachment from purpose was the sign that he was meant for something else, something higher?

For Lettice, too, life had settled into a pattern, and though it was not the pattern she would have chosen, yet in many ways it was more comfortable than she had expected. She saw little of Rob—he came home rarely, once in the summer to hunt at Birnie Castle for a week or sometimes two, once in the winter, to spend the twelve days of Christmas at Aberlady with his family. Apart from that she hardly ever saw him or even heard from him. She guessed it was partly to protect her: she knew in some obscure way that though he was within the Council, he was not in accord with them, that his idea was to remove Morton, whom he hated, and replace him with the ex-Queen as Regent for her own son. Though he had not discussed it with her, Lettice understood now something of the way his mind worked, and she could almost hear his voice saying, "The Queen would wield no power, but she would prevent anyone else usurping that power."

She had to learn to bear with his long absences, to look forward to and to live to the full the few days he was with her. When they were together their passion knew no bounds, and every moment when they were not alone together was a pain to them. He talked to her, too, as no one else in her life ever had, talked as though to another man, a friend. It never occurred to her to wonder what he felt about her, to ask herself if he loved her. What she felt for him and what she felt when she was with him was so different from anything that she had ever witnessed or heard tell of that she did not trouble herself to give it a name. It was the breath of life to her. When he was not there, she lived on her memories and her anticipations of the next time.

Despite their great physical passion, she did not conceive again, and that was grief to her, though Rob never spoke of it and never mentioned their two dead sons.

Kat was still with her, and, unexpectedly, she had great pleasure in the company of her stepdaughters. Jean was now seventeen and should have been married, but Rob would not do anything about a match for her. He seemed indifferent to her fate, and Lettice learned not to ask him, for angering him wasted their precious time together. But Jean was a good friend to have, though she was strong-headed and quick-tempered, reminding Lettice strongly of Rob. Lesley was twelve now, and, having been more under the influence of Kat than had Jean, she was gentler and more womanly. She was devoted to Douglass and petted her and played with her like a kitten or a toy child.

Douglass was five, a very pretty child, with the Morland blue eyes, dark hair and high cheekbones, though to Lettice she had a great look of Rob about her, particularly when she laughed. She was a happy child, always bubbling over with good spirits, and the grim silent corridors of Birnie Castle rang with her laughter and chatter as never before in their history. She was the only one of his daughters that Rob had the inclination to play with when he was there, and he would swing her up above his head in his strong hands for the pleasure of hearing her squeal with delight. She had no fear of her father, not even in his rages, and perhaps that was why he loved her.

"You're as bold as you are bonny, my wee bird," he would say to her. Sometimes he would take her out with him when he rode in the park and would hold her with one hand before him on the saddle while he galloped flat out. Douglass would part her lips, drinking the air, her cheeks and eyes bright, trusting absolutely that he would not let her fall. When he at last drew his horse to a rearing halt, she would look up at him, hair tangled and bonnet gone, and cry, "Again! Gallop again!" and he would laugh exultantly at her fearlessness and her beauty.

So Lettice spent her days in reading, sewing, organizing the household, bringing up her daughters, riding out in the park and waiting for Rob. All fear had not left her: she knew that it was dangerous to be his wife, that at any time he might slip and stumble from his precarious position, and that in falling he would take her with him. She wore, always, an Italian blade tucked into her jeweled belt, and the sound of horses outside always brought her to attention, listening warily for the sounds that might signal her death. But that fear was part of her life's pattern now, and her spirit stretched to accommodate it, just as it did to accommodate the fear of discovery when she said her prayers.

Lord Hovenden's Men, like the stars in their courses, moved along a fixed route through the year. Of Lord Hovenden they saw nothing. He was their patron only in the sense that he allowed them to use his name, as the law demanded. They were the means of spreading his fame abroad, he was their guarantee of respectability, but he gave them no money or support, and had they disgraced themselves or been thrown into prison, he would have hastened to repudiate any connection with them. This was the way of things, and they accepted it. Once in a while they might be called upon to do a performance in his house for his guests; otherwise they were the Trinity Players still.

William's love affair with the players lasted two years. At the end of that time he had begun to detect a sameness about the days, about the performances, about the plays, even, for though plays rarely appeared more than once, they were written by the same few overworked, underpaid writers, revolving about the same few scenes. The actors all had their idiosyncrasies and there was a tiresome familiarity about their effects, a mannerism, a way of pronouncing a phrase, a toss of the head. As he fell out of love with them, he began, as a man will who no longer loves his wife, to ignore them, to think of other things while they were talking, to think of other things even while onstage playing his parts.

His love affair with Jack Fallow lasted a little less than two years. He had begun to suspect Jack of double-dealing even before Austin began to drop ill-disguised hints. He understood that Austin wanted him and was willing to do anything short of risking physical violence—for Austin was a coward—to get him, and the veiled hints he had ignored. But there was a change in Jack which William's musical ear detected long before he had any reason to suspect what it was. No man could ever lie successfully to William, because he heard the sound of what they were saying before the words.

Then, at Christmas in 1572 when they arrived at Fulham again to play at the Three Feathers, the truth was revealed to him. Jack had excused himself on business, saying that he had to see a gentleman about a possible engagement. William, left to his own devices and unhappy about the sound of Jack's excuse, decided to spend the evening repairing his costumes, which were all in need of some attention after a long time on the road. He went to the little shed in the stable yard where they stored their gear when staying in Fulham, carrying a glim—a rushlight—with him. He flung open the door, and by the light of the glim saw the gleaming pale mounds of Jack's buttocks and the angry glint of his eyes as he turned his head over his shoulder to look at the intruder. Under him, naked on a heap of cloaks, was the newest and youngest of the apprentices.

The boy, Ralph, tried to speak, and Jack pressed his face down into the cloaks to muffle him. Otherwise he made no move.

"Well, my dear, so now you know," he said to William. William looked at him gravely, amazed to discover how unmoved he was. "No, my dear," he said at last, "I have known for a long time."

"Since when?" Jack asked scornfully.

"Since it began," said William, and went away, closing the door behind him so that they should not take cold. Outside in the dark starry yard, he felt a strange lightening of the spirits. He felt free, as if a great load had been taken from his back, and he paused for a moment, though it was cold, to try to determine why he should feel that way.

"I can go anywhere now, do anything," he said aloud, testing the words. But he had nowhere to go; he did not want, particularly, to do anything. And so he stayed on with the group, and by his dignified behavior towards Jack and little Ralph he would have won back the love he had lost if he had cared to lift so much as a finger. But he no longer wanted Jack; he was not sure now what he wanted; but inside the chrysalis he was changing. Another year went by, and the change became outwardly apparent. He began to grow quite suddenly, and to fill out, becoming, though neither very tall nor very big, certainly man-shaped rather than boy-shaped.

His voice deepened a little, and his beard began to grow more quickly. Some of the actors remarked on it; Kit Mulcaster took him aside in the autumn of 1573 and said, "It will be difficult for you to go on playing women much longer, my dear; have you thought of that?"

William nodded. "Over the past year—"

"Yes, we have all noticed. Well, you are a fine actor, you have an excellent voice and you still sing like an angel, albeit a male angel." He smiled, and William responded to the kindness. "I have discussed with the other sharers, and they agree with me—that we should like you to join us as a full member. Of course, you would have to put up some money, to become a sharer, too."

"How much money would I need?"

"A hundred pounds," Kit said.

It was not an impossible sum. William had some money saved already, and he earned good fees for his performances. He considered. "When do I have to decide?"

"Not yet awhile, but soon," Kit said. "I am sorry, my dear, but there are others waiting to take your place, and though you still play the Queen, the Princess is beyond you. By Christmas we shall have to have a decision from you."

"I will decide by Christmas, then. I do not yet know—" he hesitated, but Kit was benign and friendly. "I do not know what I want to do. I love to compose songs and to sing them as well as to act. Perhaps—"

"Aye, perhaps. Think about it—and, Will, say nothing to anyone. In our life we must learn to keep our counsel."

It was kindly meant. "Thank you," William said.

At Christmas of '73 they were back in Fulham, where first he had fallen out of love. The Three Feathers was a comfortable inn, and the landlord, one John Greene, a comfortable and kindly man. He had a large family, including three daughters, who helped in the tavern. The youngest, Susan, had always been a special favorite of William's. She was just turned fourteen now, and he noticed with some concern that she had put on womanly dress for the first time, and had darkened her eyebrows and turned up her hair.

"Why, Susan, how pretty you look," he said the first time he saw her. She blushed and lowered her eyelashes with pleasure at his notice, but as he watched her during the evening he saw he was not the only one to be attracted to the change in her. Though John Greene was a good father and a good Christian, a tavern was a rough place for a young unwed girl to work. Of course, at fourteen Susan was marriageable, and doubtless John Greene would be on the lookout for a suitable husband for her.

He called William over during the evening and said, "Will, why don't you give us a song, one of your own? Folks here have been asking, and I know young Susan dies to hear you." He smiled indulgently at his daughter, who modestly turned down her eyes. "Give us 'Summer's Merry Dance,' Will, we all like that one."

Obligingly William fetched his lute and sat down on a stool by the buttery hatch and sang, and from the first notes a hush fell over the taproom as everyone listened. When it was done there was applause and calls for another, so he sang again, and this time, looking around, he caught Susan's admiring eyes on him. She was pretty and fair, with bright eyes and parted lips, like a little squirrel, he caught himself thinking. While he sang the last verse he looked around and wondered who John Greene would marry her to, and discovered it distressed him a little to think of that little, fair, soft thing being married to any of these great hard-handed louts she was serving with ale.

When his song was done he declined to sing another, and John Greene beckoned him over to thank him and give him a tankard of ale.

"No, no—this is a thank you," he said when William would have paid. "By Our Lady, Will, but you've a powerful sweet voice—and your songs are mighty pretty. People from miles around ask about you. I wonder the Queen hasn't called for you to sing in Court. God's beard, I wish you'd stop here and sing your songs

very night. The Three Feathers would be famous from
ere to Scotland if you did."

"Well, and perhaps I may," William said idly. But
that night and the next day he thought about it. Was
that what he wanted to be in life—a composer of songs,
a musician? He had been a Court musician, and he had
been happy. Perhaps he would be happy again. At any
rate he must do something, and he no longer wanted to
be with Lord Hovenden's Men. So two weeks later
when the troupe moved on, William stayed; he stayed
to become the landlord's son, assistant and resident
singer. He grew his beard, wrote his songs and married
Susan Greene, because she loved him and because he
did not like to think of her being married to anyone
else, and in the autumn of 1574 when his first child, a
son they named Ambrose, was born, he thought he was
happy again, and forever.

CHAPTER FIFTEEN

On Lady Day 1574 Nanette, accompanied by Matthew
rode over from Watermill to Morland Place. They rode
slowly, Nanette ahead on an aged palfrey, Matthew half
a pace behind, watching her covertly. He wished that
his mistress would consent to ride pillion behind him,
but she was too proud and had almost snapped his
head off while he had been persuading her not to try
out the new gelding Jan had just broken. She had consented in the end to take the palfrey, but she still rode
cross-saddle and still used the crimson-dyed, gold-
tooled tackle decorated with gold swags and little bells
that her high-bred horses had worn for almost forty
years. And Matthew had to admit, as he kept close
enough to grab a rein should the need arise, that his
mistress still looked every inch a Queen's lady. The little horse held his head up as she rode, and she sat as
straight as a sapling in her French blue velvet gown and
bear's-ear silk dress, with a much-feathered cap over
her linen coif.

It was a sign of how much things had degenerated
that there was no one to meet them when they rode

hrough the barbican into the courtyard at Morland
Place. Matthew had to dismount and tie his horse to a
ring so that he could lead Nanette's horse to the mount-
ing block and help her down, and then she had to wait
while he led her horse away and hitched it. Matthew
could hear her tutting under her breath like a death-
watch beetle, and he composed his face into a suitable
disapproving gravity before rejoining her.

"It's Quarter day, you see, Matthew, and no sign of
any cleaning," she said as they walked into the great
hall. There should have been a great bustle of servants
changing the rushes, washing the windows, taking down
hangings, scouring the trestles with silver sand on this
day; but there was nothing but silence and a slightly
musty, deserted smell.

"Shall I go and look for Master Morland, Madam?"
Matthew asked. "You could walk about the herb garden while you wait—it's pleasant outside."

"No, I can guess where he is. He'll be in one of the
gardens. Come, we'll look together," Nanette said, and
she flicked him a glance that said she knew perfectly
well he was trying to save her exertion but that she
would not be saved. And in perversity she always did
more than she had intended, as now she led the way at
a brisk pace that was quite an effort in her heavy gown.

They found Paul, as she had guessed, in the kitchen
garden, and he looked up vaguely as they came in and
did not seem surprised to see them, although it was not
a planned visit. Paul was almost twenty years younger
than Nanette, but now in age and sorrow he had caught
her up. He was bent and gray, his face oddly shrunken
under his bushy gray beard; saddest of all, to Nanette,
was that he who had always been such an elegant
dresser was now wearing a plain long gown of the sort
that he used to upbraid his son John for wearing.

"Ah, there you are," he said, as if he had known they

were coming. "Look, look here—all the little thing[s] springing up. How wonderful it is. And there, where th[e] sticks mark, there is nothing to be seen yet, but it is a[ll] growing away under the earth there. I come every da[y] to see the progress. Sometimes I lie down and put m[y] ear to the ground and listen to them growing."

Nanette looked about her. Everything was orderl[y] and well tended here, and she guessed much of it wa[s] done by Paul. Since he had felt Morland Place to have become deserted, he spent more and more time out o[f] doors, as if he could not bear to be in there. She understood—here, in the gardens, there was still a sense of renewal and purpose. Things grew here.

"What have you planted?" she asked kindly.

He waved a hand about proudly and straightened a little. He had never been a tall man; now he looked directly into Nanette's eyes.

"Melons, cucumbers, pumpkins, radishes, carrots, turnips, parsnips, and two kinds of cabbage," he said, rattling them off. "And around the walls I'm trying peaches and almonds as well as apricots and figs. The price they have been charging for almonds in the Thursday Market is scandalous—"

"And you do so love that trout with almonds and honey that your cook does so well," Nanette said, smiling. "Which brings me to the point, Paul—your house needs to be set in order. Don't you know it is quarter day today?"

"Is it?" he said, surprised. "Then I must go in. The servants' wages have to be paid, and the tenants will be coming in with their rents."

"And the house should be being cleaned," Nanette said severely. "And why was I not met when I arrived? The gatekeeper let me in, but there was no one in the inner yard at all. You are not running Morland Place as it ought to be run, Paul. It is dirty and ill managed."

"Now, Aunt Nan," Paul said defensively.

She tucked her hand through his arm and turned him toward the door of the garden. "Come, coz, we'll walk back together and sit a little in the herb garden and talk. It is time we used our wits, you and I. Matthew, go on ahead and see if you can find anyone in the buttery and have us brought out a pitcher of cold ale. And then you had better see if the horses are being taken care of. And then come back to me and see if I am ready."

Matthew bowed his head and hurried off—Nanette liked all her orders to be carried out with an air of urgency—and the two old people walked back to the house together and went through into the herb garden, or Eleanor's Garden as it was sometimes called, after Eleanor Courtney, the founder of the Morland line, who had planned and planted it. Here, too, everything was orderly, the gravel paths neatly weeded, the low gray-green and silver mounds of the herbs neatly trimmed back. Nanette led the way to the bower, where a stone bench stood under a trellis, over which grew an exotic flowering creeper brought back years ago from Cathay, and two bay trees grew in tall stone crocks— Hezekiah's father, Ezekiel, had brought those back from the Mediterranean. Nanette sat down on the bench, spread her skirts carefully, took off her feathered cap and began.

"Paul, I think it is time I came back to Morland Place. I am not happy at Watermill. You know my children do not follow the Old Faith as we do, and I think it troubles them to have me there. I catch them looking unpleasantly at my poor Simon. And then I cannot keep from criticizing the way Mary runs the house, and that causes unpleasantness. I have not so much longer to live, and when I die, I want to die in my home, where I was born. And so I have decided to come back to Morland Place."

Paul opened his mouth to reply, but she went straight on, lifting a hand to silence him.

"Now, as for you—you obviously need someone to run the house, and I have a lifetime of experience in that. Also, it is not seemly that the two little girls should have no female influence in the house. You are responsible for the little Butts girls. I'm sure you govern their inheritance correctly, but what about their persons? I know Jane keeps an eye on Margaret, but she is not always free to take charge, and as for little Celia—she must be taken away from school at once and given to me to instruct. She is ten, and it is almost too late, but she is a docile child and I shall make something of her. How do you think you will get her wed if she runs wild like a Hottentot?"

Paul blinked at the severity but said nothing. He was feeling, among other things, a great relief that someone was proposing to take from his shoulders a burden that he had been finding more and more difficult to bear. Nanette had stopped talking for the moment, for Matthew had returned with a serving girl, bringing the pitcher of ale and two pewter tankards. He served them and then withdrew, and Paul noticed that Nanette was looking about her distractedly.

"What are you looking for?" he asked, glad to have something neutral to say.

Nanette turned her head sharply and then laughed lightly at herself. "Foolish of me. I was looking for Zack. I still miss the sound of him pattering along behind me. It is the first time I have been without a dog since Anne Boleyn gave me a spaniel. Dogs' lives are so short," she said sadly. They drank some ale, and their minds wandered for a little. From time to time Paul glanced across at her and felt how comfortable it was to have a companion again, someone of his own kind, who thought like him and who obeyed the same rules of behavior.

At length Nanette recalled herself briskly to the point. "Well now, I must be gone. You will have things to do today. I shall come at the end of the week—that should give you time to arrange matters—and I shall bring Simon leBel, Matthew and Audrey, and Digby if Jan will let me have him. Otherwise some other footman. As to their status in the house—they will be my personal servants, but under the general discipline of Clement. And you know it is high time poor Father Philippe gave up his duties—he is too old to be running the risks he runs, not to mention riding out in the night to visit estate servants on their sickbeds. I propose that Simon take over his duties and Father Philippe retire. Then Simon can live in the priest's room, and Philippe can have one of those little cottages down by Micklelith House. Or if he prefers to live in the city, Jan will give me a property for him. One of the Lady Row cottages is empty, and since he will have Watermill House, which is mine, the least he can do is give me a cottage for an old friend."

"Very well—if he agrees," Paul said.

Nanette smiled. "I will speak to him. He will agree. He will see that Simon is much more suited to the onerous task. Now I shall not bring much with me—a few items of furniture and plate. I must have a bed, of course—where is Eleanor's bed?"

"In the solar. Arthur has begun to sleep there."

"And you sleep in the Butts bed?"

"In the bedchamber, yes."

"Who sleeps with you?"

"A boy."

"Well, then, Arthur had better come in with you, and the boy can sleep on a mattress. It is not good that Arthur should be unattended in the solar. It is too easy to slip out of there at night—you can get down by the roof of the kennels, and Arthur is of the age to go a-roving.

I'll have Eleanor's bed in the solar—and I'll have the
unicorn tapestry hung in there, too. You have it in your
room, I suppose? But it is mine, made for me, and I
have a fancy to be with it again. Audrey can sleep in
with me, and Digby and Matthew can have the truckle
bed in the solar—that will save trouble. Now is there
anything else? Let me see—"

"I think you have covered everything," Paul said
dryly.

Nanette raised an eyebrow. "You do not sound satisfied. Do you think I have not thought of you in all this?
You need a companion; you need someone to guide
you. I will run your house and order your servants. The
food, I know, has always been good here," she added,
smiling, "so I do not need to do anything there."

"And will be better when all my vegetables are growing up," Paul said with a spark of eagerness.

Nanette patted his hand and then looked serious.
"But, Paul, you must be careful. With Simon in the
house, we shall have the Mass as we have always had it,
but times are changing, and we must be circumspect.
When the Mass is held, there must be a reliable servant
on the chapel door and one on the outer gate, to be
sure no strangers slip in. And you must go to church—
yes, I know you have been avoiding it and paying the
fine, but it draws attention and makes bad blood. If you
will but make your once-weekly attendance, they will
leave you alone. You risk the safety of all your servants
and household, as well as the future of the Mass at
Morland Place."

"But Aunt Nan—" Paul protested, but she overrode
him firmly.

"You *and* Arthur. God understands. Simon will talk
to you about it—he will absolve you. It is for the best,
believe me."

"Very well then," Paul said listlessly.

Nanette looked at him sideways and gave her most charming smile. "Now tell me about your horses," she said. His face brightened at once. "We shall have such lovely conversations; you'll see. And music in the evenings. You have been too quiet, too long alone."

And now he smiled, too, and she saw in his face the realization of what it would mean to have a female companion again. He began eagerly to tell her about his horses—the Morlands had always been passionate breeders of horses—and was still talking when Matthew came back half an hour later, followed by Clement to tell him that the tenants were arriving.

A week later the move was effected. Tensions had been growing at Watermill House, and though Nanette believed that Jan had not yet told Mary the secret, she knew that sooner or later he would, and then conflict would be inevitable. Jan was both sorry and glad to see her go, feelings that she shared. They parted with loving embraces and swore to meet often, but there was the unspoken knowledge between them that part of the reason she was going to Morland Place was to be on hand to help Paul should Jan and Mary hatch any plot to usurp the inheritance. The thought even of that potential conflict hurt them both deeply.

She rode to Morland Place, Matthew riding with her and Audrey and Digby traveling on the ox cart that carried Nanette's possessions. Though she had been quite rich at various times of her life, she had never traveled with very much, and one cart was enough for the things she wanted to take with her. There were two chests of clothes—one of them the little silver-oak chest Old Paul had given her when they wed and that was supposed to have belonged to Eleanor Courteney—and her mirror, which was made of a sheet of burnished silver and was framed in silver-inlaid ebony, a very beautiful piece. There was a pair of oak stools, a little triangular low-back chair made of mahogany and much carved, and a set of oak boxes for storing things. Then there was her plate—six silver plates and six gilded silver—and her beautiful crystal and silver goblet, which had been James's wedding present to her, and her silver-inlaid drinking horn, which had been one of Old Paul's presents to her, and her ivory crucifix on the rosewood stand that always stood on her dressing table wherever she slept.

It was not much to show for a lifetime, she thought, but so much of her life was preserved in other ways, in people and in the fabric of the places where she had lived and in memories. She was glad to be back at Morland Place, where she had been born, where she had lived in happiness with her beloved father and mother, where she had known the brief bliss of love and marriage with Old Paul, the conflict of life with Paul Amyas eased by the knowledge that she was needed. Now, in the December of her life she came back to know again a little peace.

"Will—are you still there, then? Look, the candle is almost burned out, and you know what they cost. Why must you sit up all night working?"

William looked up from the music over which he was laboring and said mildly, "I thought you were asleep."

Susan, hugely pregnant and with a counterpane wrapped around her shoulders over her nightgown, stood in the doorway of the tiny attic he had taken over for his study. Her long hair was braided for the night, and with the long fair ropes hanging down from her nightcap; she looked absurdly young, like a child dressed up with a pillow. She looked at him with exasperation, searching in her mind for something on which to hang her grievance.

"Why can't you work in daylight instead of burning up candles night after night?" she said.

"Because during daylight I am working at other things. Your father needs my labors," William said reasonably. His patience irritated her. It galled her that she could not get through to him, that he treated her always with the same bland courtesy, whatever she said or did, never affectionate, never cross. She would have preferred him to knock her about than to ignore her like this—even now he was simply waiting for her to leave him alone again. He would never abuse her or order her to go.

"I couldn't sleep," she said. "It's so hot in that room."

"It's over the kitchen," he said—as if she didn't know. "Is it the pain again?"

"It's always the pain," she said. She moved restively, like a horse smelling thunder. "My back hurts."

"Sleep on your side, then," he said.

"Come to bed, Will," she wheedled. "Then I can lean against you. I can't sleep when you're up working."

"I will, soon," he said.

"The babies will wake up soon, and then you'll get no sleep." He did not answer, and his eyes, as if drawn irresistibly, went down to the piece of paper covered in words and music that lay defended between his hands.

"What are working on, Will? Is it another song?"

"Yes," he said noncommittally. She took a step forward, craning her head to see, and without even realizing it he closed his hands a little to shield it from her.

"Is it for me, Will? Is it a song for me?" Once, in the early days of their marriage, he had written a song called "Little Susan" and had dedicated it to her. She liked the distinction.

Now he said, to be rid of her, "Yes, if you like." She

smiled, looking less peevish but somehow also less childlike.

"Will you write my name on it? Write 'Susan' on it, at the top, like they do."

"All right," he said, and she came around the table to watch as he dipped his goose quill in the ink and wrote "Susan" in large letters at the top of the page. She was not book-learned, but he had taught her to read and write her own name.

"And the rest," she insisted. He wrote "Shawe" beside "Susan," and she smiled at him happily.

"And now you had better go back to bed. I'll be in soon. Go on now; you need to rest. It will be daylight soon."

Reluctantly, but knowing it was no use staying longer, she sidled out, closing the door behind her, and he waited in silence until he heard the creak of the bedroom door and the click of its latch. Then he relaxed, sighing heavily so that the candle flame twitched like a cat's tail. He leaned forward and pushed the shutter of the window open a little. It was still dark outside, but with that luminous darkness that precedes dawn, and the air smelled of morning. His concentration was broken. He looked down at the paper and then, with a grimace, pushed it from him and opened the shutter fully and blew out the candle. At once the dark outside grew less dark. He stared out over the jumble of rooftops to where the sun would be, and a blackbird, the first of the dawn chorus, began to sing somewhere near, liquidly and joyfully. The sound made him feel immensely sad; he wanted to weep, though he did not know what for, and he clasped his hands together and found his mind sliding into a prayer.

"Oh Lord God of Hosts, almighty, everlasting God,' his mind said, but there was no more. What was he doing here? What was his life? What was he for? What were men for? He had the feeling that he was wandering in a wood, so close to the path that one step would reach it and yet so unable to see it that any step he took could as easily take him away as toward. Down in the yard he heard the sharp rattle of the watchdog's chain as it came out of its kennel, and then it barked once, experimentally. William braced himself, expecting to hear a baby cry, but there was silence in the house.

He thought then of Susan. He knew she was unhappy, but he did not know why, or what, if anything, she had ever expected out of life. She had married him because her father had told her to and perhaps also because he was good-looking and a cut above the usual young men she met. Their sexual relations had been very meager. William had lain with her, because it was the thing to do, and had performed adequately without particularly enjoying it or finding it repulsive. Susan had conceived at once, and he had stopped having sex with her. The pattern had been repeated three times: Ambrose was born in the autumn of '74, little Susan in the summer of '75 and the next babe was due in a month's time. It seemed hard that Susan should be always either pregnant or giving birth, but it was never that that she complained about, and he saw that the lot of other women in their society was no different. It was something else that made her peevish; he did not know what.

For himself, now, what was it that he wanted? He worked hard every day helping Susan's father with the tavern, serving in the taproom and singing his songs, and Will Shawe had indeed became famous for miles around, and his songs were copied out and sold by chapmen up and down the country. He liked John Greene, he had a vague affection for Susan, he played with his babies with as much pleasure as he would have played with a nest of kittens, he did not find his work irksome. No, it was the music, the music that made him feel so often that he was grabbing at and missing a lifeline. There was something he should be writing and was not. He looked down at his work of that night—not a song, precisely, though the feel of it in his mind suggested it should have words. When a thread of music drifted into his mind, he could tell whether it belonged to the lute or the trumpet or the hautbois or the human voice. What he had before him was a number of separate threads that should in some way be together, entwined or overlapped or—the words slipped through again, Lord God of Hosts, Almighty Everlasting God. Three in one. The Trinity. Southbank Trinity Players. Three persons in one God—in some way, that was the clue to it. Three strands in one thread. The twist of a rope—

The sound of a baby crying brought his mind back to the present, and with a start he saw that it was luminous gray outside, light enough to read by. The birds were singing wildly, with that fierce desire for life that made it seem that their efforts alone dragged the sun up above the horizon; only the blackbird, nearby, sang effortlessly, his golden liquid notes bubbling upward in the cool, scented dawn like the fount of life. Tears filled William's eyes and brimmed over, and he felt them first hot, then cold on his cheeks.

"God, what shall I do?" he said aloud. Then he heard Susan cry out, loud and anguished in pain, and he jumped to his feet and ran to the door, knowing what it meant. The draft from the door to the window plucked the paper with her name on it and switched it off the table so that it planed down to the floor and settled in the dust under the stool. Two days later it was found by a servant who had noticed from outside the open shutters and had gone in to close them. He brought it to William, thinking it might be important.

William, sitting by the fire in the parlor, looked at it, having forgotten it completely, read the notes, won-

ered and rejected and, crumpling it up, threw it into
the fire. He did not notice Susan's name written at the
top. His jerkin was dressed with fluttering black rib-
ons whose shiny side caught the firelight as he
stretched his arm forward; for Susan was dead, had
died giving birth to their third child, a daughter, Mary,
who mewled in the crib on the other side of the fire,
waiting for a wet nurse to be found for her to replace
her mother.

In the autumn of 1576 Nanette discovered that Arthur had gotten a village girl pregnant, and she brought
the news to Paul in some agitation.

"I cannot think when he had the time—I thought he
was always within sight of one or other of us," she said.

Paul did not seem unduly concerned. "A lad will always find a way of wenching," he said, going on with
his accounts. Nanette reached across the table and took
the pen from his hand.

"Paul, this is not to be taken lightly. The conse-
quences of sin have a way of coming back upon this
house. The girl must be sent away and provided for—
provided for comfortably, of course, but at as great a
distance as possible. You don't want Arthur to get no-
tions about her and the brat, do you?"

"No, of course not," Paul said. "I'll see to it. You
need not worry any further."

"See it done," Nanette said, dissatisfied. "See to it
today. And, Paul, you must now see that it is time for
Arthur to be married. He is eighteen—no wonder he
has sired a bastard. Wonder he has not sired a dozen.
He must be married and beget an heir. I am surprised
you have not thought along those lines yourself."

"I have," Paul said, getting up and walking about the
room, seeing that he was not going to get any more
work done. "But marriage negotiations take so much
time, and I have so little."

Nanette snapped her fingers in irritation. "You do not see what is under your own eyes. Do you not have an heiress under your own roof? Are you not guardian? Will it be difficult to negotiate with yourself? Come, Paul, if Margaret does not marry Arthur, whom will she marry? Will you have the Butts fortune severed from ours after all these years?"

"Arthur and Margaret to marry?" Paul said.

"She is almost seventeen," Nanette said grimly, "and if *she* presents you with a bastard it won't be so easy to deal with. That girl is beyond me to supervise. Marry them at once and let us be done with it. She can give Morland Place an heir by next summer."

So it was arranged, and Arthur, a little sulky, was married to Margaret, a little rebellious, in the chapel at Morland Place at dawn on a fine October day, and then again officially in the Church of the Holy Trinity. And on the same day, in the Church of St. Mary in Fulham, Will Shawe married Margery Cheadle, the wet nurse who had come to take care of Mary. He was a widower with three chidren, she a widow whose posthumous baby had died, and so it seemed to every one a good arrangement and a happy union directed by heaven for their mutual comfort. Only John Greene wondered a little resentfully how his youngest and favorite child could have been forgotten so easily; but it was not in his nature to think ill of Will Shawe, so he decided that Will was one of those folk who, for some reason, hid their emotions, and that Will had married again solely to secure a good mother for the bairns.

Arthur's marriage with Margaret Butts was evidently successful, for Margaret conceived almost at once, which quieted her down considerably and gave her new cause to queen it over Celia, while it made Arthur put on manly airs, don a stuffed doublet and take a great interest in the running of the wool business and the estates. The babe, a son, was born in August 1577, and Paul had it christened with the dynastic name Edward, but by the time it was born, it had already been eclipsed in Arthur's mind by the other great topic of conversation that summer—the proposed trip around the world by one of Hezekiah's sailor friends, Francis Drake. The plan was to sail via the Straits of Magellan to the Pacific side of the isthmus and to put in a serious challenge to Spain in the New World, and also, incidentally and not unimportantly, to make the fortune of everyone involved.

Drake and his brother had been to visit Hezekiah at Shawes during the summer, and most of the family had gathered there in some excitement to meet him and hear talk of the scheme. Drake was a typical sailor—short, broad and barrel-chested, enormously powerful, with arms and neck like a bull, too short and powerful for grace but with a quiet dignity that prevented even his rolling gait from seeming ridiculous. He had a round face, broad at the forehead and balanced by his full, close-clipped beard and mustache. His eyes were gray and clear, his eyebrows arched so that he had a look of innocence and alertness that was strangely appealing; his nose was short and straight, his mouth humorous but firm; altogether his face was as strong as his body—there was not a weak line anywhere, and he was evidently a man born to command.

His brother John was with him, and a Captain Winter, a friend who was to command one of the vessels. The object of their visit was to persuade some money out of the Morland purse.

"It is not to be officially sanctioned by the Council, you see," Drake said after dinner when the tablecloth had been drawn. There had been little talk during the meal. Drake was a good trencherman, as was Hezekiah, and when both of them were silent, it did not behoove anyone else to speak.

"But I thought that the Queen was in favor of the

plan," Nanette said. "I heard from a friend at Court—discreetly, you understand."

"Of course," Drake said with a bow in her direction. "It is all very much the secret everyone knows about. And yes, you are right, the Queen is in favor—but there is a strong pro-Spanish element in the Council, and it would not be politic to outrage them openly."

"Pro-Spanish?" Hezekiah questioned.

"Those who want peace with Spain," Drake elucidated. "So I am to have unofficial help from the Council. That means they will put up a little money, and if everything is a success they will share in the sweets, but if aught goes ill, I shall have the pains to myself."

He smiled as he spoke to rob the words of their sting. He was a practical man and saw no reason to trouble himself over things that could not be helped.

"Frank and I are putting up most of the money ourselves," John Drake said now. "Our own ship, the *Pelican*, will lead the way; and the Queen's ship, the *Elizabeth of London*, will be fitted out and financed by the Council, under Captain Winter here. But two ships are not enough for such an expedition. We would really like to start with a flotilla of half a dozen sail."

"And that," Hezekiah said, laughing, "is where I come in."

"I sincerely hope so," Drake said, reaching out to slap his friend's chest with the back of his hand. "I want to charm the gold out of this purse of yours. It is a purse, is it not? This bulge—you never used to wear bran stuffing."

Hezekiah put his hands up defensively. "Only a sailor would know where another sailor keeps his purse. Well, you shall have what I can manage—but come, tell us more about your plans."

"Such as what return you can expect on your gold?" Drake said.

"Return on my gold? Why, Frank, I'd assumed I'd never see it more. If there's profit in it, you might even persuade my cousin Paul here to put up some money."

Two days later the Drakes and Captain Winter went away with money promised from both branches of the Morland family, and through the autumn they heard news of the progress of the scheme. In late September it was announced that *Pelican* and *Elizabeth*, together with two sloops and a pinnace and a crew of 160 all told, would be sailing from Plymouth—Drake's own country—in November; and there was an invitation for Hezekiah to go along.

"And sorely tempted I am, too," Hezekiah said when he told the news at Morland Place, "but my dear wife thinks I am too old, and truly I cannot wish to leave her for a year or more—for Frank does not know how long the trip will take."

"Then—oh Cousin—let me go in your stead!" Arthur cried out, and before anyone could say anything, he turned on his father with a face bright with excitement. "Father, let me go with them! Someone from the family ought to go, to keep an eye on the investment. Suppose there is a great fortune made, and no one tells us about it?"

"Are you suggesting that Frank would cheat us?" Hezekiah growled.

Nanette shook her head at him. "It's only an excuse," she said. "You can see in his face that he has thought of nothing else since your friends first came here, Hezekiah."

"It's true—I even dream about it," Arthur said, made suddenly frank by her understanding.

Paul scowled at him. "No wonder you have paid so little attention to the estate, then. Well, you can put it out of your mind. Of course you cannot go! Nonsense!"

"But why?" Arthur asked passionately. "Father, this is the greatest opportunity that anyone is ever likely to have. Cousin Hezekiah, you would have gone, would you not, if this had happened when you were young?"

"Well, yes—of course—but—"

"You see!" Arthur said to Paul. "He understands. You must let me go, Father."

"In God's name, child, you are the only one of my children left to me, you are the heir to Morland Place. How can you go?"

"But I have done my duty," Arthur said, not without bitterness. "I have married and given you an heir. You do not need me to help you with the estate. You cannot punish me for what my brothers and sisters have done."

There was a silence at this. Nanette saw the justice, but not for worlds would she speak.

Paul glared at his son. "Punish you? How is it a punishment to be heir of Morland Place and all that that entails? You should be proud of such an inheritance."

"I am proud, Father," Arthur said desperately, "and one day when it is mine I shall be glad to stay home and watch things grow. But I am young, and I want to see things while I am young. This is a new age—new things are being discovered. There is adventure everywhere, and I want to be part of it. You have always kept me at home, shut me away here because I was the only one left. Well, I have done everything you wanted, and I have given you little Edward. Now you must let me go, to live my own life and be part of my world, not lock me up in your world, in the past."

He stopped, panting for breath, and the older people looked at each other painfully, as though to acknowledge the truth of what had been said would hurt. Paul looked stunned, Hezekiah thoughtful, Nanette anxious. Only Jane looked at Arthur, and though her face was as serene as always, her eyes were full of sympathetic sadness for him. Rebellion, she thought, was so painful.

She was imprisoned in her faith, her lot in life, the fact of being a woman, and she understood Arthur's yearning for wide horizons very well. If it had not been that her prison was bigger on the inside than on the outside, she would have fretted, too.

"Does it mean so much to you, then, to go?" Paul asked at last with great difficulty.

Arthur's eyes met his with a mixture of defiance and sorrow, love and rebellion. "Father, 'if you deny me this," he said very quietly, "I shall hate you forever."

Much later Nanette found Paul sitting alone in the chapel; not praying, just sitting. He did not look up as she came in, and she sat down beside him and was silent for a while. At last she said, "He is right, of course. As you are. You are both right, but in different ways. You will have to let him go." Paul said nothing. She thought of Jan, of Alexander. "Children are a sorrow to us. Through them we live again, and die again. Each time a little more of us dies, each time we see that they are not as we were. It is not given to us to live forever, and yet always we hope that we will." She stopped, and after a moment, glancing at Paul, she saw by the light of the altar candles the tears sliding down his cheeks and into his beard. How softly, inconsolably, an old man weeps, like Priam for Hector, she thought. She could not reach out to him in any way; she could only say, "You will have to let him go. In his heart, he is gone already."

"I know," Paul said. And still he wept silently, an old man weeping for his son.

CHAPTER SIXTEEN

On a June day in 1578 the *Pelican* and the *Elizabeth*, followed by the sloop *Marigold* and the pinnace, crept cautiously into the harbor of St. Julien on the coast of Patagonia, but no hostile reception awaited them. Everything was quiet and deserted, so quiet, in fact, that the spirits of the crews were dampened and one or two crossed themselves nervously, and when a lookout let out a yell, they all jumped and cursed.

"Look, sir, on the foreshore—a hanged man, sir!"

"Ugh, that's all I need," a sailor muttered to Arthur. "Enough to give you the creeps, this place—and ain't a hanged man the symbol of death?"

Arthur silenced him with a glance. Drake was training his telescope on the gallows, from which an undoubtedly human figure dangled, not stirring in the still-damp air.

"It's been there some time by the look of it," Drake said, unconcerned, and then he folded up his telescope with a snap and said, loudly enough to be heard right down the deck, "I'll tell you what that is, lads—that's a man that was hanged for mutiny, must be fifty years ago—one of Magellan's men. I've read it in his diary."

"It's a sign, that's what it is!" someone called out, and others joined in nervously.

Drake looked stern. "It's a sign, all right—a sign that this is the place for us to hold the trial for the traitor. As soon as we've anchored, we'll set up a court here on deck and be done with it."

It cheered the men and took their minds off signs and portents; Arthur knew also that Drake considered it bad for the men's morale to have the traitor aboard ship unpunished. The traitor was one Doughty, who had captained the other sloop; he had turned out to be in the pay of the Spanish ambassador. A couple of weeks earlier he had tried to make a run for it, but *Marigold* had gone after him and captured the sloop. Drake had emptied it and burned it and had kept Doughty prisoner in his own cabin ever since.

The three ships and the pinnace anchored in clear water, and an armed party was sent ashore to investigate and to look for fresh water—what was left in the hogsheads was stinking and so thick with green things that it would scarcely pour. They came back to report that there was no sign of Indians and a clear stream a hundred yards up the beach, so the work of anchorage began. A boat was sent off with the hogsheads and a working party to wash them out and fill them; a guard was set up between the water's edge and the stream in case of attack; another party was sent off to hunt for fresh meat. Meanwhile, on board, the carpenters and sail makers gathered their assistants and began on the minor repairs that were necessary.

The trial was held at sunset, after the evening meal. Drake presided, the ships' officers were the jury, and all the sailors stood around to witness justice. There was no doubt of the outcome—Doughty was condemned by his own actions and out of his own mouth—but Drake would have everything done properly. When sentence

was passed, Drake with his own hands administered
the sacrament to the condemned man, kissed him on
both cheeks and then called for a sword.

"You don't mean to execute him yourself, sir?" Captain Winter demurred quietly. "Surely someone else——"

Drake's eyebrows went up, his clear pale eyes widening. "No, Jim, I would not ask any man to do what I
would not do myself. I am captain, and in a ship the
captain is King. It is for me to do."

The sailors near enough to hear the exchange murmured their approval—it would be passed on to every
ear in the flotilla in half an hour's time. They watched
in seemly, solemn silence as Drake unflinchingly cut off
the traitor's head, and when the body had been dragged
away, he faced the crew, still with the bloody sword in
his hand, and addressed them.

"Lads, you have seen justice done. You have seen
the punishment meted out to a traitor. A harsh punishment—the final punishment—and why? Because the
life of every one of us depends on complete unity
among us. There must be no division, not of word or
thought or action. You are obedient to me not just because I am the captain and I pay you, but because any
deviation from absolute obedience could mean the
death of everyone here, down to the smallest cabin
boy." His eye swept around the sea of faces turned up
to him, and there was absolute silence. Behind him the
sun was going down in a blaze of gold and crimson as
rich as a royal caparison, and no eye strayed toward it
from the face of the little barrel-chested man before
them. "We'll be running into danger, lads—but the
danger of the body is nothing to the danger of the soul.
Keep faith and you'll have nothing to fear. And now I
shall administer the sacrament to every one of you, so
that we shall all be united in the Body and Blood of
Our Blessed Savior."

He did so, and the men dispersed in a quiet, thoughtful mood to their evening occupations, and soon there was singing from the fo'c'sle, gentle, pensive singing rather than the usual loud and bawdy noise the hands made. Boats were taking the crews of the other ships back. Winter went last, and Arthur, holding the rope for him, witnessed an exchange between him and Drake.

"You see that sky?"

"Aye, Jim. Cold weather coming."

"And it'll get colder the further south we go. Maybe it would be better—"

"To stay here?" Drake grinned and shook his head. "What do you think we'd do for six months, friend, sitting around here? No, no, the longer we leave it the worse things will be. As soon as we've finished repairs and we're all fit again, we'll be off."

Winter nodded. "You're right, of course. It's just that something about that sky—" He looked past Drake's shoulder. "Golden and bloody."

"Don't you start talking about signs. Look upon it as a sign that we're all going to be rich. Now off with you. And I want a report on the crews' health tomorrow morning."

Arthur, scratching at his flea bites, could have answered the captain right then. They had managed to eradicate the lice, but the fleas and bedbugs were harder to catch. Then there was the scurvy and the various kinds of rash the men passed one to another—Arthur hadn't stopped itching since three days out of Plymouth.

They stayed six weeks in St. Julien, during which time Drake ordered the pinnace burned, for he decided it was too small to get through the rough seas he was expecting, and by the time the three ships weighed anchor, there was no doubt in anyone's mind that it was winter. On the twentieth of August they reached the Magellan Straits.

"Seventy miles of hell," Drake commented cheerfully to his officers. "That's what I've heard it called. And that land there"—he pointed toward the southern shore of the straits—"goes on wild and inhospitable to the southern end of the world. Awesome thought, eh?"

The sea was gray and forbidding, and a strong westerly wind was blowing.

"Not going to be easy sailing against this," one of the officers commented.

"Wouldn't it have been better to wait for a favorable wind?" Arthur asked John Drake, who was standing next to him.

John shook his head. "According to Magellan, in these latitudes the wind blows from the west all year round. There's no good time or bad time."

It took them three weeks to get through the straits, the ships' boats going ahead taking soundings—for there were no charts—and the three ships following slowly behind. Snow fell heavily and continually, packing treacherously to ice on the decks, steathily covering the quartermaster and his mate, freezing the sheets and halyards so that they cut even the sailors' horny palms like knife blades. On either side icy mountains overhung them menacingly; wild and wonderful scenery could be glimpsed between snowstorms, and in the brief gray daylight they saw seals, with their strangely human-looking heads, swimming near them, and sometimes a hardy bird.

There were little islands here and there, and sometimes they stopped and rested on them, for it was bitterly hard work for everyone. The sailors killed seals and penguins to eke out their stores and reveled in the fresh meat after living so long on salt, though with sailors' perversity they complained that it was not pork or mutton. There were birds' eggs to be had, too, with a strong and strange flavor, and one or two of the hands became skilled at spearing fish.

It was when they were through the straits and into the Pacific that their troubles really began. The seas there were higher than any of them had ever known, and the tiny, frail ships climbed what seemed like mountains of gray-green glassy water and shot down into the trough so that it seemed they would never stop but go plunging to the bottom of the sea. Sometimes a great wave would crash over them, sweeping the decks from stem to stern, and the ships would groan and creak as they shuddered free of the load of water. There was no hope of making any progress; all they could do was go with the seas, for if they tried to fight them they would have been smashed to pieces. So they furled their sails, and the gale-force winds and mountainous, running seas drove them southeastward, away from their objective.

Drake stood firm on the quarterdeck, refusing to show concern, occasionally training his telescope on the other two ships. *Elizabeth of London* was well up to windward of them, and though she disappeared regularly in the trough of the waves, she rode up again, her bowsprit pointing almost vertically at the sky as she shed the white water. But the *Marigold*, lighter and less weatherly than the two ships, was running further and further to leeward, where the purple and gray smudge of the shore lay like a lurking predator, ready to smash the little sloop on its rocks. There was nothing in the world anyone could do to help. *Pelican* herself could well be in the same trouble soon.

"Cap'n, sir!" a lookout called. "The *Marigold*, sir— I think she's trying to set sail."

Drake's telescope swung around on her, and everyone on deck strained their eyes toward the distant dot.

Sure enough there was the merest gleam as she tried to show a scrap of sail, just enough to counterbalance the pressure of the wind and water blowing her down onto the shore. It was a wild scheme, and her captain must have been driven to it by desperation. No one even attempted to speak; everyone's thoughts and prayers were with the men who were struggling to claw their way back up to windward and away from certain death. It seemed that she might make it; but a freak wave, a sixty-foot cliff of water, rose out of the trough of the wave before it. *Marigold* had had no time to regain her bouyancy. She set her bow into the side of the mountain and disappeared under its tons of falling water. For a long time the crew and officers of the *Pelican* watched, but she never rose again, and after a while Drake shut his telescope and made the sign of the cross, and everyone on deck followed suit.

The wild seas drove the two ships six hundred miles off course to the southeast, and they would surely have suffered the same fate as the *Marigold* except that, as they discovered, the south coast of the Magellan Straits did not belong to a solid land mass that stretched on right to the South Pole but was the coast of a small island, so they were saved the menace of the lee shore. Then the storm worsened. They would not have thought it possible, but the wind grew wilder, the sea rougher; and as darkness came on the visibility closed down abruptly, and the two ships lost sight of each other. Captain Winter's last view of the *Pelican* was not comforting. She was far down to leeward and seemed to be laboring more heavily than *Elizabeth*—presumably caught in a worse eddy of the the storm than her sister. When dawn came at last, there was no sign of her at all. The weather seemed to have moderated slightly, and Captain Winter decided to attempt to show a scrap of sail and begin to beat back to the northward.

There had been a procedure agreed between the Captains in case of separation, and having regained the straits, Winter worked his way around to Valparaiso and there rested his exhausted crew and effected much-needed repairs to the damaged ship. They waited there three weeks, and every night they lit a fire on the headland as a beacon to Drake and the *Pelican* if she should be anywhere near, but she never came. At last Captain Winter decided that she must have been destroyed, for otherwise she would surely by now have rejoined them at the rendezvous. He and his crew joined together in a memorial service for the lost ships and then, in a subdued and sorry mood, set sail for home.

The news that the *Pelican* had been lost at sea with all hands came to Paul in the summer of '79 in a letter from Captain Winter. Paul did not weep, and Nanette understood why: he had said good-bye to Arthur long since, had mourned him that day in the chapel as already dead, and there was no call for further grieving. After a memorial Mass the family retired to the winter parlor for a little privacy, and Nanette watched Paul anxiously as he walked, slowly, like an old man, to a seat by the fireplace. His face was devoid of all feeling. Arthur's son Edward had died last November, and the desertion of Morland Place was now complete.

All eyes were dry that morning. Margaret, the widow, had managed to squeeze out a dutiful drop or two when she heard the news, but she had long since given up expectations of seeing her husband again, and she had wept far more over the loss of her baby, of whom she had been genuinely fond. Now she wondered how long it was before dinnertime, and she hoped they would not have to sit in solemn silence for too long. It was embarrassing and unnecessary, especially on her part. She had not expected to see Arthur again, and at least now that the news had come she could marry again, when a decent period of mourning was over. She fidgeted and looked around at the others.

There were few enough of them: Jan and Mary and the boys, Jane and Hezekiah, Celia, Nanette and Paul—that was all that was left of this once-large family.

It was Margaret who broke the silence by asking, "Well, what now?"

Paul looked up and saw the expectation on every face, though for different reasons. It was what everyone must be thinking.

"I suppose," Margaret went on, not without bitterness—for she had looked forward to being mistress of Morland Place for a very long time, until her son married—"I suppose you will have to send word to Hare Warren for Mary and Daniel Bennett's son."

"If he'll come," Mary said.

"Of course he'll come," Nanette said sharply.

Jan and Mary exchanged a glance, and Jan said gently, "Why look so far off? Are there no young people nearer to hand?" He caught up Paul's glance and directed it with a nod of his head toward his own sons—Nicholas sitting on the floor beside Celia and trying, covertly, to gain her attention, and Gabriel leaning on his mother's shoulder and playing with a curl of her hair.

"What do you mean?" Paul asked sharply. "What have your sons to do with it?"

"Let the young people go further off and we will speak," Jan said. Paul hesitated and then nodded, and Jan said, "Nicholas, take Celia and Gabriel out into the garden and stay until you are sent for."

When the children had gone, Paul said, "Am I to understand that you are suggesting I make your sons my heirs?"

"Why not?" Jan said lightly, hoping to keep the tone friendly for as long as possible. He avoided his mother's

ye. "You know you have always been very fond of my
oys. At one time you looked upon them almost as
our own grandchildren."

"Until you took them away," Paul pointed out.

"But they were brought up here for a long time.
They are born and bred to this place—not strangers,
lmost foreigners like the Bennett boys. Would it not be
etter for Morland Place to be cared for by someone
who has lived here all his life?"

"You have had them brought up as heretics," Paul
aid, using the harshest word he could find.

Jan did not flinch. "That is not a word I would use,"
he said calmly. "But though they have been taught
ideas a little more advanced than your own, they are
good boys, with sound principles. And you could marry
Nicholas to Celia and let her influence guide him."

This, Nanette saw, was all part of the plan. "Why not
Margaret?" she said.

Margaret made a face, and Jan said quickly, "Surely,
Mother, you can see that Nicholas is too young for
Margaret?"

"Thanks, but I don't want to wed a child," Margaret
said huffily, and she glanced at Nanette to see if she
would take up her cause. It would be galling indeed for
her younger sister to inherit what had been hers.

"Margaret or Celia, what matters it?" Paul said irritably. "Your boys may be very good boys, but they are
not Morlands. There is no more to be said." He stood
up to go, and Nanette braced herself in vicarious antici-
pation of the blow she knew was about to be dealt him.
She glared at Jan, but she knew he would not stop now.

"Oh, but there is," Jan said. "Though he is not a
Morland in name, Nicholas has a Morland for a father.
He has Morland blood all right."

The silence was almost tangible. Paul had reached
the door and had stopped when Jan began to speak.
Now he turned very slowly, and from the terrible ex-

pression on his face Nanette knew that he had *know*
all these years, had known and had hidden the know!
edge from himself, shut it away with other fears too te:
rible to be spoken of.

"Who is this Morland father of your brats?" he sai
in a voice low with menace.

"You know," Jan said, discovering it for himself
"You know, don't you? I am John's brother, John's
elder brother, your wife's firstborn son. And my father—"

"No, Jan!" Nanette cried out, and Jan turned to
look at her, startled. "No, Bear-cub," she said,
"enough." For she knew, as did no one else, that Jan's
father's identity was a secret from everyone.

Paul looked from Jan to her, turning his head slowly,
his expression terrible, like a bear goaded almost to
death. "You know *that*? You know who did that terrible thing? In the name of God," he cried out suddenly,
anguished, "does everyone know except me?"

"*I* don't know anything," Margaret said peevishly. "I
don't know what you're all talking about." No one even
heard her, still less paid her any attention.

"I'm sorry," Jan said to Nanette. "I didn't realize—"

"You didn't think," Nanette said angrily.

"Oh, for God's sake," Mary said irritably, "what difference does it make now? She is dead long since."

Paul stared at her as if he could not believe that anyone could bring him such pain. "She's right—what difference does it make?" he said. "You had better tell me
the rest."

"Paul—" Nanette said, putting out a hand to him.

He moved his head slightly as if to avoid her touch,
though he was across the room from her. "No, let him
tell me. Come then, Jan Chapham, who was your father?"

Nanette could see that he did not at all want to go

on, and in the end it was Mary who burst in, breaking past the barriers of Jan's reticence and shame. "His father was your grandfather's bastard son, your father's half-brother. So now you know. Morland blood on both sides, you see? My Nicholas is the great-grandson of Paul Morland of Morland Place, just as your children were."

She looked around triumphantly. Jan's eyes were on the floor, Margaret was looking both puzzled and bored, Paul was staring at her in an extremity of anguish.

Nanette said in a low voice, "How could I have brought up a woman so heartless, cruel and greedy? Oh, Mary, your mother would weep to see you now."

And Mary flushed with anger and embarrassment. "It's the truth," was all she could say.

Paul slowly drew himself together, reassembled the shattered pieces of his life. "Take your children and go home," he said, his voice little more than a whisper. "Tonight I will write to John in Northumberland. He shall send his son home."

That night when Nanette came out from the chapel after her evening devotions she found Paul waiting for her in the passage by the stairs up to the solar. Audrey had gone on up, and it was the first time they had been alone together that day. Nanette waited for him to speak.

"You knew all along who his father was. You told him and not me?"

"I would not have told him, except that he and Mary guessed between them."

"Did she know?" He meant Elizabeth, of course. Nanette shook her head.

"No one knew but me. She never saw his face."

"But you protected him all these years," Paul said bitterly. Nanette said nothing. It was not for Paul to know the full complexity of the story and her own part in it. In the face of her calm, his bitterness changed to sadness. "You should not have hidden the child. What did Elizabeth think?"

"I told her the child died."

"Would to God he had! Would to God you had never taken him from that obscurity. Why did you?"

"It was wrong, I suppose—but I loved him. He was not to blame for his father's faults. He is a good man, Paul—he does not mean to rob you of anything. He truly thinks it would be for the best for his son to inherit. And who knows, perhaps it would."

Paul made a wry face. "For the best that the blood of that man, the man who violated Elizabeth, should inherit Morland Place? How can you think it?"

"They are not to blame," she said again.

"Perhaps not, but they carry the taint," Paul said, and turned away and left her.

It was a sharp, dry morning ablaze with autumn colors, lovely to look at but poor for scent. John stood on the top of Oh Me Edge, looking out over the burnished country with wonder, while Kithra beside him snuffed the air hopefully. The old hound was gray-muzzled now, being past thirteen, and was sometimes stiff on first waking in the mornings. But he was still king dog in the household, as his many scars bore witness, and there were more of his children stalking about the fires than John could count. Finding no scent of interest, he pushed his muzzle up under John's hand, and John scratched his head and fondled his ears and turned back to Mary.

"Strange that something dying should be so beautiful," he said. She knew what he meant, as always— their years together had brought their minds as close as any two minds could be, and whatever they did— sleeping, eating, working, fighting, hunting, playing— they did as one person. Yet, thought John in wonder,

ne freshness never tarnished and the closeness never
loyed. Every time was as the first time, and an hour
apart from her was grief to him. She was sitting a little
away from the edge on Houlet, holding Jupiter's reins
for him, and he was reminded of the first time he ever
saw her, sitting just so, framed against the sky, still as a
statue on Houlet's back, the same thoughtful frown between her fair brows. The Princeling, he had called her,
and she looked scarcely any older now, for hers was not
the kind of beauty that depended on youth. Her pure
carven beauty, her clear gray eyes, the flash of gold
that was her laughter, her stillness, as if she were a god-
dess fashioned out of crystal—all were the same. Down
the pale gold of her cheek ran the faint silver line of the
sword scar, and there was another across her temple,
newer, jagged and pink, where she had been struck by a
flint thrown during a gallop by the horse in front: they
were the only differences.

No, that was not quite true—they were the only material differences. There was also the difference inside
her, and it puzzled and troubled John, for in all their
lives together there had not been anything hidden between them. But now there were silences, reserves:
there was a sadness that came over her from time to
time, and when he asked her about it, she would not
speak but would shrug it off and change the subject.
Sometimes he would wake in the middle of the night
and find her kneeling by the bed, praying silently.
When that happened he would not disturb her or let her
know he had woken, but she never mentioned it afterward, or the candles she lit before the statue of the
Blessed Virgin in the little stone, turf-roofed church
they attended. He could not account for it, except to
think that perhaps she was praying for another child—
but then why could she not speak to him of that? He
did not understand—he only knew there was some sor-

row in her that she wanted to hide from him, and while
she wished to hide it, he would not shame her by letting
it be known he had noticed.

She said now, "It is as if God wished to give us some
beauty to compensate for the long winter. A burst of
flame, leaving ashes afterward." They stared a moment
longer in silence, and then Mary's bitch Kai yawned
long and loud and sat down to scratch her neck noisily,
breaking the mood. Mowdie was dead, had died in
trying to give birth to a litter of huge puppies, too big
for her small body. Kai was one of Kithra's daughters,
bold but still young and unreliable.

"Shall we go on, Papa?" Thomas asked. He had been
waiting with well-concealed impatience and was glad of
Kai's intervention. "The horses are getting restless." To
make this slight falsehood true he nudged Hawk with
the heel furthest from his parents, and when the colt
moved forward, checked him ostentatiously.

"Yes, of course," John said and took the reins from
Mary and mounted up. They rode down toward Girdie
Fell, rounding the head of the Kielder Burn and making
for the woods, the men coming behind them with the
leashed hounds. Thomas rode with his parents, tense
with excitement. It was the first time he had been allowed on a boar hunt, and he was very conscious of the
honor and the responsibility it laid on him to behave
like an adult, so he rode a little stiffly, with a stern
frown between his brows that made him look, to John,
absurdly like his mother. At eleven he was already very
tall and strong, able to handle a horse rather than a
pony, and he rode on a half-brother of Houlet's, a gray
gelding called Hawk, who was no child's ride. He carried a spear, the butt ground on his foot in approved
style, and he rode with the same upright carriage and
springy ease as Mary. John glanced back from time to
time at the two of them riding side by side, and his
heart ached with love at the sight of Thomas's eager

...ce and his straight pale hair blowing back off his fore-
...ead above the crystal-gray eyes.

The boar they were hunting was a big one, and it had
...een attacking the flocks and doing considerable dam-
...ge among the outlying villages; those people who had
...een it said it was a monster, but even allowing for ex-
...aggeration it was necessary to be rid of it, so Mary and
John had gotten together a hunting party. They rode to
the place where it had last been seen and then put the
hounds on to cast about, but it was Kithra who found
the place where it had been lying—a long oval of flattened grass. The smell made his hair stand on end, and
he began a high, singing growl that soon fetched the
other hounds to the place. Mary leashed Kai, for she
was not to be trusted loose, and with Kithra running on
ahead and the foot servants with the leashed hounds
close behind him, they began to track the quarry.

The trail led them over the high ground just below
the crest of Girdie Fell, and it was there that they sighted
the boar. At a command from Mary, the servants
slipped the hounds, and with the pack hunting by sight,
Mary, John and Thomas and the mounted servants galloped after the hounds, leaving the foot servants to
catch up as they could. The boar, after staring for a
moment, turned and ran. Boars move fast, but they are
not built for long chases, and this one headed straight
for cover, leading them down off the exposed tops toward the thickly wooded ravine of the Kielder Burn.
Once they were in the trees hunting was slower, and the
hounds got their noses down and hunted by scent again.
Sometimes the riders had to dismount and lead their
horses through the more tangled undergrowth, and the
foot servants caught them up again.

Finally the boar went to ground in a dense tangle of
briar, gorse and whin, and the hounds ran back and
forth on its margin, snarling and singing at the dense
pig smell but unwilling to go after it.

"We'll made an end here," Mary said. "We'll net the other side of the thicket and drive him out this way, where there's more room." One did not want to be trapped with an enraged boar and have no room to maneuver. The servants unpacked the nets from the horses and set them up all around the thicket, driving the stakes hard into the crumbling loam with flat stones, against the boar's strength. Thomas and two other servants took the horses away to tether them at a safe distance, while John and Mary examined their spears and disposed the servants with the killing knives to either side. When Thomas came back, Mary gave him Kai's leash to hold and told him to stand back.

"But Mother—" he began to protest, fearing some slight to his dignity. Mary's brows drew together, and John interposed.

"Thomas, get up there on that rock—yes, take Kai with you—and keep a lookout for us. Give a yell when the boar breaks. Come, it is no shame to you. You are not strong enough to hold a boar on a spear, and that is all there is to it."

A little sulkily, Thomas obeyed, climbing up onto the outcrop. Watching him to safety, John's eyes traveled on upward to where the trees and ravine side broke for the sky, and he saw, with a vaguely troubled sensation, a rounded, bare outcrop of rock high above them. Why did it trouble him? he wondered. But there was no time to search memory—Mary had ordered the dogs put in at the far side, and grounding the butt of his spear, John readied himself, his eyes fixed on the thicket where the boar would emerge.

There was much noise from the thicket—hound noises and plenty of crashing about. It was a fairly large area, and the boar would run this way and that, coming up against the nets on each side, before he found the gap and decided to break for it. Mary, beside John, was as tense as a drawn bowstring. The big, heavy hounds were singing, held by their collars by the knife men; all but Kithra, who, head to John's knee, quivered in silent excitement.

Then came the rending crash of small wood, and simultaneously with Thomas's shrill cry, the boar broke out straight at them. He came faster than an arrow, a small black boulder, big for a boar, big enough to justify the peoples' talk of monsters, his tushes gleaming white against his dark mask. The hounds broke behind him, driving him on, but at the sight of the spears and the men and the great snarling dogs ahead, he skidded almost to a halt, turning his head this way and that to seek escape. Then he came on again. The pause had been only for a second, but in that time John had relaxed just enough for the renewed charge to take him unaware. His spear wavered, his aim was faulty, and he took the boar in the shoulder, turning it aside and snapping the shaft against the ground. The boar reeled, skidding a little on the soft earth, and turned toward John.

He heard Mary cry out in warning and saw Kithra leap to meet the animal and stepped back hastily, losing his footing. For a moment he smelled death; but then Mary's spear flew past him, missing the boar and thudding into the ground as with a wild shriek of pain Kithra was thrown up into the air from the flashing white tusks. As the hound's body hit the ground, the boar, unnerved, ran through the gap he had created and disappeared into the undergrowth behind them.

"Are you all right?" Mary asked him anxiously.

"Yes, I turned my foot, that's all," he said. He scrambled to his feet, and as Mary bent to retrieve her spear, he limped over to Kithra. The old hound was lying on his side panting; his belly was slit open from end to end, and the gleaming coils of his entrails were spilled on the ground. As John hunkered down beside him, the hound tried to lift his head and then beat his tail feebly on the ground in apology. John reached out and stroked his head, and Kithra licked his hand.

"There, old fellow," he said.

Mary came up behind him, and he heard her breathe a soft sound of distress and pity. "It's hopeless."

John nodded, unable to speak, and Kithra made a small whine of distress, looking up at him in puzzled entreaty. Mary silently offered him her knife, and he took it, his hand strangely slow and unwilling.

"There, old fellow," he said again, lifting the gray head to stretch the hound's throat taut. "You've been a great hunter in your time. Good hound. Good dog." Kithra's tail thumped again, and John held the brown eyes with his own and quickly thrust the knife home. Kithra died without a sound, and John crouched over him, stroking the gray-scarred head, with the unexpectedly soft, velvety place between the eyes. Kithra had been with him so long, he did not know how to leave him; but the servants were coming up, clamoring about the boar.

"He has your spearhead in him; he won't have gone far," one said. Another cried, "He's in those bushes there, toward the river. We can drive him out again from this side." And another, "He's wounded—he'll bleed to death if we leave him."

Then Thomas came scrambling down from his rock, Kai tugging him ahead, and John stepped between him and Kithra's body—Thomas had learned to walk by pulling himself upright on Kithra's patient tail. But for now he was too excited about the boar to have noticed anything else.

"I could see him, Papa, from that rock. He is only just through those bushes there—there's a clump of rocks, and he's lying among them."

"We'll take him from the other side," Mary said,

throwing John her spear and reaching for another from the servant who had brought up the spares. They skirted the tangle and found themselves unexpectedly at the burn side: they had not realized that the water was so near.

"We don't want the river at our backs," Mary said. "We'll go on around——" but at that moment the boar broke cover, heading straight toward them.

It happened so quickly that it was impossible to tell exactly what happened. John was taken by surprise, was swinging his spear into place and feeling for foothold on the smooth turf of the natural lawn and thinking, without any great fear, this, then, is the end—for it was impossible for him to take the boar squarely— when Mary leaped forward under the line of his blow, her spear shortened for close work.

She had seen John's unpreparedness, seen the curve of the boar's neck expose a vulnerable place and had jumped; in the same moment the boar, its eye caught by the flash of color her movement made, altered its line a little and swung its head up at her, and its tushes entered her at the groin as her spear went in between its forelegs. They fell together in a threshing, struggling heap. Mary smelled the stink of the animal's pain and anger and the hot reek of blood, felt the knifelike pain searing her body in a hundred places, saw a tumbled confusion of earth and trees and sky, the smooth lawn, the tall menacing cliffs beyond the Standing Pool, and high overhead the gray, round rock face of the Old Man; and as clear as the flash of a kingfisher across a summer river, her mind said, "That is why I have always known this place. It is the place of my death."

The confusion went on for a long time until at last there was silence, and she was lying with her cheek pressed against the cool moss of the lawn; and then there was blackness.

* * *

The boar was dragged off with half a dozen knives in it as well as the two spears and the broken spearhead, and John crouched over Mary, thrusting the servants back with one hand as one pushes off hounds from a dead stag. She was not dead, though her eyes were already blind with death, wandering. Her cap was gone, and her hair fell, soft and tangled as flax, on the bloody turf. John smoothed it back from her face, talking to her, unaware of what he said. Her hand moved, grasping at the moss, and when he took it, the fingers tightened on his own. He saw she did not know him but was glad of the company, held in the loneliness of dying.

"You should not have done it," he said over and over. "I could have struck it and stood aside. You should not have done it." Behind him Thomas was sobbing with fright, and a little way off the hounds were making worrying noises over the boar's body. Beyond again was the small cold voice of the stream. Someone put into his hand a rag soaked in water, and he wiped her face with it, uselessly. Her eyes opened wider, she stared past his hand into the sky and her lips moved, but no sound came from them, and in a moment she gave a convulsive shudder, as if something had broken inside her, and her eyes grew clear and blank, and she was gone.

He carried her home in his arms like a sleeping child, though it was near three miles, and would not relinquish her, though his injured ankle ached and the dead are heavier than the living. Her head lolled, the long hair trailing the ground; behind, the servants walked with the hounds, leading the horses, Thomas still holding Kai's leash, Kithra's body wrapped in a cloak and tied across Jupiter's saddle.

The steading was hushed with shock at the news, and then the weeping began, the whole household mourning her with unrestrained grief, for she had been beloved of everyone. She lay in state in the church for three days, and then they buried her where the stone wall marked off the churchyard from the fell, and covered the mound with turf until the master should give orders for a stone.

John buried Kithra with his own hands, choosing a site under a rowan tree near the place where he had first seen Mary, when she had set the dogs on him. He dug a deep, oblong hole and laid Kithra down in it, his paws out straight and his nose on his paws as he used to lie by the fire. He stroked the gray head once more and then filled in the hole with the earth and covered it over with the carefully cut sods, and heaped stones over the place for a marker and so that it should not be dug up again by scavengers. And then he sat down and wept, his arms around his updrawn legs and his head down on his knees, rocking a little back and forth. For Mary he shed no tears at all: his grief was too great for weeping. He had loved his mother too much, and his mother had died; he had loved Mary too much, and Mary had died.

The damp, peat-smelling wind blew down off the fells, moving his hair like fingers, and there was a hint in it of the oncoming winter. John lifted his head and stared at the damson-dark hills, and the tears dried on his face. She was gone; he did not know what to do to fill even this one day, and there was the rest of his life to come.

BOOK THREE

THE PHOENIX

The wheel is come full circle; I am here.

King Lear, Act V Scene 3

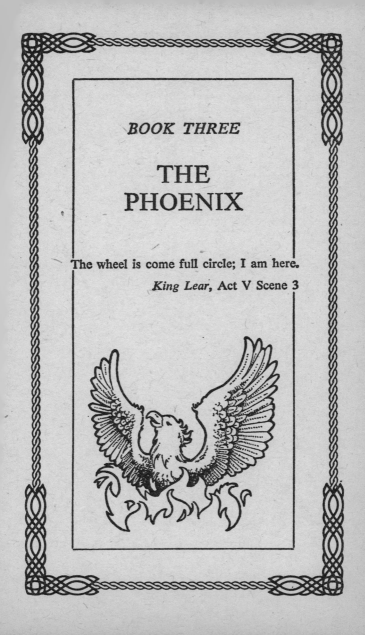

CHAPTER SEVENTEEN

The *Pelican* was not sunk, although to those who endured and survived the storm it seemed a miracle that she was not. As soon as they were able to set sail they began to beat back northward and reached at last the inadequate but welcome shelter of the little rocky islands scattered about Cape Horn. There they dropped anchor and waited for better weather, supplementing their dwindling stores with seal meat and fish and observing from a safe distance the comings and goings of the natives on shore, who, to their astonishment, went naked through the ice and snow without appearing to feel any discomfort.

"What do you think happened to the *Elizabeth*?" Arthur asked John Drake.

"Who can tell?" he said. "Probably sunk—but she might have survived, as we did, by some divine chance. We are all in His hands. And if she did survive, she could be anywhere now."

"But if she went to the rendezvous?" Arthur said, pursuing a line of thought of his own. "Captain says he means to hold out here until spring."

"If she went to the rendezvous, and we don't turn up,

she'll think we went down. We were well to leeward of her when we lost sight."

"And what will Cap'n Winter do then?"

"Go home," John Drake said, his teeth showing white through his beard in a sudden smile. "Lucky beggar! Still, we shall have the laugh on them—we'll be the ones to pick up all that Spanish treasure lying just over the horizon." He jabbed his thumb to the north.

"He'll go home and tell them we were sunk?" Arthur mused, and the slight questioning note in his voice resolved itself into pleasure. It gave him a strange sense of freedom and elation, the thought that at home they would consider him dead. He was a dead man, a no-person; he could do anything, go anywhere, with no need ever again to consult the will of his father or what was good for the family. The weight of his inheritance dropped from his shoulders like a burden; now if he could only change his name, too—

"Aye, and won't they be surprised when we turn up again like a ship full of ghosts. Very rich ghosts, however," John Drake was saying. Arthur did not like that idea—going back, however rich, to resume the burdens he had just seen tumble overboard.

"But perhaps we won't ever get back," he comforted himself aloud. John Drake misunderstood, and he patted Arthur's shoulder reassuringly.

"Don't worry, young 'un, we'll get back all right. Cap'n has the golden touch—we got through that storm, and we'll get through everything else. Why, half the crew already worships him as a god! I'll wager my head on it that we get back safe and sound. And when I hit Plymouth with a pocket full of ingots and pearls—!" He left the rest of the sentence to imagination, which was probably as well, Arthur having led a sheltered life.

Fortune seemed out to win John Drake's wager for him. The *Pelican* finally set sail in clement weather for

Valparaiso, and though, of course, they did not find the *Elizabeth* there, they met almost immediately with a huge Spanish galleon coming from Peru, hull down with treasure. Long security at sea made the Spanish careless: seeing another ship, they took it for granted she was Spanish and began the elaborate ceremony of greeting, hoisting the colors and beating the drums. All this gave the *Pelican* time to get around the unhandy side of her and fly up alongside, whereupon the English sailors poured over the gunwales and disarmed the Spaniards without loss of a single life. Drake hated bloodshed and ordered no violence, and the Spaniards were allowed to jump overboard and swim for the shore. It set the tone for the journey north up the coast of America. At every halt there was treasure to be taken—almost to be picked up, for they met with no resistance—the weather continued clement and the health of everyone aboard continued good. In March 1579 they reached the Canoas Bay in California, and there it was decided, on account of the pleasant climate and the abundance of food supplies, to stop and refit.

A stockade was built on the shore, and into it was conveyed the treasure, the stores and everything. the ship contained, and an armed guard was set up. Then food supplies were laid in; fruit and grain and some fresh meat—men were detailed to hunt every day—and the water barrels were refilled. The ship, light and empty as a paper boat, was warped up to the shallow, shelving beach, turned over on her side on rollers and dragged up onto firm sand to have her bottom cleaned. It was a long job, for she had to be scraped and then recaulked and tarred—men were picking oakum for a week for that job—and every rope in the rigging was replaced. Drake wanted to make sure that it was a perfectly sound ship he took northward into the unknown.

There was work for every man, long hours of it, and

hard work, too, for no captain can be happy with his
ship lying helpless on her side, and Drake wanted the
task finished as quickly as possible. But there were also
many pleasures to be tasted, not the least of which was
eating fresh meat and fruit every day and drinking water that tasted of water. They did not see much of the
natives, who lived in the wooded hills above them, but
though the dark-haired, dark-skinned people were
wary, they were not unfriendly and were sometimes induced to exchange bread and meat for small matters of
cloth and beads and wooden artifacts that the men
knocked up sitting around the campfires at night.

It was here that Arthur began to think seriously
about his future. It seemed that John Drake was
right—at least so far. The cap'n had led them victo-
riously halfway up the coast of America, had beaten
every ship he encountered and collected enough treasure to make every man Jack of them rich for life. But
what lay ahead, he wondered one day as he sat in the
sun on a hilltop, leaning his back against a rock and
looking down over the thick green forest to the spar-
kling blue sea on which, tiny as a toy, the *Pelican* was
being warped out again by ships' boats almost too small
to be seen.

He was leading the hunting party, and the men under
his command lolled at a little distance from him, roasting some joints of rabbit meat over a small fire. They
had stopped for their dinner, and a good dinner it
would be—the meat (it had been hard to acquire a
taste for flesh black on the outside and raw in the middle, but he had acquired it) and some good white
bread, not nearly stale yet, and some of those peculiar
roots that the natives here ate, cooked by being thrust
into the embers of the fire, and a skin of wine to be
mixed with water and shared among them.

They were talking among themselves of the natives

they had encountered that morning, who had watched them shyly from a distance and then run away. They did not talk about the future—sailors hardly ever did, Arthur had discovered. But he was not a sailor, though life at sea had hardened him and given him the skills he needed to survive that arduous life. What he was, he realized suddenly, was an escaped prisoner. Morland Place seemed very far away, but he could just about imagine it, and the imagination made him sick. He did not ever want to go back there. He had enjoyed the trip so far, even in a strange way the hazardous parts, but he had no desire to go on with it. Ahead lay the trip northward into hostile and dangerous waters, searching for the northwest passage. They might all die on that trip—and Arthur had no desire to die—but if they survived it, whether they found the passage or not, they would return to England, and Arthur had no desire to return to England.

Death or imprisonment faced him if he went on in the *Pelican*. He stretched his legs and squinted up at the heavenly blue sky. There was a logical answer, was there not? The climate was wonderful here, food was sufficiently abundant not to need much working for and the people were a simple, friendly people who would make a man like him their leader for the sake of the things he knew. And the women—he had seen, only that morning, among the group of natives they passed, a young girl just on the verge of womanhood but still young enough not to hide the frank admiration of her stare as she looked at his tall, strong body, his blue eyes and his reddish, salt-bleached hair.

When they had finished their meal he stood up, stretching, and went around the rock to make water, and when he came back he said, "I've just spotted something down there in the trees I think I ought to investigate. Wait here for me. I won't be long."

The men were too glad to continue to relax to ask any questions, and they watched him through slitted, slumbrous eyes as he picked up his spear and gun and disappeared downhill into the trees. It was hardly to be wondered at that in the drowsy peace of the afternoon they fell asleep, waking only when the sun slid around far enough to cast a shadow on them that chilled their hot flesh. They woke in confusion, to find their leader not yet back. They searched a little for him, casting to and fro in the edges of the woods and calling, but they had no idea where he might have gone or even in what direction. Soon it would begin to get dark, and they had been warned not to stay away from the ship after dark. Besides, they were getting hungry again. After a quick consultation they trotted back quickly to the stockade, there to report with suitable expressions of anxiety and regret that Mr. Morland had gone off alone to investigate some danger and had not returned.

There was little that could be done, though what there was Drake did. But the refitting was complete, and he was anxious to press on, and so on April the sixteenth 1579 the *Pelican* set sail again northward with "discharged dead" marked against Arthur's name in the ship's register, since "lost at sea" hardly seemed to cover the case.

The refusal of John Morland to allow Thomas to be sent to Morland Place was softened for Paul in the new year of 1580 by the news that Jane was, at last and against all expectations, pregnant. She had been on a pilgrimage the autumn before to the shrine of Our Lady of Walsingham, which, despite all government attempts to suppress it, continued to flourish and to be visited by barren women. Jane was confident that it was the pilgrimage and the offering she had made that had given rise to her happy condition, and she would not be upset by Zillah's gloomy prognostications of the difficulties that would attend a woman giving birth for the first time at the age of thirty-two.

Nanette was very brisk and at one point had to be restrained from slapping Zillah's face by a glance from Jane.

"Nonsense," she said. "Look at me—I was far older than your mistress when I had my first child, and it went very well with me."

Jane smiled inwardly at that, for though childless herself, she was well aware of the mysterious but benevolent conspiracy of nature by which women forget the pains of childbirth. Nanette obviously sincerely believed that all had gone very well with her, but there were servants enough still who remembered the difficulties that had attended Alexander's birth, and Jane had heard the story of how it turned Nanette's hair white. Still, she looked forward to that with the same calm as attended her every day.

"What God wills for me will come," she said. "There is no point in worrying. Besides, I feel in my bones that I will be all right. And how happy Hezekiah is!"

"And no doubt already looking for a name for the bairn," Nanette grumbled. "It was well enough, before we left Rome, to choose names out of the Bible, but now it makes you sound like Protestants. Why cannot he give the child a saint's name or a good, old-fashioned English name? It was bad enough when Bartholomew called his girls Faith, Hope and Charity, but I fear Hezekiah will come up with something worse—Revelation if it is a girl and Apocalypse for a boy."

Jane laughed. "Oh, Aunt Nan, you do exaggerate! But tell me, now, what has my father said about it?"

"Oh, my dear, he is so delighted you cannot imagine; though he has been worrying about the name, too. He sees the day when this boy of yours—you cannot have a girl, you see—when this boy of yours will inherit everything, and he thinks a great deal of the dignity of the family. He wants you to come to Morland Place for your pregnancy and confinement, so that the child can be born in the bed where he was born."

"No, I cannot do that," Jane said, surprisingly firmly.

Nanette hid her reaction. "And so I told him, my dear—most unsuitable. Besides, John may yet change his mind."

Jane's expression softened at once. "Oh, poor John—my heart aches for him, Aunt Nan. He loved her so much—I can imagine how much, as much as I love Hezekiah. I think how I would feel in his place, and it makes me grieve. I don't think he will ever let Thomas go. He will want to keep him near, to remind him of her. The boy looks very like his mother, so it's said."

"You are too soft-hearted, child—you forget that years among those people will have changed him. He is not the John you remember, the gentle boy who was your slave when you were a child. We are none of us what we were then," she added, and in the bleakness of her face Jane saw reflected the bitterness of death and desertion that she had witnessed in her long life. "Sometimes," Nanette went on very quietly, "I think that I have lived too long."

"Don't say that," Jane said quickly, crossing herself. "We are all in His hands. And things will get better— see, already new life is coming to us. My baby will be the beginning of renewal for us all. The cradles will be filled again and the fires rekindled on the hearth."

"And the Morland family will rise again from those fires like a phoenix, you would say?" Nanette said, smiling wryly. "Well, perhaps it may, my dear. At all events, your happy condition has already eased matters between Paul and Jan. I pray it may be a boy, then we can all live in peace again."

* * *

It was a boy, a healthy boy, and Hezekiah called it Nehemiah, at which Nanette grumbled that she supposed it could have been worse, although not much worse. Paul was rapturously happy and gave one of the best feasts in living memory for the occasion of the christening and was so far mellowed toward Jan by what he saw as an insuperable block to the Chapham plans that he allowed the match to go ahead between Celia Butts and Nicholas Chapham. Nanette wisely did not comment on this *volte face* and set herself to keeping Margaret's sour comments as inaudible as possible. If Margaret did not marry again, all her half of the fortune would go to Celia's children, and she did not relish the idea. Matters were not made easier for her when the rumor reached England that Drake's ship had not gone down, that it was sinking Spanish ships and taking their treasure, which meant that she was probably not a widow at all; and then in the late autumn of 1580 the *Pelican* reached Plymouth, and the news was sent up to Yorkshire of the second official death of Arthur Morland, so Margaret was back in mourning again. When she heard that he had not actually been seen dead and properly buried but was merely missing, a strong conviction, born of irritation, seized her that he was not dead at all, but she kept the thought to herself. She wanted another husband, and if at some later date Arthur came back and found her married to someone else—well, that possibility could be taken care of if and when it became actuality. She certainly did not intend to spend the fine years of her youth and fruitfulness keeping faith with a husband who had so little sense of his duties toward her.

There was one consolation that winter, which was that Arthur's share of the treasure was sent and, even after a proportion was given to his father, it still made

her a very wealthy and therefore a very desirab
widow. With the help of Mary Seymour, with who
Margaret had become quite friendly now that there wa
so much coming and going between Morland Place an
Watermill House, Margaret had a very expensive an
ostentatious new outfit for the Christmas season tha
year, which made even Celia's bridal finery look poo
in comparison. Celia and Nicholas were to live at Mor
land Place, since Watermill was too small to hous
them comfortably, and Celia put up a spirited defens
with her married status against Margaret's attacks or
the subject of wealth and feedom. Altogether, it made
for a lively Christmas.

When Margery, William's second wife, died in labor
of a stillborn child early in 1581, William hardly noticed. His father-in-law, John Greene, had died a few
months before, and he had since that time been losing
touch with the Three Feathers, spending more and
more time in his attic, while his former brother-in-law,
John Greene's eldest son, took over the running of the
inn. Seb, the new proprietor, was willing to be charit-
able toward his sister's widower and particularly toward
her children, but when a reasonable period for mourning
had passed and William still had not resumed his duties
around the tavern, Seb decided it was time to have a
talk with the young man in the attic.

Accordingly, one day in March he went up the stairs,
puffing a little because he was good and stout—it
would have been a poor advertisement for a tavern if
the landlord had a lean and hungry look to him—and,
despite himself, knocked on the attic door before enter-
ing.

William looked up from his work and smiled
vaguely. "Ah, Seb," he said, and his eyes went straight
back down to his paper. "The trouble is, it seems to be
impossible to make a musical instrument that is quite

eliable, and if one cannot be quite sure what sound will emerge, how can one determine the polyphony? Also—"

"Will," Seb said firmly, cutting across what was to him pure gibberish, "I have to talk to you. I've been patient—I'm a patient man, as you know—"

"So your are, Seb; I have often noticed it," William said.

"Have you, then? I wouldn't have thought you noticed anything. Did you even notice your wife died? You did not seem surprised by it—but then neither was anyone else. You know why she died, Will?"

"I suppose it was the will of God," he said, a little surprised at the turn the conversation seemed to be taking.

Seb shook his ponderous head in what was for him quite a brisk gesture. "She died giving birth to a dead baby, because for months she had been doing your work so as not to disturb you. It does a pregnant woman no good to be carrying great pails of water up and down stairs and bringing in coal for the fires. But you would not do it, and so she had to. And what about your poor children?"

"My children? What is the matter? Are they ill?" He was quite fond of his children: Ambrose, Susan and Mary, and Margery's son Will. He liked to listen to them chattering to each other while they played, and sometimes the little girls would dance for him.

"They're not ill, though I don't suppose you'd notice that, either. But they are growing up wild for want of attention. Ambrose shames us all, running about the streets with no shoes on."

"I thought he went to school," William said. "Why does he have no shoes?"

"He plays truant. And he sold his shoes to a boy in exchange for a pair of ferrets to go rabbiting with."

William considered that. "That seems enterprising. I daresay ferrets are more interesting to him than shoes."

Seb lost his patience once and for all. He thump
his big fist down into his palm. "Now you listen to m
Will Shawe! I've put up with you since Father died b
cause you were my sister's husband, but enough
enough. I've my own family to feed, and my unmarri
sisters, and I've enough to do without worrying abo
you and your brats. Now either you can start to pu
your weight around here or you can get out and tak
your family with you. What kind of man are you, to le
someone else provide for your children? You sit her
scribbling your nonsense—aye, I know Father though
a lot of your songs, but fine words don't butter no pars
nips, so you can get off your backside and do a day'
work or I wash my hands of you. And them's my las
words."

Another possible meaning of the last phrase crossed
William's agile mind, and he crossed himself without
thinking. Seb frowned at the gesture.

"And that's another thing," he said. "I don't want
none of that Papist stuff in my house. I've watched you,
and I don't think you're a proper Christian like the rest
of us. Well, now the new act's gone through, it'll make
an end of the Romans once and for all, and if you're
one, I don't want you here, understand?"

William looked at him, puzzled and thoughtful. "Oh,
yes, Seb, I understand. You've said everything beauti-
fully clearly."

"Right, then," Seb said, feeling a little deflated, for
the lack of resistance threw him off balance. He was
not used to people who allowed him to shout at them.
"Well, then," he said, shifting from foot to foot. "I better get back downstairs then." He hesitated, and William smiled politely and inquiringly at him. "Supper'll
be ready soon," Seb said in almost his normal voice.
"Soon as the children get back from school."

"I'll come down and give a hand," William said, getting up and pushing his papers aside.

Seb looked more put out than ever. "All right," he said. "Thanks, Will." He led the way downstairs, stepping softly, and William followed behind him with a slight smile on his face, which he concealed quickly at the turn of the stair.

Two weeks later he came to Seb while the latter was tapping barrels and said, "I've been thinking about what you told me, Seb, and I've come to a decision."

Seb straightened up, wiping the sweat out of his eyes on his sleeve. "What's that, Will?" he asked uneasily.

"It's quite true you have a family to support, and there's no reason you should support me and mine, too. So I'm leaving, and I'll take the children with me."

"Now wait a bit, now, Will, there's no need to be hasty," Seb said. "I didn't mean you was to leave us— just that you should give a hand a bit about the tavern. Course, I know you got your songs to write, but—" Seb had already regretted his outburst, for he was essentially a peaceful and kindly man.

"No, you were right," William said firmly. "I've decided to go back to my old trade—acting. My old troupe are in need of an experienced man, and I should like to get back on the road again."

"But what about the children?" Seb asked, perplexed. "You can't take them with you, man, traveling about like gypsies, and Little Will not three years old yet."

"They'll be all right," William said. "As you pointed out, Ambrose is running wild already. I'll be able to keep an eye on him."

"But the girls—and what about their schooling?" Seb was thoroughly upset now. "Look here, Will, I'm sorry if I spoke out of turn the other day. I didn't mean nothing by it—you know me. Let's forget all about it and let bygones be bygones, eh?"

William smiled and took Seb's large calloused hand in his in a cordial shake.

"My dear Seb," he said, I'm not leaving because I'm angry with you; don't think it. It's just that I have the feeling that I need to go traveling again. There's something evading me here—something I'm not quite getting hold of—" He frowned, his words wandering off vaguely into silence.

Seb stared at him in distress and bewilderment. "Well at least," he said, realizing that William meant to go, "leave the children here. We'll take care of them."

William laughed. "Ambrose would never forgive me if I left him behind. Come, Seb, cheer up—they'll be all right."

Nothing Seb could say would change his mind, and when the children were told they were so wildly excited at the idea that there was no going back on it. So a few days later William set out to rejoin Lord Hovenden's Men, and Seb and the whole family turned out to watch him go. His belongings were packed onto the large white mule, and the two little girls, Susan and Mary, rode in front of the bundles. William carried Will in a canvas sling on his back and held Ambrose, too excited to speak, by the hand. At the corner of the road he turned to wave and then plodded on toward London and his new life—or back to the old one, perhaps.

There were changes in the troupe—Austin Hoby was dead, Jack Fallow had set up as a tavern-keeper and Dick Johnson had gone to another troupe—but Kit Mulcaster was still there and welcomed Will as a kindred spirit.

"It will be so good to have someone intelligent to talk to again," he said. "And your singing and playing will give us distinction. There is so much competition these days, one needs something to single us out. But what of these poor children of yours? Can your lad sing? He's pretty enough to play the women's parts if he can learn the lines."

William smiled. "Ambrose will be an asset to us, and as for the girls—they are young yet, but they can sew, and I daresay they'll make themselves useful around the place."

Kit frowned slightly. "That's well enough, but I think you'll need a woman to look after the child, will you not?"

"As to that, there are always women," William said carelessly, "but I don't see why I can't look after them just as well. It doesn't seem to me there's anything very mysterious in it. Just feed 'em when they're hungry and see they wash from time to time. They're like animals—they let you know what they want. They bellow when they want food, and when they want sleep—why they lie down and take it."

Kit laughed. "A whole new philosophy of education," he said. "I dare say they'll be happier for it than most children."

"And now," William said more enthusiastically, "let's talk about important things—what plays have we to come? And since you mention Ambrose, I've been working out a very pretty song that would sound well if there's a part that fits it—"

Thus began a strange and wonderful life for the children, moving about from place to place, from tavern to tavern, riding on the white mule or in the swaying baggage cart with the costume hampers; sleeping in cheap lodgings or in attics above taprooms, even sometimes in haystacks or, if sleep overcame them before anyone had thought to put them to bed, on benches or floors or wherever they happened to be sitting. They grew used to foraging for food and knew how to play upon the sympathies of a moist-eyed landlady or tavern wench, and many's the time they were cared for by a kind-hearted doxy or a sentimental slut when Papa was too busy to look after them.

They watched the plays and helped out in man ways, moving stools, prompting, sewing costumes, copy ing out parts; Ambrose, to his intense delight, wa soon playing small parts and singing songs, while Susa and Mary provided thunder and battle noises offstag and played drums and pipes. They saw many strang sights, witnessed inexplicable behavior, took part in wild flight or two from the bailiffs; and sat in innumerable taverns by candlelight, with drunken men all around them singing vulgar songs, whores plying their trade on either side, while Papa and Uncle Kit discussed plays and music, until they fell asleep in the sawdust or were whisked off to bed by some disapproving innkeeper's wife. It was a wonderful life, and none of them would have changed it for all of Lombard Street.

In the autumn of 1581 Celia gave birth to twins, a girl and a boy who were named Aletheia and Amory. Jan and Mary were delighted, and Nanette agreed a little grudgingly—for she disapproved of the names—that they were the prettiest babies she had ever seen.

"Of course they are," Jan said teasingly. "They are your great-grandchildren. They will obviously be not only the most handsome children that ever were but also the most intelligent."

Gabriel, leaning over the crib, stared at them in perplexity. "I think they are ugly," he said, "all red and wrinkled. And how can you tell if they are intelligent when they can't speak or anything?"

"Never mind, one can tell," Nanette said. "And push the crib a little closer, child, and lift that frill out of the way so that I can see." Gabriel obeyed—he was wary of Nanette's sharp tongue. Nanette looked at the babies with secret longing. She could not hold them in her arms, for of late her hands had become so swollen and twisted and painful that she could barely lift a spoon

nd had sometimes, when the pain was really bad, to
etire to her room and be fed like a baby by Audrey, an
ndignity she felt the worse because she had always
peen a little vain of her white hands. Those that live by
:he flesh shall perish by the flesh, her teaching reminded her—but she wished she could have held the
babies.

"It is good to have new young ones in the house,"
she said. "A house without babies in it is hearth-cold. I
wish Jane would let us have Nehemiah here—it would
cheer Paul so much, and he has been so low recently."

"Do you think he is ill?" Jan asked.

"I don't know. I think perhaps he may be. He seems
to be eating less and getting thinner all the time. And
then—" she stopped and would say no more, but she
had been about to say that Audrey had heard from
Clement that Paul was often sick shortly after eating,
would suffer terrible pains in his stomach and then
vomit. There had been loose talk of poisoning—
servants will always talk of poisoning in cases of sudden
illness or death—but there was no one who could possibly have any interest in killing poor Paul. Except—it was
the except that stopped Nanette. Nicholas and Celia
and their children were established in Morland Place,
and Jane kept Nehemiah at home, at Shawes. If Paul
died while Nehemiah was still an infant—yet it was a
monstrous thought. It would need a person not only un-
scrupulous and greedy—which Nanette believed Mary
Seymour might be—but also utterly depraved and lost
to decency, which she could not believe of her. Mary
had been well brought up, and Nanette could not believe she would turn herself to wickedness, even if she
had left the True Faith and become a Protestant.

Paul, once he had taken to his bed, sank rapidly,
flesh falling away from him almost visibly as it became
more and more difficult for him to keep anything

down. Nanette, taking over the reins of the busines
from him, took time to have his food carefully watched
brought directly from the kitchen by the cook who had
prepared it and tasted by that cook in her presence before it was fed to Paul, for she wanted to be quite sure
in her own mind that there was no truth in the rumors.
Her precautions made the servants surer than ever that
the master was being poisoned, and in the end she was
forced to call them together in the great hall and to
speak to them severely on the subject of loose gossip.
But the precautions made no difference to Paul. Shortly
all he could keep down was thin gruel or lentil porridge,
and after a day or two he turned his head away from
that and would take nothing but a sip of wine from time
to time. It was evident that he was dying, and Simon
told Nanette that it was time he made his peace with
God.

Nanette and Simon went in together to Paul's room,
the great bedchamber, where he lay propped on pillows
in the Butts bed, and Nanette saw at once that they had
left it almost too late. Paul was so wasted away that he
scarcely made a shape under the counterpane, and his
face was like a skull on the pillows, even his lips shrunk
back against his teeth, nothing living in his visage but
his eyes that burned with a sullen anger, as if they were
the spokesmen for his trapped and cornered soul. He
did not want to die. Clement was there beside the bed,
weeping and trying to hide it. He had been with Paul all
his life. Simon went to the bed and took the lifeless
hand and spoke the words, the familiar, comforting
Latin, and Nanette knelt with difficulty and folded her
twisted, painful hands together. Behind her, others
came into the room, other members of the household,
Celia and Nicholas, Jane and Hezekiah, and Nanette
shut from her mind the pity of the death that was attended by only one of Paul's many children.

Simon asked Paul for a sigh of repentance, but Paul

uld not speak or move, and only the dully burning
es moved from face to face, fixing at last on Simon's
ce in what the latter chose to interpret as the required
gn. He anointed the dying man with the chrism and
ade the sign of the cross and then came to help Na-
tte to her feet so that she could come to Paul's side.
ne took Nanette's other elbow and gave her first
ace, acknowledging a senior right to her own.

"Paul," Nanette said, kneeling again at the bedside
that they were on a level, "I know you die in the
rue Faith. I'll see that Mass is said for you as long as
here is a chapel at Morland Place, and that your fu-
eral is properly carried out. "The burning eyes fixed
n her face. "Is there something you want to say? What
s it? Is it Jane you want?" The eyes did not move from
hers. "Is it about your will? You leave everything to
Jane's children, don't you?" But there was no response,
only the harsh sound of his breathing and the stare of
his eyes.

One by one the servants and family said good-bye to
him, some weeping, some solemn, many kissing his
hand and calling on him in gratitude for his long and
just dealing with them. But there was no way of telling
if he even knew they were there, and all through the
day and into the evening he lay motionless, his eyes
open and staring, as he struggled inwardly with death;
until at nine in the evening, when the candles were
being changed for the second time, Paul Morland of
Morland Place drew his last breath, and his daughter
Jane closed his eyes.

CHAPTER EIGHTEEN

Middle age came gently to Lettice. In 1585 she was thirty-eight, a handsome and dignified woman with the fears and doubts of youth behind her, settled, it seemed forever, into the routine of her life. She lived now at Birnie Castle, never visiting Aberlady, and time and custom had made Birnie her own, her home, run in accordance with her wishes. As the old servants died, she replaced them with others of her choice, and the atmosphere grew easier so that it was not necessary to be so circumspect in behavior. Lettice still gave an outward show of being a Protestant, but she and Kat and Douglass now said their prayers together in the old form in her chamber, and it was unspoken knowledge in the household that they did so.

It was very much a woman's household. Jean, Lettice's stepdaughter, was thirty-one, still unmarried, for Rob had never troubled himself to find her a husband, and she, as well as being a companion to Lettice, was her lieutenant, doing much of the running of the household rather like a steward. She had a mind for detail and a prodigious memory and was moreover very thrifty: Lettice often thought how sad it was that she

ad been born too high in rank to marry a country gentleman, for she would have made an excellent wife to
someone of limited means. As it was, she used up her
considerable energies making lists of stores and laun-
dry, running back and forth from pantries to cellars
with an enormous bunch of keys in her hand or ruining
her eyes darning linen by candlelight.

Lesley, who was twenty-four, was more quiet and
docile and in fact almost lethargic. Her passions were
music and food. She had been a plump girl, and as a
woman she grew fat, comforting herself for her unmarried state by eating sweetmeats and dreaming of the
man who would one day ride up to the castle walls on a
white horse and rescue her. Rob laughed at her on his
occasional visits, called her his Easter hen and threatened to have her killed and dressed for dinner. Lesley
accepted the gibes placidly, taking them as fun, for she
adored her father and could not have supposed that he
did not love her, too. She would never allow Jean to
criticize him for leaving them unmarried, always finding some excuse for him.

"He would have wed us if he could," she would say,
nibbling a sugar violet. "It is hard to find a suitable
person of our rank. He must be very distressed that he
has failed so far."

And Jean would shake her head impatiently. "You're
such a fool—so far indeed! We are unwed because he
does not care a plucked hen for either of us, but you
are too stupid to see it." Jean, too, adored her father,
waited with trembling for his visits, was stimulated by
his sardonic humor; but she was too clear-sighted to
suppose her love was returned by the father who had
ignored and despised her for most of her life. He was
coming, now when it was too late for her, to like her a
little, and would sometimes speak kindly to her. When
he did she would, despite herself, reply coldly or
sharply and leave the room. His kindness was harder to

bear than his cruelty: she could not let him pity her. T
Lesley he would bring gifts—boxes of sweetmeats
ribbons for her lute—and ask her to play and sing f
him, and she, withdrawn into her own world of fantas
accepted the attentions without irony; but Jean cou
not do that, and she both despised and envied her hal
sister.

Lettice noticed all this, and noticed also, which wa
strange and wonderful to her, that both of her step
daughters loved Douglass and were never touched b
jealousy that she was her father's favorite. Douglass a
seventeen seemed blessed with everything a young gir
could hope to have—startling beauty, high spirits
grace, charm, wit and intelligence. She had a swee
singing voice, could play three musical instruments
could ride as well as a man and would gallop about the
park every fine day on the pretty little chestnut mare
that Rob had bought for her, coming in with her cheeks
bright with blood, her curls tumbled and her eyes like
stars, laughing with the sheer joy of being alive. And
then Lesley would cry, "Oh you pretty thing!" and hug
her and offer her the best sweetmeat from her box, and
Jean would say gruffly, "Your hair is all awry, child—
come let me pin it for you"—attentions that were equal
in their intent and accepted by Douglass with equal
charming facility. If she had not had a naturally sweet
temper and a loving heart she could have been horribly
spoiled, but she loved everyone and everything, right
down to the least spit dog in the kitchen, and everyone
loved her, willy-nilly.

Lettice was a little afraid that Rob meant to leave
Douglass unwed just as he had done his other daughters, for, though he evidently loved Douglass best,
brought her presents, seemed to like simply being in her
company—often he would take her out riding alone
with him, without even a servant to attend them—yet
he had never spoken about marriage plans and never

ntroduced any eligible men to Birnie Castle. As Dougass reached marriageable age, Lettice intended every :ime he came to bring up the subject, but somehow she never got around to it. Her times with him were so few and so precious that she could never think of anything when he was there other than that he *was* there.

The quiet house buzzed like a disturbed swarm when the master came home. He would always send a messenger on ahead with a day's warning, sometimes more, and then there would be scrubbings and beatings of hangings and changings of linen, and bathing, and taking out best clothes, and such activities in the kitchen that you might have thought the King himself was coming. And then, always an hour or two before he was looked for, Rob would ride up and stride into the house, bringing the smell of the outdoors with him and making the atmosphere crackle like lightning. The dogs would go mad, racing back and forth and barking fit to burst, and in the din the women would run down to the hall to greet him, and Rob would shout orders, and the servants would bob and grin in embarrassed delight.

"Where are my women folk? Get down, Bran, down Fich—Fergus, call these dogs off! And tell Wullie to see to the horses. Ah, there you are—Douglass, my pretty sparrow, here is a *boîte* for you—go open it quick and tell me if you like it. Lesley, you have been fatting yourself up for my return, like the prodigal father I am—ah yes, says Jean, *prodigal* is the right word. Will you send for wine for me, daughter? And Lady Hamilton, how goes it with you? How do you endure this soft, woman-scented world? Come here till I look at you."

Lettice trembled at his touch, came forward for a formal salute upon the cheek, looked up into his eyes and was lost again. Their passion for each other did not wane, although as Lettice grew older, Rob took time to settle in before dismissing the servants and taking her to

bed. Sometimes when he came home he brought frien
with him, and then they would not be able even
touch each other until after the feasting was done a
everyone retired for the night. But the constant facto
were their physical joy in each other and the wonderf
times afterward when, lying sated and exhausted t
gether, they would talk. Sometimes, in the long montl
between his visits, Lettice would try to bring to min
their times together, and it seemed to her that it was tl
talking she really missed most. When he had been gon
some time, she found it hard to bring his face clearly t
mind, but she could without any difficulty remembe
what it was like to lie in the dark, her body sore an
tingling from their lovemaking, her head on Rob's bulg
ing, muscular shoulder and his big, hard hand idly o
her breast; and she could hear as clearly as if it wer
really there the sound of his voice talking on endlessly
telling her everything that had happened to him since
they last met, telling her his plans, his thoughts, his
pains, all the small dross of his days, knowing without it
ever having to be said that everything was interesting to
her, asking her opinion as if she were a man—no, better than that, as if she were he and there were no distinction in the dark between his self and hers.

And Lettice's soul fed upon it, upon the talk. She
loved the sound of his voice, its deep, rich timbre, its
flowing, sonorous beauty, as if it were a new kind of
musical instrument; she loved it even and sensible,
rudely mocking, hoarse with passion, ringing with
laughter, sharp with anger; when he spoke, she felt the
touch of his voice with her skin, and when she recalled
it in his absence, it made her hair rise on her scalp and
her spine tingle. She knew that it was wrong for a Catholic to love anyone as much as that, that such love
should be reserved for God alone, but when she prayed,
that part of her mind closed itself off despite her, and
she could not mention it, could not pray for forgiveness

lest, forgiven, she ceased to love. If I pay for it afterward, she would think when she rose from her knees,
yet I will have it, for it is life to me.

When he came for his summer visit that year, 1585,
Lettice felt that there was something troubling him that
he was not telling her about. He seemed quieter, and
though he behaved much as usual when in public, there
were fits of abstraction that were not like him. He spent
more time with his daughters than was usual, too, and
Lettice noticed that he was being kind to them—his
teasing of Lesley held almost a crooning note, he spoke
to Jean with a gentle respect, and Douglass he took
upon his knee as he used to when she was a child and
looked at her with what seemed almost like wistful admiration.

Lettice watched him, feasting her eyes; he was growing older, she noticed, his face more heavily lined,
streaks of gray in his beard and hair, and the mocking
humor in his eyes no longer concealed what was underneath—a sadness, was it, or a weariness. She studied
him, saw with a touch of apprehension how sharp the
lines were around his eyes, how when he was not thinking about it his mouth drooped at the corners and his
shoulders stooped a little. She had a sudden awareness
of what her life would be like if he were to die, and she
shivered at the bleak emptiness of it and thrust it from
her mind, as one will shut out the night and the cold in
winter and draw nearer to the fire. Rob saw the movement and looked across at her, and his mouth curled in
his old sardonic smile.

"What does her ladyship? Are you cold, Madam?
Have you not yet lost your English squeamishness? Or
was it a goose walking across your grave, a *memento
mori*, sent by God no doubt to remind you that the fair
are especially mortal. Aye, God has always had a predi-
lection for the young and the fair. The old, gnarled and
ugly, like the wicked, he leaves to flourish in this

unweeded garden of a world." He hugged Douglass abruptly, making her grunt with surprise. "So beware, my pretty little finch, and do not go jumping that mare of yours over any more thorn hedges. Are you aware, Madam," he said to Lettice sternly, "how this baggage has been risking her tender body and pretty face jumping hedges three feet thick and more bristling with thorns than an angry sticklepig? For shame, Douglass, how shall it be with thee if thy face be scratched? All thy lovers will desert thee." He kissed her hard on her rosy cheek and then slapped her behind, pushing her off his lap.

"And now, away with you—away all, I would speak with Lady Hamilton alone. Go to bed. Good night, children. God bless you."

Lettice waited with growing apprehension as they slowly cleared the room, curtsying to their father, gathering up their little belongings; and when they had finally left and she and Rob were alone together, he stood up, stretched and met her eye, raising an eyebrow in sardonic inquiry.

"Well?"

"Lord, but you're in a strange humor tonight," Lettice said nervously.

He smiled and began to walk about the room. "I like to be unpredictable. It is the essence of survival. And survival is very much on my mind tonight."

"Rob, you're not ill?" she asked anxiously.

"No, child," he said absently. He walked about awhile, clasping his hands behind his back. "You know, don't you," he said at last, "that I have been working for some time to place Queen Mary on the throne of England?" He had never actually told her that, but she had pieced together hints and fragments of information he had dropped from time to time.

"I guessed it."

He smiled briefly. "Aye, lassie, I expected you would. An intelligent woman is a dangerous companion. Well, well—you know at what, and perhaps why, I have been occupied these years. Things have gone badly. People promise, and do not keep their promise. Now the English have passed an act to say if their queen is murdered, Mary shall never have the throne— ah, no," he added quickly as Lettice opened her mouth to protest, "I never gave the nod to a plan of murder, though there's others would. But Mary is now imprisoned and well watched. Sir Amyas Paulet—do you know him?"

"Yes, he was a distant relative of my father," Lettice said.

Rob nodded. "Well, he has been given charge of the Queen, and he seems incorruptible, hard though that is to believe. And now, my child, now I have come by the information that our dearly beloved King James is treating in secret with Queen Elizabeth."

Lettice made a small noise of surprise. Rob interpreted it without difficulty.

"For money, I suspect," he said. "He would give a great deal to have an income that does not go through the Council. So you see, times are hard, and we must move soon, and firmly."

"But Rob, why are you telling me all this?" Lettice said.

He cocked his head at her. "Intelligent woman, she goes straight to the heart of the matter. God, if you had only been born a man, what a friend, what a companion you would have made! I would have ridden to the ends of the earth, dared anything with such a one as you at my shoulder. But as it is—" he turned away from her with an abrupt and oddly uncalculated movement, as if he had been surprised by himself, and Lettice clasped her hands in fear.

"Rob, what is it? What are you going to do to me?"

He had his back to her, his hand to his face, and his voice was oddly muffled. "Hurt you. Kill you," he said.

Lettice grew very still and very cold, and after a long moment he turned again to look at her questioningly. She met his eyes, trying to express in a look all that she could not say, of her love for him, and trust, and consent in his will.

He gave her a crooked smile. "What?" he said, "why do you not scream? Call for help? Have you no normal decent fear? What"—he came toward her, stretched out his hands and closed them on her throat above her soft ruff—"what if I strangle you now, squeeze the life out of you right here and now? Or —I have my dagger in my belt. You are so little and weak I could hold you still with one hand and stab you to the heart with the other."

His hands moved from her throat to her body, gripping her to either side just below her breasts. "Will you not scream now, my lady?" he whispered, holding her gaze. She grew weak with longing and felt her body trembling—or was it his trembling, communicated through his hands? His crooked smile broadened. "Why, you shameless slut," he murmured, "you are not trembling with fear at all. It is something else, is it not, Lady Hamilton? I might kill you, if I swive you first." He bent his head with a deadly movement like a bird swooping and kissed her, and she unfolded outward at the touch of his lips like a ripe fig. She felt him change, felt him wanting her, and he picked her up and carried her to the bed and lay her down there, and she looked up at him, dazed and drowsy with longing like a pollen-drunk bee. But he did not climb onto the bed with her to make love. He sat down on the edge of the bed beside her and took her hands in his and looked down at her with such sudden naked pity that she was shocked instantly out of her languor, and she knew that what he had said was true—he was going to hurt her, kill her.

"Child," he said, "I am in increasing danger, and I

must have a son. I want to get a son before I die, and so I need a new wife. I am going to divorce you."

Lettice jerked upright in shock, and he pushed her back down gently. She searched his face for the truth, and it was there in that same deadly pity.

"But you can't!" she said at last.

He smiled without humor. "Oh yes I can, my little Papist. I am a Protestant, remember, and a highly placed member of the Council. I can divorce you, and I will."

"But—but—Rob—" Lettice could not assimilate the idea. She had expected pain and death, but this she could not comprehend.

He stroked her hair sadly. "I shall miss you, you strange thing," he said. "I never knew, when I plucked you like a meadow flower, how you would stick to me like a burr, stick in my mind, irritating but—God alive, I shall miss the irritation. I am sorry to hurt you, my child, but it must be."

"But what will happen to me?" she managed to ask.

He grew brisk, practical. "I have a house in England, in Kendal, and I shall send you there. You may take the children if you wish, and servants. I will send you money, of course, but I must have Birnie and Aberlady for my new wife."

"Have—you chosen her?" Lettice asked, her mouth dry.

He smiled. "It cannot interest you to know that," he said gently. He waited for the next question, watching her tenderly.

"When?" she said at last.

"Soon," he said. "You will be at Kendal by Christmas."

"And you? Shall I see you?" That was the hardest question to ask, because she already knew the answer.

"No," he said gently. "Not for a long time. Perhaps never."

"Oh God," she said, and she began to cry. He held her silently while she wept, the great sobs racking her body as if her heart were literally breaking, some vital cord snapping inside, leaving her broken and deranged. He made no attempt to calm or soothe her, just held her as he might have held a dying comrade on a battle-field until the storm of grief was spent, and he lay her back exhausted on the pillows. Tenderly he wiped her face with his kerchief, and as his hand passed away, she caught it with hers and carried it to her lips, and her drenched, swollen eyes looked up into his.

"Please," she said.

He knew what she was asking. He smiled ironically. "Why not? It can do no harm." He undressed her and took off his own clothes and lay down on her, naked flesh to flesh, and made love to her, slowly and ten-derly, quite unlike their usual passionate encounters. There seemed healing in it, and they clung together softly with underwater movements like strands of wav-ing weed, until he came in her, shudderingly, but almost without movement. She slept then like a worn-out child, and he pulled the covers over them both and lay awake, holding her in his arms. The candles sputtered and went out, leaving only the fire glowing, for the bed curtains were not pulled. She woke then and turned to him hun-grily, and he made love to her again, and again and again through the night, in the blackness of the dead hour, in the thin gray of before-dawn, to the shrilling of the dawn chorus, they turned to each other in passion, trying to assuage a hunger that was generated by what it fed on.

At six he drew away from her at last and stood up and began to dress. She watched him from the pillows, so exhausted she seemed flattened, barely denting the mattress. Dressed, he turned to look at her, and a whole world of sadness, like all the grief there had ever been for mankind rolled together, passed between them, severing them forever. She knew that he was going then, that very minute, and that he would not come back, and there was nothing in her that was capable of comprehending so vast a loss. Without speaking, he turned and left her. It was the first of September.

By Christmas the small household was settled at Kendal. Lettice discovered that things had been in train for a long time before Rob had spoken to her about them, and she guessed that he had wanted to leave her happy for as long as possible. The divorce was granted in October, Lettice was exiled from Scotland for Papism, and on the same day that the divorce was dated, he married the young girl he had chosen, a rich gentleman's daughter who was already six months pregnant. Lettice understood and approved the caution that had made Rob wait to see that his new choice could conceive before marrying her; it was the same kind of ploy he had used with her and, who knew, perhaps his first two wives as well.

She was still dazed at the change in her life, added to which she was feeling unwell, tired and sick, often vomiting, and feeling strange pains in her back and sides. She wondered vaguely if she were being poisoned and found she did not greatly care. In January Rob's new wife gave birth to a son, the news reaching Lettice indirectly through the servants and that strange network of information that always exists among the serving classes, and the news left her unmoved, though she was glad for him and hoped he would not be disappointed again.

In February Jean, who had been increasingly worried about Lettice's condition, asked to speak to her privately, and when they were alone, she said, "Madam, forgive me, but I must speak plainly. Your health has not been good recently?"

"No," Lettice said dully.

"And you did not have your flux last month?"

"No—but—"

"Madam, has it not crossed your mind that you might be pregnant?"

Lettice's eyes opened wide at that. It had not.

"Count back," Jean urged. "And I have noticed that though you eat very little, you are growing stouter. Surely it must be—"

"But my fluxes have been—irregular—for a long time. And I have not—I mean"—she blushed—"it was in August, September, when your father and I last—"

"And you have had a flux since then?"

"Not a normal one, no, but there has been a little blood from time to time."

The two women stared at each other. The more Lettice thought about it, the more it seemed that Jean might have come upon the truth. That last night between her and Rob—her flux had been due two weeks later, and in the daze of grief and the confusion of moving home, she could not remember if she had seen it. In November there had been a spot or two of blood—and in December—the truth was, she had been too lethargic and unhappy to notice particularly.

Suddenly she put her hands over her face and began to laugh hysterically. Jean came closer and put her arms around her stepmother in concern, and the laughter changed to tears. Jean held her soothingly, murmuring words of comfort until Lettice was quiet again, and then, as the latter pulled away and began to collect herself and dry her face, she asked, "What shall you do?"

Their eyes met, exchanging silent question and answer. It was too late, too late. "What is there to do?" Lettice said finally. She moved restlessly, like an animal in pain, looking around the small, bare room in distaste. Outside, the February wind howled bitterly over the Kendal hills. "I hate it here," she said vehemently. It reminded her too much of what had happened. Suddenly she thought of Morland Place, its snug rooms, lazed windows, great log fires and charcoal braziers, warmth and comfort, the way it was in her childhood. A flood of tiny memories fell into place in her mind like fragments of mosaic—her mother brushing out her hair before her silver mirror, her father saying grace before dinner, the smell of mincemeat pies and spiced wine at Christmas, John helping her pull her bow on Sundays, the smell of her own hot skin when she sat on the grass of the Italian garden in summer.

Jean, watching her face, saw it light and change, and she said anxiously, "What is it? What are you thinking?"

Lettice stared at Jean, wondering why she had not thought of it before. The longing came over her, stronger and stronger, quite simply to go home.

"Why not?" she cried out, holding her hands out to Jean and beginning to laugh. "What a fool I've been! We'll go home to Morland Place, all of us, as soon as the weather is better. I shall be well again there, and everything will be all right."

Her sudden joy was so infectious that without really understanding why, Jean began to laugh, too. Lettice seized her hands and in a moment the two middle-aged women were whirling around the room in a mad dance.

It was a very different Morland Place Lettice returned to in early April from the home she had left as a young girl to go to Court: the place was as different as the woman who returned to it. Her father was dead, her brothers and sisters all gone except for Jane, all the Butts cousins gone, and the house seeming empty and deserted by comparison to her childhood days. It was not empty, of course, but there were silences and tensions where there should have been laughter and conversation, and Lettice, who had grown sensitive to the things people did not say, soon worked out what the situation was.

Nanette was still there—astonishingly, for she wa[s] incomprehensibly old, almost eighty, shrunken an[d] twisted by her swollen joints so that she could no longe[r] walk or dress herself, but still living by her will, stil[l] sounding the same, except that her tongue was sharp-ened by pain now, still running the house and oversee-ing the business, her mind unclouded by the deteriora-tion of her body. She was moved from place to place in the house in a chair with long handles carried by two footmen, for she would not retire to bed, knowing that she would lose her grip on the reins if she did so. Let-tice understood that, having run a household of her own, and Nanette responded quickly to the sympathy and likeness of experience she perceived in Lettice. Na-nette had herself woken early in the morning so that two maids could wash and dress her in time for her to be carried down to the chapel for the early celebration, and from then on she seemed to be everywhere in the house, always with her four attendants—two young maids and two strong footmen (Audrey and Matthew were both dead now)—so that her moving seemed as significant as a procession.

The household over which Nanette grimly kept con-trol was much reduced. There were Nicholas and Celia Chapham, who seemed in awe of Nanette and avoided her when they could, to live a curiously mouselike exis-tence in hidden corners of the house, and Gabriel Chapham, a tall, handsome and incorrigibly lazy youth of eighteen, who preferred to live away from the stern eyes of his parents and had enough boldness and charm to amuse Nanette and keep her from noticing his ex-ploits. In the nursery, under the tuition of Simon leBel, were the twins Aletheia and Amory, who were five, and Nehemiah, who was six, and that was all.

Margaret Butts had married an elderly merchant and lived with him in York in a large house on Fossgate. Jane and Hezekiah still lived at Shawes and came over once a week, on the Sabbath, for Mass and to spend the day and visit their son. Lettice was surprised that fhey did not come more often, until she noticed how frequently Jan amd Mary came over from Watermill House. Of course they had more excuse—there was not much of an estate to run at Watermill, and their mother and children were at Morland Place, to say nothing of the grandchildren. But Lettice found something brash and nervous about them that made her uneasy, and she soon saw the conflicts that existed between them and Nanette and understood why Nanette clung so grimly to a life that must long since have become wearisome to her.

Most of the conflicts were unspoken ones, but that of religion came up time and time again. Since Paul had died, Nanette had defiantly replaced all the forbidden religious items in their places and had the Mass said as before, three times a day in the chapel, for all the Old Faith followers in the household and on the estate; and there were many Faithful in the villages round about who had taken to coming in to the Mass, emboldened by Nanette's courage. Of course, it was forbidden and dangerous and had inevitably attracted the attention of the authorities, but when the Justice of the Peace in person had come to remonstrate with Nanette and warn her, she had faced him out and talked him down, and neither he nor anyone else had dared to proceed further against the Morlands. Of course it would be different when Nanette was dead, but while she was alive the force of her personality conferred some strange kind of immunity on them.

For Lettice it was blissful to be able to practice her religion openly again, and in a proper chapel with a proper priest. When they discovered that Jean and Lesley were Protestants, the Chaphams tried to enlist their support in the battle against Nanette, but Jean refused to have any part in the quarrel and made sure that Les-

ley, who was silly enough to have been persuaded
took no part, either. Their loyalty was to Lettice. The
felt very comfortable at Morland Place. For Jean ther
were all her old duties waiting for her, and Nanette
brought out the best in her and conferred authority on
her, which she had never had at home; Lesley was
happy as long as she had a modicum of comfort and
plenty to eat, and there was a very fine clavicytherium
to be played, and an appreciative audience in Nanette.

And for Douglass there were fine horses, hounds and
hawks, and such freedom, such wide open spaces to be
ridden over, plenty of servants to accompany her, good
hunting, no need to keep within the demesne lands and
no fear of being ambushed and murdered when she set
foot out of doors. Also there were young men around,
and young men were a commodity she had had little
chance to enjoy. Gabriel was very attentive to her,
flirted with her, danced with her, fetched and carried
for her, hunted with her and often took her for rides
over to Watermill House to visit his parents. It was obvious that his parents approved strongly of their friendship, and Douglass was innocent enough to think it was
because he visited them more often in her company.

Lettice watched her closely and soon discovered she
was in no danger, even from so handsome and charming a wretch as Gabriel. He had not what it took to
move Douglass's heart, and though she enjoyed being
fussed over and flattered, as was quite normal, she had
a sweet temper and sound enough principles not to have
her head turned by his attentions.

By the end of April Lettice and her household had
settled in at Morland Place, and Lettice could turn her
attention to the approaching birth of her child. She was
very large, and the month of May was very hot. She
was glad not to move around much and spent much of
the time sitting talking with Nanette in the shade out in
the gardens or by the open window in the solar or win-

ter parlour. Lettice generally had some piece of sewing with her, but Nanette of course had no diversion for her hands and liked to talk or read aloud to occupy herself, and in their long hours of conversation Lettice talked for the first time to another person about her relationship with Rob, while Nanette told Lettice all that had happened in the family since she went away, and of the problems facing it now.

"I dread the winter," Nanette told her one day. "The pains in my joints grow worse in the winter. In summer sometimes they go away completely, with doses of willow-bark extract, but in the winter the pain is almost more than I can endure. And then when one is old, one is more vulnerable in the cold weather. I am afraid I will die."

Nanette looked down at her clawlike hands, the fingers drawn in to the palms as though by strings. "I have written again to your brother John," she said abruptly. "I am seventy-eight, and I may not survive another year. He must send us Thomas, if he will not come himself. I hope he will come. I have told him that you are here, and I pray his curiosity to see you will bring him. But at all events, he must send us Thomas. The boy is eighteen in July, just the age to take over."

"But perhaps he does not want to take over," Lettice said.

"If he sees another's hands reaching for what should be his, it will wake the instinct in him," Nanette said. "The thing is to get him here. Once he is here, trust me for it."

Lettice's pains began nine months to the day from the last time she lay with Rob, and in the afternoon of the first of June her child was born, a large, healthy-seeming boy with a great thatch of black hair. He was not red and wrinkled, as new babies often are, but, as Gabriel remarked when he saw the infant, "He's

smooth and golden, like a ripe fruit. He's a handsom
baby, Grandmother, not like the twins when they wer
born."

He was born in Eleanor's bed, which Nanette ha
vacated for the occasion, and Lettice lay there in som
state while people came and went, admiring the baby
asking kindly after her health. She felt exhausted physi
cally and emotionally and was grateful simply to hav
around her so many that she loved. There was dea
Jean, who had been with her all through the labor and
had been the greatest help and comfort, though she had
never borne a child of her own. She seemed to know
exactly what Lettice wanted without being told and
would see to it quietly and without fuss.

Lesley was a comfort, too, for she was happy to sit
for hours beside the bed, saying and doing nothing,
without growing bored or restless, and she was charmed
by the baby and promised to be a most doting sister.
Douglass came and went from time to time, bringing
her mother flowers and scraps of news from the outside
world, shy about the baby but charming in her youth
and beauty and happiness. And Nanette in her sharp-
grained way was a comfort, too, and knew when to shoo
everyone but Jean away so that Lettice could sleep.

The baby Lettice held in her arms hardly seemed to
be hers at all, but his beauty and his helplessness moved
her deeply, as did the anomaly of his position in the
world.

"It is hard for you, I know," Nanette said. "In the
eyes of the church you are married still—and yet what
of the child of the new wife? I lived through it, my
dear, with King Henry, and the Princess Mary and the
Princess Elizabeth. Divorce is a dreadful thing, and no
good can come of it. It is a game in which there are no
winners and everyone loses."

But it was to Jean that Lettice spoke her mind at last.

Jean came in to bathe Lettice's face and found her
rocking the baby in her arms and weeping, great hot
tears falling on the child's robe and leaving gray marks
on the white linen. Jean took the baby from her and
laid him in his crib, and then took Lettice in her arms
and rocked her like a child.

"Oh Jean—my poor little boy—and Rob—all for
nothing," she sobbed incoherently.

"I know, I know," Jean said, holding back her own
tears. So much sorrow, and for what?"

Lettice lifted her face, swollen with weeping, and
said, "It is the irony of it that hurts so much—the irony
of that last night together. And yet if he hadn't already
been suing for divorce, it might not have happened. But
I keep thinking—what if—"

"It doesn't do," Jean said, stroking the hair from her
stepmother's face. "No one can ever know what would
have happened. What is, is all that counts. Come, hush
your crying, you'll make yourself ill. How hot you are!
Your forehead burns—you have given yourself a fever
with crying. Be still now, rest, and let me bathe you
with cool water."

Lettice lay back on the pillows, and gradually her
shuddering stopped, and she felt only terribly weary.
"What will become of him?" she murmured. Jean did
not answer, not knowing if she meant the child or the
father. "Should I tell him, Jean? Should I write to him
and let him know? Would it be cruel? And yet he is the
father—perhaps it would be crueller not to."

"I can't advise you," Jean said, "except that it would
serve no purpose." She brought the cool cloth and began to wipe Lettice's hot face.

Lettice sighed. "That feels good. I think I will write,
Jean, because you see, whatever happens, I am his wife.
And he loves me—he wanted a son. I will write. I'll
write tomorrow."

But when the morrow came she did not write, for she

was burning and shaking with fever. The fever cam
and went, each time leaving her a little weaker, and stil
she spoke of writing, and still she could not get the
strength to sit up. At the end of the week she lapsec
into unconsciousness, and when she awoke she found
Simon leBel beside her, holding her hand.

For a moment the significance did not dawn on her,
and then she whispered, "Simon? Am I dying, then?"

He nodded, squeezing her hand, unable to speak. She
looked from him to Jean, who was standing behind
him, and saw the tears running down Jean's face, and
knew the truth.

"My child, you must cleanse your mind of earthly
cares and think on your Savior," Simon said gently.
Tears stung Lettice's eyes, but she was too weak even
to cry, and they rolled from under her lids heavily like
drops of blood. I do not want to die, she thought, not
while Rob lives. And yet I am so tired. But there is my
baby—who will look after my baby?

"Jean," she said. What an effort it was to speak. And
how dark it was in here. Why did they not light the
candles? "What o'clock is it?"

"It is ten o'clock a' morning," Jean said. She looked
at Simon, and he let her come to Lettice's side. Lettice
sighed. She was not afraid, only tired, and sad.

"Jean, look after the baby for me. And promise
me—"

Jean leaned forward to catch the words, for her voice
was weak and drowsy. "Yes?"

"Promise you will write to Rob and tell him."

"I promise."

Simon touched her shoulder, and she held Lettice's
hand more tightly. "Shall I bring the others—Lesley
and Douglass?" But Lettice could only just shake her
head. She was too tired for more. Jean gave place to
Simon, who gave her the last unction, and awhile later
she died, like one falling asleep.

* * *

Jean kept her promise and wrote to Rob Hamilton, telling him of the birth of his son and the death of his wife, but she never knew whether her father received the letter or not, for in July the latest in a series of bizarre plots involving the Queen of Scots was uncovered. It became known as the Babington Plot, for Anthony Babington, a former page of the Queen's, living in France, had been a principal correspondent. Letters had been smuggled in to the Queen hidden in the bung of a beer barrel, and the plan had been to assassinate Queen Elizabeth and put Queen Mary on the throne. But it soon transpired that the whole matter had been engineered by Walsingham, Queen Elizabeth's agent, for he himself had intercepted the first of the letters and had allowed it to reach Queen Mary in this secret way to entice her to compromise herself.

She had done that thoroughly, and entrapped many of her leading supporters in doing so. In August Walsingham began making arrests, and in September fourteen conspirators were tried, convicted and executed. One of them was Robert Hamilton. His three daughters wept bitterly for him.

"He would never have agreed to killing Queen Elizabeth," Douglass said. "He would never have killed anyone."

"I hope they execute that wicked Queen Mary," Lesley cried. "It's all her fault."

"They will," Jean said. "That was what it was all for. Our father was just a victim of circumstance." And in her heart, but not aloud, she added, "Thank God Lettice did not live to know of it." For despair is the final sin, and a world without Rob in it would have brought Lettice to despair.

CHAPTER NINETEEN

The years had drawn John inexorably away, as if Mary had stood still while he was rushed faster than a galloping horse, so that when he stared back, she grew smaller with distance until he could barely see her. The seasons had come and gone, indistinguishable in their endless pattern of seed time and harvest, calving and killing, sun and rain, heat and cold. The turf was old and dark upon her grave now; Houlet was long dead, and Kai was gray-muzzled—it was one of her pups, Kee, who ran at John's heels now. Mary seemed so far away, beyond reach, like sunlight to a blind man. The sun had gone from his world that day, and he had lived the years since in darkness, doing what he must and looking for her everywhere, helplessly, like a dog that cannot understand and keeps returning to its mistress's grave.

Was it any wonder, then, that he would not let pass from him the only token she had left him? When his father wrote, begging him to allow Thomas to be brought up at Morland Place, he had not even considered it. He could not live without Thomas, even though in the boy, as he grew, she died again for him, there where she was most recalled. Perhaps that was why at last he consented, when Aunt Nan wrote that sad, desperate letter, to take Thomas back for a visit, in the hope that it might make the change in the boy. He thought about that letter as they made their way south riding along the old Roman Road toward Corbridge. It had been a long letter that had told him things his father, from pride, had never told him.

Aunt Nan was proud, too, but she had a different sort of pride that saw necessity and outcome. It pained him to hear her speak critically of Jan, knowing how much she had always loved her son. John remembered Jan more clearly than anyone else at Morland Place. He had always loved him and admired him, and he felt matters must be grave indeed for Aunt Nan to so much as hint that all was not well between them. Perhaps it was that which had persuaded him to do as she asked.

All around them were the colors of autumn, all the shades of gold, and that indefinable scent in the air like wood smoke; his horse, Kestrel, was already growing his thick winter coat. It had been autumn when John first came to the Borderlands to wed Mary. He glanced sideways at Thomas, riding beside him on Hawk, and his heart leaped with that strange mixture of joy and pain that never grew less intense, for Thomas at eighteen looked absurdly like his mother on that first day. A young prince, he looked, with that clear-cut profile, the firm chin and high cheekbones; he went shaven, as his father had as a youth, and his skin had the same pale gold color that hers had had; his eyes were the same wide, gray, clear eyes, surrounded by fair lashes, that hers had been. He was wearing high boots and a leather jerkin for this journey, and under his velvet cap his pale hair—her hair—blew softly in the damp autumn wind.

He rode well, having ridden before he could walk, and his straight, slender body and long, narrow hands were as still and confident as hers had been. John could

glance sideways and see, unobscured, a living ghost:
Mary riding beside him. But it was not Mary; Thomas
was not a princeling, except in looks. There was a light-
ness about Thomas, a facility, an easiness. He was indo-
lent, liked comfort, disliked struggle, effort, endeavor.
He would agree with anyone for the sake of peace, accept anything rather than try to improve it, espouse any
opinion rather than think for himself. The fierceness,
the strength, the pride of his mother had died with her
and would never come again. Times were changing,
here in the last stronghold of the old ways, and men
were not what they had been. The power of the Percys
had been broken at last; the forces of law and the
Crown were bringing their new kind of order to the
wild country.

In John's youth it used to be said that the Queen's
writ did not run in the Borderlands: north of the wall,
no king but Percy. Now it was said that the rebellion
had been a battle not for the True Religion but to preserve the old way of master and man, loyalty to one's
lord, and that the rebellion had failed because the old
days were gone. John remembered his father-in-law's
words on that subject before he rode away to his death.
Tod's Knowe was one of the last strongholds, and John
would keep it to his last breath because he found himself now, like Black Will before him, facing the end of
his world, and he did not know what else to do. But
Thomas would not be king afterward in John's small
kingdom: Thomas belonged to the new world.

The ballad that the Tod's Knowe harpist had made
for Mary had been a lament not only for her but for the
passing of the times; it was like the lament made for a
dead king or warrior rather than for a woman:

Oh where, oh where is Mary Percye?
Where oh where is our ladye sweet?

She lies in the shade of yond rowan tree
With her sword in her hand and her hound at her feet.

Thus ran the chorus. The plaintive tune of it ran
through John's mind to the rhythm of the horses' hooves
on the turf, and for a moment she seemed close, with
the burning brightness of rowan berries and the wood-
smoke smell of autumn and the youth on the white
horse riding beside him. Then Thomas, as if he had
picked up his father's thought, began to hum the song
absently and lightly, and she was gone again, dissolved
like mist, taking the brightness with her.

It was as they were riding over Knapton Moor in the
last stage of their journey that one of the men rode up
alongside John and murmured, "Man on a horse, Master. Over there."

Instantly wary, forgetting that they were in the civilized south now, John looked, his hand reaching for his
sword. And then he laughed and relaxed.

"It's all right, Jed, it's only one man, and this is
Yorkshire, not Redesdale. We shan't be attacked here."

"He looks as though he's waiting for us, Father,"
Thomas said. "Perhaps he's been sent to guide us."

They rode nearer. The man was sitting on a bay
horse, his back to the small copse of trees that was familiar to John for some special reason he could not
bring to mind. It was a good horse, well caparisoned,
and the man was no servant by his dress; a middle-aged
man with a little of the stoutness of wealth to his figure
under his bombasted waistcoat and stuffed britches; a
bearded man with two streaks of white in his beard so
that he looked like a badger.

When they were near enough to be hailed, the man
called out, gesturing behind him, "Harewood Whin.
Where we caught the fox. I thought it would be appropriate," and then John spurred Kestrel into a trot,
laughing with pleasure and because he had not at once

recognized the badger-bearded man. The bay hors-
started back as Kestrel reached him, and there was a
moment of circling and fretting before the horses were
still enough for the two riders to embrace.

"Jan! Bear-cub! I didn't recognize you."

"Big John Morland, come home at last! God's
beard, but it's good to see you! I've had everyone for
miles around keeping watch for you so that I should get
word which way you were coming. And look, you come
over the moor with an army at your back, like an invading king. Have they made you King of Scotland,
that you come with swords behind you?"

John was laughing, but there were tears in his eyes,
too. "Jan, Janny, it's so good to see you again. It's so
strange, I have thought about you ever since we last
met as you were then. I seem to forget that people
change, get older."

Jan reached out and scuffed John's fair beard. "You
want to get some gray in that, give you an air of distinction. Aye, there are changes enough," he said sadly, but
added more brightly, "though some are changes for the
better—for instance, that strapping young Greek god at
your side must be your son Thomas. Well met, my
boy—give me your hand."

Thomas came forward, smiling, and leaned across his
saddle to shake hands with Jan, who gave him a piercing look, as if gauging his mettle, before slapping his
shoulder and returning his attention to John.

"Come, brother, let's ride on, and if you will, ride a
little ahead with me, because I want to talk to you before we get home."

John looked at him quizzically. "I have been wondering if there was any special reason you met me out
here, and alone."

Jan smiled, his old wicked smile, white sharp teeth
through dark beard. "I could not wait to see you, that
was all! Come, let's on."

John signaled to his men and to Thomas to fall back a pace or two, and after some threatening snaps and laying back of ears, Kestrel consented to walk beside Jan's bay on a loose rein, and John said, "I suppose you want to tell me about the situation at Morland Place."

Jan nodded. "Things have not been easy for some time. There have been great changes, mostly sad ones. Your father dying—"

"God rest his soul," John said, crossing himself. Jan's lips quirked in an ironic smile.

"Aye, and that's another change. Look, John, I know my mother wrote to you, and I wanted to have the chance to speak for myself. Everyone seems against me and my poor Mary. One of the reasons is that I have left the Old Faith. Well, the new religion seems good to me; it seems right. I know many of us have a bad name for persecution and interfering, killjoy ways, but I am not like that. I don't want to change you or stop you believing what seems good to you—all I ask is to be left alone for the same thing."

John looked uneasy. "These things are beyond me, Jan. I can only refer to the teachings of Holy Mother Church and follow what the priests tell me."

"There, you see, is one of the differences—I like to think for myself. But the other thing I wanted to talk of is the Morland inheritance."

"Ah, yes," John said.

"I don't know what my mother told you—"

"Only that you seemed set to steal Morland Place from the rightful heir," John said dryly.

"Which is—who?" Jan reined his horse and faced John, looking directly into his eyes. "I'm not a thief come by night, John. Everything was in chaos; one by one everyone seemed to be deserting Morland Place. There was no one to carry on after your father died except outsiders, and it seemed to me for the best that my children should take over rather than a foreigner from the south who did not care about the place."

"What about Jane's child—Nehemiah, is it?"

"Jane and Hezekiah don't want him to take over. They want him at home, to inherit Shawes, just as you want Thomas at home to take over Tod's Knowe. So who is left? My Nicholas is a good boy, married to Celia Butts, and already they have a son to follow them. What is so wrong?"

John looked at him quizzically. "What I do not understand is why you think your child has any right to the place—I know Aunt Nan is a Morland, but it was James Chapham who legally adopted you, not her."

· Jan's gaze wavered for a moment but then steadied as he determined to speak. "When I called you brother awhile ago, it was not a mere convention. John, I am your brother, your elder brother. I am your mother's eldest son."

There was a long silence filled only with the sounds of the horses grazing, the crunching of grass and the chinking of bits. Kestrel, who had been standing quietly, suddenly jerked at the reins, wanting to get his head down, too, and John checked him automatically and then sighed and dismounted.

"You had better tell me everything," he said. "Sit down on the grass awhile." He gestured to one of the men to take the horses, and he and Jan sat down a little way off and Jan told him the whole story. John listened in silence, his odd-color eyes never leaving Jan's face; from a distance Thomas watched them idly as he lolled across Hawk's back, his feet out of the stirrups, one elbow propped on the firm white rump, wondering what in the world could be so important as to make two middle-aged men look so grave. Older people, his experience told him, had strange divisions between classes of event and behavior, strange compulsions they named honor and duty and virtue. Thomas's world was sim-

er, there being only two sorts of things in it—those
at were pleasant for Thomas and those that were not.

At last John sighed and said, "I can see that you
ave some sort of reason, some justification, albeit a
range and twisted one. If there were no one else, it
ould be right for your children to inherit. But there is
lways someone—if not Nehemiah, then Mary's chil-
ren. And then there is Thomas—"

"Yes," Jan said thoughtfully. "There is Thomas.
What do you intend with regard to Thomas?"

"I want him to come home with me, to take over at
Tod's Knowe when I die. But when I am dead, who
knows what he might do? And now had we not better
ride on? I for one am hungry." He stood up and
snapped his fingers for his horse.

Jan caught his arm and turned him so they faced each
other. "What will you do?" he said, low and urgent.

John looked at him sadly, seeing, as daily he saw in
Thomas, that the past was dead and those who peopled
it gone beyond recall. This was not the Jan he had
grown up with.

"As in everything, I will try to do what is right. I can
do no more."

They mounted and rode on.

Because everything looked the same—the house, the
furnishings, the gardens—the changes were the more
painful. To see Aunt Nan, who had always been so
beautiful and elegant, such an energetic horsewoman,
shrunken and twisted, confined to a chair, her face
marked with the harsh lines of continual pain, and
old—above all, old—was painful in the extreme. His
father was dead, his sister Lettice dead, the house was
being run by Jean Hamilton, a stranger; the business
and the estate by Jan Chapham under the stern and bitter eyes of his mother, because there simply was no one
else, for the only possible heir was a child of six. John

felt disturbed, bewildered—and above all, bereft. Th Morland Place of his childhood, the order, the rightnes of everything, the sense of life and purpose, the sense o the indestructibility of the Morland family, was gone. I had been the Morland Place of his mother, and she died again for him that day. He wished he had no come. He knew he had been right all these years not to come.

For Thomas everything was delightful, and he wondered why his father had never let him come to visit before, The spacious house; the luxurious surroundings; the wonderful food; the beautiful, elegant, soft-spoken, sweet-smelling people were all so different from the low, dark, dirty, comfortless huddle of buildings he knew as home and the dark, unwashed, coarse people he lived with. The servants were so numerous and well trained; meals were an elaborate, almost ceremonial procession of delicious dishes; his bed was so soft, and a hot bath was easy to obtain, and he knew at once he had entered an environment where pleasant-for-Thomas far outweighed unpleasant-for-Thomas.

He liked everyone. The twisted little old woman who lived in the chair and was carried from place to place did not frighten him, for he saw, with that instinct for feeling behind words that he had inherited from his father, that she wanted him to be here and respected him in some obscure way, wanted him to be pleased. The tall, dour Mistress Hamilton who organized everything he soon won over by admiring her efficiency, and in the plump little Mistress Hamilton he recognized something of a kindred spirit. Nicholas and Celia were wrapped up in each other and in the children and lived in a world apart, from which they looked timidly and ingratiatingly upon the inhabitants of the real world. There was Gabriel Chapham, who was amusing and good to look at and liked Thomas as soon as he admired his

at; and Jane and Hezekiah Morland, who were the
kind of grave, goodly people who could be won by
quiet speech and decorous deportment.

There were strange little undercurrents that Thomas
felt, though he did not understand them, and because
he did not want to understand them he was not upset by
them. There was some conflict, for instance, between
the Old Lady and Jan, who was her son, it seemed.
They bristled like cats when they were together, and yet
when his back was to her, her eyes would follow him
with sad and tender longing, like a girl looking at a lad
she loved and could not wed. Then there was the odd
behavior of Gabriel, who pursued Douglass Hamilton
for all he was worth, despite the fact that Thomas soon
perceived he had a deep and secret desire for her sister
Lesley. This was strange to Thomas on two counts, for
first he did not know why, if Gabriel wanted Lesley, he
did not have her, since she was unwed, and second he
could not understand anyone's preferring anyone in the
world to Douglass.

For Douglass seemed to him the most beautiful thing
God had ever made and put upon the earth. It was not
quite true to say that nothing at Morland Place disturbed him, for Douglass disturbed him deeply from the
moment he first saw her. She was like a creature from
another world—so full of vibrant life she seemed to
hum with it like a plucked harpstring. She bubbled over
with happiness all day, enjoying everything that came to
her, always laughing, talking, singing, rarely standing
still—if she was not out riding or walking in the gardens, she would be walking around the rooms, playing
games or dancing, her little feet barely seeming to touch
the ground. Her voice was gentle and sweet and always
dappled with laughter like a running stream dappled
with sunlight, her figure light and graceful so that every
movement seemed like part of an endless dance, and

her face was so alarmingly beautiful that he wanted to
kneel and adore her, the way he saw his father kneel
before the Blessed Virgin.

She was, most undoubtedly, pleasant-for-Thomas,
and he contrived, as was his way, to be with her or near
her for most of his waking hours; and when he was
with her, even in chapel when her eyes were very properly bent on the altar or on the floor, he could not
take his eyes from gazing at her. It seemed unexpectedly easy to secure himself of her company. She loved
to ride, and he was an excellent rider, and so he offered
his services as her lieutenant, guide and protector when
she rode out; when she walked in the garden, he would
offer to carry her basket or book, and she always, with
a charming blush, agreed. In the house he would always
volunteer when she wished to organize a game, and
though he could do nothing but listen admiringly when
she played or sang, she seemed to like the attention.
And when she danced, he was her first choice of part-
ner because he excelled at dancing.

There was some rivalry for her attention from Gabriel, but the Old Lady and the elder Mistress Hamilton
seemed for some reason to be on his side and generally
found some way to oust Gabriel, and, as Thomas had
observed, Gabriel was not entirely unwilling to be
ousted, since his real interests lay elsewhere. Thomas
did not trouble himself to wonder why gaining his objective was so easy. His life was ruled by such simple
principles, he never found the need to wonder about
other motives. That Nanette and Jean wanted to help
him, and that Douglass was willing to have his company, were pleasant facts, and that was enough for him.
So, when the weather began to change and his father
asked him if he was ready to go home, Thomas said, "I
would sooner stay here, Father, if you don't much mind
it?"

He did not think his father would want him to stay,

he was agreebly surprised when John said, "I cannot
e longer away and must go home. But if you wish you
an stay here for the winter, and I will come and fetch
ou in the spring. If you do not come with me now, the
weather will be too bad for you to come until then."

"I'll stay, then, and thanks," Thomas said. The
pring was months away. He would worry about the
pring when it happened.

"He wants to stay," John reported to Aunt Nan.

She smiled, relieved. "I guessed that he would, but I
am glad all the same. It is not for the reason I expected,
but that will come, in time."

"I warned you," John said sourly. "I told you he
would have no ambition to rule. He cares for nothing
but pleasure."

Nanette reached out a twisted hand to him but withdrew it before she had touched him. She hated the sight
of her hands, knotted like tree roots. John pretended
not to have noticed. "Now, John," she said, "don't be
bitter. There is no harm in him, and there may be much
good. He is evidently much attracted to Douglass, and
that shows he knows the best when he sees it."

"I cannot imagine what she sees in him," John said.

"He is a pretty lad and likes to please her," Nanette
said.

"So is Gabriel," John pointed out.

Nanette shook her head. "Gabriel seeks not to serve
but to be served. He wants Douglass to admire him and
offers only a token admiration to her. Besides, Douglass
is a virtuous girl, and Gabriel is a rake. She could not
love him."

"Love? You think she might love my Thomas?"

"You sound so surprised. Yes, why not—and that
would be the best solution of all. Come, John, what do
you say? Would you be unhappy for your boy to marry
Lettice's girl and settle here? It is his place, you know."

"I don't know," John said, sighing. "I wanted him t[o] inherit Tod's Knowe. But he is not her son, after all.["]

"The heir has come back to Morland Place," Na[n]nette said gently, as if she were speaking to herself a[s] much as to him. "God knows best, and the patter[n] works out as it must. Douglass is strong and good, an[d] she will have ambition enough for both of them. If the[y] wed, she will rule him in everything, he will be virtuou[s] for her sake until it is such a habit with him he will no[t] know how to do any differently. God's grace works i[n] many ways, comes upon us where we do not look for it, and in disguise. But we are His, to be held in His hand, not spilled like grain. We may stray from Him, but if we wander to the world's end, He will bring us back at last."

John stared past her, out of the window at the sky as gray as Mary's eyes, but never so clear. "But what of me?" he said. "All seems pain. There is no balm in my soul to keep it soft. I am afraid of the bitterness I feel. I am afraid that if I lose Thomas, I will lose all human feeling."

Nanette longed to touch him comfortingly, but she kept her crippled hands in her lap and tried to put the caress she could not give him into her voice. "All is for a purpose," she said gently. "Thomas's place is here, and if yours is elsewhere, that is where grace will find you. Pray for it, John. You know that prayer is given us for that. Pray, and it will come, though it may not be in the way you expect."

Sighing, he knelt suddenly beside her, as if he were too tired to stand anymore, and he put his arms around her and rested his head on her shoulder. He was silent awhile, and then he lifted his head from her shoulder and kissed her, and smiled.

"You do me so much good. I wish I had your acceptance."

Nanette smiled, the ghost of her girlhood beauty

howing in it. "I am very old," she said. "It is the only
hing left that I can do gracefully. God bless you, John.
Come back in the spring to bless your son's wedding."

"If I come, it will be to see you again."

"But if I am not here, come anyway," she said, and
he nodded consent, and she smiled.

At Christmas Thomas and Douglass were betrothed,
and the twelve-day festival was celebrated more heartily
and gleefully than it had been for many years past. The
servants threw themselves into the preparations with a
will, for they had been as much affected by the uncer-
tainty and gloom as any of the family, and there was
scrubbing and baking and brewing such as many of
them had never seen before. The hall was decked with
boughs of holly, and mistletoe was hung over the doors
and windows to keep out the Evil One, and the fires
were built up in the chimneys until even the dogs had to
move away from them. The air was heavy with the
scents of roasting meat and spice pies, and the children
ran wild in the sudden atmosphere of festival, roasting
so many chestnuts and apples on the metal rims of the
braziers that when it was time for them to rehearse their
parts in the songs and mummeries and masques that
were being planned, they could barely move or speak.

Everyone was happy with the solution. Jane and Hezekiah now felt assured of their son's eventual return
home and ceased to begrudge him to the Morland nurseries. Nicholas and Celia felt a weight lifting from them
and felt that at last they could enjoy their life together
here openly, without anyone thinking they were covet-
ing what should not be theirs. Even Jan was glad of the
way things had gone, for he had felt of late that he was
being forced further and further along a path he had no
real desire to tread. Having once taken up a position, it
seemed to be part of human nature to defend it and not
abandon it. More than anything, he wanted to be rec-

onciled with his mother, whom he loved and respected and on Christmas Day when he came to her with hi gift, he knelt in front of her and put his hands over her and said, "Now, Mother, all cause for conflict betwee us is over. Say you forgive me and give me your bless ing."

"Not all cause, my son," she said. "There is still the matter of your faith."

Jan's blue eyes met hers frankly, and she saw, as she saw every time she looked at him, how much of a Morland he was. "There I cannot meet you, Mother. But you have a generous and forgiving heart, I know, and you cannot condemn me for doing my conscience, as you do yours. I have a faith that is to me as good as yours is to you. So will you not bless me?"

Nanette's face softened. "Bear-cub, perhaps there may not be so much difference between the two," she said. "And when we die and our hearts are opened and all is seen, it may be that we call the same thing by two different names. Of course I forgive you—and God send a mother's blessing to you." He leaned forward and she kissed his forehead. "God knows," she said, "I have missed my son since this trouble started between us—and you are my son, my very dear son, whom I love."

Jan laughed aloud in happiness and relief. "Oh, what fools we mortals are, to let so much come between us! Now, Mother, we shall have the best Christmas that ever was since the first one."

So it was, with no shadow to mar it, and Nanette enjoyed it more than any feast she remembered, for she had feared more than anything that she would die unreconciled with her son. Jan was more like himself than he had been for years, laughing and playing in wild high spirits, putting on an impromptu masque that was wickedly funny, in which he, as a pun on his nickname, played a bear that was baited by Morland dogs, represented by Douglass and Thomas and Nehemiah and the twins, until he fed them sops and wine and they fell asleep, allowing him to escape. Nanette laughed with the rest, crossing herself covertly to avert the blasphemy, but knowing that what was done in love would not be punished.

Another piece of happiness was in store that day, for Nanette had been a little worried as to how Gabriel would react to losing Douglass to his rival, and she remarked to Jan once when the dancing had thrown him up like a piece of jetsam into her corner that it was good to see Gabriel dancing so happily with Lesley and showing her such pleasant attentions.

"Why, yes," Jan said, "and it's good to see how she has improved since she came here. I think looking after her baby brother has given her a new interest in life. She is looking very pretty now."

"She is eating less and taking more care of her appearance," Nanette said, with a faintly surprised tone in her voice. "Perhaps it is not impossible that Gabriel might fall in love with her."

And Thomas, passing at that moment and pausing to see if Nanette's cup was empty, caught the words and smiled at her.

"But he has been in love with her all the time," he said. "He only paid attention to Douglass because he did not think she cared for him. But now, by the look of them, there will be nothing to come between them."

Jan stared at Thomas and laughed. "Why, you notice everything, don't you? Will they wed, do you think?"

"Why not?" Thomas said, sounding surprised, for it seemed to him the obvious, inevitable outcome.

"She is a little older than him," Nanette mused, "but that will be to the good. He needs a steadying influence. The wonder of it is that he should have fallen in love with her in the first place."

Thomas said indifferently, "Perhaps he likes plump

women," and went on his way, leaving Nanette and Jan
to laugh. The joy, she thought, of being able to laugh
with her son again, of being able to look forward with
confidence to the future of the family, of knowing that
she would be able at last to lay down the burden she
had carried through such pain and trouble for so long.

Jan's hands were on her shoulders, and he leaned
down to rest his cheek against hers for a moment as he
said, "Are you happy, Mother? Is there anything I can
get you?"

"No, Bear-cub," she said. "I have everything I
need."

February, the month of her birth, was cold and
damp, the worst weather for the old. Nanette suffered
greatly from the pains in her joints, and she began to
have trouble breathing, too, and on the day after her
seventy-ninth birthday she did not rise from her bed but
lay propped on pillows, struggling to get her breath. It
felt as though her chest were filled with thick, liquid
mud, through which she dragged in air with enormous
effort. Jean stayed by her, doing what she could, which
was little enough, and watching with pity and concern
as, her eyes staring with the effort, Nanette's life narrowed abruptly to that one concern, breathing.

The next day she was a little easier, but when Jean
spoke cheerfully about getting better, Nanette shook
her head and said, between breaths, "We both know
better than that. I should like to see Simon."

It was not a bad way to die, Nanette thought as she
waited for her chaplain, with some pain and trouble,
but clear-minded and knowing it enough in advance to
prepare herself. The children's wedding was not
planned until April, and she knew she would not live to
see it, but she found now, at last, that she did not care.
She had no more curiosity. She had laid down the burden
at last, and God was calling her home.

There was time for everything she wanted to say, though speaking was difficult. There was time to pass over the reins of government to Jean, to speak to Douglass about duty, about the role she would have to play and about the guidance she would have to give to her husband. There was time to say good-bye to everyone, from the least servant upward, and ask their forgiveness for any slights she had given them. There was time, sadly, lovingly, to say farewell to Jan, who, even through his tears, left her with a joke, and whose lips, lingering on her cheek, smiled, though they were wet with tears. Her son, yes, always her son!

Then, when they were all gone, there was time to pray with Simon, to repent, to cleanse her heart and to receive the absolution that would make her fit for the long journey home, to the loving arms of her Father who would make her well again. Peace came to her, dropping like slow balm into the wounds of years, and in that peace, like a last unexpected gift, there was time without pain or struggle to think, to remember and be glad. Her long life stretched back before her, clear now on the edge of the dark, with that pure clarity of the sky between sunset and night.

Out into the dark she drifted, into that luminous sky where the last of the light was draining into the west, and the first stars shone, preternaturally bright, low on the horizon. He was there, the one person she longed to be with, his strong arms promising comfort, his heart full of love. The face was the face of Paul; the dark eyes were his, but the arms that folded her in and the love that warmed her was a greater love than that. For in the end, all loves are one, and she flew to His arms who loved her best, and had always known her.

CHAPTER TWENTY

Despite the sadness over Nanette's death, and over the death of Hezekiah at sea in March, the wedding took place, as planned, in April, and turned out to be a double wedding, Gabriel and Lesley marrying at the same time. Mary was not much pleased by Gabriel's choice, for because of Lord Hamilton's remarriage, Lesley had no dowry but the small bequest left her by her mother, and Mary did not consider her to be much of a match for her handsome son. She tried to dissuade him from the marriage, and when he merely smiled and ignored her advice, she tried to persuade Jan to forbid the marriage or at least to disinherit Gabriel if he insisted upon it. Since the return of Thomas and his reconciliation with his mother, however, Jan had lost much of his driving ambition, and he had, in any case, always had more interest in Nicholas. He told Mary that he had no intention of preventing Gabriel from marrying who he wanted.

"Lesley will steady him," he added. "I am only glad he has been caught by the nose at last. A ne'er-do-well can be an expensive son."

He and Mary quarreled violently on the subject, but

Jan would not be budged, and Mary could do nothing but refuse to dance at the wedding. She had been ailing for some time and had been taking a large number of potions and simples for her ailments, which had made her short-tempered. After the wedding she began to suffer from the strangury and declined rapidly, and by the end of April she was dead. Jan was deeply afflicted by her death, for though in later years they had not lived peaceably together, yet he had known her almost all his life, had grown up with her, and she had been the only woman he had ever loved or wanted. Had she not married him, he would probably have remained single.

He felt lost and bewildered, looking for her, listening for her voice, continually finding himself thinking, I must tell Mary that, or That will amuse Mary. A part of himself, and a large part, was missing. Her portrait in the parlor at Watermill House was hung with laurel and wreathed in black, and Jan, whenever he saw that fresh, confident young face looking down at him, felt stricken with remorse and regret for all the times he had denied her things or quarreled with her or simply missed an opportunity to please her.

Watermill House was haunted for him now, and too large for him alone, so it suited everyone for him to move into Morland Place and give Watermill to Gabriel and Lesley. They wanted a place of their own; Thomas and Douglass welcomed Jan's experience and guidance in running the estates; and Jan could be with his grandchildren. It occurred to him afterward as ironic that he and his eldest son and his grandchildren had ended up living at Morland Place after all, and he smiled a little to think of Paul looking on from heaven with disapproval and Mary with satisfaction.

On the nineteenth of November 1588, the Queen ordered a day of thanksgiving for England's safety after the failure of the Spanish Armada. It was celebrated with much feeling by the residents of Morland Place because it coincided with the confirmation that Douglass was pregnant. Douglass was particularly delighted, since Celia had recently become pregnant again, and she had been worried that there had been no sign of pregnancy, though she had been married in April. Then at Christmas Lesley announced with many blushes that she, too, was pregnant. The babies were due in April, May and June of the following year, 1589.

"Then we shall really have a houseful, with little Rob, too," Thomas said pleasantly. "I shall enjoy writing to tell my father. He will be glad to know that the house is coming alive again." Jean shot him a strange look and forebore to point out that since Nehemiah had been taken away by his mother to live at Shawes, only one of the babies in the nursery would be a Morland. Thomas wrote to John and asked him to come and visit, and John did reply this time and said that he would visit, if he was able to leave Tod's Knowe at the time, for the christening when the new babe was born, provided it was a proper Catholic christening. Thomas, true to his nature, did not tell Douglass about this, not seeing any reason to meet trouble before it arrived. Time enough when the babe was born to worry about the christening.

Meanwhile, in a burst of unaccustomed energy generated by his approaching fatherhood, Thomas enclosed a piece of intake land on the edge of Hob Moor for grazing and revealed to his family that he intended to start breeding horses for sale. Breeding horses was second nature to Borderland folk—horses and cattle were their wealth, and sheep still came strange to him. They weren't in his blood as horses were.

Douglass, happy in the glow of her pregnancy, smiled at him indulgently when he told her his plans. Like him, she had grown up in horse country. She had no feeling for sheep, either. "Well, I hope you can make some money with them, anyway, my young cattle lord, because after last year and all that business with the ships, our coffers are empty."

Thomas reached out to touch her hand. He could never pass her without touching her or be near her without looking at her. "You shall have gold, my princess, and jewels, and everything that's fine, if I have to turn to alchemy for it."

Out of the corner of his eye Jan saw Jean's hand move, and because his mind was elsewhere he thought she was going to cross herself, as his mother would have done at the mention of magic. But she only pushed a thread of hair back under her linen cap, and Jan reproached himself smilingly. Those days were gone, the days of ignorance and superstition, but all his life he had been accustomed to the devoutness of women; and more, it worried him that the chapel was empty, the priest's room uninhabited, and that Douglass and Thomas did not seem to be making any effort to find a new chaplain. He made a mental note to speak to them about it at some convenient time.

Spring came, green shoots thrust up out of the dark earth, the world was filled with the many-voiced din of lambing time, and Thomas, out guarding the flocks on the higher ground, taking his turn with the rest, killed a brace of foxes and took the pelts to a furrier in Stonegate to have them cured for trimming a new gown for Douglass when she had had her bairn. The three women grew large and slow, especially little Celia, who was so great with child she could hardly move and had to wear a loose, shapeless mantle like a shroud, for nothing else would fit her.

The long, bitter Lenten fast ended with the sacred mystery of the Passion and the Easter feast, and on Easter Monday Celia went into labor and was hustled away by the women of the house to the solar, which

had been set aside and prepared as a confinement
chamber. It was a long, hard labor, and try as they
might, no one could ignore the groans and cries of pain
from the upper chamber. Nicholas, who had always
been quiet, seemed to shrink even further into himself,
creeping about the house with a haunted look in his
eyes, shuddering in unison with the cries of his wife. At
last there was the wail of a baby, and Nicholas went to
the foot of the staircase to be ready as soon as the word
came that he could go up, his eyes turned hopefully upward like a dog at a kitchen door.

The call did not come, but after a while the baby
wailed again—and the voice was joined by another.
Twins! His heart rose in gladness, even while he ached
for Celia, for the pain she had to bear. The children's
voices sounded lusty. His hands hanging by his side, his
eyes fixed on the turn of the stairs, he waited. Meanwhile in the solar the midwife was wrapping the second
child with an air of satisfaction, as if she herself were
responsible for the fruitfulness of her patient.

"That was well done, mistress," she said. "A fine little girl, to go with the little boy. It's well that the boy
came first, for they are always weaker than the girls. I
doubt not we'll keep both of these babies, God willing.
Lord but you were big, mistress! I tell no lie, I've never
seen a woman with so fair a belly on her as you had,
and I've delivered more women—Lord, now, child,
don't cry. It's all over now."

"Such pains," Celia sobbed, turning her head from
side to side on the pillow as if seeking to escape it. She
cried out, drawing her knees up and trying to turn onto
her side. Jean looked at the midwife in concern, reaching out to stroke Celia's head. The midwife was brisk,
putting her hands to Celia's shoulders to push her onto
her back again.

"Now then, chuck, lie down—it's only the afterbirth.
Once you've rid yourself of that, all will be comfortable

again. Why, it's only a little pain—such a fuss to make!"

"No, no, it's not a little pain!" Celia cried desperately. Her body arched in a spasm, and she groaned with it and then clutched at herself, rocking and crying, "It hurts, it hurts."

The midwife frowned and, pushing Celia's hands away, placed her own over the belly and pressed around. Jean watched her anxiously.

"What is it?" she whispered.

"Lord, missus, I don't know. I've never come across a state like this before. You'd think she was still to be delivered, the size of her belly. Now then, child, now then—" as Celia began to cry out again. She drew her legs up, pressing her heels into the bed, and arched again in spasm. The midwife stooped and peered, and gaped. "Lord bless us and save us, if she hasn't another bairn in there! Well, I've never seen the like of this before in all my days. What—? Why, master, you can't come in here! Get you gone right this minute!" For Nicholas, frustrated and frightened by the sequence of noises from above, had finally lost his nerve and rushed into the chamber.

The midwife inserted her considerable bulk between him and the bed, and he could only call out, "Celia! What is it? What's wrong?"

Celia was too far gone in pain to wonder what he was doing there. She screamed at him, sobbing. "It's a judgment on me, for leaving the Faith! Nicholas, pray for me, pray to the Blessed Virgin, and St. Anne, and St. Celia. Tell the Lady that I'll see her chapel made fine again if she'll help me. Oooh!" She broke off as a pain ripped through her, and the midwife, growing anxious, pushed Nicholas toward the door.

"You must go," she said firmly. "There is work to be done here."

The urgency of her voice got through to him.

"I'll pray," he said, sounding bewildered. "Nurse, don't let anything happen to her. She will be all right, won't she?"

The midwife had no time for him. She thrust him away without looking at him. "Lord, yes! You go and pray, sir, just so long as you go away now."

Nicholas went to the chapel. He had no experience of praying for the intercession of the saints, but with a full heart and a dry mouth he knelt down in front of the altar—denuded of its ornaments and statues but still covered with its fine cloth, embroidered by the hands of Morland ladies long since dead—and folded his hands. The sanctuary lamp burned unflickering, like the presence of God. He tried to pray as she had asked him, to call on the help of the saints, but in the end he could find no words, only saying softly, "God—please—"

The third bairn was laid wrongly, and Celia struggled in vain for hours, while the midwife sweated and panted, trying to bring it out. At last the thing was done. The baby was born dead, suffocated and strangled by the birth cord, and Celia was exhausted, torn and bloody, but alive. There was no chaplain on hand to baptize the new twins, so two days later they were taken to the village church of St. Stephen to be christened, and Celia was carried there on a litter for the ceremony. Opinions as to the wisdom of that differed, and Jean insisted ever after that it had nothing to do with it, but the next day Celia had a high fever, and the day after that she died.

Douglass and Lesley, both awaiting the birth of their first child, clung together as they wept.

"I'd sooner have just the one," Lesley said, "and keep it and my life. Oh Lord, I'm so afraid."

"I am, too," Douglass said, hugging her for comfort. Inside her she was cold and still. She could not help wondering if it was a judgment—and if it was, was her turn next?

* * *

Easter 1589 found Lord Hovenden's Men playing *The Moor and the Pusill* in the Sun Playhouse, next door to the Sun-in-Splendor tavern. It was a theater newly built on the south bank opposite Blackfriars, handy for the ferry that brought the pleasure seekers out of Puritan London to the excitements of the outlying villages. The play was proving successful and seemed likely to put a little long-awaited money into the pockets of the players. Last year had been bad—the sharers had put all their money into the building of the playhouse, only to run into trouble with the Master of Revels over their first production, with the result that the playhouse was closed for six weeks and a heavy fine imposed. The sharers considered themselves lucky not to have been put into prison, and the hired men and 'prentices could hardly expect wages when the sharers themselves were out of pocket.

But *The Moor* was doing well; for several reasons, one of which was the death scene, for not only was the Pusill herself horribly murdered, her severed head being brought in on a platter, but the Moor was then butchered by her brother and father, but not before he had caused them considerable injury, involving the use of almost two buckets' full of sheeps' blood, obtained daily from the abattoir two miles away.

Another reason for the success was the performance of William's second son, Will, who at eleven was proving an even better actor than Ambrose had. Will played the Pusill, and his death shriek offstage was so authentically horrible that ladies in the upper gallery had been known to swoon. Ambrose, now fifteen, played the maid's brother. His voice had broken, so he could no longer play women's parts, but he had a fine tenor voice, and that together with his popularity with women had compensated him for the loss of the female lead to his younger brother.

Cynthia Harrod-Eagles

Apart from Ambrose and Will, there was a third son now, Rowland, the child of William's third wife Gill Hooper, whom William had picked up in a tavern years ago and had married in order to have someone to look after the children. Rowland was six and had a small role as the Pusill's younger sister and also walked on as a page and a maid in other scenes.

Even William's daughters were employed by the company. They could not, of course, appear onstage, but they formed an essential part of the production by playing the hautbois, gittern and drums offstage. Susan was fourteen now and a very comely young wench who would have caused any other father much concern; Mary was thirteen, bolder in temper and so used to getting her own way that Gill used to ask her opinion before doing anything, because it was better to have Mary's objections beforehand than for days afterward. Gill was a good-natured, gentle, hopeless slattern, and it was Mary who in reality kept the family together, saw to it that everyone got fed, that clothes were mended and washed and that Rowland went to bed instead of sitting under a table in the taproom swilling ale like the men and making himself sick by experimenting with tobacco smoking.

In spite of everything, they were a close and loving family. Ambrose was Mary's willing lieutenant, and between them they organized Gill, protected Susan, encouraged Will, attempted to discipline Rowland and were united in adoring and being exasperated by their father, who loved them all equally and indifferently and increasingly inhabited another world. It was Ambrose who fought off the young bloods who hung like panting dogs around pretty, blushing Susan and who made sure that his father was changed in time for his entries; just as it was Mary who scolded Gill into cleaning their rooms upstairs in the Sun-in-Splendor and buying a piece of mutton for Father's supper and the boys' when they had finished the play.

On Easter Sunday there was no performance, and Mary, coming through from the inner room where she and Susan and Rowland slept, found her father sitting at the little table by the window writing. A glance at the fair stubble on his cheeks and the marks under his eyes told her that he had not been to bed.

"Really, Father," she said, coming across to him and pushing at the scraps of paper on the floor with a contemptuous foot, "look at you. You'll be fit for nothing, sitting up all night with your nonsense."

William looked up at the sound of her voice; his eyes focused slowly and he smiled. "Oh, it's you, child. Is it morning? Do you know, I can't quite decide whether I have been asleep and dreaming or whether I have been awake all the time, but I have had the most extraordinary harmonies running through my mind——"

"Oh, Father, music again!" Mary said. "As if your music did us any good. Why, you don't get any extra shares for the songs we use in the plays, and you won't sell your music outside or try to get one to someone in Court, and there's Rowland needing new hose, for I'm sure Gill and I have darned them until there's more darn than hose, and he's growing so fast I'm never sure in the morning if he'll get into them again, and then there's the fair tomorrow at Camberwell, and you promised we would all go together, and there's no fun in a fair without a fairing, and we can't walk all the way and so that's a wagon to hire, and I don't know what else, until I'm sick of wondering how we'll pay for the rooms, let alone the price of beef and we can't eat mutton every day—and you talk to me of harmonies!"

William stared in amusement and delight at his little, bold girl, as neat and trim as a summer dunnock and as small, and as brave; and his eye took in her small, plain face, her linen all as white and starched as if it had

never been worn, her red woolen gown and black stomacher, all serviceable, tidy and neatly mended, but with
a touch of finery about it all the same, for she must
have leaned out of the casement window and plucked a
rose from the rambler that grew up the back of the tavern—a white one, still beaded with dew, was tucked
into her bodice pin.

His heart melted for her, and he found himself thinking suddenly of his mother, clad in silk and velvet, and
a string of priceless black pearls around her white
throat; this little dunnock of his had never known the
touch of silk, but when she stood on his foot and
chirped and shook her wings at him, it was not for finery but for new hose for Rowland that she berated
him.

"Why, Mary, my hinny, if you were a boy, what a
part we could make for you in the play," he said. Mary
eyed him with exasperation. When he looked sentimental and used the Yorkshire endearments of his youth,
she knew he had stopped listening.

"It's Easter Sunday, Father, and we are all going to
church. Let you wash and shave and put on your best
britches. Come on now, and shake up Gill and send her
down to mend the fire, for I have to get Rowland up
and dressed. You let him drink sack again last night,
and you know how stupid it makes him in the morning,
she added accusingly. There was a stirring behind the
curtains of one of the beds, and in a moment Ambrose's
tousled head came through.

"And the voice of the turtle was heard through the
land," he said. "*Dominus tecum*, little sister. It's Easter-
tide, and happiness abounds."

Mary rolled her eyes expressively toward her father
and marched back into the inner room to wake her
drink-bemused brother. An hour later they were all assembled downstairs, dressed in their best and ready to
walk along the riverbank to the church—all except

William. When the bells began and he still had not appeared, Ambrose went looking for him, only to return and report that a servant had seen William walking off along the bank downriver, in the opposite direction to the church, half an hour ago.

"He was hatless and waving his hands about," Ambrose said, "and you know what that means."

They knew. "I should have guessed when I saw he hadn't been to bed last night," Mary said. "Well, it's no use waiting for him—when he's in his music mood he can walk all day. I wish you had kept an eye on him, Gill. He is your husband, after all."

Gill looked reproachful at the attack, for she had never had any influence with William.

"Hadn't we better go?" Will said impatiently. "We don't want to be late again."

"Yes, come on," Mary said. "Really, it is too bad of him. As if everything weren't bad enough, without fines for missing church."

"Perhaps no one will notice," Susan said placidly.

Mary shook her head. "Father's too conspicuous. Everyone notices when he isn't there."

William was walking through the long grass along the edge of the riverbank path, and his shoes and hose were soaked with dew. With one part of his mind he was noticing the flags and asphodels, bright happy yellow like the essence of Easter and sunshine, and the paler primroses, massed and tight in their bright circles of leaves, and the banks of cowslips, and the new tender leaves on the chestnut trees, and the bright flash of birds darting here and there gathering moss and twigs for their nests. The tide was making, and the river was flowing stongly against it so that long arches of ripples flung back the sunlight and chuckled against the stems of bulrushes and the roots of willows. Two swans regarded him cautiously from a distance, holding their position against both tide and current with strong strokes of their black feet.

But that was the smaller part of his mind. The other part was absorbed in the music he had been working on all night, and it was that part that had driven him out of doors and kept him walking, for he could not be still when this fever of creation was upon him. He crossed the river by London Bridge without noticing it and carried on through the narrow, stinking streets, his feet trampling cabbage leaves and ordure as indifferently as they had trampled mud and grass. The crowds all seemed to be moving the same way, and he allowed his body to go with them because it was less of an effort.

He walked up some broad steps, and as a member of the crowd he slowed to a shuffle and in a moment passed in out of the sunshine into cool gloom. He sat down on a bench because there was nowhere else to go, and the fact that he was no longer moving brought him back to himself, and he looked around him irritably to discover that he was in a church. Moments later increasing awareness identified it as St. Paul's. He stopped scowling and smiled. So he had gotten to church after all—Mary would be pleased!

The great old cruciform church with its shadowy beams and dark corners filled with the rustling wings of the prayers of thousand upon thousand worshippers, past and present, soothed him. He stared about him, feeling the old tug of familiarity of sight and smell and sound. The choir came in, and as they began to sing the Processional, William grew still, and there seemed inside him a great well of silence opening up, into which the pure treble voices fell like shining stones. The ripples ran swift and gleaming as quicksilver, expanding until he felt so filled with light he must burst open. He clasped his hands to his chest, for he thought he was dying, so strange and wonderful was the feeling.

It was truth, it was light, it was knowledge, it was

eation! He was filled with such exaltation that he was
t aware of anything around him, only a great break-
g pain inside him as if his soul had grown too big for
s body and was tearing him open to escape, to fly
)ward into the sunlight and that great, breathtaking
lence at the heart of music. That was the anomaly,
lence at the heart of music, and music at the heart of
lence. That was what he had sought; and it had found
im at last.

The Litany, of course, the Litany! That was why the
ongs and ballads he had been writing had frustrated
lim, left him feeling cheated and sick, as if he had
:aten too much mutton fat. The Litany was the medium, and the music was the grace and the glory. And
that was what he was for, he, William Morland, Will
Shawe the actor—it was to lead down the glory of God
to men on earth through that talent that God had endowed him with. For why else had he been gifted so? It
was obvious, beautiful and clear and true as a bell. He
listened, enchanted, and when the service was over and
the crowd shuffled him back out into the sunshine, he
sat down on the steps and stared up at the sky and
smiled like a lunatic, having no desire to go anywhere
or do anything else.

It was not the first time that William had wandered
off, but he had never been away so long before, and
when he did not come home on Sunday night, Gill was
tearfully certain that he was dead while Mary was
equally certain that he had been picked up by the
Watch and packed off to jail. Half a dozen of the men
went out with lamps to search for him, but they did not
go very far and never thought of crossing the river. In
the morning they proposed resuming the search, but
Mary said firmly, "We are going to the Easter fair.
That was all arranged long ago."

"And leave poor Father?" Susan said.

"He's dead—I know he's dead," Gill wailed.

Mary stood firm. "Either he'll turn up again, or we get news of him. I don't see what good it does any of ˌ to stay here."

"Oh, you are a hard-hearted, wicked girl!" Gi cried, wringing her hands. "You don't care about you poor father at all!"

But Ambrose, looking with sympathy at his small sis ter, knew better. She was as worried as the rest o them—certainly more worried than either Gill or Su san, for she had more sensitivity—and he put his hanc on her shoulder in a brief gesture of comfort.

"Leave her alone, Gill. She's quite right. Father will come home when he's ready, and I for one don't want to miss the fair. I've heard there's a troupe of tumblers there who make a tower of themselves ten people high, and a fire-eater, and a man with three legs—"

"I want to go," Rowland shouted.

"Me too," Will added.

"Right, then," Ambrose said quickly, "we must get ready. Washed and dressed—best hose—hurry now. Come along, Gill, you have to help Mary put up some food for us—bread and meat will do—"

So between them Mary and Ambrose hustled the family along, and by seven o'clock they were in the wagon, which they were sharing with another family, bumping along the rutty lanes towards the village of Camberwell.

William, with the luck of the utterly careless, had not been either murdered or picked up by the Watch. He had spent the night sleeping in the Cathedral church-yard, and when the Watch came by with their lanterns on poles, he had merely covered his face with his arm, and they had not noticed him. As soon as it was light he went back into the church for the first celebration. He stayed there all day, sitting through every celebration,

d at six o'clock he suddenly realized that he was both
ngry and lonely, that he wanted to go back to the
n-in-Splendor and eat and drink and sit with his fam-
y and tell them what had happened, and then go to his
ble under the window and start to write. He felt enor-
ously energetic and happy, quite different from his
ormal vague, almost lethargic self. He came out into
e cool evening light and started to walk briskly home-
ard.

The family was heading homeward too. The wagon
olted violently over the ruts, flinging them about so
hat they had to hold wearily onto the sides to keep
hemselves from going overboard, but they didn't mind.
Happy, sticky, dusty, tired, their faces flushed and their
eyes half-closed, they were going home after a day of
great pleasure and excitement; their heads were full of
the sights and sounds of the fair. They had gaped at the
freaks, cheered the tumblers and the fire-eater and the
stilt-walkers, applauded the musicians, shrieked at the
morrisers, eaten hot pasties, pawed over the ribbons
and toys and cheap, pretty, tawdry goods of the chapmen, danced until their feet were sore, laughed until
their sides ached, stared and pointed and chattered until
their brains reeled.

The cart jolted on, the old horse plodding half
asleep, the carter on his high seat flapping the reins
against its bony rump more from habit than because he
expected any result from it, and the people behind leaning against each other or against the sides of the cart
and shifting from foot to foot with weariness. It was
growing dark—they had left it later than they had
meant to come away—and chilly, and the horse seemed
to go more slowly every moment, but they were all too
sleepy to care much or to think how overgrown the
hedges were along this road.

Disaster struck as suddenly as lightning. A man
jumped out from the hedge in front of the horse, star-

tling it out of its normal lethargy so that it snorted a
half reared, and then screamed as the man cut its thro
with his large, gleaming knife. The cart jerked forwa
as the horse sank down in the dust, and the passenge
were thrown violently against each other, some losi
their footing. Meanwhile two other men had jumpe
out behind the cart, rough-looking men, gaunt enoug
to show that they were starving and desperate.

"All right, good people, let's have your purses a
Come on, come on, hurry up about it! And those ea
rings, missus, and anything else you've got about yo
Come on now, or do we have to come up there and ge
them?"

Frightened and bewildered, they stared at each other
unable to move either to obey or attack. The man who
had spoken spoke again, more impatiently, as othe
dark forms crept like rats out of the hedgerow.

"Why, you are all dazed sick! I can see we'll have to
help you. Come on down, all of you, one at a time, and
we'll see what you've got. Come on—it'll be the worse
for you if we have to come up and get you."

They began to climb down from the back, dazed and
stupid; all but the carter, who had clambered down
over the front of the cart and was sitting in the dust by
his horse, weeping and stroking its gaunt white head.
As they reached the road they were seized roughly by
the men and searched, their purses and any other valu-
ables being snatched away. One or two put up a struggle, but a knife held to the throat was a strong per-
suader against objection.

"God's breath, but we've got a poor crew here, Mak,
and that's the truth. This 'on't keep us for long. Cut
that purse there, Bill, don't wait for him to untie it.
Wait, now, what have we here?"

Susan had jumped down, stumbling a little as she
landed, and the man who was the leader caught her un-
gently and straightened her up. Her cheeks were pink,

er hair slightly disheveled, and she was wearing flow-
rs pinned in her curls, faded wild flowers that a young
man who danced with her had picked for her. She
looked at the robber, too frightened to look away. He
smiled unpleasantly.

"God's ears, but you're a soft 'un," he breathed. Ambrose threw himself forward, and the man made a gesture to fend him off as he was caught by two of the
others. "No you don't, my lad, or you'll get your nose
slit. Jed, have you got all? Well, we'll go then. Thank
you, kind people, for your generosity. We'll remember
you in our prayers. Get along now. No, not you, my
girl," he jerked Susan back. "I've a mind to have you.
We'll take you along with us."

At that both Ambrose and Will started forward, but
to no avail. There was a brief struggle, and Gill
screamed as Will fell to the road, hit on the head from
the side by a rock in the hand of one of the robbers.
Mary ran forward but was thrown easily to the ground,
and Ambrose sank to his knees with a choking cry,
clutching his middle where he had been stabbed. None
of the others moved, and the men went through the
hedge the way they had come, taking Susan with them,
thrown like a bundle of rags over the shoulder of one of
them.

It had all taken no more than half a dozen heart-
beats. Mary crawled over to Ambrose and pried his fingers away from his wound and said, "You're bleeding
like a pig. Is it bad?"

"Hurts," he said tersely. "But I don't think it's bad.
Quick, we must get after them. Oh, God, for a light! Is
the horse dead?"

"Wait, I must look at Will," Mary said, scrambling
up.

He was beginning to come around. He sat up, groaning, and said, "Oh, my head. What happened?"

Mary pushed his head to one side. There was a nasty

flesh wound, and it was bleeding copiously, as suc
wounds will, so that his face looked a terrible sight
streaming scarlet.

"They hit you with a rock. They've got Susan," Mary
said.

Will tried to get to his feet and reeled back. "Dizzy,"
he muttered.

"Ambrose, you mustn't go alone, they'll kill you!"
Mary screamed, seeing him head for the hedge. She
looked at the menfolk of the other party with contempt.
"Help him, can't you?"

The carter suddenly came forward, his tear-wet face
suffused with anger.

"They killed my old Mayflower. I'll go with you," he
said.

"In God's name, then, be quick," Ambrose cried in
anguish, and he and the carter went through the hedge,
followed after a second's hesitation by the other two
men.

Will tried again to rise and began to vomit, and Gill,
for once shaken to sense, grabbed Rowland as he was
about to follow. "You go, Mary," she said. "I'll look
after these. Go on!"

The robbers had not had much start, but it was
enough for them to be out of sight. Beyond the hedge
was a marshy, tussocky fallow leading down to a stream
fringed with osiers and thorn tangle, and beyond it a
ragged wood. The ground showed no footprints, and
there was nothing to tell them which way they had
gone, but the wood was the obvious direction for
fleeing men to choose. They searched in the growing
gloom, calling to each other, calling for Susan in case
she should be near enough to call back. They cast up
the stream and down, and it was a little upstream that
they found the brambles beaten down and branches
snapped off by a hasty flight of several heavy bodies.
There, in a brake, they found her, lying on her back by

...e water's edge, one hand flung back so that her fin-
...ers trailed the water. Her bare legs gleamed white
...gainst the dark leaf rot, her head was turned away,
...nd the hard pearl of her teeth showed through her
...arted lips. She looked as though she were wearing a
...lark scarf around her neck, and when Ambrose, sick
...nd shaking, knelt and turned her head gently toward
...im, it almost came away in his hands, for her throat
...ad been cut right through, so savagely that only her
...neck bone held it in place.

They were met some way out from home by a group
of people with lanterns, led by William, who had grown
almost frantic when darkness came and his family had
not come home. Everyone knew they had gone to the
fair, and at last he had managed to gather a dozen men
together willing to go at least part of the way along the
road, and when they had gone about a mile they met
them. It was a pitiful sight, the weary, dusty, tear-
streaked and bloodstained people plodding along, taking turns to pull the cart on which, wrapped in a cloak,
was the body of Susan. Will, much against his desire,
also rode, keeping his eyes firmly turned away from the
rolling bundle. He was still too sick and dizzy to walk,
though he had tried several times.

They were all too shocked and tired to talk, and it
took a long time to get the story from them, and when
they got back to the tavern there were still questions
being asked while the womenfolk were bandaging Ambrose's and Will's wounds and laying out the body of
the girl. For William the shock came later, after everyone was at last in bed, sleeping the dead sleep of those
tired beyond endurance; for him sleep was impossible,
and he kept vigil over his daughter, too grieved and
horrified to weep.

He had admired Mary, but Susan he had loved in a
special way, the particular way a man loves his first-

born daughter, a tender, protective kind of love. S]
had always been dutiful, sweet and good, and of la
had grown into a delicate and blooming prettines
Soon, he knew, some great lout would have wanted 1
marry her, and he would have had to give away his li
tle maiden to the grossness of mankind, and he woul
have mourned her, though seeing the necessity. Had sh
died of fever or pox, he would have mourned her, too
but this death went beyond mourning. He could not ri
his mind of the horror of her last moments, seeing ove
and over again her terrified struggles as she was carrie(
away into the dark and flung down among the snapping
twigs, and ravished, and murdered. It was as if her terror still reverberated on the air, so clearly could he see
and hear it.

And he was to blame. He should have been there to
protect her instead of wandering in London, absorbed
in his own selfish pleasures. He should have taken his
family to the fair; he should have made sure they left
early enough to get home safely in daylight; he should
have been there, armed with a sword, to keep them
from harm. He had failed in his duty, and Susan, soft,
gentle Susan, had paid. He put his head in his hands
and pressed his eyes with the heels of his hands. He was
exhausted, not having eaten for two days, and though
he could not sleep, he must have drifted for a moment
or two, for he heard a voice saying, "Father."

His spine grew rigid with terror. It was Susan's voice.
She had come back to haunt him! All the old supersti-
tions, so shallowly buried by the modern-thinking man,
rose up in him. Slowly, in terror, he raised his head and
took his hands from his eyes.

There by the door, a pale gleam in the candle-
shadowed room, was a female figure in white. William
could feel the hair lifting on his scalp, a cold, prickling
sensation. The candle flames dipped sideways in the
draft from the door, and Mary said again, "Father."

William let his breath out carefully. The dead lay till, and Mary's voice had always been very like Susan's. "I've come to help you keep watch. Are you tired? You look as though you haven't slept for a week. You still haven't told us where you were yesterday. Let me see to the candles first—they need trimming, and that one's nearly burned out. It must be the draft from the window."

Talking gently, as one will to reassure a horse, she moved about her little tasks, and William's weary eyes followed her, feeling the calm and comfort flowing out from her. Then she came and stood before him and looked at him kindly, head a little to one side, and he told himself she was a child of thirteen, and his brain refused the information.

"Are you come to chide me, chuck?" he said at last.

She put a hand up and smoothed his hair from his brow. "No, Father. I've come to sit with you."

William shuddered. "Mary, hinny, berate me, chastise me, call me bitter names—I deserve it all. But don't be kind to me. Your kindness breaks my heart."

She sat down beside him and looked at the still, white-clad figure of her sister lying on the trestles. The hands were folded over the breasts, the thumbs locked and tied to prevent the arms straightening as they stiffened, and a white cloth was tied tightly around the throat to keep the head in position. Mary kept her eyes on the cloth and the piece of tape around the thumbs. The little details kept her from thinking about Susan. That body was not Susan—Susan was on her way to glory now, winging upward like a white pigeon let out of the cotes at dawn, with her upspotted, maiden soul. But without the piece of tape and white cloth, it looked so like Susan, lying between four candles, that she might at any moment get up and walk toward them.

"I can't chide you," she said at last. "I don't know

that you are to blame for anything. She is gone to Go
now, Father, and we can't call her back, even if w
should want to. I'm only afraid——"

"What, chuck?"

"That she will walk," Mary whispered, fearful eve
of the words. William, without even knowing he did it
crossed himself. "They say," Mary went on, "tha
women who die that way won't rest until their murderer
is brought to justice. And we don't even know who he
is."

William said nothing. He could not comfort Mary,
because his own thoughts had gone that way. He tried
to think of something else, and the only thing to hand in
his mind was his experience of Sunday, so he told her
that. For once she listened to him, and he was surprised.

"You never thought it was important, my music, did
you?" he said in the end.

"No," she said simply.

"But life has to be more than this—this human
clay," William went on, pinching up a fold of flesh on
his hand; gesturing toward the corpse of his daughter.
"More than *this*. We strive and struggle, work, get our
bread, beget our children, see them die, die ourselves,
and there had to be more to it than that."

Mary looked puzzled. "But we are told, from childhood——"

"Yes, we are told, but it doesn't mean anything.
Mary, it meant nothing to me, though I was brought up
in it, in the Old Faith, the celebration—but it meant
nothing until yesterday—Sunday—when I *felt* it. I *felt* it,
chuck, with my bones and my bowels and my breath,
and now I know."

"Yes, I see," Mary said. "I don't understand, but I
see. So what will you do?"

He drew a breath shudderingly, discovering he had
tensed every muscle in the effort to make her under-

nd. "I have hardly had time to think. I must write, I
ist have time to write. I can't go on with the com-
ny; it takes up too much time and energy."

"But how will we live?" she asked with a child's sim-
city, accepting that he would do what he said. He
oked at her with love. An adult would have argued
th him. She would simply accept what he chose and
ake it work.

"This is no life for you," he said abruptly. "I should
ver have—"

"What?" she said, for her father was staring at her
ith his mouth open. "What?"

"I have just seen it. We shall go home, Mary child. I
on't know why I didn't think of it before. I may have
o beg forgiveness, but after all these years, surely
hey—"

"Home?"

"To Morland Place," he said. "Where I was born.
And the chapel—what an inspiration! You'll love it,
inny, I promise."

He thought of the red-brick house, the tall chimneys
and cool gardens, the fresh wind off the hilltops, the sun
shining on the glazed windows, the holy beauty of the
chapel. He looked at Susan—it was too late for her. "I
wish she could have seen it," he said. But every truth
had to have a sacrifice. Her blood paid for all. Already
he heard the opening phrases of the litany in his head.
Mary looked at him with affectionate exasperation,
seeing he had gone off into one of his dreams again.
Her mind was already jumping ahead to preparations,
packing and traveling. Of Morland Place she thought
nothing. She was not of a temper to question the inevitable.

CHAPTER TWENTY-ONE

Though it was the best and most convenient room fo
the purpose, Douglass did not want to give birth in the
solar after Celia had died there, and Thomas quelled
Jean's arguments with a glance and at once gave orders
for the preparation of the bedchamber.

"It is better that way," he said. "After all, both our
parents were born in that chamber; and in the Butts
bed. It is right that the Morland heir should be, too."
So he converted her nervous whim into a dynastic decision, and she looked silent gratitude at him. It was only
when she was low that he became decisive and master-
ful. The bedchamber was cleared, the other beds moved
to other rooms, new rushes spread on the floor, the suit
of childbed linen laid ready in the chest at the foot of
the bed. A store of candles was placed ready, and the
silver ewer and basin Thomas had ordered arrived and
were taken up to be placed on a tripod in the corner.
Finally he ordered the unicorn tapestry to be taken
down from the solar and rehung in the bedchamber,
and fresh flowers to be arranged around the room for
as long as it was being used, and these little touches
Douglass noted with gratitude and love.

On the day after May Day the baby dropped inside
er, and she retired to the chamber with her women.
ane came from Shawes to attend the birth, and Jean
vas there, of course. Lesley was at the other end of the
ouse, keeping as far from events as possible. It would
ot have been lucky for her to be present. She occu-
ied her time in playing with her little half-brother
Rob, for whom she had a great fondness, and in admiring Celia's surviving babies, Hilary and Sabina, who
were contented now with a wet nurse, a young girl
called Meg on whom the courtesy title "Mother" sat
oddly.

The labor began late in the night of the fifth of May,
and just before noon on the sixth Jane came downstairs
into the great hall bearing the new baby on a cushion.

"A son!" she said to the assembled family and servants, and a great cheer went up as Thomas came forward to receive his child into his arms. He looked down
at the swaddled bundle, at the crumpled red face,
tightly sleeping, and such tenderness and gladness swept
over him that he could not speak for a moment. Then
through the noise of congratulation and comment one
voice was raised louder than the rest.

"What shall you call 'im, Maister?"

Thomas looked up, and his eyes met Jane's, and he
smiled.

"Edward," he said, and a new cheer went up. "And
now I must go and see how my lady does."

"God bless her!"

"Give her our best respects, Maister!"

"Eh, what a bonny bairn."

"The little day star."

Through a torrent of cries he made his way to the
stairs and mounted to the bedchamber with Jane following behind. Douglass had been washed and tidied,
and the mess had been cleared away, but the room still

smelled of blood. Douglass was propped on her pillow
looking tired but otherwise rosy and healthy, and there
was a smile of pure triumph on her face. Her dark hair
hung curling loose all about her, and her blue eyes were
as bright as stars. She and Thomas exchanged a long
look of love and accomplishment, and then he came
over to her to kiss her and place the bairn in her arms.

"I think we should call him Edward," Thomas said
as they gazed together at the sleeping face.

Douglass smiled. "It is a good name. And his device
should be a phoenix." She looked up suddenly into
Thomas's eyes, her expression grave but not unhappy.
"Thomas, husband, while I was in labor, I prayed for
deliverance—"

He pressed her hand, shuddering lightly. "Thank
God you are safe."

"I prayed," she went on, "not only to God and Our
Lord, but to the Blessed Lady and the Saints. It
seemed—natural, somehow." She looked apologetic,
but beyond Thomas, Jane nodded slightly as though
agreeing that it was what one would do. "And, Thomas,
I promised the Lady that if I was brought safely
through, we would restore her chapel to her."

She looked at him anxiously and pleadingly, and he
leaned down and kissed her forehead. "Whatever you
promised shall be fulfilled," he said softly.

She relaxed visibly. "Husband," she said, "I have
been thinking for a long time that we ought to have a
chaplain in the house. The children will need a tutor as
they grow up, and I cannot bear to have the chapel unused."

"Of course, you are right," he said. "We will find
one as soon as may be—there will be a man somewhere
who will satisfy both our consciences and the law.
There is no need for us to endanger anyone or anything."

"Except for the Lady-chapel," Douglass said in a
small voice. "I promised Her that Her statue would be
put up again."

Thomas smiled. "One little statue—no one will per-
secute us for that."

"I promised Her a new crown," Douglass said in an
even smaller voice.

"She shall have one—of gold and pearls," Thomas
said. The baby began to cry, and Jane came to take it
from Douglass to the wet nurse, and as she bent over to
pick the bundle up, she gave Douglass a most peculiar
and sweet smile and kissed her.

"Bless you," Jane said softly. "Phoenix indeed!"

A chaplain-tutor was found by the end of the month,
a scholarly young man called Ashcroft, who had been
born nearby at Aksham and had studied theology at
Cambridge. He was an intelligent and humane man, of
Cranmerian bent, and he agreed with Thomas that
there was no need to challenge the law but that the offi-
cal celebration could be used without violating the conscience. He looked with indulgent amusement at the ancient wooden statue of the Virgin in the Lady-chapel in
its gown of blue silk, tied with golden cord, and its new
crown of gold set with little seed pearls, and suggested
building a secret compartment behind the paneling for
the sudden concealment of such things should the need
arise.

Thus it was when John arrived from Northumberland
for his visit to see his first grandson that the chapel was
once again in use, and the only criticism that he could
make was that compromise was never a good thing. It
was good to be back, good to ride out on his own moors
again. Thomas showed him his new horses with pride,
Jan took him to visit the school and the hospital and
displayed the improvements that had been made there,
and hunts and masques were organized for him. It was

when he and Jan were coming back from a visit t
Shawes, riding back down toward the ford accompanie
by young Nehemiah, that they saw the strange proces
sion up ahead of them heading toward Morland Place

There was a white mule drawing a two-wheeled car
in which rode a woman, a young girl and a boy o
about six. Hitched to the back of the cart was a little
gray ass loaded with bundles, beside which walked a
boy of ten or so; and leading the mule, one on either
side of it, were two men. They were neatly but plainly
dressed, all in black, and wearing mourning ribbons,
else they might have been taken for Puritans. The
younger of the two men had a very long crimson
feather in his bonnet, which he wore at a jaunty angle;
the older man was bareheaded, and his hair shone pale
as water in the sunlight. The sight of that moonshine
hair tugged at John's heart, recalling Mary so abruptly
and vividly that it served only to remind him how long
it was since he had laid her in the dark earth. His hound
Kee, who ran at his heels, was a mature dog now;
Mary's Kai was dead; and Mary's son had a son. John
had been pleased with the improvement in Thomas and
recognized that it was the work of Lettice's daughter.
He wondered if age was mellowing him, for he was beginning to think it had been a good thing for Thomas to
come here.

Kee ran out ahead of him with a warnng bark, and
the fair-haired man turned to look and then halted the
cart to wait for them, in courtesy.

"Now who do you suppose that could be?" Jan murmured, scratching his badger-striped beard. "They
hardly look like gypsies, yet I would not be surprised to
discover that that cart holds all they own."

"I don't know, Bear-cub," John said. "But they are
waiting for us, so we had better go and see. Perhaps
they have lost their way and want direction."

"They don't look dangerous, at any rate," Jan said. "You had better call off your dog."

John touched his heel to Kestrel's flank and they trotted down the slope toward the ford. As they approached, the fair man gave the reins of the mule to the younger man and stepped out to stand in the road facing them, his hands a little out from his side and palms forward, as if to show he had no ill intent. John noted with a prickle of misgiving that not only was he bareheaded, he was also clean-shaven, as was the younger man, which was odd: even Thomas had grown his beard now he was married.

The pale, shining hair and clean-shaven face made the man look young, and yet as the two horses were reined in in front of him, John saw the lines of age and of new grief. A strange, old-young face, and strangely familiar. It was tugging at him in a way that had nothing to do with Mary.

"God's day to you both," the man called, and then, starting and staring closer, he cried out, "as God lives, it is John and Jan Chapham!"

John and Jan exchanged a glance, and seeing it, the fair man said, "Why, don't you know me? Have I changed so much? John, brother, it is William—I am your brother William—don't you remember?"

John was very still. "My brother William is dead," he said. The fair man laughed suddenly and struck his palm to his forehead.

"I had forgotten. Yes, that's what was agreed—Aunt Nan was to say nothing. Father thought I was dead. But Aunt Nan will tell you all about it—she will speak for me."

"Aunt Nan?" Jan said cautiously.

William smiled up at him, squinting against the sunlight. "Your mother, Jan. Come now!"

"My mother is dead," Jan said. He saw surprise and

shock register on the fair man's face, and then saw him rally himself.

"Then—Matthew, her man—he will speak for me. He was the one that found me after I ran away."

"Matthew, too, is dead," Jan said.

The man put a vague hand to his face "Yes—yes—it has been so long. One must expect it. But—I had not thought." He looked up suddenly. "My father—is he—dead too?"

It was that which convinced John—the way he said "My father." "Yes," he said. "And Lettice, and Arthur, and Hezekiah. I have lost too much family to refuse to know you. William, brother, let me embrace you."

He swung down from his horse and stepped up to William, and the two embraced hard. Jan leaned from the saddle to catch Kestrel's rein and watched expressionlessly.

William looked dazed. "So many—so many. I had forgotten how long it was. John—tell me—is Jane—?"

"Jane is well. This is her son. And Lettice's daughter and my son are married, and have Morland Place now. There will be much that is different to you. But where have you been all these years? Why did you never come home?"

"It's a long tale," William said. "I dare say we'll have enough tales for months to come. We had better wait until we get home to begin."

"Home," Jan echoed. They looked up at him. "Who are these people you travel with, William?"

He laughed. "Lord, yes, I must introduce you all. My wife and children—"

"Ah," said Jan. "And you have come home—for good?"

"The prodigal returns," William said and laughed, hugging John again. "Lord, but it's good to see you."

John, however, was looking up at Jan. "What is it, bear-cub? What troubles you?"

"I just wondered why he comes like this after all this time," he said.

John frowned, and William, looking from one to the other, appeared suddenly enlightened.

"Ah, you think I am an imposter, a pretender to the throne? For shame, Jan Chapham, to think so ill of a cousin. No, I do not come to change anything or to claim anything. I wanted only to come home. If John's son does not want me, then I'll away again. But as to why I have come—that, too, is a long story, and stories are best told with all comfortably sitting. Will you refuse a party of weary travelers rest and food? My father would not have turned any man hungry from his door."

John looked at Jan reproachfully and said, "Of course not. We will go home at once, and there will be food and drink in plenty. Come, let us go."

The procession moved on. The others had watched quietly, apprehensively even, while the conversation was going on, and now they followed obediently as Jan and John rode past them across the ford, their eyes taking in everything warily. Rowland stared enviously at Nehemiah's horse as the latter rode past, and Nehemiah grew a little warm and self-conscious under the not entirely friendly gaze. Mary sighed as the cart jolted on again, flinging her against the side on places already bruised almost numb, and Gill, having noted the fine apparel of the mounted men, stared at her dirty fingernails and work-scarred hands and wondered who there would be in this new place to scold and bully her.

There was so much to be told. Not only had William to tell all of his story, but he had to be told everything that had happened since at Morland Place and Shawes and Watermill, and what had happened to John and to Lettice. There were all the new people to be assimi-

lated, and that was not without its problems. Gill, fo
instance, seemed to belong more happily with the ser
vants, and yet she was William's wife—though no on
knew or liked to ask what, if any, form of marriag
they had gone through. Rowland was boisterous an
displayed so many bad habits that it was hard to believe
he was William's son. He soon quarreled violently with
Nehemiah, who disapproved of him and told him so,
and got into trouble with Nicholas because Amory began to imitate his bad language and swaggering airs.
Will felt compelled to side with his little brother, and
he felt sad that they were such outsiders, for he loved
Morland Place already and did not want to have to
leave, though he foresaw that they would be turned out
if Rowland continued to make trouble.

Others managed better. Mary, though she was in-
clined at first through nervousness to be a little sharp
and bossy, soon found a friend and defender in Jean,
who admired the child for her energetic endeavors to
keep the family together while she pitied her for the
hardships of the life she had led. Ambrose had mixed
with gentlemen and acted them often enough to be able
to fit in with any society, and both Nicholas and Gabriel sought out his company in order to hear the tales
he could not tell in front of the women.

Then, in the middle of all this, Gill and Rowland fell
sick with a pox, and Lesley went into labor. The house
seemed in chaos, lights burning all through the night,
people running about with ewers of water and cups of
physic, no one where they should be, nothing done to
routine. Jean had to be with Lesley, who grew hysteri-
cal if her sister left her, and so the organization of the
care of the sick fell naturally on the shoulders of Mary,
and after the first few hours it no longer seemed strange
to anyone that a child of thirteen should be the one to
whom all questions were referred. Douglass was mis-

ress of the house and made the overall decisions, but he had always left the day-to-day running to Jean, as o a steward, and she was glad enough in all conscience not to have to take up that task again.

Besides, Thomas had caught the pox, and though lightly, he had never been ill before, and she was so worried that she would not leave his side for a moment. Suppose he dies? she kept thinking, and life without him appeared so barren that she sat with him day and night, holding his hand tightly as if he might be snatched from her.

Lesley was delivered in the middle of the night of a boy-child. Gabriel was delighted and offered to name it after her father for her. She smiled but said nothing, seeming flushed and feverish. By the morning the spots had appeared, and it was plain she had caught the pox, too. The baby was removed to the nursery by Mother Meg, where, with a second wet nurse who had been hired for Edward, all four babies were suckled. With the wisdom of hindsight, Jean afterward said that was what was done wrong, for though it did not occur to anyone at the time, it seemed that Lesley's baby had the infection from her, and passed it on, and soon every child in the house was sick. It was not the smallpox but the lesser sort, and the strong survived it without difficulty. Aletheia and Amory had it lightly and hardly noticed it; Rob and Rowland had it more severely but after a week were mending; but with the babies it was serious. Lesley's baby lived only a day, and Edward and Hilary died two days later, and at the end of the week, when it began to appear that Sabina might recover, Lesley herself died; though Jean said that it was not the pox but the childbed fever that had killed her.

Though the pox also proved fatal to poor Gill, Thomas recovered with nothing but a few pockmarks on his forehead to show for it. But other scars there were,

though they did not appear. He was more distressed t
the death of Edward than Douglass was, and inwardl
he felt that in some way the failure was his. He love
Douglass and wanted to give her everything, and in thi
case he could not give her anything. For a long tim
after he rose from his sickbed he moped, until his fa
ther, exasperated, took him to one side and spoke t
him firmly, telling him that he must shake himself u̧
and get his wife with child again.

"I had hoped she might be with child again before .̧
left," he said, "but I cannot stay much longer away.
Still, I expect to hear from you in a letter very soon that
an heir is expected."

"Father, must you go?" Thomas said. "Cannot you
stay here with us all the time? You know Jan would
wish it, and surely you want to be with your brother
after all this time?"

"But someone must look after Tod's Knowe."

"You could put in a steward—or better still, let it to
a tenant."

John smiled at that. "It is not that kind of place,
Thomas, as you should know. Well, well, perhaps one
day, when I am too old to keep it; I should like in some
ways to live here. But I cannot leave your mother."

"Oh," Thomas said, turning his head away.

John touched his shoulder. "You must get a great
many sons, so that one of them can come to Tod's
Knowe and take over from me when I grow too old.
That is the best way."

"But you will visit?"

"Of course. It is not so far, now that the roads are so
much safer. Every time you have a son to christen, I
will come."

Thomas smiled. "Then I hope it will be every year."

John stayed to the end of summer in order to see a
little more of William. He found his brother strange,
but there was a level of communication between them,

r they seemed both to be searching for the same
ing, though by different means. Once he had settled
own in the house, William spent much of the time in
he chapel and the rest walking alone on the moors or
isiting other churches, especially the Minster, or sitting
a a corner of the winter parlor writing. Sometimes he
would play small sections on the clavicytherium or lute,
nd sometimes he would call Rowland or Will or Ne-
emiah to sing phrases to him, but otherwise he shared
his work with no one. Mary took it philosophically, as
he took everything, and explained to anyone who
sked that it was always thus with Father. To John
alone, William made a comment on his work.

"It will be my masterpiece," he said. "When I have
completed it, I will have justified my life, and I will
know God has done with me."

"I envy you," John said.

The autumn colors were just beginning to be apparent when John and his small retinue arrived home. The
place had been well run in his absence by the steward,
but there were many small matters that needed his attention, and it was not until the third day after his ar-
rival that he had leisure to walk up the hill to his favorite vantage place, the rowan tree under which Kithra
was buried. He sat down on a granite outcrop, pulled
Kee against his knees and, idly caressing the dog's ears,
looked out over his kingdom.

It was darkening, and rain was coming, the skies
heavy with great rolls of plum-purple clouds, and a
fresh damp wind was blowing toward him down the valley, singing against his ears. To the north, toward Scotland, there was a break in the clouds, invisible to him
except that through it a great silver band of light was
falling with edges as straight as blades, lighting the
round flanks of the hills and the thick woods, still at
this distance late-summer green. Kee sighed comfort-

ably and leaned harder against him, settling himself, an
John's hand slowed and stilled.

He was home. He realized it now, though when h‹
was at Morland Place the familiarity and old associa
tions confused him into thinking that that was home
But it was here in Redesdale that he had lived mor‹
than half his life, here married and begotten his son,
here laid his wife to rest. Jan had given him his first
hound; his first horse had been bred at Morland Place.
But the horse he rode now was a Borderland horse, and
his hound was buried here under this dark turf.

He still did not understand; there was no pattern apparent, no direction for the future, any more than there
had been that day when he buried Kithra, and still the
long days stretched empty before him, like a trackless
waste in which there were no landmarks or directons.
But if grace was to be found anywhere, it was here, and
like William, it was grace that he was seeking. He
sought it through his life and the life of his people and
of the Church; and in the little, turf-roofed church he
attended, dark inside and crowded with statues and
paintings and relics and glittering with the pinpoint
lights of candles like the starry sky on a moonless night,
he took comfort. He did not know anymore how to go
forward—he could only retrace his steps and try to find
where he had gone wrong.

By Christmas Douglass was pregnant again, but in
the early summer of 1590 she miscarried. Thomas converted his grief into a furious burst of energy about the
demesne lands, reading every book he could find on
husbandry, in unconscious imitation of Paul, and turning
his mind and skills toward improved farming methods.
The horses were eating most of the hay and sainfoin he
could grow, and the problem of winter feed, which had
always been a severe one, was exacerbated by them.
The sheep that were kept through the winter survived

what they could graze, though in a severe winter
eir flocks were reduced most dangerously; the cattle
rvived on what hay was kept for them and otherwise
browsing on the tree loppings, eating the moss and
:hen and even the bark off the trimmed branches.

Fitzherbert in his *Book of Husbandry* and Tusser in
is *Five Hundred Points* had little to offer in the way of
elp; but there was a Dutch book by a man called Heres-
ach, which had been translated into English by one
arnaby Googe, and when Thomas managed to get
old of that he found a very interesting suggestion,
vhich seemed likely to solve or at least alleviate the
roblem. Heresbach said that horses and cattle could
urvive and remain fit by eating turnips, and that turnips, if properly stored, would keep right through the
winter. It was a revolutionary idea—cottagers grew turnips in their gardens, but only for their own consump-
tion, and it had never occurred to anyone before to
grow them as cattle feed. But, so Heresbach said, not
only did cattle thrive on turnips, but the turnips seemed
to do the ground good, and cereal crops grew better if rotated with turnips.

Thomas determined to try it and eagerly read other
suggestions in the book. Another advantage of keeping
the cattle through the winter was that they made a lot
more manure, which helped the ground. Heresbach
spoke very forcibly about the importance of manure.
Thomas threw himself into it with a will. He could not
bring himself to be interested in sheep, and luckily for
him, Jan was perfectly content to oversee that side of
the business for him. Horses and cattle were what
Thomas understood, and he was learning about husbandry. The first crop of turnips proved a success, and
from then on the cropping of the demesne lands was
reorganized on a four-year rotation instead of three:
rye or wheat, then turnips, then barley, and then fallow.

The people round about thought him mad to change
system that was hallowed by time and custom, but whe
they saw his fat kine at the Shrovetide killing, they r
vised their opinions.

In the spring of 1591 Douglass miscarried again, an
in the February of 1592 she bore a son who lived ju:
three days. In the spring of that year Thomas turned hi
frustrated energies to improving the house. Its mai
fault by modern standards was that the upper floo
could only be reached by means of the spiral staircases
which were steep and narrow and difficult to manage
carrying a burden. Thomas's idea was to build a proper,
open, modern staircase at the north end of the Hall.

"By using the musicians' gallery as its landing, we
can save a great deal of work," he told Douglass enthusiastically. "The estate carpenter can do most of it, and
we can get that man in from York to do the carving—
what's his name?—the one who did the work for the
King's Manor."

To please him, Douglass tried to show interest, and
as the work proceeded the pretense gradually became
reality. It was something to keep her mind off their lack
of an heir. In the autumn of '92 she conceived again,
but in March '93 she miscarried and in the following
year bore a stillborn son. That year, 1594, Thomas had
the great chimney rebuilt and the fireplace enlarged. In
'95 there was no pregnancy at all, and in September '96
Douglass conceived again, only to lose the child at the
end of January, whereupon Thomas planted young
trees all along the Long Walk and engaged a miniaturist
to make the portraits of every member of the family for
hanging on the wall of the winter parlor. In July 1597
Douglass entered upon her seventh pregnancy and her
thirtieth year, and William started upon the last section
of his polyphonic Mass.

CHAPTER TWENTY-TWO

The harvest in 1597 was poor again, for the fourth year
in succession. The poor starved: it was not unusual for
old or sick folk to die in the winter from lack of food,
but in York that winter four people who should have
been in their prime died in the streets from hunger. The
hospital on the south road was full, and the Morlands,
like every rich family, gave out alms and food at the
door daily. But there was little enough to eat, even for
the Morlands, and when the turnip crop, planted at
mid-summer for winter feed, was ready, the cattle got
only the tops and leaves—the rest went for human con-
sumption.

Despite that, despite the cold and the empty bellies,
everyone was cheerful within the house. Douglass had
passed the dangerous fifth month without slipping her
child, and though she had lost flesh until her bones
seemed like to come out through her skin, she seemed
healthy and comfortable. Thomas's reaction to hunger
and hardship was to arrange entertainments, masques
and pageants and games of all sorts, and since the family was largely confined to the house, there was no lack

of participants. He turned always to Ambrose for ide
and for the practical details, and Ambrose never fail
him. He called in Will and Gabriel as his faithful lieute
ants, and Mary's nimble fingers would devise co
tumes or props out of whatever was available, just
she would bully the cook into making meals out of th
most unlikely ingredients when everything ran sho
Jan, looking on, saw how the families had settled in t
gether and wondered if Paul would have been surprise
at the love between the heir and the pretenders.

Everyone made a special effort at Christmastide, fo
after that would come the really lean time, the dead o
winter and the long Lenten fast. Mary and Jean ha
been quietly putting things aside for the twelve-da
feast. Corn of all sorts might be scarce, but from thei
own growing there were dried figs and currants and
apricots, stored apples and pears; Jan and Amory had
taken joint responsibility for the hives and had carefully
moved them to the best grazing places, so there was
upland thyme and lowland clover honey to make up
for the lack of sugar; and in his pen in the sheltered
part of the orchard the Christmas goose was living the
life of a king in preparation for his big day. Some things
could be bought for money—oranges, for instance, and
spices—though wine was scarce and ale scarcer; but the
hunting expedition that went out on Christmas Eve
morning came back with a buck in very good condition,
and a bull calf that was born early provided veal for
pies and stews as well as tender offal. No one was likely
to refuse to eat humble pie this Christmas.

At New Year the presents were exchanged, and
Thomas made the biggest impression with his present to
Douglass, which was a new tapestry for her bedchamber, specifically for her lying-in. He had sold some
plate to pay for it and had ordered it from the same
family in York who had made the unicorn tapestry;

ey were still the best in that country. It was a long,
arrow cloth that would admirably suit the gallery wall
f the chamber, and it portrayed the four seasons, in-
eniously united by a hunting-and-hawking party that
ode through the four from left to right. In the center,
t the place where spring gave way to summer, a
voman in a blue dress with her black hair streaming
down her back rode upon a dainty white horse with a
golden bridle.

"That's you," Thomas told the admiring Douglass.
'Look more closely." She did so and exclaimed with
delight. The white horse was so cunningly woven that
when you looked closely you could see that what
looked like a part of the tree behind him was in fact a
golden horn: the maiden was riding on a unicorn.

The family feasted and made merry for twelve days.
Then came Epiphany and Plough Monday, and a dead,
bitter, black cold set in over the country, and belts were
tightened again around already lean waists. Firewood
became hard to find, especially with the continuing
snowfalls, and so what warmth there was was concentrated in one room—the winter parlor, which was always the warmest room in the house. There, there was
always a good fire and, when needed, extra braziers,
and there Douglass sat, sewing, reading, playing the
clavicytherium or the lute, talking and laughing with
her companions. Thomas would not allow her to be
cold, and since that room was always kept warm for
her, everyone gathered there, so it was a companionable winter if a lean one. Despite the fact that he had
always said he could not work with other people near
him, William was always in the winter parlor, sitting
near the window with his feet buried in the rushes for
warmth, writing. He was generally still there when they
went up to bed and was there, unshaven and crumpled
but working again, in the morning.

Lambing time came, and for the first time in year
there were wolves on the hilltops, and their strange, spine
chilling singing could be heard after dark. Every ma
had to take his turn at guarding the flocks, for lamb
were the prey of every flesh eater; wolf, fox, raven, ea
gle, kestrel—even stoats and owls would go for new
lambs if their dams were dead. Douglass's bairn wa
due in March, and Thomas hated to leave her, bu
though others told him he need not take a turn, he wa
too conscious of the weariness of everyone else and too
guilty over his lack of interest in the sheep to miss his
duty. The only person who did not turn out was William, and somehow it never occurred to anyone to ask
him. He lived so much in a world of his own that it was
as if there were no contact with him. Mary saw to it
that he ate from time to time, and otherwise he was left
alone.

The thaw came suddenly in the middle of lambing,
turning the earth in the course of one day from a white,
frozen blanket to an impenetrable ocean of mud. Douglass had taken advantage of the first sunshine in months
to go out into the herb garden for a gentle walk and
some fresh air. Returning to the house, as she passed
through the great hall she trod on a bone that a dog had
left lying hidden in the rushes after gnawing it, and fell
heavily. A servant passing through moments later ran to
help her as she tried to struggle to her feet, and
blanched as she cried out with pain. She was too heavy
for him to lift, and in a panic he ran to the winter parlor and called William.

"Oh, sir, quickly, the mistress has fallen, and I think
the babe is coming."

William followed the imperative, though he had not
properly taken in the message, but when he saw Douglass on her knees, hugging her belly, silent though there
was sweat on her face, he was shocked out of his dream
and ran at once to help her. Between them they got her

her feet and walked her slowly toward the bedcham-
r. For the first time William saw the benefit of the
oad, elaborately carved staircase that had replaced
e old, narrow spiral—using the latter, they would not
ave been able to support her one on either side in this
ay, and she would have had to climb unaided.

Having helped her lie down on her bed, William said
o the servant, "Run and fetch Miss Mary and Mistress
Hamilton, quickly now."

"Miss Mary is out, sir. She went into town this morn-
ng to the market."

"Miss Mary did? Alone?" William was shocked.

But, sir, there wasn't anyone else to spare. Everyone's
out at the lambing."

"Fetch Mistress Hamilton then, and someone will
have to go for the midwife," William said. "And get
one of the women to bring linen and water. Hurry up."

The man ran out, and William busied himself making
Douglass comfortable and giving her sips of water from
the ewer.

"It should be wine," he said, "to strengthen you, but
no matter. Perhaps on an empty stomach wine would
be too strong."

Douglass turned her head fretfully on the pillow and
said, "It's coming, the baby's coming. Oh dear Mother
of God, not another failure!"

"Hush! Don't say it. Look, the bairn is due to come
now. Perhaps it was already on its way when you fell.
All will be well, child. Trust in God."

Then she cried and clutched his arm, and her eyes
bulged. "It's coming!" she said, and he knew she meant
now, this minute. Where was Jean? Where were the
women? He tried to disengage his arm, but she would
not let him.

"No, don't leave me!" she cried out.

"But I must not be here—I must not see—"

"Help me!" she cried, and braced her body with the

fierce contractions that were gripping her, plucking fee
bly at her heavy skirts.

William stared at her in helpless horror. "What mu
I do?" he whispered.

"Push against my legs," Douglass said. The urgen
of her body prevented her from the shame that wou
otherwise have overcome her. Averting his head, Wi
liam put his hands to her upbent knees and pushe
back to her pushing. He was amazed at her strength
She was groaning, not, it seemed to him a groan of pai
but the long-drawn-out groan a man might make as h
tried to lift a heavy weight; then it ended in a cry c
mingled pain and accomplishment, and the pushin
stopped as abruptly as the cry. He could not stop him
self from looking down, and he saw, where she had
pulled her skirts back, saw with mingled horror and dis
gust and shame, the black-haired and bloody head of
the child protruding from her body, between her
woolen-stockinged legs.

"Oh Lord God," he muttered, trying to drag his eyes
away. "Oh Holy Mother of God preserve us."

Douglass was panting shallowly, her eyes closed, but
moments later they flew open again and she gave him a
warning cry, and he took up the strain again. This time
he was watching, and his shame and disgust gave way
to a terrified wonder as, turning and slithering a little, a
whole, complete and perfect mannikin slid out of her
body, face upward, with a great thick striped cord
sprouting from its middle like the thick stem of a
flower. As the bairn's skin came into contact with the
rough of Douglass's skirt, it opened its tiny, budlike
mouth and yelled, an astonishingly loud yell that seemed
to William to express something like anger: the child
was angry at being born, as though it knew the condition
of the world it had been forced into, and its soul, trapped
for a lifetime in a prison of flesh, to be subject to all
the ills and pains and discomforts that flesh is heir to,

made that one, furious protest before the sound became only a baby's wailing.

"What is it?" Douglass asked hoarsely.

"A son," William said, his eyes fixed on the tiny, perfect thing, its delicate nacreous fingers, its smooth, unused skin. "Oh Sweet Mary, a boy, you have a perfect little boy."

And it was at that moment that Jean and two of the older women servants rushed in and cried out in shock when they saw William, and in a moment, clucking like hens at the presence of a fox, they had hustled him out and shut the door with a hasty bang as if he might try to slip in again. Stunned and joyful, William went no more than a few paces and then sat down on the top stair of the staircase and put his elbows on his knees and his head in his hands, and simply sat there, smiling.

He was still there some time later when Jean came out to call for wine, and she looked down at him with an odd expression.

"Merciful God," she said, "but that was the quickest delivery I ever heard tell of."

"Will they be all right?" William asked eagerly. "The little lad looked so perfect—and is my niece all right?"

"Both as well as a spring day," Jean said, "and looking to thrive. Quick deliveries are always best for mother and child. You should not have been there. You should not have seen what you saw. What would people think? Poor Douglass will be mortified when she thinks about it."

William smiled the sweet smile that had earned him the title of angel in his youth. "I never saw anything so wonderful in all my life," he said.

"Nevertheless, you should not have seen it at all."

"God disposes, Jean," he said. "It was meant so, otherwise it would not have happened." He stood up, and Jean was touched by the wonder of his smile. "One cannot really comprehend the Passion and death of Our

Lord, but look, one can see the bliss of His birth! I
never knew before—not with all my being, only with
my mind. Now I *know*! You should not keep us out,
you women; you should not forbid us to see. Even thus
was He born—don't you understand?"

"Aye," Jean said, her head a little on one side. "I
never knew a man like you," she added after a moment.
"It would not do, you know—but after all, I'm glad for
your sake you were there, seeing what it means to you.
Only for pity's sake never mention it to anyone. And
never speak of it to Douglass."

"No, I won't," he said. They continued to look at
each other, and then, hesitatingly, Jean began to smile,
and William, in his joy, took both her hands in his and
pulled her to him and kissed her on the lips, and then,
smiling still, released her and went down the stairs.
Jean stared after him, her hand going up to touch her
lips in surprise. They were of an age, she and William;
he was still a handsome man; and she had never been
kissed like that, on the lips, by a handsome man; so it
was not until he reached the bottom of the stairs that
she recovered her wits enough to call after him—

"Will you find a servant to bring up some wine for
Douglass?" He turned and looked up at her, and she
felt her face begin to redden.

He only said, "For you, too. You deserve it," but she
had never noticed before what a beautiful voice he had.

The thaw made the roads impassable, and neither
midwife nor wet nurse could be brought to Morland
Place for more than a week after the child's birth. The
men got back from the fields late that night, exhausted
by the long day and the hard traveling, and were astonished to find a new child in the house, Jean and William radiating quiet joy, and Douglass having had so
easy a labor that she was already sitting up, smiling and

looming like a June poppy, with her son in her arms. Thomas was so overjoyed that he burst into tears, though afterward he recovered himself quickly and made a joke about having given the boy a salt christening. The house was filled with a riot of joy all evening and late into the night, and the only sadness was that Mary was trapped by the mud in town and could not be here to see it all.

The boy seemed perfect in every way, small, healthy and lusty, and since there was nothing else to be done, Douglass suckled him herself. It made her love him all the more, and when at the end of the week the roads improved enough for Mary to come home and a wet nurse to be brought in, Douglass was very reluctant to give up what had become a great pleasure to her. Jean was shocked and told her sternly that no lady ever suckled her children, let alone spoke of enjoying it, and Douglass replied that nothing about the birth of this child was usual and that he was obviously destined to be a great man. Thomas wanted him to be called Edward, but since Douglass was uneasy about it, seeing that her first baby Edward had died, they compromised and had him christened Edmund. Mary was delighted and thrilled with the baby and was only sorry to have missed all the excitement of his birth and the joy of his christening.

"Never mind, little coz," Thomas said, putting an arm around her thin shoulders. "We shall have a special celebration Mass and feast as soon as Lent is over and the weather is better. I want my father to come, you see, so it will have to wait until traveling is easier. But that will give us all the more time to plan it and savor it."

There was also the unspoken reason, that it was best to wait and see if the child survived, but there was every hope of that, it being so obviously healthy.

"Oh, Thomas, you do think of such nice things," Mary said. "We must think of something really special for the occasion, otherwise it won't outshine the Michaelmas fair."

Thomas smiled. "The presence of my little day star alone would make it outshine any feast there has ever been," he said. "But you are right—we must have something special."

The next day the something special appeared. Thomas and Mary and Ambrose and Gabriel were walking in the herb garden, discussing plans, when Will came hurrying out from the house to them.

"Mary—'Brose—quick, I think my father has gone mad. Come quick."

"Why, what's wrong?" Mary asked, hastening to join him. The others fell in behind.

"I went into the winter parlor just now, and he rushed past me, actually running—and you know Father never moves out of a walk—and I followed him, and he's sitting in the chapel on the altar step—weeping!"

"Oh God, what's happened?" Ambrose said anxiously. "Has he had bad news? Has a letter come, or a messenger?"

"Nothing that I know of," Will said. He glanced at Thomas. "Nothing is wrong in the house," he added for his sake. They had gone in through the door into the great hall, and as they came out from the shadow of the staircase, William appeared at the screen door at the other end. He stood quite still, his hands hanging at his side, his shoulders slightly stooped as if he were very tired, but as Mary ran forward she saw that his face was peaceful and happy, and she knew what it was that had happened.

"Oh, Father!" she cried, and he opened his arms to her, and she ran into them and they hugged each other tightly. "Oh, Father, you've finished."

"Yes, thanks be to God," William said, pressing his cheek to her head.

"I'm so glad," she said, her voice muffled by his chest. She released herself and turned to the others, laughing with pleasure. "It's all right," she said, "it's good news. Father has finally finished his great Mass."

There was a moment's silence, and then Ambrose and Will looked at each other and let out a great yell of delight and linked hands in a mad dance of joy, flying around and around, hooting and laughing and scuffing the reeds everywhere. Thomas, to whom it meant less than the others, nevertheless smiled his pleasure and said, "Your great work, Uncle? I am so glad. Is it good? Are you pleased with it?"

William, smiling with pleasure and at his sons' antics, tightened his arm around Mary's waist and said in a voice that shook a little with emotion, "Yes, I am pleased with it. That seems inadequate, somehow. I think it is good; better than good. It comes from God— He directed and inspired it, and I am only grateful that He chose me to be his instrument. But yes, I am pleased with it. It is—what I wanted to write."

Mary looked up at him, knowing the strength of those words, and then she turned to Thomas and Gabriel with shining eyes.

"Thomas—this is it! The special thing you wanted— don't you see? It must be. It's been designed so."

"Why, yes—a first performance, on the occasion of the solemn celebration of joy," Thomas said. William looked questioningly at them, and Thomas said, "We have been discussing the celebration we wanted to hold over the birth of Edmund—"

"Exactly the right occasion for the first performance of your Mass, Father," Mary finished for him.

William smiled slowly. "You don't realize how right an occasion it would be," he said. "It was the birth of the child that inspired me to finish the Mass."

Ambrose and Will slowed in their dance for lack of breath, and then Ambrose flung an arm around Thomas's shoulder and said, "It will be the best thing we'v ever done. Come, let's go with Father and see the grea work and talk about it." He gathered up Will and hi father and went into the winter parlor.

Gabriel lagged behind, and when Mary turned to see where he was, the expression on his face stopped her still. She folded her hands at her waist and said, "What is it, Cousin? Did you want to speak to me?"

"Yes—I did—Mary, I—" The bold, bad Gabriel, at thirty years of age and with the first three gray hairs carefully plucked out of this beard that very morning, found himself completely disorganized in the face of that neat little sparrow of a woman with the plain face and the eyes like the innocent speedwell. He felt his ruff too tight around his neck, and he cleared his throat nervously. "Mary, I—" he began again, and two women servants came through from the kitchen passage with ewers of water and went up the stairs to the bedchamber, chattering lightly. He could not talk here. He held out his hand to her in abrupt entreaty. "Will you come out into the herb garden with me?"

For a long moment she looked up into his face with an expression that was both grave and merry, like a child, and then she put out her hand and placed it in his. His heart seemed to beat all over his body at once, and he knew that what he could never have deserved had been given to him as a gift, and that the question he was taking her outside to ask had been answered already.

On the day after May Day the celebratory Mass was held in Morland Place, with Master Ashcroft officiating and a number of other clergy attending out of interest, for there had been a great deal of talk about the new work since William had started rehearsing it. He had been forced to go far afield for musicians and singers whom he felt were good enough for the performance, but he was quite satisfied with the location. The chapel at Morland Place was to him the most beautiful in the world, and though the Minster was greater, yet there was an intimacy about the beauty of the chapel that suited the intimacy of the occasion.

Edmund was two months old and still thriving. Douglass had recovered her normal health and was so happy that her beauty had been enhanced to dazzling proportions. Mary was looking unexpectedly pretty, too, in the happiness of her betrothal to Gabriel—they were to be married in June, at the same time as the official betrothal of Nehemiah and Aletheia. The weather was good, and the corn was sprouting so strongly that it looked as though there might be a good harvest this year at last, so everyone was happy.

On the day after the Mass the young people all went out hunting, and Jan and John, declining such energetic sport, rode over to visit Jane at Shawes to discuss the settlement for Aletheia and Nehemiah. Afterward, by unspoken consent, they did not ride home immediately but went on up to Popple Height and there waved their attendants back and sat in easy companionship, leaning on their saddles and looking down over the Morland lands.

"We may see the hunt pass," Jan said idly. "I think it will be a good match, don't you? They will be happy together."

"Jane is not sure," John said, "but I think so. Jane is so old-fashioned. It seems time makes us more of what we are."

"It is good for my children," Jan went on, tugging his beard reflectively. "It means that Amory can have Watermill House when he marries."

"What about Gabriel and Mary?" John said in surprise. "I thought that you would have wanted them to live there."

Jan smiled. "Ah, you haven't heard, then, the latest plan? It was Ambrose who came up with it. He and Gabriel want to run a tavern. There's one on the South Road, not far from the hospital—you know it, I expect? The Green Man?"

"I have passed it. It never seemed worth going in, for one was always on the last lap home when one passed it."

"They both need something to do," Jan went on, "and they were both at home with taverns, so the idea occurred to them. Ambrose is to supply the ability and Gabriel the money."

"Where will that come from?" John asked.

"Nicholas is giving him one of the Butts houses, and he will sell it and buy the tavern. William, of course, has nothing to give. He feels unhappy about that, but Gabriel says Mary is a dowry in herself, and Nicholas is only too happy to see his brother settling down. It will be interesting to see how they manage."

"What energy these youngsters have," John said.

"You are right. They'll make a success of it. They are going to rename it—it's to be called the Hare and Heather." He laughed at that, and John smiled, trying the name over in his head.

"It's a good name. So there'll be another christening, then?"

The two men were silent for a while, thinking back over the ceremony yesterday, and then Jan said in a gentler voice, "It was magnificent, wasn't it? You know, we really must get the manuscript to the Archbishop. It ought to be performed in the Minster—nothing less is enough."

John nodded. "Who would have thought our little brother—and yet he always sang like an angel."

Jan noticed that *our* and smiled. "He has already be-
un a new work," he said. "I'm glad for him. It would
e hard to have done that and have nothing more to
rite. Thomas says that it is an honor to have him in
he house. He is going to pay for Rowland to go to uni-
ersity in Antwerp in the autumn, to study law."

"That's good," John said vaguely.

"It is good. Rowland needs to be occupied. He has
oo much energy and not enough to do. Unlike us older
nen. I never have enough for what I want to do. To-
norrow you must come and see my horses. Thomas
nd I are keeping the brood mares at Watermill. There
eems little point in trying to keep the two estates sepa-
ate. Look, you can see it from here, the water shining
n the sun."

They looked down, their minds flooded with memories. Their childhood had been spent together, divided
between Morland Place and Watermill House; how often had they shared the task of breaking a horse? John
glanced at the gray-bearded man beside him with the
merry eyes and felt such a tug of love and reminiscence
that it was fortunate he did not have to speak just then.

In a moment Jan said softly, "My mother brought
me up here when I was just a child—six or seven, I
don't remember—and showed me Watermill and told
me it should have been hers. It would have been the
portion your great-grandfather settled on her. I remember her so clearly that day. Douglass has such a look of
her sometimes."

They were silent again, and this time Jan glanced at
John and saw the marks of age and sadness on the
younger man's face and felt in a great surge all the pity
of life and of man's striving. "Will you come home,
now there is an heir?" he asked suddenly. "It would be
good to have you here again—I miss you. And you
could watch your grandchild grow up. Must you stay in
exile?"

John smiled a little. "Is that how you see it? Yes, suppose it is exile—but I chose it for myself when I stayed there against my father's will. And now it calls me when I am not there, like sleep beckoning. I could not sleep here."

"It breaks my heart to think of you alone there," Jan said, "but I see that it is what you want. One man's delight is another man's torment." He looked down again at the distant shining of Watermill House and the great spread of Morland land. "After all the striving and contriving," he said quietly, "God turns it all His way in the end. Though you ran away, it is your son and grandson who will rule here, and my grandson will have Watermill, which is all that is his, and your father and my mother need not have striven and fretted all their lives after all. The wheel turns, John, and we are all back where we started."

John smiled, lighting up his tired face, and he reached out and clasped Jan's hand. "Not quite, brother," he said. "We have grown in grace."

Jan smiled, too, returning the pressure, and then with one accord they gathered up their reins. Kee sprang up from his comfortable bed of heather and ran out ahead, barking, and with a nod to the servants to follow, they turned their horses homeward.

The glorious saga of *The Morland Family* will continue with *The Crystal Crown*, the fourth book in Dell's exciting Morland Dynasty series.

The Crystal Crown is set in one of the most turbulent periods of English history. When the novel opens in 1630, Morland Place is occupied by Edmund and his beautiful second wife, Mary Esther. They raise their children on the vast estate, keeping Edmund's eldest son Richard at home to be trained as the next master of Morland Place, sending Kit to Oxford and securing a place for Ambrose and his lovely wife Nell on an emigration ship bound for the new land of America. But while the family is expanding its sphere of influence, embracing the untamed land on the shores of Chesapeake Bay, the British branch must survive a bloody storm that threatens to shatter its existence.

Brought up as an Anglo-Catholic, Edmund is ambitious and power-hungry, ready to adopt the Puritan-backed Parliamentary cause against Mary Esther's strong-willed protests. And in a land torn by the British Civil War in a time when Royalists square off against

Puritans and the King loses his head to Cromwell's sword, the Morlands must create a strong bond that will survive such cruelly divided loyalties.

Here is a preview of The Crystal Crown, *to be published by Dell in February of 1983.*

Edmund turned and walked away, but at the door he stopped, and after a long hesitation he turned back. He did not quite meet Mary Esther's eyes, and his voice was stilted and shy, but he made a great effort and said, "Thank you—for staying with me."

Warmth spread through her, and she went forward and took his arm and looked up at him, and slowly, slowly, his eyes met hers and he allowed her to draw his arm around her shoulders.

"Will you go in to bed? There is still a little of the night left."

"Yes," he said. He cleared his throat and said awkwardly, "Will you come, too? I need you, Mary."

Together they crossed the quiet yard and passed through the sleeping house to the bedchamber. In the dark safety of the curtained bed, he was bolder.

"You are too cold, my dearest. Come closer and let me warm you." She snuggled in to him, and he held her and stroked her head.

"You do warm me, Edmund," she said. "You are the warmth of the sun to me." She felt him quiver under her words and in a moment turned her face up for his kisses. The tension of the long night, the pain and sadness of loss, broke through his restraint, and he kissed her passionately, her brow and eyes and lips, lifting her fingers to his mouth, drawing her long curls again and again through his fingers. He did not need to ask permission, nor she to give it, nor did their garments hinder them; flesh to flesh they found again the freedom that their lives and his nature had so rarely granted. To give himself as completely as she gave her-

elf was so nearly impossible that now when it happened it seemed to open his soul and turn it inside out
like a ripening fig; a joy so intense, so piercing, that he
felt he might die of it, that a wrong word could kill him.

But she said only, "I love you—" and, shuddering,
he yielded the last bastion of his spirit, and their joy
was accomplished.

They drifted together in the darkness for a long time,
and then he roused himself enough to say, in a voice
unlike his own, it was so warm and so easy, "Mary—
my own love."

The warm darkness claimed them; cheek to cheek,
breast to breast, they slept. Mary Esther was still
wrapped blissfully in his arms when in the gray of the
January morning she was woken, dragged unwillingly
from the sweet dark sleep by a voice she wanted to ignore. Never had she so little wanted to wake.

"Madam, Madam." It was Leah's voice. "Wake,
Mistress, wake up."

"Oh, Leah—what is it?" she mumbled sleepily. "It
can't be important."

"Oh, Mistress—oh, Mistress, I'm so sorry." The
words pierced the delicious fog—ah, painful, painful to
be woken! "A messenger has come. Oh, Madam, I'm
so sorry."